Readers think **VIXEN** is the cat's meow . . .

"Plenty of delish details." —*Booklist*

"Filled with wicked fun."
—*Tales of a Ravenous Reader*

"I loved this juicy, fast-paced novel by new author Jillian Larkin." —*The Book Buzz*

"*The Luxe* plus *A Great and Terrible Beauty* smacked into the 1920s. I really, really loved it."
—Bloggers Heart Books

"A very good debut novel!" —*The Cerebral Girl*

"*Vixen* was everything I hoped it would be—fun, flirty, sexy, naughty, and full of surprises."
—Examiner.com

"If you're ready for a slightly darker look at life in the Flapper era, then *Vixen* is for you. If you're looking for a coming-of-age read where the prices are high, then *Vixen* is for you. If you're a great lover of a wonderful story and great characters, look no farther."

—*The Reading Frenzy*

"This book is for ALL ages of readers who are interested in scintillating adventure, and a fiery romance, that will leave them breathless."

—BookPleasures.com

"Jillian Larkin's take on the Roaring 20s gives it a glamour that no one can resist. *Vixen* is well-written and has all the makings of a great read—coming of age, the losing of innocence, heartbreak, action, romance, and truth paired with the dark world of speakeasies."

—*Flippin' Fabulous*

"Glamorous and dangerous and fun and dramatic."

—*The Mimosa Stimulus*

"Get yourself a copy and settle down for a good read."

—*The Book Faerie*

"Couldn't put the book down." —*The Darcy Review*

"I can't stress how much I enjoyed the first book in this smashing new series. *Vixen* was captivating, dangerous, sexy, and beautifully written . . . I can't recommend *Vixen* enough. If you're looking for a 'totally jake' read, here's your best bet."

—Bookwormlovers.com

Also by Jillian Larkin

INGENUE

# VIXEN

Jillian Larkin

EMBER

This is a work of fiction. All incidents and dialogue, and all characters with the exception of some well-known historical and public figures, are products of the author's imagination and are not to be construed as real. Where real-life historical or public figures appear, the situations, incidents, and dialogues concerning those persons are fictional and are not intended to depict actual events or to change the fictional nature of the work. In all other respects, any resemblance to persons living or dead is entirely coincidental.

 Published in the United States by Ember, an imprint of Random House Children's Books, a division of Random House, Inc., New York. Originally published in hardcover in the United States by Delacorte Press, New York, in 2010.

Ember and the colophon are trademarks of Random House, Inc.

**theflappersbooks.com**
**www.randomhouse.com/teens**

Educators and librarians, for a variety of teaching tools, visit us at www.randomhouse.com/teachers

The Library of Congress has cataloged the hardcover edition of this work as follows:
Larkin, Jillian.
Vixen / by Jillian Larkin.
p. cm.
Summary: In 1923 Chicago, seventeen-year-old Gloria Carmody rebels against her upcoming society wedding by visiting a speakeasy, while her Pennsylvania cousin, Clara, hides similar tastes and her best friend, Lorraine, makes plans of her own.
ISBN: 978-0-385-74034-0 (trade) — ISBN: 978-0-385-90835-1 (lib. bdg.) —
ISBN: 978-0-375-89908-9 (ebook)
[1. Conduct of life—Fiction. 2. Social classes—Fiction. 3. Cousins—Fiction. 4. Prohibition—Fiction. 5. Nineteen twenties—Fiction. 6. Chicago (Ill.)—History—20th century—Fiction.] I. Title.
PZ7.L323154Vix 2010
[Fic]—dc22
2010030406

ISBN: 978-0-385-74035-7 (trade pbk.)

RL: 6.0

Printed in the United States of America

10 9 8 7 6 5 4 3 2 1

First Ember Edition 2011

Random House Children's Books supports the First Amendment and celebrates the right to read.

For the two finest modern-day flappers,
Beverly and Wendy:
You've got all the moves.

## ACKNOWLEDGMENTS

A girl needs partners when she dances,
and I've had some of the best. My thanks to Ted Malawer
and Michael Stearns at The Inkhouse; and Krista Vitola,
Barbara Perris, Trish Parcell, and the whole brilliant
chorus line at Delacorte Press and Random House
Children's Books. Special thanks to Chip Gibson,
Beverly Horowitz, and Wendy Loggia for believing
in The Flappers from the very beginning—
you are all the cat's pajamas.

# PROLOGUE

She didn't feel like wearing a garter tonight. Her gold-beaded dress, cascading in waves of crystalline fringe, covered the intersection between her sheer stocking and bare thigh.

She slipped her right foot into one of her two-tone Mary Janes, her left foot into the other. The thin black straps went across her ankles, the silver buckles tightened with a pinch.

From the munitions strewn across her vanity, she carefully selected her weapons and placed them in a gold mesh evening bag: vamp-red kiss-proof lipstick, silver powder compact, tortoiseshell comb, ivory cigarette case.

She stared into the mirror. Everything was perfection: green eyes smoldering, cheekbones rouged and accented, lips outlined and plumped. Tonight, even her skin shimmered with something almost magical.

As she dabbed a final drop of perfume into the crease

where her shiny bob skimmed her neck, she decided the garter would be necessary after all. Of course it would.

And then, before snapping her bag closed, she added the small black handgun.

Now she was ready.

# PART ONE

# SPEAK EASY

All life is just a progression toward,
and then a recession from,
one phrase—"I love you."

—F. Scott Fitzgerald ("The Off-Shore Pirate,"
*The Saturday Evening Post*, 29 May 1920)

# GLORIA

They found the entrance exactly as instructed: just before the cracked sign for Malawer's Funeral Parlor, between the tailor and the barbershop, through the rusted gate, eleven creaky steps below street level. After they'd knocked precisely three times, a tiny slit in the boarded-up door slid open.

"What's the word, doll?" One dark eye blinked at them.

Gloria opened her mouth and froze. This was the moment she had practiced endlessly in front of her bedroom mirror: saying the secret password to be admitted into the hottest speakeasy in Chicago. So what if it was the first time she'd ever snuck out of her house, lied to her parents, or been in the city alone? Not to mention that her dress—which she'd bought only the day before—was so short that one gust of wind could turn her from flapper to flasher like *that*.

"Come on, I don't got all night!" the Eye barked.

Sweat began to bead on her upper lip. She could almost feel it caking the layers of her meticulously applied makeup and cracking the surface of her finishing powder.

"Ouch!"

Marcus, her best friend—who'd taken on the role of accomplice/chaperone for the evening—jabbed her in the side. "Just say it already!"

Gloria inhaled sharply: It was now or never. "Ish Kabibble?"

"Wrong. Now *scram!*"

And just like that, the Eye disappeared.

Gloria glared at Marcus. "You have *got* to be kidding me."

"It was 'Ish Kabibble' the last time I was here!" he said. Steps below the street, the bluish night softened the harsh angles of his golden-boy features—his sharp cheekbones and jaw, the habitual smirk he wore—and made him look infallible. Trustworthy. Swoony, even.

Gloria could see why girls threw themselves at him, of course, but her own relationship with Marcus was three parts brother-sister to one part sexual tension—a healthy, balanced equation for any male-female friendship.

"You've been here a total of . . . wait, let me count—one . . . one. Once. Right, *one time,* Marcus. And that was merely because you *paid* your friend Freddy to take you."

"Well, at least I've actually *been* inside," Marcus said, crossing his arms with a sigh. "Let me take you home."

Home? A few miles away by car, only it felt more like a

few thousand. Her father's gleaming Mercedes—sneaked from the garage after the family's driver went to bed—beckoned to her from beneath the streetlight. Maybe she *should* just return to the quiet, safe, *boring* tree-lined Astor Street that she knew so well. She could make it into bed scot-free by one a.m. and even fit in a few flash cards before her European history exam tomorrow. But wasn't that exactly what people always expected her to do? Make the safe, good-girl choice?

No, she couldn't leave now, not when she was one door away from carrying out the first and only rebellious act of her entire life. She was already here. She just had to get inside.

Gloria pounded on the door again.

The slit opened up a crack. "You again? You got a choice chassis, kid, but if you don't go home to your daddy's this second, I'll call security—"

"*Wait.* All I ask is one single clue." She pouted her brightly painted strawberry lips because, well, pouting always worked in the movies. "If I get it on the first try, we're in. If not, we disappear."

The Eye squinted menacingly. "Does this look like some kinda party guessing game to you?"

"I wouldn't know," Gloria said coolly. She could hear the band inside begin to play, its jazzy rhythms spilling out onto the street in muted tones. "I don't go to parties. And I save my games for men."

The Eye glanced at Marcus. "This one's a real bearcat, ain't she?"

"*Glo?* A bearcat? Ha!" Marcus said, laughing out loud.

"Fine." The Eye rolled. "Here's your clue: It's a dirty deed you're too young to do."

Marcus jumped in. "That's easy, it's—"

"The girl's got to get it, or I shut this door in your face forever!"

The phrase was on the tip of Gloria's tongue. Oh yes, her best friend, Lorraine, had written it in a note during biology yesterday: "Oh my gawd—Welda, my lab partner, was just suspended . . . she was caught in the bathroom during last wknd's dance with the CAPTAIN of the football team giving her a good—"

*"Barney-mugging,"* Gloria whispered huskily. Then she blushed, embarrassed to have said out loud the dirtiest term she knew for sex.

The Eye's slit closed and the door opened. "Welcome to the Green Mill."

◆◆◆

It was as if she had walked right into the rebel side of heaven.

A dense cloud of smoke hung near the ceiling of the windowless room—everyone seemed to be holding a lit cigarette. The smoke was shot through with dazzling beams of light from the stage, and from the sequined dresses and the crystal *coupes* of champagne. At the front of the room, a mahogany bar overflowed with debonair men in suits and tuxedos, nursing tumblers of amber liquid and puffing thick cigars. And in the plush green booths along the walls were more men, shifty-eyed and menacing even as they chewed on hamburgers and slapped down cards.

And moving among all the men, flitting about in glittering flashes: flappers. That's what today's independent women called themselves, Gloria knew. As carefree and glamorous as if they'd been ripped straight out of a glossy fashion spread in *Vogue* or the set of some extravagant Hollywood movie. They were everywhere. Lazily dallying, dangling long cigarettes between their jeweled fingers, showing off their Charleston moves on the dance floor, and flirting shamelessly—all pouty lips and cocktails. With their fiery red boas draped over their bare shoulders, peacock feathers shooting out of silver headdresses, oxblood lipstick painted in perfect bows, and strand upon strand of creamy pearls, sequins, and rhinestones, they looked like exotic birds. And there was so much *skin.* More exposed skin than Gloria had even seen at the beach.

She had never felt so out of place. At Laurelton Girls' Preparatory, she was the president of the Honor Society, an example for the rest of the girls. But here, Gloria was that poorly dressed, unwashed foreign exchange student from wherever—Arkansas, maybe—whom nobody bothered to eat lunch with. Her peach chiffon sleeveless dress, with its delicate lace on the shoulder and billowing skirt, was positively flapperesque in the store yesterday. Now it not only looked entirely too long, too plain, but *pink,* of all colors, in this dim lighting! She felt like a Victorian.

She tried to locate Marcus—at least he could give her some consoling compliment he didn't really mean—but he was nowhere in sight.

A tuxedoed waiter passed with a tray of mismatched teacups, coffee mugs, and glasses. "Do you have any water, by any chance?" she shouted over the music.

He handed her a teacup, and she drank down the clear liquid in a single gulp. It wasn't until after she swallowed that a sharp burning sensation flooded her throat. She wheezed, and tears leaked from her eyes. Then she remembered why a spot like the Green Mill existed in the first place: so that people could drink. *Illegally.* She had been fourteen when the Prohibition began, so she'd never had alcohol and didn't know what she was missing. Now that she'd had her first drink—it tasted like a bottle of her ancient grandmother's perfume—she couldn't imagine why anyone would miss it in the first place.

Until about two minutes later, when it hit her. Hard.

Everything began to spin: the twirling dancers and swishing glasses and dazzling dresses. Gloria stood paralyzed at the edge of the dance floor, not knowing quite what to do with herself. Feeling and looking like she did, she certainly couldn't join the Charleston-crazed flappers, no matter how much she wanted to. She watched them enviously, their lithe bodies gyrating with blissful abandon in an almost reckless loss of control.

Gloria swayed to the melody, trying to memorize the steps. Suddenly, she had the strange sensation that someone was watching her. From the direction of the tiny stage. It was filled by a group of black musicians accompanying the vocalist, who looked stunning in a skintight sequined scarlet dress. Gloria skimmed her eyes across the band: drummer, bass, trumpet, saxophone . . .

His fingers never strayed from the keys, but the pianist was staring at her. Under the bright stage lights, his face seemed to glow with its own radiance. There was something sensual in the way he played, his entire body rocking back and forth, following his roving hands. His fingers struck the keys like lightning.

As much as she wanted to, she couldn't look away. When he stopped playing, a flock of girls pressed in around her, blocking her view. Gloria elbowed her way toward the front of the crowd.

"You spilled my drink!" one girl shrieked, holding her mug out in front of her as if it were a ticking bomb. Lustrous strands of pearls were haphazardly wrapped around the girl's swanlike neck.

Gloria suddenly felt like a gawky ugly duckling. "I'm really sorry, I was just trying to find my friend—"

"Do you even know *who* you're apologizing to?" asked

another flapper, who was wearing enough black kohl around her eyes to scare a raccoon. "You just spilled Maude Cortineau's martini. You're lucky if she doesn't claw your face off right this second."

Gloria had heard this name before. Allegedly, Maude had dropped out of school during her junior year and become the unofficial flapper queen of the Chicago speakeasy set. She fit the part—skin like a porcelain doll, in an opalescent taffeta dress that hugged her curveless body, and a jet-black sequined headband as a dramatic contrast to her wispy blond bob.

"It's copacetic, beauts," Maude cooed, handing her glass to the mousiest girl in the group. She fingered a lock of Gloria's hair. "But Rapunzel here better let down her hair somewhere else next time. Somewhere far, far away. *Tu comprends?*"

"Oh no!" Gloria's hands shot to her head. The inconspicuous French twist—which she'd obsessively secured with only a million bobby pins—had come undone, and her long, wavy locks were loose. She realized that each and every one of the girls was bobbed. Blond or brunette, straight or crimped, it didn't matter—their hair was cut short. She might as well have showed up wearing her gray and white school uniform and called it a night.

Humiliated, she ducked toward the back of the club and the only refuge: the powder room. En route, she had to pass through a group of men at the far end of the wraparound bar. As Gloria took a step closer, she saw that these were no ordinary men. Blue pin-striped suits, tilted-up fedoras, clouds of cigar smoke: These were most definitely gangsters.

She recognized one of the men from the tabloids. Carlito Macharelli, the twenty-year-old son of one of the mobsters who owned the place. With his bronze skin and oiled black hair, he looked almost exotic.

Gloria met his steady gaze and felt a damp chill creep over her. She almost thought he was about to say something.

In the powder room, Gloria gazed into the mirror. Her reflection seemed faraway and blurry. *This is what* drunk *must feel like,* she realized. She found a few bobby pins in the bottom of her purse and pinned her hair back as tightly as she could. She would have to hold her head like a statue for the rest of the night, but it would do. Then she readjusted her breast-flattening bandeau brassiere—essential for achieving that boyish flapper figure, but it was cutting off the circulation in her upper body—and fixed the smudge of kohl that had started to bleed onto her cheeks. Now she was ready. Or at least, as ready as she could be.

Fighting the surging tide of the crowd, Gloria stumbled to the bar, grabbing on to an empty stool as if it were a life raft. She closed her eyes, relieved. The only thing calming her was the feathery tranquility of the band's song, wafting through the room like a sad summer breeze:

*The world is hungry for a little bit of love,*
*As the days go by.*
*Someone is longing for a pleasant little smile,*
*As you pass him by.*

*Some heart is aching, some heart is breaking,*
*Some weary soul must droop and die;*
*The world is hungry for a little bit of love,*
*Even you and I.*

The singer's buttermilk alto sank deep into Gloria's skin. The song was one of her favorites. Gloria's voice lessons were strictly limited to operatic arias, but whenever her mother wasn't home, she turned on the family's brand-new radio and sang along with the latest popular tunes. Even though she'd only performed publicly for school events and the occasional society party, Gloria was overcome with a fierce longing, wishing it were *her* up there instead, soaking up the spotlight's beam.

"Hey, no sleeping allowed at my bar!"

Gloria's eyes shot open. The bartender was leaning over the long mahogany counter, his face inches from her own. "And beauts are no exception to that rule."

Something about his wild shock of hair, the shade of a dull penny, against the crisp white tuxedo made him seem more like a cartoon character than a real person; strangely, she felt she could trust him. "I wasn't sleeping, I was listening." She forced a half-smile.

"In that case, there's no *dry* listening allowed at my bar." He tapped the bar like a drum. "What'll it be?"

"Um, how 'bout a . . ." Gloria hesitated. What did a proper flapper ask for in a bar? She was used to ordering a cream soda at the movies. Besides, hadn't that one accidental drink been enough? "I just came here for the music."

"That right?" He mopped at the bar with a rag. "If you enjoy the music so much, tell me the name of that singer, and your drink is on the house."

Gloria's stomach churned. After the eyelock she'd had with the pianist, she couldn't bring herself to glance at the stage again, though she could hear the sharply struck notes from the piano rising above the clamor of the crowd.

"I'm Leif, by the way. But everyone calls me . . . Leif," he said, raising his chin.

Gloria forced a little laugh.

"How come I don't recognize you?"

"Because," she confessed, "it's my first time here."

"A virgin!"

"No! I said it's my first time *here.*"

"Right. A virgin."

"Just because I'm new doesn't mean I'm a virgin!" she said, raising her voice as the blasting music came to a sudden halt.

A roar of laughter rose from the crowd. Gloria felt her face grow hot. Would people notice if she crawled underneath the bar stool? She couldn't have felt more humiliated.

"You just earned yourself that free drink," Leif said, chuckling. "Though you should know, for next time, that her name is Carmen Diablo. And her accompanist is the best piano player this side of the Mississippi: Jerome Johnson. They say he's the next Jelly Roll Morton."

"Jerome Johnson," she repeated to herself. "I knew that."

"Sure you did. So, what'll it be?"

"She'll have a dirty martini." The voice, filled with cigar smoke and Southern privilege, came from behind her. She turned. He was startlingly handsome, with slick salt-and-pepper hair and eager eyes.

"So confident for a man who knows nothing of my taste," she said, keeping her eyes glued to Leif as he shook her martini. After a minute, he strained the liquid from the shaker into a mug, added a spear of olives, and slid it across the bar.

As she picked up her drink, Gloria caught the man glaring strangely at her hand. "Would you like the first sip?" she asked, thinking maybe that was polite in speakeasies.

He frowned. "I think that privilege has been reserved for somebody else."

Then she caught the focus of his gaze and felt the blood drain from her cheeks. On her left hand sat an enormous diamond and platinum engagement ring. She had forgotten she was wearing it! But even worse, she had forgotten she was engaged. And if her fiancé, Sebastian Grey III, saw her now, the engagement would be called off. Immediately.

Bastian.

Gloria took a huge gulp of her martini, wincing as the strong, salty liquid slid down her throat. Getting sloshed wouldn't change the fact that Bastian was a proclaimed leader of the Prohibition's "Dry Camp." Or that he condemned speakeasies and all they represented: flappers ("floozies"), bootleg liquor ("Satan's $H_2O$"), black jazz ("voodoo tom-tom witchery"), and yes, barney-mugging (well, Gloria and Bastian avoided this topic altogether).

Of course, none of this had really mattered before tonight. She had always overlooked Bastian's conservative values because he was at the top of the "B List"—the unofficial ranking of Chicago's most eligible bachelors. (The formula was high-level calculus. Among the variables were x = wealth, y = industry, a = estates, b = family, c = swooniness, d = education, and q = size of his [ego, trust fund, etc.].) Bastian was also a blue-blooded import from the British royal family (how distant in relation, nobody really knew), and therefore about as close as one could get to Chicago aristocracy.

But, Gloria rationalized, she had six months before her diamond turned from promise to vow. She twisted off her ring and slipped it into her purse with an uncomfortable laugh.

Salt-and-Pepper gave her newly bare hand a squeeze. "I know what'll look better between those little fingers of yours." From the inside of his suit coat, he retrieved a silver cigarette case, which he flipped open like a traveling salesman.

She was actually starting to enjoy this new role—alluring flapper—so why stop now? "Butt me," Gloria said as he planted a cigarette between her lips, torching the end with a sleek silver lighter. She inhaled deeply. Her throat burned and she coughed uncontrollably.

"Whoa, easy does it there," he said, gently patting her back. "Cough any louder and your fiancé will hear you."

Gloria smiled weakly. "You know what they call a woman who smokes?"

"A *(cough)* hussy?"

"I was going to say a smoke-eater. It's nicer."

"What if I'm *(cough)* not such a nice *(cough)* girl *(cough cough)*?"

"You can't fool me. You're the nicest tomato in this joint. Cash or check?"

Her head felt filled with smoke. Which one meant *now* and which meant *later*? "Cash?"

He pecked her on the cheek and disappeared into the crowd. Gloria pretended to smoke her cigarette as she surveyed the room. Scantily clad girls chatted with men in every corner, exchanging witty repartee over drinks, over song, over nothing. The Flapper Way was all about style, the way a hand moved or a chin was thrown back in laughter or a girl sipped a drink with a dark smile and a sidelong glance at her date. It was about peering into someone else's eyes and letting the hot jazz say what words did not. Could not.

Gloria left her drink and drifted toward a dark corner, trying to catch her breath and collect her thoughts. She wished she could find Marcus. She wished she could crawl into her own bed—

Wait. What was wrong with her? This should have been the best night of her life—she had consumed illegal drinks in a notorious speakeasy! Flirted with a highly unsuitable man! Smoked! (Well, sort of.) But still she couldn't shake the feeling of being an outsider. She would be shunned by her parents and Bastian if they found out, and yet she had also been shunned by Maude and the very flapper girls she so desperately wanted to be like. If only her best friend, Lorraine, were here—she would know exactly what to do and how to act.

Suddenly, Gloria felt a wave of body heat beside her. She didn't dare turn around, but she didn't need to. Somehow, she knew exactly who it was.

Holding a cigarette were those same strong, dark fingers that had darted out to sting the piano keys. Up close, he smelled of sweet tobacco and Brilliantine. How she wanted to take those hands, press them into her cheeks, and . . .

What had gotten into her? This was a strange man she was thinking about. A black man. She was white; she was engaged; she was—

"Why weren't you dancing?"

She was startled by his earthy, rich baritone voice. "What?"

"My music not good enough for you to dance to?"

"No! I mean, your music is"—her heart was beating so loudly, pulsing through her entire body, that she wondered if he could feel it in the sliver of space that separated them. "I've never heard anything like it."

As she met his soulful eyes, she wanted to—needed to—say something else (only what?), but the sudden impact of a heavy hand on her back sent her wheeling around.

"Glo, where the heck have you been? I've been searching all over for you!"

"Marcus?"

He examined her critically as if he hadn't seen her in years. "Are you sozzled?"

Before she had a chance to turn around again, Gloria knew Jerome Johnson was gone. Back into his underground world of blues and booze, leaving her to face the only person in that room who knew who Gloria *really* was: president of the Honor Society, varsity tennis player, debutante daughter of Beatrice and Lowell Carmody. Good-girl, private-school-virginal, soon-to-be-married Gloria Carmody.

"I'm ready to go home," she muttered, pulling Marcus in the direction of the door.

"What happened to you?" he asked. "You seem . . . different."

"Oh, please, you left me for something like five minutes."

But truthfully, she knew it might as well have been a lifetime. Something *was* different about her, something terrifying and transcendent, but she couldn't say what.

As they made their way across the dance floor, she spotted *him* again out of the corner of her eye. Jerome. He was at the edge of the stage, his arm around the waist of a gorgeous black girl in what looked like a silver negligee. They were laughing, and the girl enthusiastically planted a kiss on his cheek.

Gloria couldn't bear to watch for another second. She pushed her way through the hordes of flappers and waiters, past the booths of gangsters, past Leif at the bar, past the goon at the door, who smirked as though amused. She tumbled outside and inhaled hungrily, filling her lungs with the crisp autumn air.

But even as she climbed the steps back to the street, the faint cascade of the first notes followed—"All Alone," a tune Gloria knew well. She found herself humming along as Marcus draped her coat over her shoulders. The melancholy music warmed the night air, and she could tell that something had begun to shift inside her, something unstoppable. Her life felt brighter now, more valuable than before. Even the piano seemed to be playing just for her.

# CLARA

Clara had been staring covetously at the same outfit on page forty-six of *Vogue* for the past ten minutes. (Jeanne Lanvin *Robe de Style,* black silk taffeta tier, peacock tail embroidery.) Not as if this dress—or anything revealing that much leg—was something she'd be wearing once her train pulled into Chicago Union Station. Which was exactly why she was trying to mastermind a plan to sneak onto one bound for New York City instead. No matter that her ticket was one-way—no refund, no exchange—or that she didn't have enough cash to make the transfer *legally* . . .

*Legal* had never stopped her before. In fact, legality had always been the last thing on her mind—until she ended up in jail back in Manhattan. But she'd been bailed out, so really, what was one more time?

No. She had to look on the bright side: At least she had gotten out of staying in Pennsylvania with her parents (which was a different sort of jail). They were the reason she'd run away to New York City in the first place, during her senior year of high school—to leave behind everything she'd known: her family, her worthless high school diploma, her "good Christian" values. She couldn't bear living in a place where the girls got excited about the prospect of a church mixer, after pledging their chastity and swapping pie recipes.

The month she'd spent back in Pennsylvania—after her parents found her and dragged her, by her triple strand of pearls, back to their farm—had been the worst of her life. She could barely get out of bed in the morning, let alone put on lipstick. It wasn't that she cared so much about being ridiculed and ostracized in town; more that she couldn't face the idea of defeat.

So when her parents proposed she stay with her aunt Beatrice in Chicago to help plan her cousin's wedding, she agreed.

Now Clara gazed out the window at a nauseating stretch of cornfields whizzing by. The only noteworthy sight for miles had been one sweaty, muscular farm boy, his tanned arms bulging as he thrust his hoe into the field. He'd been pretty, but probably as dumb as the soil he worked. To think that only a month before, she would have looked out of her Bank Street apartment window to find well-dressed businessmen hailing taxis with their leather briefcases while bohemians lounged on the stoops, debating the artistic fad of the moment and chain-smoking.

What were her roommates, Leelee and Coco, doing this very minute? The girls would probably be meeting up for a lunch break in Washington Square Park, Clara imagined, sitting outside and gossiping about last night's dates and parties and adventures. Clara couldn't bear it: The intoxicating, madcap swirl of urban life would continue, with or without her. Even though she knew, deep down, that a break from the city was probably for the best. After all, that year had nearly ruined her.

What she would do for a smoke right now. *Kill,* she thought. She took out her case: one cigarette left and two hours to go. The train ride from hell. At least she had her flask of gin, securely tucked into her favorite red garter. She'd have to drink it in the bathroom; unchaperoned young ladies getting tanked on trains was frowned upon. Mostly because it was illegal.

Clara rose and made her way up the aisle. Most of the seats were filled by chubby businessmen absorbed in their *Wall Street Journal*s. But then, a gift from heaven, Seat D20: an absolutely striking young man, with strong features, dark eyes, and dangerous-looking lips. He was reading the paper. She slowed her pace and sent a smoldering stare intended to burn a hole through his sports section. But he didn't so much as glance up. Ugh, men! They were so naïve.

"Whoops!" she exclaimed, stumbling and chucking her cigarette directly under his seat. As she bent to pick it up, she squeezed her arms together slightly to amp up her cleavage. Crouching at his feet, Clara looked up at him. He was even more gorgeous from this angle. "It seems as though my cigarette has fallen underneath your seat. Would you mind terribly retrieving it for me?"

"I don't mind retrieving it for you," he said, bending down so that his face hovered mere inches from hers. "But I do mind you putting something that filthy in your mouth."

"It was my last one, so I have no other choice."

"You must want it badly, then."

"Unless, of course, you have something better to offer me?"

He pulled her up from the floor. "I hope you like it unfiltered."

They walked down the cramped aisle toward the next car. Clara paused at the door so that they were pressing against each other for lack of space. As he flashed her a knowing grin, the cleft in his chin suddenly reminded her of someone else.

*Him.* The boy she'd left back in New York. The one she had so surely (and tragically) fallen for. The one who was responsible for—

"I'm glad we agree there's only one way to make a cigarette truly worthwhile," Seat D20 whispered into her ear, his hand reaching up toward her blouse. Clara intercepted it just as the train went over a large bump. He stumbled backward. "I shoulda known you were the type of girl who likes to play rough," he quipped, approaching her again.

A wave of disgust rose through Clara's body. Back in Manhattan, she *never* would have shied away from being naughty with a handsome stranger. But that was then. Now she needed a break from her old life. From *boys,* those disgusting, horrid little creatures who had the ability to toss her heart in the air and then smash it into the ground. Now D20 seemed repulsive. She didn't even know him. Or was it herself she didn't know?

"I guess I'm not the type of girl you thought I was," she said. Then she slid out of his grasp and walked away.

◆◆◆

Clara stood in the middle of the foyer with two suitcases and an open mouth. She hadn't visited the Carmody estate since she'd been a little girl—she didn't remember it being *this* palatial. She could fit her entire Greenwich Village block inside this mansion and there would still be room left over.

As she waited for her aunt to come downstairs, she walked along the wall, checking out a series of boring portraits that ended in a large gilded mirror. Clara caught a glimpse of herself and winced. Her face was a bare canvas: no kohl around her eyes, no scarlet lips, no fake fringe of lashes. Her blue-gray eyes were puffy from lack of sleep, with a smudge of bruised purple beneath each of them. Her honey-blond hair hung thin and dull, blending into her complexion, which was the wrong kind of pale—not Botticelli porcelain, but pasty and sallow. She hadn't realized how hard this past month had hit her.

Anger surged in her throat, and she quickly averted her eyes. Her ex-boyfriend—if she could even call him that—was probably off laughing over drinks at the Waldorf, not giving Clara a second thought. And here she was, shipped off and baggy-eyed and *still* thinking about him. This needed to stop. Now.

"Clara, dear, is that you?" Her aunt was at the top landing of the grand staircase. What *was* she wearing? She looked as if she'd been swallowed by a beast made entirely of dark ruffled crinoline.

"Aunt Bea, hi," Clara said in her sweetest tone. "It's so good to see you!"

Aunt Bea swept down and gave her a chaste tap of a hug. As she pulled away, her eyes carefully scanned Clara's face. "Why, my dear, I barely recognize you. What a . . . woman you've become."

"I'm only a year older than Gloria."

"And yet, interestingly enough, she's the one getting married," her aunt replied. It was a barb intended to sting, Clara was sure of that. "You must be exhausted after your long journey. Claudine, Gloria's maid, will unpack your luggage for you and—"

"No! I'll unpack it!" Clara practically shouted. She didn't know what would be worse: the maid finding the bottle of gin or her diaphragm. Not as if she planned on using the latter. "I mean, I would prefer to do it myself," she said.

"Of course." Her aunt raised a suspicious eyebrow. Clara guessed her parents had told Aunt Bea almost everything, but she wasn't entirely sure. "Why don't we have some tea while we wait for Gloria to come home? It's the perfect opportunity for us to get reacquainted."

Her aunt led her down an endless hallway into a mahogany-paneled drawing room. A table was set with an elaborate spread of tea, coffee, pastries, and a variety of finger sandwiches, with a maid waiting to serve them. Her aunt, uncle, and cousin were New Money, that much Clara knew. And New Money, as opposed to those who had been rich for decades, had a tendency to put everything—including themselves—on display.

Her aunt beckoned for Clara to sit beside her. "Tonight I will be hosting a small dinner party for Gloria's fiancé."

"Oh yes, I'm excited to finally meet him," Clara said. "Since I'm here to help plan their wedding, of course."

Aunt Bea's smile vanished. "There is no use *pretending* with me, young lady. We both know I am doing you the biggest favor of your life by taking you in."

Clara almost spewed her coffee. As if slaving away for prissy Gloria and Aunt Bea were a favor to *Clara*. "You talk as if I were a stray dog—"

"At this point, my dear, you are little better than one." Aunt Bea lowered her voice to almost a growl. "I know all about what happened in New York. *Everything.*"

Clara felt something tighten in her stomach. What had *really* happened to her in New York was Top Secret—no one besides her roommates knew. Not even her parents. The booze, the jazz, the men, getting thrown into jail—that was all common knowledge. But the Cad . . . well, her roommates would never tell anyone. A city sister's oath. Surely her aunt was bluffing. "Aunt Bea, I don't know what you could possibly mean."

"Don't be smart with me, Clara. I know all about the arrest, and your night in the New York City penitentiary."

"Oh. *That.*" Clara breathed a sigh of relief. Not that her jail time was something she was particularly proud of, but at least Aunt Bea didn't know her darkest secret.

"It is no small matter," Aunt Bea said with a wave of her hand. "Gloria, *my* Gloria, knows nothing of your year of sin. And I fully intend to keep it that way."

"As do I, Aunt Bea," Clara said. "I fully intend to leave my 'year of sin' in the past."

"You can't fool me that easily. A leopard doesn't change her stripes."

"You mean spots?"

"I mean what I say!" Her aunt placed her teacup in its saucer with a shrill clatter.

"But I *have* changed. I mean, just *look* at this outfit!" Clara protested, referring to the pink blouse that was buttoned up to the base of her neck.

Her aunt cleared her throat. "I certainly hope your behavior is not as cheap as that blouse. If it is, I have no qualms about putting you on the first train out of here."

"You mean, back to my parents' house?" Clara asked hesitantly.

"I mean," Aunt Bea said with a calculated pause, "to the Illinois Girls' School of Reform. A boarding school for 'lost girls' such as yourself."

Clara put a hand to her chest. "Surely you can't be serious, Aunt Bea!"

"I already have your parents' instructions. They have given a deposit to the headmistress, guaranteeing your place at any point during the year. *That* is how serious I am." Her aunt selected her words as if they were bonbons on a silver platter. "Of course, you can avoid this fate by helping to ensure that your cousin Gloria turns from *Carmody* to *Grey* as smoothly as possible. Is that clear?"

"Yes, ma'am." Clara wasn't entirely sure what her aunt meant by all this marriage business—hadn't the engagement been finalized? And had her parents really paid in advance to send her to a reform school without even telling her? How could they? Clara was about to further question her aunt, but she felt the contents of her stomach roiling—coffee, whiskey, cigarettes, train food. If she didn't escape within the next 8.2 seconds, it would end up all over the Persian rug beneath her feet.

She quickly excused herself, sprinting out of the room and up the grand staircase, dashing into a room that was marked with a golden *G* on the door—*Guest?*—and took a deep breath. Now she was feeling better.

Until, that is, the blitz of carnation-pink *everything* actually caused her to gag. The room reeked of rose water and French soap and looked like a life-size dollhouse. The quickest scan of the room confirmed that *G* stood for *Gloria:* An essay on *Great Expectations,* with an A+ marked in red on top of the desk; a silver hairbrush and a pair of pearl studs atop a crystal tray on the vanity; and on the nightstand, a gilt-framed photograph of cherub-cheeked Gloria gazing adoringly at a blandly handsome man, whom Clara could only assume was Sebastian Grey. If her stomach hadn't already began to settle, Clara would have lost it all over this pink hell.

She slumped down on the pink tulle bedspread, feeling overwhelmed.

Already in this new place, this new city, her Manhattan self—the one she had taken such pains to create from scratch—was slowly slipping away. And though she was reluctant to admit it, perhaps there was something to be said for that. Would taking a break from playing the Fearless Flapper be such a bad idea? Maybe it was the key to finally getting the Cad out of her head. For good.

She would prove Aunt Bea and her parents wrong. Of course she could change! But it would require her to create a whole new role for herself. She would have to improvise as she went along. If this were a play, how would her character be described?

Clara Knowles (18): Sweet-as-pie and innocent-as-a-lamb farm girl, with aspirations to be a humble schoolteacher, comes to the big city for the first time. Country mouse. Wide-eyed and naïve.

Didn't all the movie magazines say that reinvention was the secret to a "new, improved you"? Perhaps that was the ticket: reinvention. She would leave behind her seedy New York ways, her lost love, her tarnished heart, and don the hat of a Chicago society girl like her cousin Gloria. Out with the old Clara, in with the new.

And God help anyone who got in her way.

# LORRAINE

Lorraine had watched her best friend, Gloria, pace frenetically beneath the red and white barbershop pole for the past ten minutes. Frankly, she'd had enough.

"Glo, *calmez-vous!*" Lorraine caught her friend's petite shoulders, bringing her to a jolting halt. "You're acting as if you're going in for surgery!"

"At least they'd put me under if I was," Gloria whined.

"A true flapper shows more guts than *that*!" Lorraine said, steering Gloria to the door. "If we hang around out here any longer, they'll start to think we're a couple of streetwalkers."

"They'd only think that about you, Raine."

"Because *I'm* the only one who's dressed like an adult," Lorraine said. "Now let's go!"

A bell clanged as the girls entered the shop. A long row of

men—cheeks covered in marshmallowy lather, suits covered in black smocks—gawked at them in the mirrors that stretched along the wall. Lorraine watched as Gloria's sea-green eyes widened in panic at the realization that she had just set foot inside a *men's* salon.

Just then, one of the lathered-up men raised a hand and began to wave.

"Speak of the devil! Well, *two* devils."

"Marcus?" Lorraine called out. "Is that you?"

Before Lorraine had cajoled her father's secretary into booking the appointment, she had done her best investigative work to find out that a certain Marcus Eastman was scheduled for a haircut on October fifth at 2:30 p.m. She had then booked Gloria's appointment for October fifth at 2:45 p.m. sharp.

*"Quelle coincidence!"* Lorraine continued, trilling in mock surprise.

"*'Quelle coincidence'?"* Gloria repeated. "Really, Raine?"

Lorraine gave a little wave to Marcus. "The best coincidences, I always say, are the ones you prepare for."

Lorraine had nurtured a huge crush on Marcus for years—the type that actually felt as if her heart would be crushed by her rib cage whenever she saw him. She sought out every opportunity to run into him—whether it was convincing Gloria to crash his baseball game, or dragging Gloria over to his house so he could help with her (already completed) mathematics homework. Marcus had yet to come to the realization that Lorraine was the One, and that their (prospective) fairy-tale romance was a classic fit for the *Chicago Daily Journal*'s Wedding Section. Lorraine blamed Marcus's almost incestuous relationship with Gloria.

But now that Glo's diamond-encrusted hands were officially hands-off, it was Lorraine's great opportunity to make Marcus at last recognize how simply *fabulous* she herself was.

Pretending to ignore Marcus, Lorraine sat Gloria down on a banquette along the wall. "Now remember, nobody's forcing you to do this. You can always come back another day after—"

"I can?"

"Well, not really. But imagine that you have a choice here."

"You're right, I can't live another day with my hair like this," Gloria said, twisting her long coppery braid around her finger. "I'm sick of being my parents' perfect little girl."

It was frustrating to hear Gloria complain about a life most girls would die for. With her peaches-and-cream beauty, immaculate grades, and angelic singing voice, Gloria had always been *that girl,* the one other parents wished their daughters could be like. But Glo also defied the principles of girl jealousy—it was nearly impossible to hate her. Gloria made life feel like a glass of champagne: sparkly and festive and luxurious. And she was completely unaware of how guilelessly charming she was.

That is, she had been until Sebastian Grey had come

along. All of Chicago was celebrating their engagement as if it were some Hollywood movie, complete with ball gowns and horse-drawn carriages. *Boring.*

Lorraine was happy for Gloria, but . . .

She'd always been Gloria's one and only—they did *everything* together. But after Gloria started dating Bastian, she began to cancel her weekly movie dates with Lorraine—a tradition for years—because she "couldn't get out of" a country club dinner or the latest gathering with Sebastian's fellow bankers. And then she wasn't allowed to go with Lorraine to society parties because Sebastian didn't approve of her being "surrounded by roving bachelors." If Gloria was already slipping out of her life *now,* what would happen after she actually got married? Lorraine feared she would be left without a best friend. Completely alone.

The week Gloria and Bastian got engaged—just before their senior year began—was the week Lorraine bobbed her hair. She was the first member of their class to go through with it, clinching her place as baby-vamp-in-residence. Lorraine could *perhaps* see a correlation between the events (the engagement came first, the bob came after), but so what? It had given the girls something else to talk about besides Gloria's fat diamond. Gloria didn't *always* have to be the one in the spotlight, did she?

Still, she and Gloria were like sisters, and Lorraine could sense that something wasn't quite right. Why else would Gloria be so determined to cut her hair, knowing full well

Bastian would disapprove? Lorraine knew that, as her best friend, she shouldn't let Gloria go through with the bob. But another, more sinister part of her was driven to push Gloria just to see what would happen.

"You're not the only one brave enough to have your hair bobbed, Raine."

"You couldn't be more right," Lorraine agreed, patting Gloria's hand. "But I'm also not the one who has to sit in the same room tonight as your fiancé, your mother, and, lest we forget, your freak show of a cousin."

"Ughhhh, don't remind me!" Gloria groaned, slumping deeper in her seat.

"What is the princess *ugh*-ing about now?" Marcus walked over to where the girls sat, whipping off his smock and jutting out his newly shaven jaw. "Ladies, what do you think?"

"Not as if you had anything there to begin with," Gloria teased.

Marcus bent down so his cheeks were at her eye level. "Go ahead, you know you want to feel."

Gloria caressed his cheek with the back of her hand. "Oh, Marcus, could you be any more of a cake-eater?"

Lorraine watched and felt a pang of jealousy. Why did Gloria get to have both Bastian *and* Marcus? Wasn't one enough?

"You've got to feel this, Raine," Gloria said, taking Lorraine's fingers and guiding them across Marcus's jaw. "Baby smooth, right?"

It was a simple movement, really, but Lorraine felt as though she were about to explode. She was touching Marcus! And he was letting her! Zing! Marcus blinked his beautiful, long lashes in her direction as she felt the cleft of his chin—so sturdy and square. Her stomach flip-flopped.

"Well?" Marcus asked.

"So . . . so . . . *smooth,*" Lorraine said.

Gloria snorted. "Marcus can't risk giving Alissa a stubble-burn tonight."

Lorraine sat up straight. "Alissa— Wait, Alissa Stock? That blond freshman who got her wiggle on with half the football team? What happened to Sybil Quince?"

"Where have you been? That was *weeks* ago," Gloria said.

Marcus ran a finger along the inside of his collar. "Sybil threatened to kill me after she heard about Muriel Trethewey."

"How many girls *do* you date?" Gloria said.

He shrugged. "My dance card is full."

To Lorraine, this news was about as indigestible as her mother's egg salad. She knew Marcus had a reputation for being a playboy, for breaking girls' hearts left and right, but there was no way she could compete with the Alissas of the world. Lorraine, after all, wasn't a quiff. She didn't sleep around. She only had eyes for one guy: Marcus.

Raine's thoughts were interrupted by François, le Barber Extraordinaire, waddling over to where they sat.

"Oh, *mon dieu.*" He pursed his lips and exhaled a very French *pffffffff*. "*Dîtes-moi:* Is le female illiteracy rate on ze rise? Or did you choose to ignore le sign that says *men's* barbershop?" He gave Gloria's braid a tug and she yelped.

"François, you don't remember me?" Lorraine asked, fluffing her bob.

He twisted his black handlebar mustache. "Ah, *mais oui!*" He leaned in and gave her a fond *bisous-bisous* on both cheeks. "You are looking like—how do you say?—one hot tomato!"

Lorraine beamed, thrilled to be complimented in front of Marcus. She pointed at Gloria and said, "She's here for the bob."

"With those finger waves?" Gloria said, her lower lip quivering.

Lorraine's eyes widened. Her own haircut was of the ordinary variation—straight and slick. "Are you sure?"

"How's the big cheese, Sebastian Grey the Third, going to feel about that?" Marcus asked. "He's always struck me as the king of the prigs."

"Well," Gloria said, eyeing her long red locks in the mirror, "if I *am* going to sin, I may as well sin badly. I mean, boldly."

"Come on, Rouge, let us make your daddy *très miserable.*" François threw a black smock around Gloria's neck and pulled her toward the back of the shop.

Lorraine and Marcus were left alone together. This was her chance to prove that she could fill Gloria's place once Gloria was married. Or even better, be something more than

Gloria ever had been. And she could reveal her big secret. It was so big, even Gloria didn't know. As of 11:57 a.m. (or 11:59, if you didn't include her attack on the mailman), Lorraine had been accepted at Barnard College. Which was the sister school of Columbia University. Which was where Marcus was studying next fall.

If only he weren't flipping through a magazine as if she weren't even there.

She moved closer, crossing her legs so that her kneecaps ("most underused erotic body part" according to *Jazz Baby Magazine*) were exposed. "Bastian is going to put her under house arrest when he sees that bob."

"Yeah, what a prune pit," Marcus said, not bothering to look up.

"I didn't have to worry when *I* got *my* hair bobbed." Lorraine selected a red lollipop from a jar on a side table and unwrapped it. "I was actually the first girl in our class to do it."

"You must have been trying to prove yourself to someone, then."

"Well, not so much to prove"—she paused, popping the lollipop into her mouth—"as to *please* someone."

At that, Marcus finally raised his eyes. "And did it? Please *him*?"

Clearly, pulling the lowest card in every girl's deck—jealousy—was the only way to up her game. "I don't kiss and tell."

Marcus leaned in closer, removing the lollipop from her mouth. "So there was kissing, then?"

Lorraine could feel her pulse quickening as she stared into his bottomless blue eyes. "I—I—I—"

He stopped her stammer by planting the lollipop back in her mouth. "I'd better go check up on Gloria."

Lorraine's heart plummeted. One second she could have sworn he was flirting with her, and then he couldn't get away from her fast enough! She couldn't figure it out: She'd spritzed herself with the Fragonard perfume her father had brought her from Paris, and she was wearing her little black Patou day dress. Everything was perfect. Or was it?

Perhaps it was the setting. A barbershop wasn't particularly sexy. Certainly not the right place to reveal herself. When she told Marcus that she loved him, everything had to be Just Right. Mood lighting. Good music. It Girl dress.

Lorraine got up to join Marcus. "Better make sure the princess is still alive," she said.

François was busy snipping the finishing touches into Gloria's hair when Lorraine approached. He swiveled Gloria around so that they had a full view of her. *"Voilà! C'est magnifique, non?"*

Gloria's hair swept across her forehead like a crinkled autumn leaf, billowing over one sea-green eye before delicately ending in a soft edge along the line of her jaw. She blinked at them with wide, apprehensive eyes. "Oh no, do I look like a boy?"

"More like a movie star!" Marcus whistled.

Lorraine glimpsed her own bob in the mirror and nearly cried. How was it that she suddenly looked like a dowdy Joan of Arc and Gloria looked like a doe-eyed starlet?

She pushed her jealousy away. It wasn't Gloria's fault that her hair turned out so smashing, right? Lorraine kissed her best friend's cheek. "You look like the bee's knees, darling!"

"You'd better not be lying," Gloria said, standing up from the chair.

François brushed the stray hairs off her shoulders. "Even if they were, is too late now."

*"C'est vrai,"* Gloria said. "All we need now, François, is a little bathtub gin to celebrate your masterpiece."

"Since when do you drink gin?" Lorraine laughed. "Wait, since when do you drink, *period*?"

"I mean . . . hypothetically speaking."

Lorraine caught Gloria shooting Marcus a furtive glance. It was the look she gave to her confidants, a look that said, *Only you know my secret.* There was nothing Lorraine hated more than being kept on the outside of a secret. Well, nothing she hated more than being kept on the outside of a secret that included *Marcus.*

"Wow. My head feels so much lighter. Is that normal?" Gloria asked nervously, smoothing her hair down with her hand.

Her *bare* left hand.

Lorraine gasped. "Why aren't you wearing your engagement ring?"

The color drained from Gloria's cheeks. "I must have forgotten to put it back on after—"

"After we went swimming yesterday!" Marcus was all too quick to fill in.

Lorraine frowned. "Gloria, you went to the library with me after school yesterday, remember? Unless the Oak Lane Country Club pool was suddenly open after five for the first time since Roosevelt was president." A thought that haunted Lorraine's nightmares came to her: "Are—are you two having an affair?"

"No!" Gloria and Marcus exclaimed simultaneously.

"That'd be like dating my *brother,*" Gloria said, horrified.

François clucked like a French chicken. "I think I'll give this *ménage à trois* some space, *non?*" He ambled away.

Lorraine sat in the empty swivel chair next to Gloria. "Spill," she commanded. "I need to know everything."

"All right," Gloria said, extending her pinkie finger. "But first you have to swear you won't tell."

Lorraine groaned. "Are we still going to be pinkie-swearing after you're married?" She hooked her finger with Gloria's and kissed the end. "Fine, I swear."

"Okay, so you know how my cousin is coming to 'help out,' thanks to the genius idea of my mother? Well, she is a total *reuben*—I mean, she's basically never left her hometown in the backwoods of Pennsylvania. Last I heard, she wants to be a schoolteacher. Maybe even a *nun.*"

"A schoolteaching nun!" Marcus exclaimed. "The horror!"

"The last time she visited, she barely did anything but read Darwin's *Origin of Species* the entire time," Gloria said. "So we *tried* to get her to at least go with us to the movies, and she said she wasn't allowed to because, get this—" Gloria rolled her eyes. "Because her parents think the movies are *immoral.*"

At that, the three of them laughed so loudly that one of the old men at the front of the shop said, "I say! You three keep it down a little!"

Lorraine was confused. "What does any of this have to do with your missing ring?" She was tired of being a third wheel to Marcus and Gloria's antics.

Gloria began slowly. "Because last night was my last chance for fun before the nun arrives, so—"

"We snuck out under cover of darkness, and we intrepidly made our way into the big, bad city, where we went to the Green Mill—"

"And it turns out not to be green at all. The only thing green in it—"

"Was our dear Miss Carmody here, and not just because she can't quite handle her liquor." Marcus grimaced. "Men threw themselves at her. *Bodily.* But every single one of them crashed against the rocks—I mean, the *rock*—on her finger."

"Which is why I had to take off my ring!" Gloria finished

with a small clap of her hands. "Not because I am interested in other men, but—"

"I beg your pardon? Stop." Lorraine didn't know where to begin with her questions. Not only had her best friend gone to the Green Mill without her, but she'd gone with *Marcus* instead? Lorraine felt like ripping the newly shortened hair right out of Gloria's head.

But Marcus was there, and she wanted him to think she was . . . nice. So she smiled sweetly and said, "I mean, you set foot in the Green Mill dressed like—like you normally dress?"

"You're wondering why they even let her through the door," Marcus said, patting down his hair. "Doubtless it was the handsome devil at her elbow."

"Hardly!" Gloria said. "Anyway, it *was* mortifying. I looked like such a bluenose. And that is why we now have to go back lickety-split, so that this time I can actually show my face. Proudly. Oh, and you can come with us, of course."

"And we mustn't forget dear Country Clara," Marcus added.

Gloria let out a little huff of disgust. "She would probably run off to the convent forever if she even heard us *mention* the Green Mill, let alone actually usher her through its doors."

"Precisely!" he said roguishly. "One prissy toe of hers in the Green Mill, and she'll be scampering to catch the next train back to Hicksville."

A wicked grin spread across Gloria's face. "Tell me more."

"So I was thinking," Marcus continued, working the pomade into his hair, "that I, say, make Country Clara fall in love with me—"

"And then you break her like a twig!" Lorraine offered. "I mean, in a nice way."

"It seems Miss Dyer and I are in agreement," Marcus said, winking at her. Lorraine could have swooned.

"I don't know," Gloria said, tilting her head and watching her hair move in the mirror. "Doesn't that seem excessively cruel? Even for you, Marcus."

"What is cruel, my little red morning glory, is that your cousin is here to ruin your life before—"

"Before Bastian does!" Lorraine chimed in.

"I was going to say before your wedding. And besides, the girls around here are such a bore. Some fresh blood will really spice up my game. I know you think I'm horrid, but it's true. Dating is like a sport, and as with every sport . . . practice makes perfect."

"Now I'm beginning to see why Columbia accepted you." Gloria leaned forward and ruffled Marcus's unmoving hair. "Besides the building named after your father, that is."

Lorraine closed her eyes, wishing *she* were the one running her fingers through Marcus's golden locks.

"Normally I wouldn't approve of such a cruel plan," Gloria mused, "but Clara is an absolute bore. The last thing I want is for her to ruin my wedding." She extended her hand

and shook Marcus's. "I applaud your plan, Mr. Eastman. Let's get Clara out of here for good!"

"Hear, hear!" Marcus said, turning to Lorraine. "Raine? You in?"

*Am I ever,* Lorraine thought. Everything began to crystallize: She would help Marcus with his plan to break Clara's heart. Only, really, she would be working to make Marcus fall in love with *her*. Against the risqué background of a speakeasy, the stage would be set for romantic sparks to fly. Their love would bloom, and they would head off to New York City in the summer. Together.

It was foolproof.

Lorraine took Gloria's hand and, along with Marcus, headed for the door.

In that moment, with her best friend and her future husband close to her side, Lorraine was happier than she'd been in ages. Everything seemed about to turn around. And in her favor, for once.

# GLORIA

Gloria was hungry. She focused on cutting her crab-stuffed mushroom into tiny pieces, avoiding eye contact with everyone at the dining room table. She could feel all their judgmental stares—her mother's, cousin's, and fiancé's—burning a hole through her bob.

The events of the afternoon had transpired as follows:

She arrived home from the barber, sneaking in through the kitchen, where she surprised her mother, who was busy evaluating the dinner menu.

Her mother's scream at Gloria's appearance deafened every living creature within a twenty-block radius of their house.

Mrs. Carmody then ordered the maids to call for a wig maker, whereupon Gloria suggested they build a bonfire in her mother's tomato garden so that she could not only burn the wig, but also every corset in the house.

This prompted her mother to threaten to cancel dinner with Bastian, to which Gloria replied: "Why don't we just cancel the wedding while we're at it?"

And then her mother slapped her. Hard.

This would all have been unpleasant but entirely tolerable, even expected, had Country Cousin Clara not suddenly intervened. The girl pertly suggested that Gloria be sent to her room. Gloria had *never* been sent to her room before! The absolute *gall* that girl had—Clara was worse than Gloria's own mother.

And now here they all were at the dining table, nibbling appetizers and faking civility like one happy family. What a bunch of top-shelf hooey.

Bastian had yet to say a word. He just glowered as if he were going to lunge across the table, knock aside the Venetian glass vase of white tulips, and strangle her with his bare hands. Weirdly, that thought was kind of exciting—she had never seen him this *heated* before. In the past, he'd always been so stable, so predictable. So dull.

Why had she ever found him appealing? Sure, on the surface she was just a prim prep school girl, but she had hidden depths. Did Bastian?

Probably not. He'd been the same way since the day they'd met at the Art Institute of Chicago's annual gala.

Tired of making awkward cocktail conversation, Gloria

had slipped away from the party, wandering around and eventually finding herself in an empty side gallery, filled with a new collection of Impressionist works.

Gloria had been lost in a small Degas pastel of a young woman bathing when a deep voice pierced the silence of the room. "She has your hair." Gloria had turned. "Only, yours is much more beautiful."

The young man was staggeringly handsome, charming, and—as it turned out—from one of Chicago's oldest and most impressive families. Her parents *definitely* approved.

Their romance unfolded over the summer: Bastian wooed her and Gloria let herself be wooed. After all, he was everything she was supposed to want in a man. Plus, every other Chicago girl longed for him, which only made him more desirable. At the end of August he proposed on his father's yacht, against the backdrop of a glorious Lake Michigan sunset, and their engagement was soon announced in the Chicago *Tribune*—just in time for the first day of Gloria's senior year.

But they had nothing in common. They rarely spoke about anything other than what Bastian wanted to discuss—finance, politics, other boring things. And perhaps most importantly, when he kissed her there was no *heat.* The kisses were soft, simple pecks. Where was the fire? The passion? When Lorraine spoke about Frenching boys, she made it sound so . . . *marvelous.*

Would Gloria ever feel marvelous about Bastian? Would

she ever feel faint when he walked into a room, the way she'd felt when she'd seen Jerome Johnson?

Gloria looked around the table. Time to break the ice. Maybe she could shift the focus to Clara, who at the very least could *bore* them all to death.

Gloria rested her knife delicately along the edge of her plate. "So, Clara, what have you been doing with yourself since graduation? You've been out of school since last June, right? Almost four months."

Everyone turned to Clara expectantly as she froze, her fork suspended in midair. "Um, let's see, I've been—"

"Why don't we let your cousin enjoy her dinner in peace tonight?" Mrs. Carmody said with an air of discomfort. "She must be awfully tired after such a long journey."

Gloria waved her hand. "She just came off a luxury train, not a wagon train."

"Gloria Carmody, where are your manners this evening!"

The words came out before Gloria could hold them back: "I must have left them in the barbershop, Mother."

"If only your father were here!" Mrs. Carmody said, throwing her hands up in exasperation. Then she turned to Bastian. "Mr. Carmody *would* be here if he weren't traveling so much for business." She glanced at Gloria's hair. "Although perhaps his absence is for the best. He would be appalled to see you like this, Gloria."

Bastian smirked. "What a wise woman you are, Mrs. Carmody."

Actually, Gloria *was* thankful for her father's absence. The last thing the dinner table needed was another conservative, old-fashioned, disapproving man. "Clara?" she said a bit sharply, turning to her cousin once again.

Clara fidgeted uncomfortably in her seat. "Oh, my recent activities don't make for terribly interesting dinner conversation, I'm afraid."

"Nonsense!" Bastian chimed in. "We are all ears." He cupped his hands on either side of his head and turned on his movie-star smile.

Gloria knew this was his way of being "silly" and "charming." His brilliant teeth were bared, a bit of white sleeve peeked from the dark cuffs of his suit, and his eyes were bright with merriment. But Gloria knew he was mocking her.

Mrs. Carmody tittered.

Gloria wanted to punch them both. Instead, she watched Clara blink a few times and start to speak: "Golly, let's see. Primarily, I have been . . . helping my father in the church and my mother on the farm. I *most* enjoy waking at four-thirty a.m. to milk the cows. I find it both physically rigorous and emotionally intimate. It's just me, the sunrise, and the cow. And the glory of a hard day's work."

Gloria almost snorted her water. She waited for Clara to start laughing and say she was only joking, but her cousin didn't crack a smile.

"That's not the only thing I enjoy, of course," Clara added.

It was a wonder the girl could speak at all, what with her blouse buttoned up so high. It was easily the ugliest blouse Gloria had seen in ages: yellow, dripping with lace, and with a tall, stiff collar that even her grandmother would have sneered at. "I also love the volunteer work I do in the pediatric ward of the local hospital."

"Pediatric ward?" Gloria repeated. Was this girl serious?

"Sick and dying children," Clara said, narrowing her eyes. "You'd be amazed at how many children take ill and just waste away. I tend to them as they give up the ghost."

"Why, Clara, I had no idea!" Gloria's mother said, her expression a mixture of shock and delight.

Gloria stared her cousin down. "What about for *fun,* Clara? Don't tell me you're really that saintly."

"Oh, hardly. Sometimes during weekends I take my favorite nag, Ginger, out for a ride." Clara paused and frowned. "Seeing you, Gloria, only makes me miss her that much more."

Gloria cocked her head. "And why is that?"

"Because Ginger is the exact same color as your hair."

"Perhaps, Clara, when you came here, Gloria should have taken your place in the country," Bastian suggested, pushing his dark hair back off his forehead. *He certainly is handsome,* Gloria reminded herself. "Your exemplary lifestyle could have prevented this . . . this . . ."

"This *what,* Bastian?" Gloria asked. "I'm dying to hear what improvements you think *country life* could work upon me."

Bastian pounded his fist on the table. "This . . . *atrocity*!"

Gloria wanted to scream. Did Bastian think he was her fiancé or her father? She glowered at her cousin's cherubic little face. But wait, wasn't Clara's golden, baby-fine hair remarkably shorter, too? Didn't it look like—well, a grown-out bob? "If you think *my* hair is such an atrocity, Bastian, then what do you think of Clara's? It's barely longer than my own."

Mrs. Carmody dabbed her mouth with a napkin. "I think it's time for the main course," she said, signaling the family butler, Archibald.

Bastian glared at Gloria. "I'm not talking about Clara—"

"It's all right, Bastian—Gloria has a point," Clara chimed in, shyly tucking her hair behind her ears. She seemed nervous for a moment, but then a visible calm washed over her face. The corners of her lips rose.

"She does?" Mrs. Carmody asked.

"Yes. Except, my intention was never to look like a flapper, of course," Clara explained. "I cut my hair off a few months ago in order to donate it to charity—so that a natural wig can be made for a woman who has lost her hair due to illness. The children at the hospital inspired me." With a smirk that only Gloria seemed to notice, Clara swigged a mouthful of milk.

"What a good Samaritan you are, Clara!" Bastian said. "Truly a model for us all!"

Was no one else sick of this girl? Gloria wanted to tell her cousin a thing or two about charity, but she couldn't risk any further punishment. Both her mother *and* Clara would be watching her, and she was determined to sneak out to the Green Mill again.

She had to find some way to return—if only to prove to herself that she had no interest in Jerome Johnson. That she'd been moved by his music and nothing more. Her attraction to him—if it was that!—had clearly been a result of the booze. And the taboo color of his skin. And how insolent he'd been. And those roving hands . . .

"Yes, Clara, you are indeed a model for us all," Gloria said. "My fiancé is right, as always."

"Well, I don't know about *always,*" Bastian said with mock humility, sitting up a little straighter. "But certainly very often."

*Men are so easy sometimes,* Gloria thought. All they need is a little coddling and they're eating out of your hand. Which gave her an idea.

She didn't have a natural spark with Bastian the way she did with Jerome. But that didn't mean she couldn't *make* one, right? After all, every fire had to start with dry wood.

Gloria listened and laughed but remained silent all the way through the canapé of anchovies, the cream of celery soup, the asparagus tips *au gratin,* the *boeuf bourguignon.* By the time everyone was devouring the last crumbs of their red velvet cake, she had devised the perfect plan: She would seduce her own fiancé.

◆◆◆

Gloria and Bastian sat at opposite ends of the silk love seat in the drawing room. The rest of the dinner party had retired, leaving the couple to themselves.

Just sitting there, Gloria felt restless. The heavy brass chandeliers above her head seemed to weigh on her. The dust from the pleated taffeta curtains made her skin crawl.

"You seem so far away over there," she said, sliding over to Bastian and settling against his muscular body. She crossed her legs so that the tops of her knees were exposed. "There. That's much better."

"We've been sitting with each other all night, Gloria," he said, readjusting himself to accommodate her weight as she leaned against him.

"But I couldn't do *this* to you before." She placed her hand on top of his, which rested on his thigh. His hands were almost twice the size of hers. As she slid her fingers between his, the dark hands of another man crept into her mind. The long fingers that had tickled the keys and taken her breath away.

She tried to rid herself of the image. She had every girl's *dream man* sitting beside her. Smart, successful, and well-bred. This was the man she loved. The man whose diamond ring she was again wearing.

Gloria let her hand glide across Bastian's thigh. "I wish you wouldn't be so mad at me," she said softly.

"I'm not *mad* at you, Gloria. I'm just perplexed."

"But I bobbed my hair for *you,* Bastian. As a surprise."

He snorted. "Why would you do a thing like that?"

"I thought you would find it sexy."

"You should strive to be respectable, Gloria, not sexy," Bastian said. "I hate to see you be like all those *other* girls. Those indecent, dime-a-dozen flappers who do nothing but get intoxicated with a different man every night of the week."

"But Bastian, I've never had a drink in my life!" *Lie.* "And besides," she said, leaning her cheek into the curve of his neck, "you're the only man I want."

*Double lie.*

Gloria tried to find something in his eyes to reassure her that this, their engagement, was the right decision. She kissed him, softly at first and then with more passion. Bastian followed her lead, his lips gliding to her neck as he lightly cupped her breast with his palm.

"I wish we could spend the rest of the night alone," she said.

She could see his eyes ignite with the promise of something he'd never quite considered before. "But, sweetheart, may I remind you that your mother is upstairs? I don't see how that is possible."

"Then we should go somewhere else. . . ."

He slid away in disapproval. "Gloria, I will not take you to a hotel, if that is what you are proposing. And if my landlord sees you—"

"No, silly, I was only proposing a date." This was the moment of truth: Now all she had to do was say the words. "Why don't we head into the city, to the Green Mill? We could dance, listen to some new music—"

Bastian stood up from the love seat in disgust. "Have you completely lost your mind? First you embarrass me with this hair of yours, and now you want to go to a foul *juice joint like that*? Do you even know who owns those kinds of places? People connected to the Mob. They use these speakeasies as their offices of corruption. Are you telling me, Gloria," he said, raising his voice, "that you want to join the ranks of those scoundrels and whores?"

Gloria could feel all the blood in her body rushing to her head. She wanted to scream "Yes!" into his face, to tell him that she'd already been to the Green Mill, and that she had flirted with men of different races and gotten tanked.

Instead, she shook her head gently. "No."

"Good. I didn't think so." Bastian straightened his navy-blue suit and fixed his tie, the checkered one Gloria had given him as a birthday present.

"I was only curious—"

"I should go home," he stated flatly, adjusting his collar. "I have an early-morning meeting. While I uphold my duties for the sake of the economy, those flappers and their swells are out every night carousing and dancing till all hours. It's disgraceful."

"Right. Disgraceful."

Gloria watched him leave. She slumped into the love seat, hugging a pillow to her chest. Her throat ached as she tried to swallow the oncoming flood of salty tears.

Of course, this was exactly when her mother chose to enter the room. Both hands were on her thick waist, and she looked angry—thin lips, red eyes, sweaty brow.

"Now that Bastian has left, there is something we must discuss."

"I'm really tired, Mother. Can't it wait till tomorrow?"

"No, Gloria, it cannot." Her mother sat down on the love seat next to her. "You're lucky you still have a diamond on your finger after this little stunt you pulled." She was referring to Gloria's bob, of course, but her tone made it very clear that she had also been eavesdropping. "Unfortunately, it's no longer just about you."

"I don't know what you're talking about, Mother."

Mrs. Carmody carefully smoothed her skirt, looking everywhere—the gilded paintings, the wooden clock, the Oriental rug—except directly at Gloria. "Your father and I are getting a divorce."

Gloria nearly fell off the love seat. "What?"

"He sent a telegram this afternoon from New York to inform me."

"A telegram?" Gloria could see by her mother's pained expression that she was serious, but the words seemed ludicrous, a jumble of misunderstanding. "He's probably just confused because he's been away so long on business. New

York must be so disorienting. He'll come back home and everything will be fine."

"It will not be fine, because he is *not* in New York on business," her mother said. Her voice cracked, and Gloria feared she was about to cry. "He's in New York with . . . another woman. Some tramp he's apparently fallen in love with."

"Wait. He told you this? In a telegram?"

"Amber. She's twenty-three. And a dancer."

"What kind of dancer?"

"The kind that has a name like Amber!" Her mother broke down into loud sobs. She folded Gloria into a tight embrace.

Gloria had never seen her mother so upset before. She'd never really considered whether her mother *loved* her father—she played the part of perfect wife with such unquestionable dedication. Gloria's mother's life had always revolved around her father—doting on him and waiting on him to make sure he was happy, comfortable, and well fed. In fact, Gloria's mother didn't seem to have any sort of life *beyond* him.

Was this what Gloria's own future held in store if she married Bastian?

"Does this mean he's not coming home?" Gloria asked.

Mrs. Carmody wiped her eyes with a silk handkerchief. "It means much more than that. The Carmody name, our entire family's reputation, could be permanently destroyed. Running off with some floozy? We'll be ruined once this gets out in the papers. Unless," her mother said, taking hold of

Gloria's hand and squeezing it tightly, "you are married to Sebastian Grey."

Gloria felt her heart sink. "I'm already engaged. Remember?"

"I do. Only, we no longer have the luxury of a long engagement. Now there is no time to lose. The second this scandal breaks is the second Bastian takes that ring away."

"But, Mother, it's 1923. Plenty of couples get divorced these days!"

"You don't understand me, Gloria," her mother said sharply. "Your father is the sole proprietor of your inheritance, which is due to you on your eighteenth birthday. But if you fail to marry Sebastian, you won't see a penny of it."

"I still don't understand," Gloria said, growing uneasy. "Daddy would never do that to me."

"I sometimes forget you're still just a child," her mother said, placing a heavy hand on Gloria's cheek. "I don't know how to say this gently, so I suppose I'll just say it: Sebastian didn't propose to you for 'love.'" She sighed. "He and your father negotiated a deal: a role in managing our steel fortune in exchange for the dynasty that is the Grey name and lineage. You know very well that being *nouveau riche* gets you nowhere these days. Your father needs the business of Chicago's elite in order to continue making a profit, and what they trust is a name—a name they recognize. But if you don't seal this bargain, you and I will be on the streets. We'll be left with nothing."

"But why does Bastian care about our money? He's practically royalty himself."

Her mother's jaw tightened. "Bastian has nothing, Gloria. He's living on credit and loans, and he's about to go under. His father gambled away all their money. All that's left is their name." She grasped Gloria's hand. "*Your name,* when you marry him. But you must do it now, before word gets out about your father. If you don't marry Bastian before then, no one will want to marry you once they discover your father's infidelity. You'll be just another penniless girl from a broken home."

Gloria's head began to swirl. She managed to croak, "But I have till June . . ."

"No. You are now getting married in a month," her mother stated firmly, folding up her handkerchief into a tight square.

"But that's not possible!"

"Sebastian has already approved. He's as desperate as we are, only for different reasons." Her mother straightened up, her face now as taut and distant as the face of a woman in a cigarette ad. "I'm sorry, dear, but there's really no other choice."

After her mother left the room, Gloria could no longer contain her tears. Her mother must have known about her father's affair long before tonight—how else could Sebastian have approved the new wedding date? Why else would

Clara have agreed to live with them like some nineteenth-century governess? Gloria was trapped, and everyone was conspiring against her. Marrying Bastian would mean the end of her as she imagined she could be—a singer perhaps, and an independent woman—but *not* marrying him would mean the end of her family. No money. No respect. How could she do that to her own mother? How could her father do this to both of them? If she'd thought there was even a chance he would change his mind, she would have appealed to him. But he was as stubborn as he was absent.

As she sat alone, crying, she found herself trying frantically to twist off her diamond ring. Before tonight, it had been a promise, yes, but a dazzling one. And a slippery one, to be put on and taken off according to her own free will.

Now her finger bulged under the platinum band, cutting off her circulation, the skin beneath turning purple. The ring was stuck.

# CLARA

Clara was bored. She'd been living in the Carmody house for almost a week, and the only evening activity so far had been cards (which she hadn't known could be played without stripping or drinking). Everyone had bought her country act so far, with the possible exception of Mrs. Carmody, who was always watching. No doubt waiting for Clara to make a mistake so she could ship her off to reform school.

Only, Clara wasn't going to give Mrs. Carmody that satisfaction.

Clara put down her book, *La Vagabonde* by Colette, about an actress who rejects men in order to retain her own independence—a fitting read for her current state of mind. Too bad she hadn't read it back in New York; she could have saved herself the trouble of falling in love with the wrong man and getting her heart broken.

If only she could see her old roommates, that might make her feel better. It was seven-thirty on a Saturday night, New York City time. Coco and Leelee would be out by now, with their *beaux du jour,* rushing to make an eight o'clock show. Then the speakeasy scavenger hunt would begin, on the trail to seek out the latest hush-hush place—housed in some millionaire's garden in the Village or in the back room of a private restaurant's basement off Madison Square. God, she missed New York. So far, Chicago had merely been . . . windy.

Just then, a peal of laughter exploded from the end of the hallway. It came from the bedroom of wedding-bell-blues Gloria, who was painting her nails (carnation pink, no doubt) with her vaguely desperate sidekick, Lorraine. It was the kind of hyena-esque giggling that accompanied gossip; there was no doubt in Clara's mind that she was the subject.

Clara almost laughed aloud at the thought of Gloria and Lorraine trying to make it in her old city life. They wouldn't survive a day in her run-down apartment building, with its bohemians and cockroaches, with its furniture scavenged off the streets, where the electric went out so often they'd had to rely on tea candles for light. They knew nothing of skinny-dipping with a bunch of drunken strangers at three a.m. in the Central Park Reservoir. And judging by the way Bastian and Gloria behaved—a polite peck on the lips, about as passionate as a smooch between an eight-year-old boy and his grandma—they knew nothing about sex. And that was one thing Clara knew a lot about. Maybe a little too much.

This was what these Chicago socialites knew: buttoned-up private school uniforms, afternoons of piano and French lessons, and the goal of a rock on their finger. Her cousin's bobbed-hair "rebellion" was no more than a fleeting temper tantrum that would last the hot minute her locks took to grow back. Then she'd marry Mr. Sebastian Grey and settle down into the coffin of her life as a wife and a kept woman.

The laughter was louder now. Clara left her room, tip-toeing toward the sound. She paused at Gloria's door, straining to overhear the conversation.

GLORIA: I'll bet she hasn't even been kissed before.
LORRAINE: As if you've done *so* much more.
GLORIA: Shut up. I mean, I'll bet she hasn't even, say, gone on a date.
LORRAINE: Definitely not.
GLORIA: Do you think she's [*gasp*] a lesbian?
LORRAINE: Who knows *what* they do on that farm?
GLORIA: Oh, Raine. She's ridiculous. So polite. So *annoying.*
LORRAINE: She's a fifty-year-old woman trapped in an eighteen-year-old's body.
GLORIA: She's practically best friends with my mother.

Clara couldn't help smiling. They had no idea. She wasn't insulted by their gossiping—they weren't really talking about *her,* but about her alter ego, the Country Rube-in-Residence. Who knew role-playing could be so much fun?

She was about to retreat to her room when something caught her ear:

GLORIA: So when do we set this plan into action?
LORRAINE: Marcus said he would take care of that.
GLORIA: Do you think it will really work? My mother is pretty intent on her being here. . . .

"Caught you!" a deep voice whispered behind Clara.

She gasped and whipped around, expecting to find a nosy servant. Instead, she saw one of the sexiest boys she'd ever laid eyes on in her entire life. She gasped again. His eyes were pools of Caribbean blue, his lips were full and perfect and ripe for kissing. His blond hair was slicked and parted at the side, his cheeks were smooth, and—oh! He had dimples!

He was totally and completely swoon-worthy.

The boy put a finger up to his lips with a faint shushing noise. Without thinking, Clara took his hand and pulled him through the hallway into her room. She shut the door. His grip was strong, and she felt an old familiar thrill at his touch. Only then did she realize that taking him into her bedroom might not have been the most in-character thing to do. Country Clara would never be so forward. She dropped his hand.

"I'm sorry, I thought you were—"

"Your dream come true?" He grinned widely, showing off his dazzlingly white teeth.

"Absolutely . . . *not!*" Clara said. Immediately, she knew this boy was Bad News. He might have been good-looking—all right, he was *insanely* good-looking—but he was the type of guy who knew exactly how good-looking he was. There was nothing more unappealing than that. More importantly, she'd sworn off boys. They weren't part of her new image.

She motioned toward the door. "Now if you'll excuse me—"

He walked closer to where she stood. "Wilt you leave me so unsatisfied?"

Clara took a giant step backward. Was he really quoting Shakespeare to her? "If you expect to impress me by *mis*-quoting *Romeo and Juliet,*" she said, "then you are sadly mistaken."

"Shows how behind I am in my English homework." The boy grinned wickedly and plopped down on the edge of her bed. He patted the empty place next to him. "I only wanted you to explain what you were doing in the hallway when I found you."

"Oh," Clara said, trying to look innocent—however that looked. He was leaning back, an easy grin on his face. Was he trying to seduce her? Her natural instinct was to pounce on him. But of course, that was out of the question. She remained standing, for her own sake.

"I wasn't eavesdropping, if that is what you are insinuating."

"I would never accuse you of such an immoral act."

"Good," she said, "because I would never think to commit one."

The boy tugged her toward the bed. She resisted slightly at first, but then happily yielded. She quickly crossed her legs, which she assumed was the sort of thing they taught in the etiquette class she'd managed to skip in high school.

His hand was warm. "You've never been tempted to do an immoral thing?"

How she wanted to whisper into his ear what she wanted to do right then and there! Instead, she withdrew. "I think that is an outrageously inappropriate question to ask of a stranger."

The boy examined her slyly. "You certainly are a strange one. *Clara*."

Clara shot him a look of mock horror. "How did you know my name?"

"You're Glo's cousin." He tilted his head. "I'm Marcus."

Marcus. Lorraine and Gloria had been discussing a Marcus . . . and some kind of plan.

"I've heard all about you," Marcus said.

"Oh? Good things or bad things?"

"I thought I knew, but now I'm not quite sure." He stood up. "There is only one way to find out. Tonight, you're coming with me. I'm taking you to the Green Mill, the—"

"The hottest speakeasy in town, I know!" Clara blurted out. She watched Marcus's face twist in confusion: How would she, Country Clara, know about the Green Mill? "I mean, I've only heard rumors about it," she said. "Very *bad* rumors."

Marcus's face softened. "So then it's settled. You'll meet me at midnight."

"I don't think that is a very sensible idea. I don't know you. I can't go somewhere with you alone."

"We won't be alone. Glo and Raine are coming, too," he said with a laugh.

"Wait a second," Clara said, genuinely shocked. "You mean to tell me that my cousin Gloria goes to places like the Green Mill?" She would never have pegged Gloria as someone who'd sneak out to a place like that—even in New York, the Green Mill was infamous. Rumor made it sound like a thrilling mixture of glamour and danger, run by young, good-looking gangsters.

"Not usually, but tonight we're celebrating her bob." He shrugged.

Clara began to put the pieces together. There was no chance Gloria would want her tagging along. If Marcus had truly "heard all about" her, surely he'd know that much. Which meant that Marcus's invitation was the girls' doing, some scheme they'd cooked up and fobbed off on him. Hadn't Gloria said that in her bedroom—something about how Marcus was going to "take care" of her? Clara couldn't figure out his intentions quite yet, but one thing was for sure: There was much more to this pretty boy than met the eye.

"I assume Gloria's fiancé is coming, too? I'm sure he wouldn't want to miss out on the celebration."

"Let's just say," Marcus said, looking in her vanity mirror and fixing his hair, "it's an early bachelorette party. No grooms allowed."

"Ah, I see," Clara said. "Perhaps you're better off if there are no cousins allowed, either."

"Give me one reason why you shouldn't go."

"Give me one reason why I should," Clara said. Even though she wanted to go, she had an act to keep up. Country Clara would never be seen at a speakeasy.

"Because I'll be there," he said. "And I've already squared this with Gloria. She really wants you to come. She even has a dress for you to wear."

And then he stood, tipped an invisible hat, and walked out of her room, leaving a scent of shaving balm and promise in his wake.

◆◆◆

The plan was that Clara would meet Gloria in her room at eleven p.m. sharp.

With five minutes to go, she made her final preparations: set her makeup with powder; threw lipstick, compact, and clove gum into her purse; double-checked her teeth. But this familiar routine now seemed faked, the remnant of some distant universe she was no longer a part of.

The last time Clara had been to a speakeasy had been on her final night in New York. The city had been abuzz with the simmering heat of August. Clara was just finishing the last sip of her martini when the sirens began to wail. "This is a police raid! Nobody move an inch!" Within seconds, the music stopped and the lights came on, exposing a blind-drunk, screaming stampede.

Before she had a chance to react, someone shoved her through a trapdoor beneath the bar. Clara found herself crawling through a damp basement crowded with cartons of liquor and full of scurrying rats, until she reached a metal door that let out onto the sidewalk. The street was still and empty, not yet disturbed by the madhouse that roared below. She was free to run home.

Or she could hijack the police paddy wagon, which was parked at the corner with one door wide open and the key dangling in the ignition and not a copper in sight.

It was easy-peasy.

She jumped behind the wheel just as the police began to emerge from the Red Head, dragging out hordes of handcuffed flappers. There were switches on the dashboard. Finding the one marked SIREN, she flipped it on, then cranked the key in the ignition and stamped on the gas pedal. The wagon took off, rattling down East Fourth Street at lightning speed, the back door banging open and closed as she swerved down the street. With no place to lock up their victims, the policemen took off after her, running down the street and blowing their whistles.

Clara just laughed and laughed and gave the wagon more gas.

She had never felt so free. She turned onto Fifth Avenue and flipped off the siren, watching the reflection of the wagon as she whooshed past the storefronts, then took a spin through Central Park, meandering past the reservoir, popping the siren on every now and then to see whom she could startle. She was coasting along Riverside Drive as the sun rose over the East Side. She found an empty intersection, parked the paddy wagon dead center, and removed the key from the ignition. She'd toss it in the Hudson when she got a chance.

It was foolish, of course, and totally reckless, but *damn,* it was exciting. She remembered wishing that life could be like that always, a wild-goose chase without a destination. A chase for the thrill of running.

Ultimately, the destination that early morning had been jail. She hadn't seen the police car trailing her, and the coppers hadn't listened to her protestations of innocence when they'd picked her up and thrown her into the backseat. She was holding the key to the paddy wagon, and that was as good as a smoking gun.

Her father arrived in New York the next day and threatened to disown her if she didn't leave behind her "immoral lifestyle" and return home immediately.

Clara didn't worry much about being disowned. But that night was the final straw. That and the boy. She had never quite recovered from him.

Of course, if her father had known about the boy, she would have been disowned already. Here, in Chicago, she was supposed to have a fresh start. Playing the Good Girl was finally becoming fun. *Especially* now that she was en route to the hottest speakeasy in Chicago.

◆◆◆

Clara crept down the dark hallway to Gloria's room and tapped on the door. Gloria opened it, her gold sequined dress pulled on halfway. She beckoned for Clara to come in and quietly closed the door behind them.

"I'm taking a big risk letting you come along with us," Gloria said. "But Marcus for some reason thinks you can be trusted not to rat us out."

"You have my word." Clara turned an invisible key on her lips. And then raised her eyebrows. "But I'm not really sure we should be going to a speakeasy! Aren't they just dens of sin?"

Gloria ignored her question. "My friend Lorraine was nice enough to bring these over for you to wear," she said, pointing to some clothes laid out on her bed. "Since I assumed you didn't pack anything appropriate for the Green Mill."

Clara picked up the peach chiffon dress, with its dropped waist ending in a layer of beaded pleats. When she held it up to herself in the mirror, she almost laughed: The hemline hit midcalf. Even her mother would find this dowdy.

Little did Gloria know that in New York, Clara's clothes had been the fabric of legend. If Clara wore a new outfit on Saturday night, flappers would storm Madison Avenue the next day in search of it. One of her day jobs had been working as a fitting model for Bergdorf Goodman's new ready-to-wear line. All irregular or damaged clothes—European or American—were hers to keep. Clara didn't just set new trends, she set *chic* ones.

She had to think of this dress as a costume, she reminded herself. Even so, it was *so* 1918. "This dress is so . . . *beautiful.*"

"We figured you wouldn't want to wear something that made you feel uncomfortable."

"I appreciate your thoughtfulness," Clara said carefully.

Gloria fumbled with the pearl buttons on the back of her dress. "Help me before you get dressed."

"Isn't this a little too tight?" Clara asked. "And too red?"

"Applesauce," Gloria said.

"Let me know if I'm pinching you." Gloria had a graceful figure, but it was moderately curvy, and the dress was clearly made for a girl without a chest. "On the count of three, suck in as much as you can. One, two, three!"

Clara managed to button up the dress all the way. Gloria exhaled loudly and then darted toward her vanity. She shimmied in front of the mirror. "Oh, wow. I look—"

"Like the bee's knees! As you crazy flappers like to say." Why not start the night out on a positive note, Clara thought, so that she could casually get the dirt on Marcus? She picked the peach dress up off the bed and slipped it over her head. "So, what's-his-name and Lorraine are meeting us there?" she asked.

"Yeah, at midnight on the street corner. We have to hurry."

"So, are they *together*? Since you're . . ."

"Since I'm *what*?" Gloria stopped applying her lipstick midstroke.

"Since you are *engaged,*" Clara said, walking over to Gloria's chair, "Lorraine and Marcus have something going on. Is that right?"

"Raine is very single. As is Marcus. And they are most definitely *not* together."

Clara fixed a smudge of kohl below her eye in the mirror over Gloria's head. "So Bastian must be incredibly jealous of Marcus, then."

"Why do you say that?"

"Because you're going to a club in that sexy dress with a single man who is *not* him." Clara picked up a pot of rouge, which was lying right next to Gloria's diamond engagement ring. "Oh"—Gloria met Clara's eyes with a distant flicker of guilt—"so Bastian doesn't *know* you're going tonight, does he?"

"Men don't need to know everything," Gloria said, slipping the ring into a drawer.

Clara frowned. "It's not healthy to keep secrets from the one you love. A successful relationship is built upon mutual trust." She'd read that in some boring magazine somewhere.

Gloria snatched the rouge out of Clara's hands and furiously applied some. Her cheeks were rounder than Clara's, whose face had narrowed from her hungry days in the city. Gloria still looked like a little girl.

After what seemed like an hour, Gloria turned to Clara. "I know my mother invited you here to help me with the wedding and everything. Which I appreciate. But I already have my own friends and my own life here, and a very important fiancé who doesn't need to be bothered with every little thing I do. So what I would appreciate *more* is if you'd mind your own business and not help me at all. Except, perhaps, to decide what flavor of frosting I want on my cake."

Clara was taken aback by this sudden outburst. It almost made her admire Gloria, seeing that there was something burning beneath her cool diamond-encrusted exterior. And, given her own past, Clara knew this spark all too well: It was a ticking bomb, waiting for the right moment, and the right person, to set it off. She decided right then that she would help Gloria find the fiery release that she herself had once found. Even if she had to light the wick herself.

"Then I hope, dear cousin, you can have your cake and eat it, too."

Gloria rolled her eyes. "Aren't you witty. Now can we go?"

"Oh, lor—I mean, rats! I forgot my purse!" Clara exclaimed.

"Ugh! You're going to make us late! And we won't be let in after twelve-thirty!"

Clara sprinted down the hall and into her own room. In the dark, she groped for her handbag, which lay right where she'd left it on her dresser. As she picked it up, she felt something fall to the ground. Her cash. She flipped on her vanity mirror's light. It was then that she saw that what had fallen was *not* money at all.

She picked up a small piece of thick cream writing paper, folded lengthwise. Where had it come from?

Tentatively, she opened the note. Scrawled in elegant black cursive were three words:

*I found you*

Clara inhaled sharply.

Suddenly the shadows in her room seemed alive, spinning her into their web of darkness. She ran to the window, looking out, but no one could have climbed to the top floor of the house without someone's taking notice. It didn't make sense. She had only left her room for a few minutes. Who had put the note there? One of the servants? Or had someone been in the house? And most importantly, how had whoever it was found her?

Clara froze, the note sticky and hot in her palm. There was someone there, hovering on the other side of her door, listening in the slit of light, as the light grew wider and wider and wider and—

"Clara! I thought you'd been murdered, you were taking so long." It was Gloria. And she was fuming.

Clara hid the note behind her back. "Sorry, I had forgotten to pack money."

Gloria let out a huff of impatience. "We don't *need* any dough. Men buy you drinks."

"Really? I had no idea. How polite of them. Oh! I must spritz on some perfume!" Clara spotted a bottle of Chanel No. 5 on her dresser, the nearest distraction, and picked it up with her free hand.

Gloria glared. "I'll be waiting in my room. For approximately one more second."

After Gloria stormed out, Clara unfolded the note again. Surely it was just a prank played by one of the servants. Or Marcus! Egged on by those scheming, devious girls! She stuffed the note into the back of her underwear drawer and slammed it shut.

Still, a cold, damp sweat had settled at the small of

her back and was rapidly inching up her spine. Deep down, Clara knew the note was not a joke. It was the exact opposite—devastatingly serious. She spritzed the Chanel perfume into the air before her, walking through it and out the door. The mist settled onto her skin, the top floral note masking the darker ones that lay hidden beneath.

# LORRAINE

Lorraine was furious. “Horsefeathers! We can’t just stand around like this! It’s not a school mixer!”

The group was perched, stiff and unmoving, at the edge of the Green Mill’s dance floor. They’d made it past the door smoothly (password: *Sugar Daddy*), but why were they all being such Mrs. Grundys? Raine was ready to drink and dance! Gloria, on the other hand, was gazing dreamily at the stage as if she’d never seen or heard live music performed before. Clara eyed the bar like a little girl scandalized by all the naughtiness grown-ups did in private, and Marcus . . . well, it didn’t matter *what* he was doing. He was a complete sheik, the sort of keen guy a girl could get dizzy over.

“Can we at least make an effort to *pretend* we belong?” Raine asked.

"Why don't I take Clara for her first real drink, and you two go dance," Marcus suggested, placing his hand on the small of Clara's back.

"No! I mean—" Lorraine fumbled. What *did* she mean? She could almost swear that Marcus had been *genuinely* flirting with Clara all night. The way his hand had rested on Clara's back—a little too comfortably and a tad too long—went far beyond the call of duty. He almost seemed to be deriving pleasure from the touch. Lorraine should have known better than to assign a man to do a woman's job. She would have to steer Project Send Clara Home all on her own. "I mean, it's only appropriate that *I* go with her instead. We wouldn't want any of the eligible men to think Clara was taken."

Clara waved her hand. "Oh, but I'm not here to meet men—"

"Why not? Do you have some secret fiancé back home that we don't know about?" Lorraine hoped Marcus would laugh, but instead he seemed to eagerly await the answer.

"I'm here to help with Gloria's nuptials, not my own matrimonial prospects," Clara said, glancing toward the bar. "Besides, I have no interest in . . . consuming illegal substances."

"But it's mandatory!" Lorraine cried. "Alcohol is to the Green Mill as milk is to your cows."

"What cows?"

Lorraine burst out laughing. "You've only been away

from home for a week and already you've forgotten your beloved cows?"

Clara twisted her gold bracelet uncomfortably. "Oh no. It's . . . um . . . if you'll excuse me . . ."

They all watched her dash off to the powder room, clearly humiliated.

Lorraine burst out laughing, pleased at her handiwork. "Well, we all know what side of the Prohibition she's on." Lorraine stepped onto the dance floor, pulling Gloria with her. "Come on," she pleaded, "we can do the Charleston."

Gloria groaned. "Oh, Lorraine, you don't know the Charleston."

"Do so," Lorraine said, swiveling her hips along to the music, trying to remember the moves. "Violet taught me during physical fitness class last week."

Lorraine hated Violet, but the girl had her uses. She had been boasting to everyone with ears how she'd mastered the steps of the Charleston. "It's the most fun I've ever had," Violet had said between exercises.

Miss Wilma had blown a whistle, and the girls had had to run a lazy circle around the gymnasium. But even that hadn't stopped Violet from talking.

"It's all the rage, you know," she'd said. "I saw it in New York."

Later, near one of the water fountains, Violet had put on a demonstration. She started twisting her feet. "Just pretend there's music!" she told the assembled girls. The twisting was slow at first and then became faster.

"It's like the Jay-Bird!" Lorraine exclaimed, nearly recognizing a dance move she and Gloria had practiced almost nightly a year before.

"No, it's better," Violet insisted, her legs moving so swiftly, her feet kicking forward and backward at such a rapid pace, that Lorraine could only watch in awe, wondering how someone so ungainly could move so nimbly. And all without music.

Unfortunately, they'd been interrupted by Miss Wilma before Violet could finish. "Girls! That's not what I call a water break!" she hollered. "Stop that immoral writhing and give me twenty jumping jacks."

Now Lorraine was trying to re-create Violet's moves and show Gloria what the Charleston was all about. "Here's how you do it," she instructed, kicking out her legs and trying not to fall on the floor. Around her, dozens of other flappers were doing the very same dance, only slightly more naturally than she was. From a few feet away, Marcus watched them and laughed.

"I don't know," Gloria said doubtfully. "You look a little . . . spasmodic."

"Oh, please! I'm doing it perfectly." Lorraine threw her arms up into the air and shouted, "Who's dry now, Chicago?" It was what she imagined a true flapper would say, a sticking-it-to-the-drys who supported the Prohibition.

"I think I'm going to take a break from the Charleston," Gloria said, still watching Lorraine. "At least until I can figure out how to do it right."

"Right, shmight," Lorraine said, out of breath. "It's all about having fun."

Marcus came forward and hooked his arm through Gloria's. "Come with me, Glo, so we can have a toast to our girl Clara's new look."

Gloria snatched a teacup from a waiter walking by, downing its contents without missing a beat. "You two go have fun. I think I'm going to watch the band for a while," she said, drifting away from Marcus and Lorraine.

Gloria had been acting noticeably strange since the night began. Lorraine had attributed it to nerves, but usually when Gloria was nervous, she talked a mile a minute; tonight, however, she'd barely uttered a word.

Either way, there was no time to worry about Gloria now. This was Lorraine's moment to have Marcus alone. She took his hand and pushed through the gaggles of flappers until they landed at the bar. Marcus immediately ordered them both martinis. There was something innately seductive when a man ordered a drink for you—Marcus *had* to be interested in her on some subliminal level.

Except for the fact that he had his eye on a willowy blonde at the end of the bar.

"I feel as if I'm on the beach in Cuba," Lorraine shouted over the music. She held her cool glass up to his cheek.

"What are you doing?"

"It looked as if you needed to cool down," Lorraine said. *That sounded seductive, right?*

Marcus smirked, clearly not picking up on her flirtatious vamping. Did he not see that she was wearing her "naked dress"—the flesh-toned one that ended in shimmery layers like a mermaid's tail, leaving very little to the imagination? He was acting as if she were dressed in a potato sack. She needed to say something, *anything* to draw his attention.

"So, Marcus, what do you think the speakeasy scene will be like when we get to New York?"

This time she caught him. His head snapped around. "We?"

She hadn't meant to let it slip. Not here, not now. But according to Freud's *Psychopathology of Everyday Life*—which she had self-consciously listed as her favorite book on her Barnard admissions application—perhaps it was her subconscious kicking in. What better time to plant the seed in his mind: the two of them, Chicago castaways, together in New York.

She leaned in closer. "I have a secret to tell you."

Marcus raised an eyebrow. "I *love* a good secret."

Just as Raine was about to reveal to him what no one else besides her parents knew, someone rammed into her from behind, sending her tumbling into Marcus's arms. She looked up into his deep blue gaze, their faces millimeters apart, and she couldn't stop herself: She leaned in and kissed him.

Their lips barely touched before Marcus pulled away. "What are you doing?"

"Oh, I . . . ," she mumbled, mortified. She hadn't expected such a reaction. "The gin must have gone to my head already."

"Since when did you become such a lightweight?" His tone was biting, cutting right to her heart.

She forced a laugh and playfully slapped his arm, but the damage was done. How could she have been so stupid? So rash? Marcus would never look at her the same way again, now that he knew she carried a torch for him.

Could the situation get any worse? Lorraine turned and grimaced. Of course it could: Clara reappeared. "What did I miss?" she asked, sliding between them. "You two look as if you've just been to a funeral."

"All the more reason for another round of drinks." Marcus beckoned the bartender.

Clara raised a hand in protest. "Marcus, I made myself perfectly clear—"

Marcus made a shushing gesture, putting his finger on her lips. "Don't you know it's impolite to turn down a drink from a gentleman?"

"Don't you know it's impolite to disregard a lady's wishes?" Clara flagged down the bartender with a flick of her hand. "I'll have a seltzer water, please. With a wedge of lime."

Lorraine was appalled. She had just made a complete fool of herself, and here Marcus was already turning up the charm with this apple-knocker as if nothing had happened!

Just as she was about to give up and go find Gloria, a tall man in a white tuxedo approached Marcus. Despite the fancy getup and slicked-back dark hair, he looked no older than eighteen. "Eastman!"

Marcus smiled broadly. "Freddy Barnes! Great to see you, old boy!" He pumped the man's hand.

"Haven't seen you outside of school since I trounced you in that doubles game last summer," Freddy said. "Where have you been? People aren't supposed to forget their high school buddies until the first year of college." To Lorraine and Clara, he said, "Eastman used to be the ultimate guy's guy, but nowadays . . ."

"Never mind Freddy," Marcus said. "He's as ugly as he is rude."

"I'm not rude!" Freddy insisted. He extended his hand to Lorraine. "I beg your pardon if I was offensive. I'm Frederick Barnes."

Marcus said, "This is Lorraine Dyer."

Lorraine loved the feel of this stranger's hand touching her own.

Freddy's eyebrows rose. "Dyer? As in your father is Patrick Dyer? As in the Dyer Building downtown?"

Lorraine coughed daintily. "Daddy does love tall things."

"And this is Clara Knowles," Marcus said. "She's from the country."

"She works with cows," Lorraine added quickly.

Freddy took Clara's hand and said, "You are like a country flower, a fresh sight in this tired gin joint."

Clara laughed, and Lorraine wanted to throw the rest of her martini on that country boob.

Marcus waved his friend off. "Don't listen to Freddy. He's so full of hot air that it's carrying him to Princeton next fall."

"You talk big for a Columbia man," Freddy said. "Care to join me and the guys for a little poker?"

Marcus said, "You're in for a fleecing."

Lorraine turned to Clara. "Oh, something you know about!" Clara shot her a blank stare. "You know, Mary had a little lamb and all that."

With a suave bow, Marcus said, "Clara, I expect your drink to be gone by the time I'm back." Then he and Freddy strolled away.

Lorraine held back tears. Not only had she been rejected by Marcus, but she'd also gotten stuck with the hick cousin.

"So, Gloria tells me you've been here before?" Clara asked politely. "Aren't you worried about"—she cut her eyes first left, then right, and whispered—"all the criminals?"

Lorraine sipped her drink and laughed as if it were No Big Deal. "Just know your onions," Lorraine said, all breezy confidence. "If you stay away from the dope peddlers, the bootleggers, the quiffs, and the police, then everything's jake."

"Who's Jake?" Clara asked, confused.

Lorraine ignored her, unwilling to explain flapper slang in the midst of actual flappers. Nothing could be more un-jake than that. "Oh! And don't go near that booth right there," she said, pointing to the plush green one in a corner of the room.

"Why? Who sits there?" Clara asked, rising on her tiptoes to see the booth.

"Don't *look*! That's the worst thing you could do!" Lorraine said through gritted teeth. "That's Al Capone's private table. He sits there so he can keep one eye on both entrances in case of a police raid—and dive into the trapdoor beneath the bar at a moment's notice."

Clara blinked her big dumb doe eyes. "Goodness gracious!"

"The guy next to him, the handsome Italian-looking one? That's his right-hand man's son, Carlito—"

"No, I was referring to . . . *that!*" Clara blurted out, her eyes widening at something behind Lorraine's back.

Lorraine turned and was unsurprised to find a black man dancing the Charleston with a white woman—of course that would shock Clara. Lorraine almost snorted at Clara's naïveté, until she peered at the couple more closely and realized who the white woman was.

Gloria.

Clara clutched her throat. "I didn't know Gloria was so . . . progressive. In terms of race relations, I mean."

"Neither did I."

Lorraine couldn't take her eyes off Gloria. She looked dazzling, like a red poppy in a field of weeds, swaying in the breeze. She had never seen Glo acting with such reckless abandon, not caring what anybody else in the room thought. What *she,* Lorraine, her best friend, thought. Gloria was smiling and laughing and exuding an effortless grace, as if she had been born on the dance floor.

"Gloria is a rare girl, isn't she?" Clara said, making it more of a statement than a question.

"I don't know if *rare* is the word." Lorraine turned back to the bar, having seen quite enough. "More like *privileged.*"

"Oh, but I mean aside from the wealthy family, the perfect grades, and the pre-Raphaelite beauty." Clara paused, squeezing the lime wedge into her seltzer. "She's rare because she's the type of girl who can have a dignified fiancé waiting at home, a handsome male best friend at her beck and call, *and* still get to dance with a famous black jazz pianist. Actually, it's more than rare. It's quite extraordinary."

Lorraine felt her heart drop through her stomach. Gloria was extraordinary, and she herself was . . . she was . . . not. There was nothing worse than that. "Well," Lorraine said, fixing her bob, "her fiancé thinks speakeasies are 'dens of corruption.' If he knew where she was and what she was doing, he wouldn't act so dignified. And Gloria wouldn't seem quite so extraordinary."

As the song ended and applause erupted from the dance floor, Lorraine watched the piano player take Gloria's hand and kiss it. Her impulse was to jump onto the floor and pull Gloria away, but something stopped her. Though she didn't quite know what.

"I admire what a good friend you are, Raine. Sometimes it takes a good friend to give us the courage to do the things we could never do for ourselves." Clara touched Lorraine's shoulder. "You helped Gloria to get her hair bobbed, right?"

"She wouldn't have done it without me," Lorraine stated matter-of-factly.

"Precisely. Gloria clearly looks up to you. And why wouldn't she? You're mature. You have a sophistication about the world that she sorely lacks. But because of that, you also have a responsibility to watch out for her."

Lorraine regarded Clara suspiciously. Of course she knew all this about herself intuitively, but why should Gloria come under her care? They were seventeen; Glo should be able to make her own decisions. "If anybody should be watching out for her, it's her fiancé," Lorraine said. As the words came out of her mouth, she felt her face flush. "But of course I *care* about her; she's like a sister to me."

"You wouldn't let your sister go farther than the Charleston with that man, would you?" Clara asked, the answer already hovering between them. "Or at least, without letting her fiancé put up a fair fight."

As much as Lorraine disliked Clara's tone, maybe there *was* something smart about this country bumpkin's advice. If Lorraine were a true best friend, she wouldn't allow Gloria to jeopardize her own future. Then again, to get Bastian involved would be a betrayal of epic proportions. If he knew that Gloria had gone to the Green Mill, and danced with another man, let alone a black man!—well, who knew what he might do?

Lorraine knew. He would break off the wedding.

"Oh, look, Marcus is back!" Clara chirped.

He was indeed. Brow sweaty, eyes glazed, his once-pressed shirt crumpled. He looked as if he'd been up to no good—and yet, he'd never *looked* so good. Lorraine's pulse raced and she held her hand to her chest.

"I'll never make that mistake again," Marcus said. "What's this?" he asked, looking at Clara. "An empty glass?"

"If you'd like to refill my *seltzer,* Mr. Eastman, you may."

"I'd rather dance," Marcus said, pulling Clara away from the bar.

"Oh no! I could never dance like *that*—"

"I won't take no for an answer!"

Lorraine shooed them away. *Let them dance,* she thought morosely. She looked around for someone to buy her another drink . . . but who?

Then something caught her eye. It was the back of

Gloria's head. Lorraine was about to call out her friend's name when something stopped her yet again. Gloria was leaning over a table in a corner of the club, deep in conversation with that same black piano player. They were staring at each other as if there were no one else in the club. She watched, in shock, as Gloria stole the piano player's glass from his hand and drained it.

Which was when she realized that Gloria was *again* not wearing her engagement ring! The room became a blurry maelstrom of color and sound. *Lorraine* was the one who had bobbed her hair first, who wasn't attached to any man, who had the world at her fingertips. Gloria had already decided her future—she'd landed the coveted ring and the coveted fiancé. And now she was flirting with some poor black musician just because she *could*? Lorraine couldn't even get Marcus to *kiss* her, let alone fall in love with her!

Everything was spinning out of control. Lorraine clutched the bar, trying to steady herself. Suddenly, she felt a warm hand on her arm. "Raine? Are you okay?" She looked up; Clara's soft face came into focus. "Here, drink this. Come on, it will make you feel better."

Lorraine took a sip of the cool, fizzy seltzer. "Thank you."

"I spotted you from across the dance floor and you gave me a fright!"

Lorraine blinked, seeing Clara as though for the very first time. Perhaps she shouldn't be so tough on Clara. So what if the girl was a hick? She was sweet and her intentions were good. She was giving Lorraine seltzer while Gloria—her supposed best friend—was off with that pianist. And if it wasn't him, it would be Bastian. Gloria was making it clear: Men Before Friends. How devastatingly rude.

"Sometimes nights like these can be overwhelming," Clara said over the noise of the crowd. "Chicago is nothing like where I'm from. Although isn't it funny how Gloria seems to be handling everything just fine?"

"Funny indeed," Lorraine agreed. Clara seemed to be the only voice of reason as her world was turning upside down. Clara truly was a Good Girl through and through. Marcus would never be seriously interested in such a wet blanket. Lorraine had nothing to be jealous of.

Perhaps she shouldn't be so quick to dispose of Country Clara. After all, if the truth about Gloria *did* need to come out at some point soon—whatever that truth might be—better it should be Clara's doing than her own. That way, Lorraine wouldn't have to get herself dirty.

# GLORIA

Gloria had been dreaming about the lights of the Green Mill. Dreaming of dropping her diamond ring into the grate on the sidewalk like a penny into a fountain. But mostly, she'd been dreaming about Jerome Johnson's hands.

But now that she'd made it back to the infamous speakeasy, she was hit with the same feeling as the first time: *What am I doing here?* The second time should be easier, she reminded herself: Her hair was the right length; she knew how to order a martini; she even had an in with Leif, the bartender. But the addition of Lorraine and Clara had unsettled her.

As soon as they'd all gotten inside, Gloria had escaped. She didn't need to see Lorraine playing the coy mistress role in front of Marcus for the thousandth time. Nor did she need to see, hear, or be within a state's distance of Clara.

The band finished its first set, and Gloria watched as Jerome Johnson stood up from the piano bench, straightened his bow tie, exited the stage, and fell into the arms of a gorgeous black girl.

Gloria's heart plummeted. She immediately recognized Gorgeous Black Girl from last time—the one in the silver negligee. This time, the girl's tall, lean body was draped in bronze silk that tapered into black crystal fringes; her dark hair was pinned with a copper leaf barrette that accentuated her luminous skin. She looked about Gloria's age, maybe a year or so younger. And her arm was now wrapped affectionately around Jerome Johnson's waist.

How could Gloria have been so stupid? What had she been thinking—that this black pianist would fall in love with her? That she could call off her engagement to Bastian and bring Mr. Jerome Johnson home for family dinner? It was unheard of in high society for any white woman to date a black man, but for a *Carmody* to even be *seen* with one? She was better off having Bastian's illegitimate child—not that that would even be physically possible at the rate their relationship was progressing.

Anyway, her future was predetermined, and there was no way of changing it now. She couldn't let her family down: It was a promise she had made to her mother, and to herself. Tonight, her sole purpose was to have a bit of mindless fun in the little time left before her wedding. She had to keep reminding herself of that.

Gloria turned away, unable to look at Jerome Johnson for another second. She should just leave *now,* before she turned back around and made an impulsive, irreversible mistake.

"Swank haircut," a baritone voice whispered in her ear. "Care to dance?"

She should have ignored the voice, or protested, or slapped him for talking to her so casually. But one look at his face made her knees weak. He firmly gripped her bare shoulders, as if he were about to play the blues on her back, just as the music changed. The speakeasy's gramophone began to swell with a slow song:

*I lost the sunshine and roses, I lost the heavens of blue,*
*I lost the beautiful rainbow, I lost the morning dew.*
*I lost the angel who gave me summer, the whole winter too.*
*I lost the gladness that turned into sadness,*
*When I lost you.*

Irving Berlin's lyrics filled in for the words she could not say.

Though, really, what *could* she say? Gloria felt as if she had lost Jerome, along with whatever potential they might have had, but she'd never truly had him in the first place. She knew nothing about this stranger whom she felt insatiably attracted to—nothing of his life or his background. She held on to his shoulders as her feet moved beneath her, almost of their own accord. His touch excited her, exhilarated her. His arms were strong and his breath was sweet and warm against her neck.

The record came to an end. The room was momentarily hushed by the scratchy static and pop of the dead record spinning on the gramophone. Then the crowd resumed its deafening conversation.

Gloria felt as if she had just emerged from a reverie. She staggered backward slightly, but Jerome caught hold of her. "Thanks for the dance, kid."

She watched as he walked off and slid into a booth by the wall without so much as a second glance in her direction. This must be his game, she thought, playing the Too Cool card. Then again, that was *everyone's* game here. But now—with her new hair to match her new attitude—who was to say she couldn't compete?

She marched over to where he was sitting and sat directly across from him. They stared at each other for a few long moments, Jerome taking drags from his cigarette in the silence. The space between them was brimming with smoke and tension and heat.

"Why are you here, kid?" he asked finally.

Gloria bristled. Just because she was younger didn't mean she had to tolerate condescension. "Why do you keep calling me that?"

"Calling you what?"

"Kid."

He smirked. "Your question just answered my question," he said, blowing a stream of white smoke rings.

"Then tell me why I'm here, since you seem to know better than I."

A waitress came over, planting a glass of whiskey on the table. He winked at her, and she blew him an air kiss in return. As Gloria caught this cheap exchange, it dawned on her: Jerome Johnson met a million girls, just like her, every night of the week. Girls who smoked and drank and laughed with him—probably other, less innocent activities, too. Besides playing the piano, his job was to play them. And they fell right into his trap like helpless mice. Just as she had.

But Gloria wasn't like these other girls—she was different. Or at least, that was what she wanted to believe.

"You're here," he began, taking a long sip of his drink, "to prove to yourself that you're not just that: a kid. Even though you know that's *exactly* what you are."

Gloria tried to keep her composure. "I'm the furthest thing from being a kid," she fumed, her cheeks burning. "How old are you? Nineteen? Twenty? You're not exactly a *man* yourself. And if you must know, I'm here for the music."

Jerome guffawed, slapping the table. "Music? What do *you* know about music? You're a spoiled rich white girl."

Furious, Gloria stood up. No one had ever been so rude to

her in her life! She knew she should walk away, find her friends at the bar, and have a good laugh about this insolent, low-class, ill-mannered—

She realized she was thinking like her mother. That alone made her want to kiss him, right then and there, to prove she was different. Instead—she didn't want to seem crazy, even if she felt it—she slid into his side of the booth. "I bet I know more about music than any girl—white or otherwise—in this joint."

He moved closer, his pant leg grazing her bare thigh. Everything about him looked strong—the shape of his nose, the cut of his cheeks, and the square line of his jaw. His eyes, though, were soft, a rich brown that almost hypnotized her. "What you know, *kid,* are the dusty old books you learn at your little girls' private school. You know how to identify a Beethoven symphony or a Mozart concerto. You know the story of *La Bohème* because your parents have box seats at the opera. You know the song we danced to because you heard it on the radio." He paused, lifting a strand of hair from her eyes. "I bet you don't even know who wrote it."

Her heart was pounding so loudly she could barely hear herself think. "It was 'When I Lost You,' and it was written by Irving Berlin."

His dark eyes gleamed, but he shrugged. "Still doesn't change the truth, pussycat. You're here because you think this makes you free. Unlike the rest of your little schoolgirl friends, sneaking out without Daddy's permission. Listening to the black man play his music and dirty your lily-white hands," he said, gripping her arm. "But your driver will take you back home to your parents tonight. To where it's safe. To where you have everything in the world. But you ain't free, kid. You wouldn't know how to be free if your life depended on it."

Gloria knew that if she cried, she would show herself to be that helpless little girl he thought she was. She could feel his palm burning into her skin. There was something alive in her, some ember that this night had lit like a match struck in the dark.

She leaned in then, her lips almost touching his neck. "Too bad you've never heard me sing," she whispered.

Then, in one swift motion, she picked up his glass, poured the whiskey down her throat, and slammed the empty glass back on the table. She wiped her mouth with the back of her hand and abruptly stood.

As she turned to make her dramatic exit, Gloria found herself face to face with the gorgeous black girl. The one she had seen Jerome canoodling with. Up close, the girl was even more stunning, her eyes a shimmering brown.

Gloria was absolutely mortified. The drama of downing the whiskey was completely upstaged by none other than Jerome Johnson's lover. "I'm sorry," Gloria muttered to the floor.

"Don't sweat it. This time," the girl said, falling into the booth where Gloria had just been seated and pinching Jerome's cheek.

Gloria wanted to get out of there as fast as she could. But then he would win, and she would look just like the kid he claimed she was. *What would a flapper do?* she asked herself. Go to the bar. Of course.

Luckily, she didn't spot her friends or her cousin—she couldn't handle explaining anything. She barely understood her own feelings. She was relieved when Leif moved over to save her.

He gave her a welcoming look of recognition. "Well, well, well, would you look at that! The virgin transformed into the Queen of Sheba!"

As miserable as she felt, she cracked a smile. "Only for you, Leif."

"For that, you get my signature martini. On the house."

As Leif was busy shaking up a storm, Gloria couldn't resist the impulse to look back at the scene she had just left. Sure enough, Jerome was engaged in what looked to be enthralling conversation with the gorgeous girl.

Curiosity was quickly becoming her biggest flaw. When Leif presented her drink, she found herself saying, "So, Leif. A question for you."

"Shoot!" he said as he dropped a spear of olives into her glass.

"I'm just wondering: Who is that lovely girl following

the piano player around all night? Is she some kind of fan?"

"You could say that." He chuckled. "That's Vera. One of the fiercest little flappers in the Windy City. Who also happens to be Jerome Johnson's baby sister."

Gloria almost choked on her martini.

Before she had a chance to fake lack of interest, there was a loud commotion from the stage. Carmen Diablo, the band's lead singer, was in a rage, shouting something that was impossible to make out over the din in the room. Gloria watched as she mounted the stage, dramatically ripped her peacock-feather headdress off, and chucked it into the crowd, screaming, "I quit!" Then she charged off.

For a moment, the volume of the room lowered to a hush. Gloria spotted one of the men from Al Capone's table—Carlito, the tabloids' favorite playboy gangster—walking over to Jerome and whispering something in his ear.

Jerome grimaced; whatever Carlito was saying to him must not have been good. The noise in the room had returned to its regular volume, and she felt a poke at her bare back.

"It's not ladylike to stare," Leif said as Gloria turned back to the bar.

"I'm a flapper now, not a lady."

Leif gave her a sympathetic look. "A word of wisdom, from the man who's seen it all? It's gonna take more than a bob to make you a flapper."

Gloria sighed. She knew what he meant but didn't want to admit it. For if it was true, she'd *never* become a flapper. Maybe she'd have a few more outings to the Green Mill, but once she walked down the aisle, there would be no going back.

Leif slid another glass of something in her direction, but Gloria waved it away. "I think I've had my fix for one night."

"Not everything's about you, Red." Leif winked at her as a black hand darted out and snatched the glass.

"He's got that right."

It was Jerome. She could feel his slick suit against her arm, but she didn't dare turn. Instead, she focused on unpinning an olive with her teeth.

"So you're a singer, huh?" he asked, taking a big swig of his drink.

She gave a sharp nod.

"And what would I hear if you were to sing?"

"My voice," she answered coldly. She could sense him smiling but kept her eyes on the olives.

"Let me ask you another question: What *song* would I hear if I asked you to sing? Hypothetically speaking. Say, one from your school choir?"

Was he serious? She'd had enough of his sassy mouth. She swiveled toward him. "I would choose 'Downhearted Blues.' Hypothetically speaking."

"Really." His dark eyes held a hint of approval. "Even our singer wouldn't have touched that one. Or rather, ex-singer."

"You mean she wasn't good enough to sing a Bessie Smith song?"

"You mean you think you're better than her?"

"Not Bessie Smith, but certainly Carmen." She stared at him unflinchingly. She wasn't entirely sure she could back it up—Carmen had a killer set of pipes. And who was she? A girl who sang songs like "Downhearted Blues"—which she'd learned from a record she hid under her bed so her mother wouldn't confiscate it—in the privacy of her own bedroom. To her pillow.

However, if there was one thing she knew about flapperdom, besides the mandatory hair bob, it was that confidence was everything. Even false confidence was better than none at all.

"Good luck to you, then, kid." Jerome finished his drink and stood up just as another black man walked up. Gloria recognized him as the band's trumpet player.

"Listen, man, Carlito's getting frisky. He says if we don't get another vocalist to front the band by next week, ready to go up and play our full set, we're done for. And I don't think he just meant in this club."

Jerome shrugged him off. "So we'll just call up my sister's friend—what's her name?—Mildred. Yeah, Mildred can really belt it out."

"Are you crazy?" The trumpet player took hold of Jerome's shoulders and gave him a firm shake. "Mildred's a beast! She'd ride us off the stage. Carlito said he wanted a pretty face, or else. And when Carlito says 'pretty face,' he means a pretty *everything.* Mildred looks like a wild boar . . . on her good days."

Gloria's heart was thumping and her hands were shaking. It was now or never. "I'll do it."

Both men turned to her and stared. The trumpet player gave her a thorough once-over. "Now, *this* is what Carlito means when he says 'pretty face.'" He grinned. "Who are you and where did you come from?" he said to Gloria. "And, most importantly, can you carry a tune?"

"I'm Gloria Car— Gloria Carson, from a hick town so hick I moved to Chicago just to find out what gin tasted like. And to become a famous singer. Which means"—she batted her lashes coyly at the trumpet player—"I hope to God I can carry a tune. Otherwise, what the hell am I doing here?"

"I like this girl! Where'd you find her?" Trumpet Player winked at her.

"He found me on a street corner, singing for my supper."

"I hope you got a nice supper."

"It would have been a lot nicer had he not shown up." She shot Jerome an I-dare-you look. *I dare you to try me. I dare you to call me a kid now. Or a rich white girl. Or a faker.*

Even though that was exactly what she was.

Gloria didn't know what had gotten into her. Or what in God's name had made her choose the name Gloria Carson. Coming from the country—well, that she'd stolen directly from Clara. Part of her felt like backtracking and immediately saying that she'd lied. Part of her was very impressed by her own quick thinking. But the dice had already been rolled. And she had rolled them herself.

Jerome stared at her for what seemed like an eternity. "Fine. I'll grant you one audition." Gloria wanted to squeal with glee at the top of her lungs, until he said: "Tomorrow night. Eight p.m. sharp."

Which was exactly the time her mother had planned for her debutante dinner. At their house. With dozens of guests and all the society papers in attendance. It would be impossible to miss. "I can't tomorrow night, it's my—"

"Be there tomorrow night at eight," he said, cutting her off. "Or else I guess I'll never get to hear your rendition of 'Downhearted Blues.'"

Then he walked off toward the stage to get ready for his next set. Which he would play well into the early dawn, when Gloria was already tucked away beneath her pink comforter, wide awake with the fear that she would never make it back to the Green Mill that next night. And would never see Jerome Johnson again.

# CLARA

As Clara gazed at her makeup-free face in the mirror, she felt a surge of nerves.

Tonight's dinner—a gathering of pompous debutantes and their mothers—was all about crossing your well-bred ankles and sounding enthusiastic about country club croquet tournaments and recent betrothals. Normally, this kind of gathering would bring out the worst in her. But it was still better than being on the farm. Plus, if Clara was going to create a new life for herself here, she had to take the party seriously. This would be her first opportunity to show off the New Clara in Chicago. Clara the Good Girl. Clara the Saint. Clara the performer.

That didn't mean she couldn't take a shot of liquid courage first. She opened her undergarment drawer, dug around, and retrieved the unassuming pink sock with the white-eyelet border that hid her flask of gin. She uncapped it and threw her head back.

But midswig, she stopped.

If Clara was going to commit to this new version of herself, she would have to get through the night sober.

The grandfather clock struck eight and was immediately echoed by the insistent ring of the doorbell. There was no time to muse. She swiped on a coat of black mascara and a dash of bright pink lipstick—a girl had to cross the line somewhere—before hurrying downstairs.

Aunt Bea was stationed in the doorway of the salon, policing incoming traffic. "Why, there you are, my dear," she said. Clara knew her aunt would approve of the blousy pale blue dress, with its delicate floral pattern and waist-cinching belt. She had borrowed it from Gloria's closet. Without asking. "I must say, you look lovely."

"Certainly not as lovely as you." Clara hinted at a curtsy, and proceeded into the next room, Aunt Bea following close behind.

Circling about the room were the mothers and daughters of Chicago's most important families. The girls looked exactly as Clara had imagined: thin and pale, with blank expressions, and wrapped up like gaudy Christmas presents in colorful frills and bows and lace. It was almost shocking to see girls actually looking their age—*sans* vamp makeup and vamp attitudes—clinging together awkwardly, acting like the schoolgirls they were.

Then there were their mothers, larger and stiffer versions of the girls themselves. The mothers gathered into groups, each trying to upstage the others with flashy diamond-encrusted baubles and equally flashy laundry lists of their daughters' accomplishments.

"Ladies, ladies!" Aunt Bea singsonged. "I want to introduce to you one of our guests of honor this evening, my niece, Clara Knowles, who will be staying with us for an indefinite length of time."

They all openly inspected Clara, as if she were a mannequin on display.

"Where is the *other* guest of honor?" a voice trilled out.

"Oh, you know our Gloria," her aunt began, turning to Clara with a flush of panic that only Clara saw.

Clara leaped right in. "She's on the phone long distance with that darling fiancé of hers," she explained. She added in a stage whisper: "He's away on business, but not even his work can keep those two apart!" The women smiled wistfully.

Clutching Clara's arm, Mrs. Carmody cleared her throat. "Why, yes—you know young love!" She croaked out an entirely fake laugh. "Now hold on to those appetites, ladies. Wait till you see what our chef, Henri—imported directly from l'Hôtel Plaza Athénée—has whipped up for you!"

The room fell into a pleased chatter, and Aunt Bea

stealthily guided Clara into the hall. "Why didn't Gloria come downstairs with you?"

Clara honestly had no idea. But as she looked into her aunt's worried face, she decided that this was the perfect opportunity to play the responsible older cousin. "Would you like me to lasso her for you?"

"Thank you, dear." Aunt Bea gave her a frightening smile. "And don't be afraid to use an actual lasso if need be."

Clara dashed upstairs, relieved to get away from the gawking. She knocked on Gloria's door.

No response.

She knocked harder, then tried the doorknob. Locked. Finally, she knelt down and peered through the keyhole. Not only was it dark, but a sharp breeze stung her eye.

The window was open.

It wasn't possible. No girl would be so harebrained as to sneak out of the house on the night of her own deb dinner. Though Gloria *had* been acting strange since last night.

After they had left the Green Mill, she had slumped in the backseat of Marcus's car with her eyes closed, presumably blacked out, for the entire ride home. At breakfast this morning, Gloria had stared blankly into her bowl of oatmeal, her face as pale as the lumpy gruel. Clara had assumed she was just overwhelmed by it all—she had felt the exact same way when she started going out in New York. But now . . .

Clara couldn't help thinking of that black jazz pianist, the one Gloria had danced with at the Green Mill. The way

Gloria had looked at him, the way his hand kept dropping to her hip, the starry glaze that had sparkled in her eyes—it all spelled trouble. And the kind Clara knew all too well.

Aunt Bea was waiting nervously at the bottom of the staircase when Clara came back down. "Is something wrong with her dress?"

This was the moment, when her aunt was at her most vulnerable, to win her over for good. Once that trust was established, the threat of reform school would have no real weight anymore.

Clara made a quick decision.

"Aunt Bea, I have some bad news. Your daughter is not in her room." She waited for her aunt to gasp before continuing. "You go and search for her," Clara instructed, taking command of the situation. "Inquire with the waiters, check to see whether all the cars are here, unlock her door. I'll take care of the guests—they won't even notice her absence." She watched her aunt's face contort, shifting from confusion to panic. "And don't worry," Clara added, giving Aunt Bea's hand a firm squeeze, "I'll call the *Tribune* and tell them not to send the photographer."

◆◆◆

It quickly became clear that Gloria was nowhere in the house or on the grounds. Mrs. Carmody rearranged seating plans while Archibald sent in a fresh round of hors d'oeuvres.

By the time Clara rejoined the party, the house was overflowing with guests. A year before, Clara's instinct would have been to shamelessly flirt with the good-looking waiter in the white tuxedo while nibbling the caviar canapés he carried. But the new Clara had responsibilities. Instead, she would have to curry favor with this witless battalion of girls and their fat mothers.

"So you're Gloria's cousin," the leader of the pack began. She was an angelic-looking girl, complete with dimples and blond ringlets. In her pink dress, she looked like a half-chewed wad of chewing gum. "How long are you planning on staying with the Carmodys?"

"At least until I don my bridesmaid's dress at Gloria's wedding—which I'm sure you already know is the main reason I'm here," Clara said. The girls murmured and shook their curls. "You girls must be the ones selected to compete in the Chicago beauty pageant that Gloria told me about."

Clara worried she was laying it on too thick, but the pink one tittered and asked, "Why would you say that?"

"Why, because you are all such *beauties*!" And by beauties, Clara really meant: *Have you ever heard of this revolutionary product called lipstick? Because you might want to try it out.*

But no matter: Each girl beamed as if Clara had offered the compliment just to her. In New York, Clara would've crushed them under the heels of her Mary Janes like the sugary rainbow Necco wafers they resembled.

This was way too easy.

"Believe it or not, we are just her friends from Laurelton Prep," one of the girls said, hiccuping. No girl with that unfortunate sallow complexion should be caught dead near the color yellow.

"Oh, Gloria has told me *so* much about you!" Clara said. "You must be—"

"I'm Virginia—but you can call me Ginnie—and this is Helen, Betty, and Dorothy—but you can call her Dot, or even Dottie." Ginnie made these introductions as she must have learned in etiquette class, leaving a two-second pause between names so each girl had time for a short curtsy. "Will you be joining us in school?"

"I graduated last year"—a lie, since Clara had skipped most of her senior year—"from high school in Pennsylvania."

"Oh, I have a cousin who goes to Macy Plains School!" Betty (the blue one) chirped.

"I have one who goes to the Grier School!" Helen (the peach one) exclaimed.

"My family all goes to school . . . here!" Dorothy/Dot/Dottie added. "Not everyone has the grades for prep school!"

Helen turned to her. "Dot, what are you talking about? You go to Laurelton Prep with us!"

Dottie laughed. "Oh, of course! Silly me!"

Clara had to bite her cheek to prevent herself from laughing at this round of boarding school name-dropping. They all blinked at her expectantly. "I went to public school in Mount Lebanon," she admitted. "But during my freshman year, Scott and Zelda rented a cottage right down the road from my house."

This was true—only, Clara had been on Martha's Vineyard for the summer, not in a suburb of Pittsburgh. Why would the Fitzgeralds bother with Pittsburgh? But she figured if she was going to lie, she had to lie big.

"Wait! The Fitzgeralds?" Ginnie exclaimed, clasping her hands together. "You mean Scott *F.*? He's the cat's whiskers!"

"Pos-i-lute-ly!" Clara said. *Though it is F. Scott, you dimwit.* She beckoned the girls closer. "They threw such outrageous, loud parties! One night, my father called the cops on them. And guess what the cops found?" The girls waited in eager anticipation. "Oh, I don't know if I should tell you this—"

"Tell us! Tell us!" they squealed.

"They found an *orgy.* Right on the back lawn! And Zelda was only twenty!" The girls all gasped at hearing such a dirty secret about the most notorious debutante of all. The deb who'd gone completely flapper.

Clara knew exactly who these girls were: Their version of rebellion was hearing the word *orgy*—whether they knew what it meant or not—right under the noses of their mothers.

"Did you actually meet them?" Ginnie whispered.

Clara was about to dive into some made-up details when the noise in the room dropped to a hiss.

Lorraine had entered the salon.

And oh, what an entrance it was! With her dark, smudged eyes and black false lashes, she looked like a scary sorceress. She was wearing a sleeveless white frock, decorated at the bottom with a wild red geometric pattern that called attention to its knee-baring length. Atop her head was a sparkly black cloche hat, a thick fringe of stick-straight bangs peeking out, and draped carelessly around her shoulders was a shiny black mink stole.

It was obvious she was tipsy. Lorraine pushed past Archibald at the door and staggered into the room, her rhinestone bangles and fake pearls clinking and clanking and her pointy-toed red high heels clacking.

"Well, would you look at what the cat dragged in," Ginnie said under her breath.

Betty agreed. "My mother would never let me out of the house looking like that. Not that I would even try such a stunt."

Helen snorted. "Lorraine, always good for a laugh."

"You know what they say," Dot said. "Laughter is the best medicine."

*Oh no,* Clara thought as Lorraine made a beeline straight for her. Everything she needed to know about Lorraine had been revealed last night at the Green Mill. A girl that desperate to be the center of attention could never be trusted.

"Fancy meeting you here, *mes chéries*!" Lorraine double-cheek-kissed each girl in the circle, pausing when she got to

Clara. "I take it you all have met our new addition, straight from the pumpkin patches?"

"You are so . . . amusing, Lorraine," Clara said.

"Where is the guest of honor?" Lorraine asked, casting her gaze around the room.

"I'm right here."

"Ha. I mean Gloria. The *real* guest of honor."

Clara sipped her lemonade. "I thought you would be able to tell us. But it's clear you don't know anything more than we do."

Lorraine's eyes narrowed. "I'm sure she'll turn up."

"Clara was just telling us about Pennsylvania," Betty said.

"Oh, I know! Isn't it just horrid? Can you imagine going to a *public* school, where everyone is the unwashed child of a farmer or factory worker? It's just simply beyond imagining!" Lorraine laughed. "We had to take her shopping the second she arrived, just to get her some proper clothes, poor thing."

"Since Lorraine is *obviously* the expert in that department," Clara said, motioning to Lorraine's zany dress.

Lorraine ignored her. "You should have seen this one last night," she said.

"Oh, I didn't see you at the country club dinner dance!" Dorothy exclaimed, her mouth filled with some type of puff pastry.

Lorraine snickered. "No, we were at the . . . oh, it's too big a secret."

"Tell us! Please," the girls begged.

"If you promise not to tell a soul," Lorraine ordered. Which Clara knew meant they should tell as many people as humanly possible. "We went to the Green Mill. Me. Gloria. Marcus Eastman," Lorraine said, snatching a glass of seltzer with lime from a waiter. "And Clara. She came, too."

The girls goggled. They looked at Clara with fresh eyes and began a succession of rapid-fire questions:

"Did you drink gin?"

"Did you meet any hard-boiled gangsters?"

"Did that rake Marcus Eastman try to seduce you?"

Before Clara could answer, Lorraine chimed in: "You should have seen poor little Clara—the whole point of going to a speakeasy is to get sloshed, and this one wouldn't even touch the stuff! Must be traumatized from all the pig slaughtering back on the farm."

"You might have been better off following my lead, Raine, considering what Marcus said about you," Clara said.

That shut Lorraine up fast. "He said something about me?"

Clara took a slow slip of her drink. "Something about how if Lorraine feels the need to fake drunk, she probably fakes everything else, too."

The girls giggled.

Lorraine looked as if she'd taken a bullet to the heart. She opened her handbag and withdrew a silver flask.

"Lorraine!" Ginnie, Betty, Helen, and Dorothy all

exclaimed. Which Lorraine clearly interpreted as disbelief—not as a warning that Mrs. Carmody was standing right behind her.

Lorraine laughed nastily. "Well, that little killjoy doesn't know what the hell he's talking about!"

Mrs. Carmody pried the flask from Lorraine's hands. "Girls, dinner will be ready in just a moment." She smiled politely but kept her grasp firmly on Lorraine's arm. "May I speak with you, please? Outside?"

Lorraine had the decency to look ashamed. "Oh, Mrs. Carmody, I'm so sorry—"

"Now, Lorraine," Mrs. Carmody said. She handed the flask to Clara. "Dear, will you dispose of that? Discreetly?"

"Of course," Clara said. She plucked a fanned napkin off a nearby table and wrapped it around the flask.

"But, Mrs. Carmody, it's my father's liquor!" Lorraine protested.

"That's enough, Lorraine." Mrs. Carmody led the girl from the room.

"I would *not* want to be her right now," Ginnie remarked once Lorraine was gone. "Mrs. Carmody is the worst when it comes to social *faux pas*. She's like the high-society Grim Reaper."

But Helen didn't seem to care at all. She looked at Clara with renewed curiosity. "Did *Marcus Eastman* really say that? To *you*? I am so impressed."

Clara couldn't believe it: Marcus was like Charlie Chaplin

to these girls—they were reduced to a bunch of drooling teenagers at the mention of him. "He's supposed to be here tonight, too, but he's late. When he comes, I can introduce you all, if you'd like."

*"Yes!"* the girls burst out in unison.

Just then, a fat little fellow in a too-tight tuxedo—Mrs. Carmody's "man," Archibald—stepped into the room and rang a silver bell. So pretentious. "Dinner," he intoned in his fake British accent, "will now be served." Then he bowed.

Ginnie and Betty linked their arms in Clara's, leading her toward the dining room.

"Oh, Mother!" Ginnie exclaimed, spotting a heavyset woman who looked identical to her save for an uncountable roll of chins. "You must meet Gloria's cousin!"

Clara curtsied. "I could have sworn you were Virginia's older sister!"

Mrs. Bitman beamed, running a finger over her pearl necklace. "How sweet you are," she said, with a heavy Southern drawl.

"Mother, we must invite her to my party next week," Ginnie said, then added to Clara, "Maybe you can even bring Marcus Eastman!"

"Why, he would be a delightful addition to your party." Mrs. Bitman grinned warmly at Clara. "Aren't you a dear for thinking of him for my Ginnie?"

"Of course, Mrs. Bitman," Clara said. "Marcus was saying to me just the other night that he longs to find a girl from a family of quality, and Ginnie is obviously a young woman of real breeding and gentility."

"Thank you," Mrs. Bitman said. "Though it appears that Pennsylvania is doing its fair share to add truth and beauty to the world." She turned to a group of nearby guests. "Did you all hear? Miss Knowles here is trying to make a match between my Ginnie and Marcus Eastman. Certainly the type of gentleman caller I approve of!" A girlish *ooooh* rose up from the assembled mothers.

"It's my pleasure," Clara said. Gentleman caller? Seriously? Had Mrs. Bitman grown up on a plantation? Probably. In the hall, Mrs. Carmody was once again directing traffic, her face now as white as her pearl earrings.

"I do hope you seated your niece near us!" said Ginnie as she passed Mrs. Carmody. "She's the berries!"

"Yes, the kitten's purr!" Betty added.

Mrs. Carmody looked at Clara with warmth in her eyes for the first time since her arrival. "Clara, why don't you sit in Lorraine's spot, which is closer to the other girls? Since she won't be joining us."

"My pleasure!" Clara said, then was carried past Mrs. Carmody into the dining room by a crush of chattering girls.

Clara had seen this room before, of course—it was the largest room on the ground floor, but one that the Carmodys rarely used. Mostly it sat empty, dark and full of dust and heavy furniture lurking in the shadowy depths. But now it had been transformed.

Shutters Clara hadn't known were there had been thrown open, and all the heavy furniture had been taken away. In its place were a dozen round white tables, each surrounded by nine finely wrought white chairs. In the center of each table was a gaudy explosion of flowers—gladiolas and tulips, zinnias and hydrangeas, phlox and carnations and roses and more. A few flowers might have been nice, but these big piles of blossoms? Tacky. Clara looked away.

But everywhere she looked, it got worse. The walls had been draped with swags of pastel bunting, and on each wall hung charcoal portraits of the couple laughing or dancing or having fun of some sort: doing things they would never have done in real life. Worst of all, in the center of the room stood a giant ice sculpture of—could it be? Clara winced—yes, icy figures of Gloria and Bastian Grey atop what looked like a big glass box. A skyscraper? A cake? Who cared.

How much money had Mrs. Carmody squandered on this circus of awfulness? Didn't she realize how desperately *nouveau riche* it was to be so showy?

Clara swallowed and excused herself from her new "friends" to go to the powder room. But really, she just needed a moment to herself.

She closed the door and leaned back against it, breathing easy for the first time in an hour.

It had been a blessing in disguise that Gloria had gone missing, otherwise Clara might not have had the opportunity to win over this crowd. And Lorraine, too—Clara owed her—though, seriously, what *was* the girl thinking?

As sheltered and shallow and irritating as these girls all were, they made Clara miss her best friends back in New York.

She left the bathroom and was about to descend the stairs, when she was intercepted by Archibald. "A note arrived for you, Miss Knowles."

When she saw the handwriting on the envelope, her entire body turned as icy as that sculpted Gloria in the dining room. "Who gave this to you?"

Archibald shrugged. "Just a messenger boy, miss. One of the maids signed for it."

"Thank you." She took the envelope, dread dropping swiftly into her stomach.

The ghosts of the past were supposed to *stay* in the past, not haunt her in the present. The only question was: Which ghost was this? And what did it want from her?

With quivering fingers, she pulled the cream-colored paper out of its gold-foil-lined envelope. The inky black letters stared up at her.

*I'm coming for you*

# LORRAINE

Every flapper knows that a fashionably late entrance must always be matched by a fashionably late exit.

Unfortunately for Lorraine, her exit wasn't by choice. But so what? The last thing she wanted to do was waste her precious time faking pleasantries with all those dumb Doras from prep school. She could barely stand them during the school day—they were the type of girls who shared a passion for those prudish Jane Austen books, in which the promise of a sexless marriage always tied a girl's problems up with a neat little bow, and then everyone had tea.

Lorraine hated bows.

What had she done wrong except show up in a fabulous outfit, take out a flask (as if no one in the room had ever seen one before!), and add spark to the dull conversation?

Mrs. Carmody should be *thanking* her, not banning her from dinner! If Lorraine's own mother had known (or cared), she would have been indignant! Maybe. And maybe even on Lorraine's behalf.

This whole unfortunate situation could have been avoided had Gloria been there. Lorraine didn't know whether she was more upset because Gloria had left her to suffer alone with those cows, or because Gloria had disappeared. So unlike Gloria. Or rather: So unlike the Gloria she used to know. Her best friend had withheld yet *another* secret from her, and Lorraine knew that when individual secrets began to add up, total deception was not far away.

Now she had to wait outside for her driver to pick her up. *Ugh.* She would have driven the spare car herself if the party hadn't been the show-up-with-a-chauffeur sort. It would take him a while to get here, so she went for a stroll. Around the side of the house lay the perfect English garden—rows and rings of flower beds and fountains and, at the edge of the greenery, a wall of towering cypresses.

It should have been peaceful. But Lorraine was in turmoil.

From the direction of the house came the clatter of dishes and the faint laughter of girls. She couldn't imagine any of them saying anything funny—except maybe some little snubs between the country club debs and country mouse Clara. And even that joke was growing stale.

Because Clara was sharper than she appeared. Oh, she pretended to be sweet as blueberry pie, batting her lashes over those big doe eyes as though surprised by everything she saw. Then she'd open her mouth and make a comment that cut like a knife. She was sharp, that Clara was. And charming. In the short time Lorraine had been at the party—she winced a little at the memory—it had become clear that Clara was charming everyone. She had totally won Mrs. Carmody's favor by being a boring good girl.

Just like Lorraine used to be. There had been a time not that long ago when it would have been Lorraine who became the party favorite, Lorraine who effortlessly charmed society's elite, Lorraine whom the boys looked for and longed to talk with.

But something had changed. And now Lorraine was being outwitted by dim little hicks like Clara, her best friend was pulling away from her, and she was alone.

She almost felt ashamed—maybe she *was* a little too flashily dressed, and maybe it *was* too much to flash her flask.

A loud burst of applause pealed out from the house.

Could Lorraine help it if she was driven to be stylish? To be daring where others were content to wear their mother-approved frills? Some women were naturally bold, and society responded only with jealousy and spite. Lorraine *was* that bold woman. Mrs. Carmody and her clique were the other sort. And that was their problem, not Lorraine's.

At least the night was crisp and clear and warm. She removed her fur stole and walked along the garden path. At the far end, she thought she spotted the tiny bud of a firefly's light, flickering on and off. As she drew closer, she realized it wasn't a firefly at all, but the lit end of a cigarette. And the person smoking it looked vaguely like—

"Well, well, well—look who it is."

That privileged accent was unmistakable. *Oh, Marcus,* she thought, *you and your impeccable timing.* "I thought you had a boys' night tonight."

"Yes, we were playing cards, but Christian got sick all over his jacks and that ended things early." Marcus was draped in twilight shadows. Dressed in a white shirt and a dark suit, his hair slightly disheveled, he looked the part of the sexy rake in some movie like Valentino's *The Sheik,* lurking outside the palace while his harem squeals.

"It seems as if we're both in exile tonight," she said, strolling calmly toward him.

"For now," he said, taking a deep drag from his cigarette. He nodded toward the house. "Though I don't think I can avoid the debs much longer."

"Don't you mean they can't avoid you?"

"I think you're talking about yourself."

"I'm clearly not a deb."

"I could tell by your skimpy outfit," he said, dropping his cigarette onto the lawn and crushing it with his heel.

"Why, Mr. Eastman, I didn't know you had a thing for girls who cover up."

"No, you're right, Miss Dyer, I much prefer scantily clad harlots like you."

At that, Lorraine gently slapped his cheek.

As she pulled back her hand, he firmly caught hold of it, and her mesh handbag fell to the ground with a loud clunk. Neither of them moved. Lorraine could have stayed in that position for hours, staring fiercely into his eyes, the scent of his cologne mingling with the tangy autumn air.

When he finally knelt to pick up her handbag, Lorraine was tempted to kick him down onto the wet grass, jump on top of him, and roll him into the mulch. But then last night's awkward, rejected kiss at the Green Mill came to mind.

So she just crossed her arms and let him work for it. "I may not be dressed like a lady, but I should still be treated like one."

"I know why I'm cooling my heels out here," he said, "but care to explain why you're not presently seated at the dining room table?"

Lorraine tried to look casual as she explained. "My drink needed a bit of a fix-up, so I took out the fixer-upper I always carry with me."

"I didn't know debutantes carried flasks," Marcus quipped.

"Yeah, you and Mrs. Carmody both," she muttered. "Good thing I have backup." She produced a second, smaller flask from her purse. "A deb must always be prepared for the best—and the worst—scenario. I believe that's a direct quote from their little etiquette handbook."

"And what kind of scenario is this, exactly?" he asked.

"One that requires bourbon."

She offered him a swig, but he raised a hand. "None for me. I'm on my way in."

"And I'm on my way out," she said. "But you *do* know that it's a deb ball, don't you?"

He smirked. "Believe me, I'd rather be anywhere else. But duty calls: the seduction of Country Clara."

"Speaking of, wait till you see Miz Clara in there—talk about un-flapper-able."

"What do you mean?" he asked with genuine interest.

"I mean, for all her drink-is-the-devil and blueberry-pie-is-the-way-to-Jesus routine, that girl doesn't flinch. At anything. Let's not forget that our original plan was to stop Clara from getting in Gloria's way. Speaking of Gloria, where is she tonight, you may wonder? At her own party? Which her mother is hosting in her honor?" she asked. "*N.O.* No!"

"Raine, drop the dramatics," Marcus said.

"I'm serious, Marcus, there's something up with Gloria. She usually tells me everything—"

"Did you ever think maybe there's a reason she's pulling away? That maybe you're being too clingy?"

*Clingy?* Lorraine was an independent woman. If anything, Gloria had always clung to *her.* She and Gloria had been best friends since they were little girls! They did everything together! Or, at least, they used to.

"If anybody's clingy, it's you," she shot back. "I know how hard it is for you to see her with another man."

"You know Gloria is like a sister to me."

"Then maybe you should start acting like an older brother! She's been sneaking around, hanging out at speakeasies—and all with that country-fried viper at her side."

"Oh, come now—Clara is hardly a viper."

"She's a snake, and I'll bet you dollars to doughnuts that she'll betray Gloria's secrets the moment she finds out about them. Unless you follow through on your promise to compromise Clara and get her to leave Chicago."

"That's why I'm here." Marcus saluted. "I am nothing if not a man of his word."

So Marcus would rile Clara up and drive her away. If that happened, great—Lorraine would be free of Clara's competition. She'd have Gloria and Marcus to herself.

But even Lorraine knew it was unlikely.

Which was why Lorraine had her own secret Plan B: Gloria was mysteriously off doing her own thing, and when Clara fell for Marcus—as she would; who could resist him?—Clara would need a friend, a confidante, someone to help her mend her broken heart. And whom would she turn to?

Lorraine. As a sympathetic ear. As an ally. As Clara's only friend in a friendless world. If Lorraine could get Clara to trust her, she would become Clara's confidante. And once Lorraine had one or two of Miss Country Clara's secrets hidden inside her Whiting & Davis mesh purse, then *she* would be the one with all the power.

She could decide whom to ruin: Marcus, for failing to see the incredible woman standing right in front of him, ready to love him; Clara, the know-it-all bit of buttermilk biscuit who'd swooped in and stolen the spotlight; or Gloria, her best friend, who'd had everything handed to her on a silver platter her entire life and was still so greedy that she was running off behind Lorraine's back and not even bothering to tell her about it.

Raine straightened the collar of Marcus's shirt and let her hands lightly graze its buttons. Which made her think of last summer at Gloria's beach house, when she had caught him changing into his bathing suit. How she'd wanted to run her hands over his tan and muscular torso, squeeze his arms, thumb the groove where his angular hip bones led down to his—

Marcus pushed her hands away, saying, "Stop fussing."

*One step at a time, Lorraine. One step at a time.*

No matter. Soon people were going to notice her. Soon she was going to shine.

# GLORIA

Without the glittering flappers and wild dancing, the bright lights and blaring music, the Green Mill turned back into what it really was: a dank basement. The dance floor seemed shrunken beneath the empty stage, and a damp chill hung over the room. It stank of stale liquor and too many cigarettes, like an ashtray full of butts. Sort of disgusting.

Gloria tried to focus on the lyrics of her audition song, but her mind kept reeling back to where she wasn't: home. The deb dinner. Her mother. The guests. One-third of the battle was already won: She'd snuck out of the house without getting caught. She'd borrowed her mother's car. Now she just needed to deliver a killer performance and get back before dinner was served.

Easier said than done, of course: It was already 8:04 p.m.

And Jerome Johnson, sitting in the middle of the room with the rest of his band, had yet to acknowledge her presence.

This was all a huge mistake.

When she'd first arrived, she'd been shocked to find the dingy stairwell lined with a half dozen girls all there to audition.

How stupid she felt. What did she think, that they'd just plucked her out of a crowd and it was a done deal? These girls looked like professionals who could sing better than Gloria even when they weren't trying. As she walked past them, she could feel their ambition rising up off their bodies like cheap perfume. There was a glint in their eyes that said *I want this more than anything.*

Luckily, when the trumpet player had leaned out into the stairwell to call in the next girl, he'd recognized Gloria. "I'm Evan," he said. "From the other night. Why don't you come on in?"

Now she was sitting at the bar inside the dark room. A row of chairs had been dragged onto the dance floor in front of the spotlit microphone. From here, Gloria could make out six men in the chairs, lazy trails of smoke rising from their cigarettes, hats tilted as they whispered about what was going on onstage.

Because yes, she had to sit there while other girls auditioned before her.

And they were all good. *Really* good. Write-this-girl-up-in-the-*Tribune*-and-alert-the-scouts good. They belted out high notes for days and made singing seem like second nature.

Gloria had tried to warm up her voice in the car on the ride over, but it was hard enough for her to drive into the city by herself without getting totally lost. Now her throat was so dry she kept swallowing, which was only making it worse.

"You look like you're about to keel over, Red," Leif said, sliding an amber-filled tumbler across the bar. He scratched his slightly crooked nose and then the top of his head. "Drink this. Little trick of the trade to calm the nerves."

Bourbon. What she really needed was a cup of tea. But she followed the bartender's orders and downed it, then coughed and gasped as the alcohol seared her throat.

Just in time for her turn. "Miss Carson? Miss Carson!" a voice called out from the front of the room.

"You're gonna knock 'em dead," Leif said, winking.

"If I don't die first."

Gloria made her way to the stage, her knees wobbling. Was she deluding herself? She loved singing, but maybe her voice was meant for her alone, and not for an audience. Whom was she fooling?

She handed her music to the piano player. "'Will You Love Me in December?'" he said. "Ain't played that one in a while."

She quietly tapped out the tempo for him. Then she approached the microphone. The spotlight was harsh, and she could barely make out the faces of the men in the audience:

Evan the trumpet player, the drummer, the bass player, two mobsters, and in the center, Jerome.

"Let's see what you got, country girl," his velvety baritone voice called out. Which made the knot in her stomach even tighter.

Later that night, when Gloria reflected on these next five minutes of her life, she would have no clear memory of them. She would remember hearing the piano begin to vamp. But she would *not* remember singing to the six men in the chairs at the lip of the stage. When she sang . . .

> *"You say the glow on my cheek, sweetheart,*
> *Is like the rose so sweet,*
> *But when the bloom of fair youth has flown,*
> *Then will our lips still meet?*
> *When life's setting sun fades away, dear,*
> *And all is said and done,*
> *Will your arms still entwine and caress me?*
> *Will our hearts beat as one?"*

. . . it was all for herself.

◆◆◆

Scattered, distant clapping brought her back to the stage.

Then the lights came up. Jerome was in the middle of his band, his gaze fixed unblinkingly on her; he didn't say a word. On either side of him, the other men all looked bored. One sighed loudly.

Gloria didn't know if that was her cue to get off the stage or to stay. So she stood there, paralyzed.

Finally, the bass player spoke. "Look, baby lark, you got a real sweet voice. Like honey. Not to mention, that hair of yours in the light looks like it's on fire. But"—he gave her a sympathetic smile—"you just don't got the sound we're looking for."

*Baby lark?* She put her entire life on the line just so some wet blanket could call her *baby lark*?

"What *sound* are you looking for, exactly?" Gloria asked into the microphone. "Just out of curiosity."

"You got this real breathy, intimate quality," the bass player continued. "But we're looking for a girl who can really wail."

"Oh, trust me, I can. Want me to try another song? I didn't bring my book, but I can sing *a cappella*—"

"You're too green, kid. Just like I thought," Jerome said. "Plus, you didn't sing 'Downhearted Blues.' Guess ya didn't have it in ya."

His words pierced her like a poison dart. She had wanted to prove him wrong, to show this holier-than-thou musician that she was a singer. An artist. Not just some silly schoolgirl. So what if she lacked what these other girls had, their big sounds and bigger presences? Gloria had something different. More seductive. Something audiences would listen to, not just dance over. But apparently Jerome Johnson didn't think so.

Gloria stomped off the stage and headed straight for the door. Halfway across the floor, she turned, looked directly at Jerome, and said, "Just so you know, I didn't sing 'Downhearted Blues' for a reason."

He smirked. "And what's that?"

"I don't give my best stuff away for free," Gloria said.

Then she turned back around and headed for the exit.

"Well, for my two cents, I thought you were a star up there," Leif said as she rushed past the bar.

She didn't even stop to thank him. She just wanted to escape, before the lump in her throat melted into fresh tears. She'd read the magazines and the stage biographies; she knew a singer's life was about rejection after rejection. She could handle that.

But there had been a cruelty in Jerome's tone, as if no matter how stellar her performance had been, she'd still never have been good enough.

She sucked in a deep breath to carry her past the girls in the stairwell and pushed against the exit door.

"Hey, Red! Bring your sweet little caboose back over here! Now!"

The voice hit her in the back as she was midway out the door. The mobsters she'd noticed before were now standing at the table. They looked young, probably midtwenties, with shiny hair and immaculate suits. They oozed confidence, and something else that made her nervous. Menace.

She turned and walked back to the table. At times like these, she hated being a redhead: She knew her skin was probably all blotchy and ugly, revealing everything. Thank God the lights were down.

Besides the occasional clink of glasses, the room was awkwardly quiet as they watched her approach.

"You forgot your sheet music." The handsomer of the two men held out three crinkled pieces of paper. She vaguely recognized him from the night before.

Gloria cringed. Her music. Of course, this was why they were calling her back! What had she been thinking? "Oh, thanks," she muttered.

She reached out to take the sheet music from him, but he snatched it away.

"Not so fast," he said.

Was it really necessary to humiliate her more than she'd already been humiliated?

"So, you want this gig, Red?" He dangled the paper in front of her. "How much do you want it?"

"I want it *that* badly," she snapped, reaching for the music again.

"Whoa. We've got a feisty one here." He let her music flutter to the floor. "Just how I like my singers."

Gloria bent down to collect the papers—probably just a cheap trick to get an eyeful. The floor had a sticky film of souring alcohol. As she picked up the last sheet, she noticed his shoes. They were covered with spatterdashers—spats like her father wore, little buttoned gray collars men used to keep their shoes clean. Even this man's spats looked expensive: They were silky and shiny and embroidered with a big *M.*

*M* for *Macharelli.* Of course. Carlito Macharelli, playboy son of the infamous Mob boss.

Reality struck like a match in the dark: She was a little rich girl, trapped underground, with black musicians and notoriously vicious mobsters. What had she gotten herself into?

"She's not ready, Carlito," Jerome said, breaking the silence. "Imagine when there are a few hundred people crammed in here, corked and shouting. Her voice is too small—it won't carry."

Carlito exhaled his cigar smoke into Jerome's face. "She's got something." He looked Gloria up and down. "Something fresh. I like her."

"Yeah, I like her, too. I like her plenty. But she needs to strengthen her vocal cords, build up her endurance. She's got no technique and no experience."

"Then you got a lot of work ahead of you, Johnson."

Jerome's eyes darkened. "What does that mean?"

"It means she's your responsibility now. Get her ready. Train her. You've got two whole weeks. That should be plenty of time." Carlito dropped his cigar into Jerome's drink. "You'll see. The inexperienced girls are always the fastest learners."

Jerome opened his mouth as if he was about to protest further but said nothing. Instead he rubbed his jaw and shot Gloria a venomous glare.

Gloria knew she should be ecstatic—she had gotten a job as a *singer,* for God's sake—but how was she going to sneak out of her house every night? How was she going to skip school for voice lessons?

But those were the least of her worries. Getting out of the occasional class at Laurelton with some forged doctor's note was not the issue. Being a rich white girl with a notable family fronting an all-black band? In an illegal speakeasy? What if Bastian found out? Surely his banker friends went to the club. Now, *that* she should be worried about.

"Gloria Carson, huh?" Carlito said, his eyes on her chest.

"My friends call me Glo."

"How perfect. Before long, your name will be *glo*-wing in lights." He took her hand and kissed it. Gloria couldn't tell whether he was being sincere or was mocking her, but his clammy hand and wandering eyes made her recoil. "Welcome to the Green Mill. Welcome to your future!" Carlito turned to Jerome. "Welcome the lady properly, Johnson."

With what looked like a great deal of effort, Jerome set down the glass with the cigar and stepped forward. "Sorry if I came off a little harsh there just now. Your voice really does have a captivating quality, Miss Carson. But that ain't nothing compared to how you're going to sing in two weeks."

Gloria was momentarily dizzy. It was that simple—a compliment from Jerome, and something deep inside her came alive.

◆◆◆

Gloria turned her mother's car into the driveway.

She was late. Too late. She was going to be in *so* much trouble. And yet it was hard to care. She was going to be a singer!

She could make out two shadowy figures near the front of the house who looked vaguely like Lorraine and Marcus. The last two people she wanted to see right now.

With the headlights out, she killed the engine and coasted down the long circular driveway and to a nearly silent stop right in front of the garage. She eased the car door open, slipped out, and gently shut it. Then she walked in her stockinged feet to the side of the house, her shoes in her left hand.

Marcus and Lorraine met her there, gawking, as if they had been waiting all night for her arrival.

"So the guest of honor decides to grace us with her presence," Lorraine said.

Gloria's first thought was: What on God's green earth was her best friend wearing? Her second was: Why hadn't she thought up an excuse before now—where was she going to tell them she'd been?

"Don't ask," Gloria said. Simple enough. She took Lorraine's cigarette out of her mouth and planted it in her own. If there'd ever been an appropriate time for a cig, it was right now.

"Come on, you think we're gonna let you off the hook that easy?" asked Marcus, jabbing her in the side. "Start talking."

What could she possibly say? As much as she loved her friends, they would never understand. She barely understood the whole thing herself. "Oh, Bastian just needed me for something," she said, coughing because she still couldn't gracefully inhale. "Some sort of business emergency, you know, dealing with stocks or bonds or whatever."

"Stocks and bonds, my ass," said Lorraine.

"Speaking of, I can practically see yours from a mile away," Gloria said, feeling Lorraine's nearly transparent dress. "What is this made out of, rice paper?"

Marcus burst out laughing. "I think Henri *le chef* mistook her for an extra piece of meat and wrapped her up to go home."

Lorraine stomped her foot. "This dress happens to be the hottest thing on the streets of Paris!"

"More like the hottest thing on the street*walkers* of Paris." Gloria laughed. She loved Lorraine, but more and more lately, Gloria sensed an edge of competition creeping between them: Lorraine was constantly trying to out-sparkle, out-bead, out-boob, and out-bob her. What was the reason behind it all?

"I'd better force myself inside before my buzz wears off. Come on, kids," Gloria said, putting her arms around their shoulders. "Escort me to my execution."

"I'm afraid I'll have to leave that thrilling task to Marcus," Lorraine said. "I've already been executed. By your mother. And I didn't even *do* anything."

Gloria could only guess what that was about, but Lorraine would have to wait. There were only so many battles a girl could fight in the world, and Gloria had to prepare herself for the one looming between her and her mother. And there'd be worse to come: She couldn't stop thinking back to how the touch of Jerome's hand had taken her breath away.

"I'll call you later," Gloria said, kissing Lorraine's cheek. "That is, if I'm not banned from using the telephone for the rest of my life." She looped her arm in Marcus's and said, "You, I need inside. Whatever I say, back me up."

"Gloria Carmody," he said. "What do you have up that sleeve of yours? Oh, that's right," he said, touching her bare arm. "You're not *wearing* any sleeves."

"All you need to know is this: We were together the entire night."

"Sheer falsehood!" Marcus said, mock-scandalized. He chuckled. "I hope you know what you're doing."

"Not a clue," Gloria said. But one thing she *did* know: From this moment on, she was going to tell one big lie after another. And she had never been more thrilled in her life.

# CLARA

How quickly a week could pass!

Ever since the debutante dinner, Clara's social calendar had been just short of full. First Ginnie Bitman's mother had invited her for lunch on Tuesday, and then on Wednesday she'd gone to Betty Havermill's estate for a fancy dinner with the girl and her parents. Betty's father was a famous Chicago architect and had designed their mansion himself, all tall ceilings and windowed walls. Thursday was ice cream with Dot Spencer at a tiny place called Harry's, where the only flavors were chocolate and vanilla and people waited on line for over twenty minutes. Clara never liked waiting for anything, but had to admit that the ice cream was pretty tasty. Afterward, she had listened to Dot play the piano in her family's sitting room. If Clara never heard another

Gershwin tune for the rest of her life, she would die happy. No offense to Gershwin, of course—just to Dot.

Getting to know these boring girls, and their equally boring parents, was the dregs. There was no jazz, no excitement, and no men. At least, no men with boyfriend potential.

Which was a good thing, Clara told herself. She didn't *want* a boyfriend. What she wanted was to move up in the world, to make a name for herself here in Chicago, and she was doing it. Slowly but surely. Yes, it involved some seriously tedious social visits, but she'd had to suffer through a lot worse in the past. This stuff was easy peasy.

Now it was Friday night, and Clara was, for the first time all week, without plans. Gloria was still grounded after her excruciatingly late entrance to her own debutante dinner. Just thinking about it made Clara grin; she wouldn't have believed Gloria's performance that night if she hadn't witnessed it herself.

Just as dessert and coffee were being served, Gloria had come traipsing in arm in arm with Marcus Eastman, a crazed look in her eye.

"I am *so* sorry! I have no excuse for my tardiness," she started, "but I just *had* to rush to the aid of one of my dearest friends—who really should learn to remember where he puts his keys!"

Mrs. Carmody dabbed at her lips with her napkin, folded it, and set it on the table in front of her. "Is that so?"

To his credit, Eastman gamely played along. He slapped his forehead and said, "Silly me, I'd forget my feet if they weren't attached to my legs." He could be the perfect man, Clara thought, if only he weren't so smitten with himself.

Marcus had turned to Gloria. "If it weren't for the large-hearted kindness of Miss Carmody, I would never have been able to—"

"Get into his house!" Gloria finished.

"Why couldn't his man let him in?" Mrs. Carmody asked. "Or his parents?"

"Sick!" Gloria said, as Marcus said, "In Mexico!"

They glanced at each other.

"That is," Gloria continued, "his parents are in Mexico and his butler is sick."

"Just sneezes all over everything," Marcus explained. "Utterly revolting. You wouldn't want him anywhere near you, really."

"But I have his spare key," Gloria said, obviously relieved to have arrived at something like an ending to the story.

"And that made you ninety minutes late?" her mother asked.

"The key didn't fit," Marcus said. "On account of . . ."

". . . the burglary," Gloria said. "Yes, they were burgled and had to change their locks."

"Quite traumatic," Marcus said.

The girls beside her tittered, and Clara had to refrain from laughing out loud.

Clara looked around at Ginnie and Dot and Betty, and at their matching mothers at the table across from them. Everyone looked confused. The dinner plates had been cleared, and the servants were pouring dark coffee into the Carmodys' perfect china cups and setting out sugar and cream on each table. The smell of the floral centerpieces was overwhelming, and Clara thought she might be sick. She looked at the ice sculpture, which was still intact, though the bride's features had started to melt. Clara wondered how long it would take before the statue puddled away entirely.

"That's very strange," Gloria's mother said, rising. "Especially as the Eastmans didn't say a word about a burglary to me—"

"They couldn't have," Gloria interrupted, redness creeping up her neck like ivy, "seeing as they are in Mexico."

"—when I spoke to them earlier this evening to wish them success at the museum gala."

"Ah," Marcus said. "They must have come home early! I'm always the last to know these things."

"They must have," Mrs. Carmody finished. "Gloria, please go up to your room. You and I shall speak more about this later."

"Yes, Mother," Gloria said. She disappeared down the hall.

Clara should have given her cousin a tutorial in the art of lying. Rule Number 1: Keep it simple. Rule Number 2: Never explain. Rule Number 3: Don't involve any other party unless he is complicit in your lie.

But Gloria's punishment became Clara's opportunity. Since then, she had filled in for Gloria at almost every social engagement. Everyone seemed to like Country Clara.

Clara put down her book, a borrowed copy of *This Side of Paradise,* and decided to compose a letter to her roommates back in New York. But she realized she had no "You'll never believe who I'm stuck on" or "I got spifflicated!" stories to report. What was she going to say? "Dear girls, guess what? Aunt Beatrice taught me how to knit today. We made the most delightful tea cozy." She could always razz on Gloria, but Clara wasn't the sort to kick a dog when it was down.

Just as Clara was seriously considering the variety of activities that might be offered to girls at the Illinois Girls' School of Reform (jewelry making? glassblowing? lock picking?), the doorbell rang. The butler would doubtless answer it—what was his name, again?—but it seemed as good a reason as any to leave her room and go downstairs.

Clara glided down the staircase, one hand on its broad white banister, and into the foyer.

It was as quiet and empty as that Lorraine girl's head.

Nothing except the gilded pictures that lined the walls and the mahogany table where Aunt Bea left her house keys and a tiny bronze dish full of mints. Where was everyone? Clara opened the front door and, much to her surprise, found Marcus waiting on the porch. He looked perfectly spiffy. He was dressed in a tailored gray flannel suit with a baby blue shirt beneath that picked up the color of his eyes, and atop his head was a soft gray derby. And his fly was undone.

Clara averted her eyes, focusing on the floor.

"Isn't the wood nice?" she asked. "I always love a good wooden floor."

Marcus looked at her curiously. "You've been inside too much," he said, striding into the foyer and taking off his hat. "Pretty girls aren't supposed to look down. Only up."

"Your"—she made vague fluttering motions near her waist.

Marcus looked down, then turned and buttoned up. "Oh, I'm sorry! I'm afraid I got dressed in a blazing hurry, I was so excited about this evening."

"Oh, what's happening this evening?"

"We're going out," he said. "Put on your finest finery—no finery is too fine for tonight."

"Who is 'we'?" Clara said, not wanting to seem like all the other girls who hung on his every word. Though it wasn't such an easy task in his presence. One lock of wavy blond hair fell over his left eye—she was tempted to brush it back, to touch his skin with the tips of her fingers. But she had to resist. "You know that Gloria is still grounded," she reminded him.

"And why is Gloria grounded? Because her tardiness was insulting to the debs of Chicago. And what do we do to remedy that?" he asked, circling around her.

"I'm confused," Clara said.

"Marcus, there you are!" Mrs. Carmody swept into the foyer and gave Marcus's cheek a loud smooch. She was wearing a tan dress that ended below her knees, and a simple yet elegant diamond necklace. Clara could see dark circles beneath her eyes. Aunt Bea looked worn out.

"How kind of you to offer yourself up to the cause. I know Clara will be in excellent hands tonight."

Clara looked quickly from one to the other. "Auntie, dear, I don't under—"

"She's been busy, you know," Aunt Bea continued, ignoring her. "Quickly becoming the talk of the town." She turned to Clara and smiled. Could this really be the same aunt who'd sat her down and threatened to send her off to reform school?

"I'm sorry, am I missing something?" Clara asked.

"Why, dear, Marcus has been so kind as to offer you accompaniment to Virginia Bitman's evening tea party. Isn't that considerate of him?" Mrs. Carmody clapped her hands together. Clara couldn't tell what, exactly, she was so excited about, but at least Aunt Bea was being nice to her.

"That *is* very considerate of him," Clara said, confused by the wicked gleam in his eye. It was not the sort of gleam usually inspired by a high tea given by someone like Ginnie Bitman.

"And since those girls took such a liking to you, Clara, perhaps you can help mend the bridges that my daughter burned? If you know what I mean."

So *that* was the reason for this whole setup. Nothing was more important to her aunt than crossing social bridges and climbing social ladders.

Clara hadn't particularly wanted to go to this wretched little tea party—she'd had her fill of Ginnie's fluffy conversation and gluey pastries on Tuesday. And whose idea had it been to have Mr. Playboy accompany her? He couldn't really want to be stuck with the debutantes on a Friday night, could he?

But whatever the reason, it was an excuse to get out of this stifling house. Grateful for that, Clara asked no more questions, but ran upstairs to put on her finest social-bridge-mending outfit.

◆◆◆

"So, admit it: How much do you love me?" Marcus asked.

Clara put her fingers together with about a millimeter of space between them. "This much?"

They were standing in line for movie tickets at the Biograph Theater on North Lincoln. The marquee overhead blinked *Our Hospitality* in fire-engine red—it was a sneak preview of the newest Buster Keaton movie.

Marcus had revealed on the way to Ginnie's that he'd

never intended to stay long at the tea party. "I'd sooner set myself on fire," he said while Clara laughed.

Clara had been happy and impressed when he'd outlined the plan—"After twenty minutes," he told her, "you will fall ill because of something you ate. Go to the bathroom, rub a bit of concealer on your face, and dampen your hairline. Come back and wobble a bit—hold on to the edge of a table while you place a palm to your head. And then call to me and I'll take care of the rest."

He'd been as good as his word, insisting to Ginnie and her group that the best thing for Clara was to take her home right away. A few moments later, they were in his car, and a few moments after that, here in line at the Biograph.

"Only that much? Come on, give a fella a chance."

She separated her fingers about an inch. This was fun. She looked good, and she knew it, and she knew *he* thought she looked good. She was wearing sheer stockings, an emerald-green skirt, and a pale pink cotton sweater that felt fine against her skin. "Is that better?"

"Come on, say it. This is a *far* better evening."

"Hmmmm, Ginnie Bitman versus Buster Keaton. Tough call."

"How can you possibly compare Ginnie Bitman to Buster Keaton?"

"Well, they both *are* kind of clownish."

"Except Ginnie wears less makeup, yet somehow manages to look more like a man."

Clara shook her head in mock disapproval. "That's not a very gentlemanly thing to say."

"If you want a gentleman, go back to the tea party." Marcus looked at his watch. "There's still time before Freddy Barnes and my friends go to see the vaudeville at the Salty Dachshund. I'll do that; you run along to your tea." He made a shooing gesture with his fingers.

"No, thanks. I think I'd rather be stuck with a cake-eater than stuck eating cake."

"Are you calling me a ladies' man, Miss Knowles?" He turned from her and stepped up to the box office. His eyes were bright, a perfect combination of little-boy eagerness and more mature masculine appeal. God, he was sexy.

"Your reputation precedes you, Mr. Eastman."

Clara was secretly thrilled that Marcus had come up with this ingenious scheme for the night, even though she was suspicious of his motives. She knew boys like him in New York. The dangerous combination of being born both wealthy and good-looking meant they never had to work for anything—girls were as disposable to them as the wads of cash in their wallet. They were all about the chase.

Clara had dated some of the most notorious ones.

There was Leo Silverman, the Jewish millionaire, who used to have her join him on his yacht in the Hamptons. There was Shawn Carroll, the banker and arts patron, who always let Clara use his box at the Metropolitan Opera, whether he accompanied her or not. And then there was

Thierry Marceau, the French heir, with his imported-cashmere empire, who filled her closets. And there were others she'd dated briefly.

*Dated* was a loose term. Mostly, she could only go to one premiere or gallery opening with a man before he started expecting something in return. Her rule with these men was: socializing only, nothing more.

But Clara had thrown the rules out the window when she'd fallen in love.

That was then and this was now, she reminded herself. She wasn't that girl anymore. She'd been broken and bruised, but she'd learned from her mistakes. And Marcus certainly wasn't going to threaten her newly minted willpower.

Until they got inside the theater.

They surveyed the seats, which were filling up quickly. She spotted two close to the screen. "How 'bout there?" she suggested.

Marcus scoffed. He pulled her toward the back of the theater and up the staircase into the balcony.

He sat her down in a shadowy corner. "Now, you stay right there. And don't you dare give away my seat to some other boy while I'm gone. Even if he is handsomer than me."

Clara was left alone, grinning like a fool. What was wrong with her? Off the bat, she should never have agreed to sit in the balcony: Everybody knew the only reason it existed was so couples could neck. She glanced around her. Yep, movie houses in Chicago were no different than New York—one big petting pantry. There were couples everywhere. In front of her, a man's arm was snugly wrapped around his date's shoulder, ready to pull her closer as soon as the lights were low. That was *not* going to happen to her.

But would kissing Marcus be such a crime? He certainly had the most kissable mouth she had ever seen, that pouty bottom lip just asking to be bitten.

The lights dimmed and the piano player began pounding out a jaunty rag—probably the theme for the movie. Marcus still wasn't back. Clara closed her eyes, as she always did at the beginning of films and plays, letting the darkness spread over her, welcoming her into a different universe.

"Are you that bored already?"

Clara opened her eyes, adjusting them to the now pitch-black cinema. A beam of light from the projector cut the darkness as the movie began.

Marcus was sliding into the seat next to her with an enormous sack of buttery popcorn. "I figure a movie is only as good as the snacks." He leaned in close to her and whispered in her ear, "Give me your hands."

Light and shadow played on his face. Clara wished she had a camera to capture the way he looked—right here, right now—forever. "Why?"

"You still don't trust me?" He reached over and filled her hands with a bunch of slick little pyramids.

Clara looked down at her cupped hands: Hershey's Kisses.

"Popcorn and chocolate together are the best combination. A little sweetness, a little saltiness."

"Shhhh!" Clara pointed to the screen. "It's starting."

Buster Keaton's familiar edge-of-panic features filled the screen. He played a character named Willie McKay, who—not unlike Clara herself—had been sent to live with his aunt. Ironically, though, Buster was sent *to* New York. Before long, Clara found herself laughing harder than she had in weeks.

Even though the film was totally ducky, Clara had a hard time concentrating with Marcus beside her. Every time he laughed—an adorable, distinct "Ha! Ha! Ha!"—he would jolt forward, and his pants brushed her leg.

But every time Clara found herself leaning in toward him, by sheer force of his magnetic pull—making it easy for him to wrap an arm around her shoulder if he wanted to—Marcus sat up a little straighter and leaned the other way.

It was starting to make her a little crazy. Wasn't that why he had dragged her up here? All the couples surrounding them were now full-on necking. She crossed her legs and rested her hand on the top of her knee so that it was exposed to him—

But he didn't make a move.

On screen, a gunman was chasing Willie, and the two of them fell into a raging river and tumbled over a waterfall, and Clara was laughing and laughing on the outside, but on the inside all she could think was: Had she gotten Marcus all wrong?

Did she think she was so much the cat's meow that every guy she met had to fall in love with her? Marcus had a million other girls. What made her think she was so special? It was then that she realized: She *wanted* him to think she was special. He was funny and charming and a little bit full of himself, but in a good way. She wanted him to rub her knee, to pull her close. To kiss her.

Then, like a wish come true, she felt him lean toward her. She held her breath.

"See?" he whispered, tucking her hair behind her ear. "I *told* you Ginnie looks more like a man than Keaton."

Clara wanted nothing more in that moment than to press her lips to his. But then she thought of her aunt, and of reform school, and of her new life as a budding socialite here in Chicago. She thought of the mysterious notes she'd been receiving, threatening to expose her, to drag her back into her old New York life. Was he here, this elusive note-sender? Was he watching her?

Clara shivered and turned her attention back to the screen.

◆◆◆

Marcus and Clara left the theater and strolled through the city. All of Chicago seemed to be out on a romantic date—they passed couple after couple holding hands and eating ice cream and kissing. She'd had no idea Chicago was such a *young* city. It made her long to be a part of the action, not just observe it from a sober distance.

In New York, her dates had always been fast-paced, more about the next activity than the person she was with. She couldn't remember the last time she'd been with a boy when she hadn't felt pressure—pressure to pretend to be someone else, pressure to be somewhere more important. Even though she was still in Country Clara mode with Marcus, she felt strangely herself. Natural. Calm. Being with Marcus was almost like hanging out with a friend—if her friend had been an incredibly gorgeous man and had made her stomach flutter with butterflies.

"I have an idea," Marcus said. "What would you say to ending this da—" He stopped himself. "This night, I mean—"

"Were you going to say the *D* word?" she teased him.

"I was about to," Marcus said, adjusting his hat. "But then I realized that this is the farthest thing from a date."

"Of course," Clara agreed, though a small part of her wished he did consider it a date, even though she would have protested. It certainly felt like one. A *good* one.

"Right. Erm, what was I saying?" Marcus let out a nervous laugh, and Clara found it kind of endearing.

"Something about ending this *D* word . . . ?"

"Right! I think it would only make sense to end this night with a nightcap."

"Marcus, you know I don't drink," she said, even though he had read her mind. She was dying for a martini. "Not only is it *illegal,* but we are both *teenagers.*" She peered at her wrist. "And I have to be back before my curfew."

"Nice watch," he said, picking up her bare wrist.

She burst out laughing, and he joined in. The streetlight cast a yellow glow over his smooth cheeks. His blue eyes were like magnets, sucking her in. "And with me, your curfew is null and void. Mrs. Carmody trusts me implicitly—unlike you."

Clara tried to suppress a smile. She seemed to be doing that a lot around him. "That's because you seem to have a way with women. *Fooling* them, that is."

"But you're not like other girls, Clara," he said. "Don't you think I know that?"

There was a sincerity in his voice, in his piercing, direct gaze. What did it mean? "I don't know."

"Come on, let me take you home." He charged ahead of her down the street.

"Wait!" she called out, and he turned to face her. Disappointment creased his forehead and made lines around his mouth. "One drink."

"I don't want to force you to do anything you don't want to do."

She could see that he meant it. "I'll even go to the Green Mill, if you promise not to tell my aunt."

He walked back toward her. "I have something a little different in mind. Someplace where we can actually talk."

"Talk?"

"Yes, *talk*. Why, did you have something else in mind?"

Boys like Marcus never wanted to just talk. But Clara didn't want this date—or whatever it was—to end. And maybe Marcus really *was* different than she'd imagined him to be. After all, if anyone knew a thing or two about unfair reputations, it was her. "Talking is fine with me."

A few blocks later, Marcus stopped in front of a bakery called Bebe's Buns.

"Follow me," he said, leading her inside the small shop.

If it hadn't been for all the chocolate and popcorn she had just eaten, Clara would have been salivating over the glass display of baked goods: row upon row of cookies, cakes, pastries, and pies. The scents of vanilla and cinnamon and sugar wafted through the room.

"Bebe!" Marcus exclaimed to a petite woman with puffy blond hair who was wearing a baker's apron. He leaned across the counter and gave her a European-style double-cheek kiss. *"Est-ce que nous pouvons entrer?"*

"For you, anytime," she said, winking, and lifted up the counter. "And you must be Patricia, right?" She beamed at them.

Clara stood there, confused.

"That was a month ago, Bebe." Marcus beckoned Clara

forward. "Come on, it's this way," he said, walking through a set of doors that led into the kitchen.

Clara followed him, even though she felt like a perfect little fool. Marcus pointed to a handwritten sign that read THIS WAY TO THE DARK SIDE over a broad arrow.

At the very back of the kitchen, he opened a metal door. Beyond was a small, dark room, illuminated by strands of white Christmas lights. Old movie posters hung over the brick walls. Eight small tables lit by candlelight stood around a little platform where a bass player and a pianist played a mellow cross between jazz and blues.

Even for a New York girl like Clara—who had seen and done it all—this place was totally copacetic. Her cheeks hurt, and she realized it was because she'd been smiling nonstop since . . . since when? It felt like forever.

They sat at a dark corner table and ordered cocktails (Scotch on the rocks for him, a Buck's Fizz for her). Clara was going to put up the expected protest, but then rationalized that even a country girl would give in to a taboo taste of champagne.

"Patricia?" she asked, trying to sound casual. "So is this the secret spot you use to impress your dates?"

"Once upon a time," Marcus answered. "But those days are behind me."

"How far behind you, exactly?"

He shrugged. "It sounds worse than it is. Yes, I have gone out with a lot of girls, but there are very few girls I meet whom I am actually interested in."

There was a couple at each table in the room, kissing or cuddling or both. She had never been a fan of public displays of affection, but something about the ambiance made Clara wish she were there with a lover, too.

Marcus started to reach for her hands across the table, but stopped himself, letting his hands rest on his glass instead. "You're not like all those other girls."

*If you only knew,* she thought.

"So tell me. Do you miss home?" he asked.

"I do." She took a sip of her drink, to prevent herself from saying too much.

"Have you been in touch with your parents? Your friends?" His cool blue eyes searched hers for an answer. "I can't imagine what you must be going through—to have left that all behind, so far away."

There was something so open in his face. As if he really cared about her. And when had she ever been out with a boy who cared about anything other than himself? She took another sip of her drink. "Want to dance?" she asked.

Marcus frowned. "Clara, I can see in your face that you're sad about something. I saw it the moment I first met you."

Clara had a brief, crazy impulse to tell him everything. She *was* sad. Or at least, she had been. Which was why being with him confused her so much—it felt as if all the sadness weighing on her from before had been replaced with something lighter, a fizziness just like the champagne bubbling up in her glass.

"You're right." She sighed deeply. "I miss so many people I left behind—my best friends, for one thing. They were like sisters to me. Of course, some people are easier to leave behind than others."

"Like who?" Marcus asked, cocking his head.

"Oh, you know." Clara peered down at her drink.

Then she felt Marcus's hand on hers, wet from the condensation on his glass. His touch—which she had been longing for all night—made her forget everything. His fingers were strong, and his grasp made her feel safe.

"I know it must have been hard to betray your upbringing and come here," he said, intertwining those delicious fingers in hers, "but I'm really happy that you did."

The line could have come off as corny, but Marcus's eyes seemed anything but. "Me too," she said softly.

"Now do you want to dance?"

"Let's just sit here for a little while more," Clara said.

She wanted to stay like this for the entire night, quiet, hand in hand, skin kissing skin.

◆◆◆

After Marcus dropped her at home, Clara walked into the house like a googly-eyed zombie. She knew exactly what this feeling meant, and it was not good. But what was worse was that she couldn't snap out of it.

She was falling for Marcus Eastman.

Marcus had definitely not absolved himself from his playboy reputation. But over the course of the evening, she'd realized there was something different about him, different from New York men. He wasn't jaded.

Clara slumped down in front of her vanity mirror. What had happened to the willpower she'd begun the evening with?

She heard Gloria's door sigh closed. What was *she* still doing up at one-thirty a.m.? At least Clara wasn't in her cousin's shoes—she would rather be stuck with her own hair-pulling confusion than Gloria's sad future. Destined to live a lousy little life with her lousy little husband-to-be—just like her aunt Bea. Dreadful.

That was the thing about Marcus: He didn't want to control her. He just wanted to be with her. Marcus wanted her to be herself. Or rather, her country self. It was so confusing.

Clara stepped out of her skirt, shrugged off her sweater, and woozily flopped onto her bed in her cream silk slip.

Something as sharp as a knife dug into her back.

Clara jumped up. She hoped, prayed, it wasn't what she thought it was. Not now, not tonight. She didn't want to let anything ruin her perfect evening—perfect because of Buster Keaton and champagne and Marcus's deep blue eyes.

But she couldn't avoid it. She tore open the now-familiar-looking envelope:

*You may look different on the outside,*
*but inside you're exactly the same.*

Something else inside the envelope fluttered to the floor.

A photograph.

On the back, in the left corner, handwriting:

*Times Square*
*September 1922*

She flipped it over.

There she was, in a speakeasy near Times Square. Her hair had been chopped into a pixie bob that was barely visible beneath a beaded headdress, and she was wearing a plunging, sparkly black toga dress. Her head was tossed back as if she had just heard the most hilarious joke, and she was wielding a long cigarette holder like a conductor's baton. A silver flask glinted in her other hand. She remembered that night vividly. The Cad had taken her out to see a Broadway show and then had rented a suite overlooking Central Park, at the Pierre. That was the night she had slept with him for the first time.

The beginning of the end.

They'd begun the night in a group, but who had taken the photograph?

She studied the photo again. It wasn't so much that she looked the epitome of a full-blown flapper, which she did.

But she was radiating something—sheer happiness?—that outshone even the lights of the marquee behind her.

Clara slipped the photo back inside the note and resealed the envelope. She stashed it in the back of her drawer with the others.

At her vanity, she began to slather thick globs of cold cream onto her cheeks. The full moon hung outside the window, its pearly glow pooling on the surface of the mirror.

She had been happy tonight, hadn't she? It was so hard to tell. Once, happiness had seemed so steady and sure, so solid. But now it was transparent—something that ran through her fingers like water.

She looked again at her reflection in the mirror. *Who are you, Clara Knowles? Which identity are you wearing now?* But her face was like the moon, just another whitewashed orb, blank and unrecognizable, lost in the darkness.

# LORRAINE

It was Tuesday night at 9:45 p.m., which for Lorraine meant only one thing: frantically trying to get ready for Wednesday morning and Madame Cloutier's notoriously brutal French *examen du vocab* at Laurelton Girls' Prep. As usual, Lorraine had forgotten to take home this week's vocabulary from *Madame Bovary,* which they were reading, but Gloria was sure to have the list.

Which was how Lorraine found herself behind the wheel of her daddy's Duesenberg, following the Carmodys' Mercedes sedan.

The initial plan was this: throw on a bathrobe, "borrow" her father's car once he was asleep, drive over to the Carmodys' house, sneak in through the servants' entrance, and copy Gloria's color-coded note cards.

The note cards were merely an excuse, of course.

It had been forever since Lorraine and Gloria had had one of their ritualistic gab sessions—razzing all the heinous girls in their school; sneaking slices of Henri's flourless chocolate cake; ranking how far they would go with each boy in the senior class at Lake Forest Academy.

But just as Lorraine turned onto Astor Street, she had spotted a Mercedes sedan, its headlamps dimmed, pulling out of the Carmodys' driveway.

Even though it was dark, she could tell that the driver was none other than Gloria. Clara was about to beep her horn when a startling series of thoughts stopped her: Gloria driving a car? By herself? On a school night? This was a mystery better than any late-night gabfest. Gloria had a secret rendezvous?

Lorraine had no choice but to follow.

She pulled over, doused the lights, and hoped Gloria hadn't noticed her.

Once Gloria had rolled the car out of the driveway and turned onto the street, Lorraine switched on her lights and stepped on the gas, gunning the sedan into the shadows and toward the city.

Lorraine trailed her friend all the way through the light traffic of Lake Forest, down through the North Shore, onto the packed streets of the city. At first she hung back a few car lengths, worried that Gloria would look into the rearview mirror and see her, but Gloria was far too self-involved to do that.

By the time Gloria nosed the Mercedes onto North Broadway Avenue, Lorraine was right on her tail, practically bumper to bumper. She toyed with the idea of stabbing her foot against the pedal and crashing into the back of the car. That would get Gloria's attention. Gloria hadn't just forgotten her best friend; she couldn't even see her when she was right behind her. It made Lorraine furious.

They passed the Wrigley Building, then the Drake Hotel at the north end of Michigan Avenue. Lorraine's only guides were the streetlamps that brightened the black sky, and the taillights of Gloria's car up ahead.

Lorraine had no idea where Gloria was going. But then, lo and behold, the buildings started to look familiar. Lorraine watched as Gloria pulled up a few blocks from the Green Mill. *Oh, how the plot thickens,* Lorraine thought. *This is unexpected*.

She watched Gloria park and hurry down the street, in perfect flapper raiment from head to toe.

From the outside, one would never know the Green Mill even existed: It was below a dark storefront between a funeral home and a shady-looking barbershop. The building looked as if it'd been vacated years ago. There were a few men in suits outside smoking cigarettes, but otherwise the street was vacant.

Lorraine parked in a spot around the corner from the club. She looked down at herself and grimaced. She'd been more or less ready for bed before hijacking the Duesenberg, wearing a silk negligee that she'd bought last summer in Paris—black silk with white French lace trim—that *might* do for a flapper dress.

Luckily, Marguerite—stupid girl—had left Lorraine's mother's dry cleaning in the back of the car. Thank the Lord her mother didn't dress like Mrs. Carmody. Lorraine climbed into the backseat and dug through it.

*Thank you, Mother, for dry-cleaning your mink stole for my benefit.* Lorraine slipped the stole over her nearly bare shoulders. *Parfait!,* as Madame Cloutier would say. At least that would be one word Lorraine got right on the *examen* tomorrow.

Her mother's emergency stash was in the glove box, as she'd hoped—coral-pink lipstick to double as cheek rouge; Vaseline to double as hair shine. She wasn't wearing the right brassiere, but considering the circumstances, this would have to do.

Lorraine descended the stairs to the door of the Green Mill and found a clutch of flappers swarming around the entrance like vultures around a corpse. They loitered here, out of view from the street, so that they'd be invisible in case the police drove by. Not as if that really mattered, anyway—most of the cops were bought and paid for by the Mob.

Lorraine hated every single one of these girls. They were all wearing actual *dresses.* They made her feel naked and cheap—and she was probably richer than all of them combined! She could have outdone their sparkly getups, if only

Gloria hadn't pulled this impromptu stunt. One of the girls had a beaded violet purse. Lorraine's own purse seemed grimy in comparison.

Insecure, Lorraine stood back in the shadows. She needed an entrance strategy before she made her move.

A rail-thin brunette in a gray fur coat aggressively swaggered up to the door.

The girl banged till the slot in the door slid open. The Eye surveyed her. "Well?"

"My boyfriend's cousin Anthony has a table in there."

"Anthony *who*?" the Eye barked.

"My boyfriend's last name is Wood, and he's inside at the table already—you must have seen him, he's tall with—"

Even Lorraine could hear the Eye laugh. "You want me to get him for you?"

"Oh, gee, could you?"

"No!" The slot shut.

Lorraine would have to resort to the oldest trick in the book: If you've got it, flaunt it. At least she could use what these other girls lacked. And that was *skin*.

She waited till there was an opening in the crowd, then tapped gently on the door.

The slit opened and the Eye gave her the once-over.

She stood tall and dramatically unwrapped her mink stole, exposing the slip.

Jackpot. The Eye blinked. "Who you here for?"

"Myself," she said, lowering her right shoulder so that the

strap slipped off it. "Oops," she said, catching the strap before it exposed too much.

"Hey!" the flapper with the violet purse called out. "We were here first!"

The Eye ignored her. "Which party sent for you?"

"My half-birthday party."

The Eye looked her up and down. "You're telling me you plan to celebrate alone, in those glad rags?"

"If you let me inside, I won't be alone."

"All right," the Eye said. "There's always room for a working girl."

Lorraine didn't really know what he meant by that—*working girl?* She had a trust fund; she'd never worked a day in her life!

But when the door opened, the other flappers yelling out in protest, she didn't dwell on it. There was no feeling Lorraine loved more than being *in.* And if Gloria was going to exclude her, she'd just be left to her own devices to make sure she wasn't left out.

Lorraine headed straight for the bar, walking along its length until she reached the end—a prime spot to perch and spy. She took a stool, slouched against the counter, and hoped she blended in with the rest of the crowd.

Stretching away to her left were the plush green booths typically filled by the wealthiest patrons and the owners of the club; to her right were small, high tables that people—mostly flappers—rested their drinks on while they went to cut a rug on the dance floor. And straight ahead lay that dance floor: tiny but packed with dancers, their heads bobbing and arms swinging as they did the Charleston with looks of bliss on their faces. Lorraine watched them and felt a twinge of envy. They were having fun, and she was having—

"Miss?" It was Leif, the bartender. "I asked you what you'll have."

"A martini," she told him. "Make it dirty."

Past the dance floor was the stage, where the black musicians were sitting, their instruments shiny with the reflected lights. They were laughing and joking with each other.

Nothing there. Lorraine began slowly scanning the smoky room for Gloria and locked eyes with a smoldering gentleman sitting at one of the booths opposite her.

*Let him come to me,* she thought, wheeling around on her stool so that her back was to him. In about thirty seconds, he had slid into the spot next to her. Men were *so* predictable.

"I couldn't help noticing you from across the room," he said, signaling Leif. "The usual for me, and mix something special for the doll."

Up close, he looked younger than he had from a distance—maybe early twenties. Lorraine was instantly drawn to his foreignness. He was so different from the prep school boys she was used to. This man had dark eyes and dark, short hair to match, almost hidden by thick black brows. His lips were thin but wide, planted around a cigar, giving him a permanent sneer—albeit a sexy one. He was a total sheik. Plus he was wearing the classic gangster getup: an impeccably tailored gray suit with a navy ascot and silver cuff links.

"What did you notice?" The bartender had set down a pink cocktail for her. Now she had two drinks. She picked one up and sipped at it.

"I noticed you look different than the other girls. With your raven hair and raven eyes," he said, dabbing with his handkerchief at a drop of her cocktail that had slipped down her chin. "Like a black bird of prey."

Lorraine liked him immediately—liked the dangerous image he painted of her, and his rough finger on her chin. She didn't really know what his banter was about, but what did it matter? She, too, could be bold; strange men could find her interesting. To hell with Marcus Eastman.

She was about to respond when she caught sight of her target: Gloria talking to—almost touching—that black jazz pianist in a far corner of the club.

Since when had Gloria ever *not* trusted Lorraine as a confidante, as an unconditional secret keeper? They told each other *everything*—or they had, until Gloria had gone off and gotten engaged to that stuffed shirt. And now she was living a double life *sans* Lorraine. Was Marcus going to pop out of the woodwork, too? None of it made any sense. Lorraine had never before felt so betrayed.

But as she observed Gloria and Jerome, a different story suddenly became clear: the way her upper body curved in toward his; the way each one's eyes were locked on the other's face, as if there were nobody else in the room. Something was going on between them. Something . . . sexual.

No, that was crazy. Aside from the fact that she had a highly publicized engagement, Gloria was cautious. Gloria was proper. And that musician was *black*.

The man next to Lorraine nudged her, bringing her mind back to the bar. "You think I'm worth your while?"

Lorraine had forgotten herself. She looked around, at the sweating faces of all these men and the desperate antics of the flappers, at the look of contempt from the mustachioed bartender—what was that about?—and then at her empty glasses.

"She'll have another," the man said.

"I'm sorry. I thought I saw someone I knew, talking to the pianist." Lorraine was already feeling a bit fried.

"You mean the club's new torch?" He pointed at Gloria. "She's some hick chorus girl—pretty, but right off the farm wagon. Coulda fooled me. I didn't know they made 'em like that out in the cornfields."

"That girl?" Lorraine laughed. "Banana oil! She's not from the—" She stopped herself. "Wait, where's she from?"

"Ohio? Or was it Pennsylvania." He shrugged. "Beats me. But I doubt a sophisticated city girl like yourself would know her."

"You're right. I wouldn't know a girl like that." Lorraine

felt sick. Gloria was singing? She had a good voice—Glo would surely be the toast of the Chicago underground. How was that fair? *Lorraine* was the trailblazer, the one who championed the flapper lifestyle, the pioneer. But, as usual, Gloria got all the love.

Wait. The mobster had just called Lorraine sophisticated. That was something, wasn't it? Lorraine found herself oddly attracted to him. Not in the way she was attracted to Marcus. This was different. Best of all, according to this man, Gloria didn't hold a candle to Lorraine's "sophistication." *How about that, Glo?* Lorraine wanted to shout across the club.

Maybe, Lorraine had to admit, what made her a sometime embarrassment among the other Chicago debs—her brashness, her say-it-as-it-is attitude—made her perfect for this world of gangsters and gin, of flappers and jazz. Gloria was trying desperately to belong, but Lorraine truly *did* belong. Didn't she?

Lorraine watched as Gloria and Jerome slipped away through the curtains near the stage. Oh, there was something going on for sure. Something *not* on the level.

"You gonna make a dent in that drink?" The man tapped her glass—the bartender had already refreshed it—and she saw then that his gold pinkie ring was engraved with the initials *C.M.*

"How 'bout I rain-check you on that one?" She stood up from the bar and the room spun around her.

"Hey there, you half overboard already?" He put his hand on her waist, steadying her. "You need someone to teach you how to hold your liquor."

"Tell me where I can apply."

"The next time you come, just say my name at the door: Carlito. Not like they would give a girl like you trouble."

"Ha," she said, and sauntered away.

And then he slapped her ass. But Lorraine didn't turn around. Clearly the outfit wasn't a total washout after all.

Especially if Carlito Macharelli—the twenty-year-old son of one of the men who *owned* the place—had chosen *her* to talk to, flirt with, buy drinks for. *Her* over every other girl in this joint.

Lorraine stomped out of the club, pushing through the desperate flappers still clogging the entrance. She wasn't one of them anymore. Like Gloria, she had an insider's key. But Gloria had already *had* her moment: her photo with Bastian in the *Tribune,* the ring every girl wanted from the man every girl wanted. She even had Marcus Eastman. Now she was going to be the toast of the speakeasy scene, too?

Gloria couldn't have everything. Or at least, she couldn't have both.

It was strictly a matter of fairness.

Lorraine would have to square things.

◆◆◆

"So this is how a bachelor lives?" she called out in the direction of the kitchen.

Lorraine wandered the edges of Bastian's living room, which was lined with windows that overlooked the sparkling Chicago skyline. It was a beautiful apartment. Beautiful and cold.

She'd only been to his penthouse once before, when he'd hosted an afternoon cocktail party after the engagement was announced. The apartment had been filled to capacity with his mostly male social circle: colleagues from the bank; fraternity brothers; tennis partners from Oak Lane Country Club—all either old men or men waiting to get old. But back then, everyone had been laughing and flirting and celebrating.

Tonight, that day felt like a lifetime ago. Lorraine was out of place in the masculine emptiness of the room. Sebastian's golf clubs were in the corner, next to a framed oar and his Harvard diploma She stopped by the mantel and picked up a photo. Gloria on a beach, looking curvaceous in a one-piece bathing suit, stared back at her. Lorraine immediately set the frame down and backed away.

Beads of sweat had begun to pool above her lip and below her eyes. Nerves. She needed to blot her cheeks and forehead before he came back into the room.

Lorraine opened a door, which she assumed led to the bathroom, only to realize that it was Bastian's bedroom. The room was dominated by an enormous, neatly made bed, decked out in a pleated red silk comforter. It was a loud reminder that she was in the apartment of an actual *man*—she and Gloria both still had single beds.

She wondered how many women Bastian had slept with in that bed. A man of twenty-three years old, who looked like Bastian and had Bastian's last name, could easily have slept with a dozen girls. Maybe more. Even though Gloria hadn't yet been made a notch on his bedpost.

The rest of the room was equally stark: a dark-colored dresser, a night table with a small ceramic lamp, and a book whose title Lorraine couldn't make out. The walls were a muted gray, and there was a framed painting of some mountains—which ones, Lorraine didn't know—near one of the windows. The carpeting was plush beneath her feet, the deep color of red wine.

"Looking for something?"

Lorraine twirled around in the doorway.

Bastian was standing right behind her, holding out two glasses of ice water. He was wearing a white undershirt and linen trousers. It was the first time she had seen him without a suit on. She'd never realized how athletic he was: His broad chest tapered to a narrow waist, and his undershirt clung tightly to his flat, muscular abdomen. His features were perfectly symmetrical, the angles of his face sharp and strong.

He walked toward her. "There's a bathroom in my bedroom, if you'd like to use—"

"No! I'm fine!" She laughed nervously, stepping back into the living room. She maneuvered around the coffee table and slid onto the sofa, resting her arm on the soft, dark fabric.

"What brings you here so late, Raine?" Bastian came up behind her and handed her one of the glasses.

"I just happened to be driving by—"

"At this hour?"

He sat down beside her, and she began to perspire again. "I was at the—a party. In the neighborhood?"

"Are you asking me, or telling me?" Bastian said, leaning back into the sofa.

"Telling."

Bastian smirked. "That would somewhat explain your choice of clothing," he said, fingering the strap of her dress. "Or lack thereof. You're quite the fashion plate."

Lorraine's breathing stopped. Compared to Carlito's callused fingers, Bastian's felt silky. When he removed his hand, her skin prickled where he had touched her. "It was practically a sauna inside this party. I nearly wilted."

"Then drink up. Or I'll have to cut your stem."

Lorraine laughed uncomfortably again, taking a long sip of water. "I'm sure you don't approve of partying on a school night, but don't worry, I won't make a habit of it."

"You're not mine to worry about."

"And if I were?"

Bastian looked thoughtful for a moment. "Then I would

give you a curfew, and punish you if you weren't in bed by a certain time."

She had always thought his eyes were hazel. Now she realized they were quite green, but pierced with pewter, steely almost. Lorraine cleared her throat. "Whose bed do you mean? Hypothetically speaking, of course."

"Hypothetical questions aside for now," he said, setting his glass down on a coaster, "let's address the more pressing question: Why are you here, Lorraine? It's late, and I'm tired. I have to work early in the morning." He studied her carefully. "And you have school."

Lorraine felt her face flush. She was here because his fiancée was living a double life as the singer at a speakeasy infested with booze and mobsters, and maybe even worse—as the soon-to-be whore of some low-class black jazz cat. She was here because Gloria didn't deserve Bastian, didn't deserve his trust—he was boring, sure, but on paper he was perfect. She was here because her best friend had betrayed her. Because she felt used, abused, and hurt. Because she couldn't believe Gloria would lie to her, would keep things from her. And she was here because she had nowhere else to turn.

"I'm here to talk about Gloria," she began, but just saying those words aloud made her throat close up. "Your fiancée?"

"Yes, I know who she is. And I assumed you weren't here to talk about yourself."

Bastian picked up her empty glass. "Let me refresh your drink with something a little stronger."

He strolled over to his bookcase, which was lined with rows of leather-bound volumes. They looked well-read—left over from his college days, no doubt. Lorraine watched as he picked out an oversized dictionary.

"I do enough vocabulary in school," she said.

"Patience, Lorraine." Bastian opened the book. It was completely hollowed out, and nestled inside was a tiny bottle filled with what looked like bourbon or Scotch.

"It's not every man who keeps his liquor hidden in a book," Lorraine said, thinking of her father. "Anyway, I thought you were rah-rah for the Prohibition."

He chuckled. "I suppose I'm not every man." Then he opened the bottle and poured two shots into short crystal glasses. "There is a difference between what you do in the privacy of your own home and what you display to the public eye."

Lorraine wondered if he was talking just about drinking. She imagined Gloria sitting in the spot where she was now, having intimate conversations with Bastian late into the night. How was it possible that he and Gloria had only ever *kissed*? If he'd been her fiancé, Lorraine wouldn't have been able to stop herself from pinning him against that floor-to-ceiling window and ripping off his clothes.

"Raine, are you well?" He handed her the drink and then

put the bottle back into the book and onto the shelf, where it blended in with all the others.

"I'm—" She avoided his eyes. "I'm a horrible human being."

Bastian placed his hand on her thigh. "I highly doubt that," he said.

She knew she should pull away—even slap him. But she hadn't been touched by a boy, really touched, in a long time.

This was the time to tell him. Now, now, *now!*

But the second Bastian removed his hand, she began to think clearly. Did she really want to be held responsible for destroying her best friend's impending marriage, not to mention her future? Lorraine could already feel the guilt brewing in her chest. No, she couldn't do that to herself; she couldn't do that to Gloria.

If she was going to get back at Gloria for betraying her trust, she would have to do so in a way that would be untraceable.

"Bastian, I'm a horrible person for not asking your permission," she said, improvising, "but I'd like to surprise Gloria with a weekend escape to Forest Lake Spa—as my bridesmaid's gift to her."

"That's perfectly fine," Sebastian said with a short laugh.

"Oh. Well, that's a relief."

"But you are still a horrible person."

She was about to say something dirty, then stopped

herself. Bastian was definitely flirting with her, which made her feel . . . unsettled.

"I really should be getting home," she said finally, standing up. The whiskey rushed to her head. "I have a French *examen* to study for."

Bastian grinned. "Since when do you study?"

She slumped back down and kneaded her forehead with her hand. "I am rather tired."

There was his hand again, warm on her knee. "At least finish your drink before you dash off."

Lorraine looked into his steely green eyes. She couldn't read them: What did he want? Was he coming on to her, or was he setting her up for a trap?

"You know," Bastian said, inching closer, "has anyone ever told you that you're a choice bit of calico?"

Lorraine nearly snorted. "Are you feeding me a line?" It was impossible to determine Bastian's motives. He was nothing like she'd thought he was. He kept booze in books, for heaven's sake!

And she didn't know what *she* wanted anymore. She didn't want to give her virginity to Bastian, she knew that much, but her head felt stuffed with cotton balls and she was definitely a bit zozzled . . . and his hand felt so nice.

"There's nothing to be ashamed of, Lorraine," he said. "Even women have needs, and I think we both know that Gloria is nothing to me but a convenience. A means to an end." He licked his lips. "There's no reason I can't take care of your needs, too, so long as you're willing to take care of mine."

He cupped her face with both hands and moved in.

Just before Lorraine closed her eyes, one of the forgotten vocabulary words from tomorrow's *examen* popped into her head:

*adulteress (noun feminine): femme adultère*

# 13

# GLORIA

Gloria stood in the center of the Green Mill.

The place was empty. No bartender, no band, no gangsters. Just chairs upside down on tables, and racks of washed glasses stacked on the bar. For a moment she felt a hot panic. Had she gotten the day wrong? The time wrong? Wasn't this where she was supposed to be for her first voice lesson with Jerome? She had found the back door propped open as promised, but where was he?

"Hello? Is anybody here?" she called out.

No answer.

It was early afternoon, but you would never be able to tell down here—the Green Mill existed in a perpetual midnight. What was she doing, wasting her time in this dank, dark, empty club? She should be in her English class that was this very minute going on without her: twelve girls sitting around Miss Moss, reading the second act of *Othello* aloud. She loved her English teacher, which was why it had pained her to present the note—with her father's forged signature—saying she had a doctor's appointment "for matters to do with her upcoming nuptials" and would be absent from class. Gloria *never* skipped class. She only missed school when she was sick, and even then she usually managed to force herself out of bed.

But now things had changed.

It was a rule that you couldn't wear street clothes on school grounds, but Gloria couldn't show up at the Green Mill looking like a student. She had changed out of her school uniform—ankle-length gray skirt, short-sleeved white cotton blouse that was positively bristling with buttons—in the gym's locker room and donned her favorite Patou floral day dress, a bell-skirted, high-waisted shepherdess-style frock. Then she had pulled a broad-brimmed hat onto her head and strolled out the back of the school. If anyone had seen her, they would have thought she was a substitute instructor, or one of the more glamorous mothers.

Gloria reached the street and found waiting the taxicab she'd arranged for early that morning.

Now Gloria crossed the dance floor, her clacking heels the only sound aside from the low drum of water through pipes. This was her third lesson, technically, since she had sat in on two of the band's rehearsals, but her first private lesson with Jerome. Alone. She hadn't slept a wink last night, she was so nervous with anticipation. It was like the feeling of going out on a first date with someone you're crazy about.

Except this wasn't a date. It was a singing lesson. And Jerome wasn't someone she was crazy about, because she had a fiancé. Jerome was a musician, and her boss, and he was nowhere to be found!

"I thought there was a tap show going on out here."

"You're late," Gloria said, wheeling around. When she saw him, her heart seemed to stop: Jerome Johnson, all long limbs and long fingers, mysterious and poised and oh so sure of himself. He was wearing tan trousers and a black shirt that was open at the neck, exposing the smooth skin of his chest. She gulped. "By twenty minutes."

"You're in the music business; you'd better get used to it." He grinned, his smile lighting up the room. "We should get started. We've got a lot of hard work ahead of us."

"I'm ready for it."

"That's the kind of attitude I like to hear from my pupils. Though they're usually about yea high," he said, marking the air at his hip.

"Oh, you teach children?"

"One of my day jobs—giving piano lessons to little peanuts." Gloria thought it was cute that he referred to the kids as peanuts; he obviously had real affection for them.

This surprised her. She hadn't pictured Jerome Johnson as a sensitive type. "What, you think I can pay my rent from this gig alone?" he asked.

"Right, of course," she said, shaking her head. But what did she mean? *Right, of course.* Gloria had never thought about paying rent before, let alone paying for anything else. Or working to survive. Or the life of a struggling musician.

"Don't tell me you were depending on this job to get by," Jerome said.

"Of course not! I've got a . . . a . . ."

"A boyfriend?"

"God, no!" She laughed uncomfortably. "I was going to say a . . . waitressing job. As a waitress. In a . . . diner."

"I thought I saw you with some blond boy at the club, so I just figured . . ."

He must have meant Marcus. "He's just a friend," Gloria reassured him. "One of the only ones I have here since, uh, moving."

There was an awkward silence. She hadn't been prepared for the boyfriend question. Jerome had noticed Marcus—maybe he'd been paying more attention to Gloria than she'd suspected.

"Come on," Jerome said, walking back behind the bar. Gloria watched as he studied the floor. It was untiled, just darkly painted wood, still dirty with scuff marks and footprints from the night before. Then he bent and hooked his finger into a nearly invisible latch. When he pulled, a section of the floor came up on hinges.

"It's where they store all the liquor," Jerome said. "Also, in case we ever get busted by the cops, there's a tunnel to the next street over."

With everything else going on—her fledgling singing career, her disturbing attraction to Jerome Johnson, the hasty preparations for her wedding with Bastian—Gloria had nearly forgotten that the only reason places like the Green Mill existed at all was because alcohol had been made illegal.

She'd been fourteen when the Prohibition started, and hadn't fully understood it at the time. Later, in her civics class at school, she'd been made to study it—its actual name was the Volstead Act, passed in 1919, but everybody called it the National Prohibition Act or the Eighteenth Amendment. Suddenly, in 1920, it was against the law to make or sell alcohol anywhere in the country. Which sounded like a good thing on the face of it.

But people weren't so eager to give up their booze. Right after the amendment passed, speakeasies began appearing—places where people could go and drink and have a good time. They were open secrets. Always hidden, with passwords needed to get in, and in places no one—especially the police—would think to look. Yet everyone knew they were there.

Not only was Gloria breaking her curfew to sing at the Green Mill, and her parents' trust: She was also breaking the law.

Jerome snapped his fingers. "You ready?" He motioned down the flight of steps. "I would say after you, Miss Carson, but I'd better lead the way."

He descended the steep staircase, and Gloria followed. On the penultimate creaky step, her heel slipped and she tumbled into the darkness.

But Jerome was there to catch her.

She clutched his sturdy arms and found her balance. Neither of them moved. His breath against her cheek, his hands around her waist. In the dark, hidden from the world above, he wasn't black or white. He was just a man.

Gloria felt that something was on the brink of happening. But then he gently released her. She stepped backward, shaken.

"Thanks," she mumbled.

"Don't mention it."

He flipped on a flashlight.

Following its narrow cone of light, she felt as if she were walking through a haunted house. Or a tomb. Corpses of cockroaches littered the floor, piled up next to soggy boxes of liquor; loose electrical wires and rusted pipes ran across the ceiling. Every so often, they passed a half-open door, and Jerome would say things like "Poker parlor," or "Conference room," or "Room I really shouldn't talk about because if you knew what they did in there you'd never want to come back to this joint."

"Here we are," he said. He yanked a chain dangling from

the ceiling and a dusty bulb lit up. The room was barely big enough for the two of them, let alone the decrepit-looking piano that filled the space.

"*This* is where we're practicing?" she asked, shivering. It felt like a meat freezer.

"Were you expecting Carnegie Hall?" Jerome lifted the cover away from the aged upright and coughed as the dust settled around him.

Gloria was used to rehearsing in the grand hall in the music wing of her school. But looking at Jerome, she felt ashamed. What did he know of grand concert halls? How snobbish of her to sneer at this practice room. "I'm sorry," she said, "this is completely jake."

"We're going to begin with some breathing exercises. Do you know where your diaphragm is?"

"I beg your pardon?" She took a step back.

"Your *diaphragm* is a muscle system, fastened to your lowest ribs. It's what singers use to control their breathing."

"Oh, right."

"See, if you breathe high in your chest, your breath is just gonna come out as air. But if you breathe deeply, all the way into your diaphragm, where your solar plexus sits, then it's gonna come out as emotion, sound, color, vibra—" His eyes narrowed. "Is that gum you're chewing?"

Her jaw froze. "I guess I forgot that it was still—" She began to rummage through her purse for a scrap of paper, for anything. "Here, let me just—"

"Give it to me." He held out his hand.

Mortified, she plopped the spearmint-green wad into his hand. "I'm really sorry," she managed to squeak out.

"If you're not gonna take this seriously, then don't waste my time." All the funny, sweet things he'd been saying earlier were instantly forgotten. "I'm not the one who needs to learn how to sing."

"I do take it seriously. I said I was sorry."

"And stop apologizing." Jerome tore a piece of newsprint from a daily paper on the floor and wrapped her gum in it. He looked up at her. "If you're gonna get up there and make every single person in that audience fall head over heels in love with you when the first note comes out of your mouth, you gotta own that stage. And your voice. And who you are, no apologies. Understand?"

"Yes," Gloria said. Jerome's intensity was infectious and unnerving—he was passionate. Bastian didn't even consider jazz to be music. Bastian didn't have an ounce of passion in him—not even when he kissed her.

"Now, are we ready?" Jerome asked.

"Ready."

"I want you to start imagining your voice as a beautiful maple tree. Here," he said, touching the top of her head, "is the top, made up of a thick bunch of rusty leaves."

"Gotcha," she said, trying to stretch her spine and stand as tall as possible.

"And here," he said, touching the sides of her ribs, "are

your branches. You wanna fill them up while keeping 'em very still."

She filled her lungs with air and puffed out her chest. "Not like this?" she asked.

"No, not like that." His grip tightened around her waist like a corset. "Try again. Inhale, but don't move my hands."

She tried, but how did he expect her to control her breathing with his hands sending out-of-control vibrations through her body?

"You need to work on that," he continued. "Finally, here's the base of the trunk—your diaphragm." He placed a hand right beneath her rib cage. "The most crucial part of your voice. Besides your vocal cords, anyway. This is where your breath begins."

Gloria began to squirm as if she'd been tickled. Though she wasn't ticklish at all, and this certainly didn't feel ticklish. It felt heavenly. Just as she had imagined his hands would feel. Strong. Intense.

"What's so funny?" he asked sharply, removing his hand from her stomach.

"Nothing!"

"Is this funny to you, country girl?" His voice was suddenly harsh. "Does this seem like a joke?"

"Not at all," she insisted. She couldn't tell him that no man had ever touched her so easily before, and that it had startled her.

"This is serious business—you're going up on that stage in

one week. And if you look bad, not only will you never work in this town again, but I'll get all the blame," he said, his eyes darkening. "Think you'll be laughing when that happens? Do you have any idea what Carlito will do to me?"

Gloria cringed at the gangster's name, and at Jerome's tone. "Do you speak this way to all the girls?"

"While you're working for me, I can speak to you however I want."

Gloria stared at him in disbelief. "You'd better watch your tongue, because I can walk out for good at any second."

"This is your big break—you wouldn't dare."

"Oh yeah? Think again." She turned toward the door. "Let's see who gets the last laugh. It certainly won't be your boss."

He caught her wrist and pulled her close. She could see flecks of gold in his eyes. As confused as she was, there was something pulsing and sparking between them like an electric current. She couldn't tell whether she loved or hated him. She couldn't tell whether he was about to kiss or slap her.

"Show me where it is again."

"What?" He let go of her wrist.

"The base. Of the maple tree. Where is it?"

Jerome relaxed. "Here," he said softly. And ever so gently, he placed his palm back beneath her sternum.

She took a deep breath in, then let it out. This time, she didn't laugh.

Jerome sat very straight at the piano bench and placed his fingers on the keys. "Why don't we just start singing?"

Then he played the first few chords of a melancholy song she had never heard before, though some part of her felt as if she were born to sing it.

◆◆◆

The more Gloria stared at her shrimp cocktail, the more she imagined that the shrimp were staring back at her with their beady little eyes.

"Darling, are your shrimp undercooked?" Bastian asked. "Because if they are, we can send them back."

"No, no, they're fine," she said. It wasn't just that the shrimp seemed alive; they seemed to be judging her. They knew where she'd spent the afternoon: at the Green Mill, in the basement with Jerome. A world away from where she was now.

Even though the Drake Hotel had opened three years before, the members-only club was still considered extremely exclusive in the circles Bastian ran in—the waiting list was two years long. But Bastian had connections with the right people.

"Let me give you some of my dish." He shoveled some of his striped bass appetizer onto her plate. He was wearing a dark navy suit, looking dapper. His hair was perfectly combed and oiled, and he was freshly shaven—he could have been a movie star. "Try this, dear."

She took a small bite and grimaced. "Ugh, I forgot how much I dislike Hollandaise sauce."

"Since when?"

"Since right this second." She considered spitting it out into a napkin, but Bastian would have an absolute heart attack at how unladylike that was. Which made her want to do it even more.

"Gloria, when are you going to stop being so fickle?" he asked, dabbing at his mouth with his napkin. "It really calls attention to your age. What are you going to do when we host dinner parties? Serve only simple sandwiches? Flush the caviar down the toilet?"

"God forbid I should do that."

He scanned the room with his icy green eyes. When they were together, she always got the sense that he was looking elsewhere—anywhere but at her.

She sighed. "Is there anything else I should learn to like while I'm at it? Parsley, cilantro, thyme?"

Bastian put down his fork. "No, I think that will be all for now."

There was a long silence, and Gloria stared at the flickering candle between them. Nothing like the silence between her and Jerome earlier, which had been fraught with possibility. This silence was just awkward. Gloria imagined dinners with Bastian for the next sixty years of her life—if it was like this now, imagine how it would be once they were married. And not just dinners: they would be *living* together. That would include breakfast and lunch. Even snacks.

Bastian cleared his throat. "I don't know about you, but I'm having a marvelous time."

Gloria burst out laughing. She took a sip of water, hoping to calm herself down. This was the second time in one day she'd laughed when something got serious. She needed to pull herself together. But then she imagined Jerome again, sitting across from her in a stuffy, straitlaced place like this, and she began to chuckle. "I'm sorry." She covered her mouth, the water dribbling down the corners.

"What has gotten into you?" Bastian growled. "Try not to be such a flibbertigibbet, Gloria."

She laughed again. "Did you really just call me a flibbertigibbet?"

He acted as though she hadn't said anything at all. "You're not going to be like this when we're married. I can't have my wife going around acting like a child. If you don't shape up, you'll simply stay home all the time. And I do mean all the time—I'll see to that."

Gloria breathed in and out through her nose, and suddenly nothing around her seemed funny anymore. The stiff couples, the cloying roses, the garish wallpaper—all of it was depressing.

Bastian folded his napkin and repositioned it on his lap. "Rudolph Wright told me that the Debutante Committee is seriously considering extending a pledge to Clara at this year's ball."

"Oh, is that so?" Gloria asked flatly, biting off the head of a judgmental shrimp.

"Clara is becoming the talk of the town," Bastian said. "Even my father asked me about her the other day."

"Well, you've always wanted to marry a debutante. Perhaps Clara would be a more suitable option."

"Don't be so *dramatic,* Gloria."

"Dramatic?" He knew she despised it when he called her that, and suddenly she realized why: Bastian wanted a wife who would serve his every whim dutifully, without so much as an opinion or a thought of her own. Or a voice. Unlike Jerome, who was trying to give her just that. "My comment was based on strict observation."

He chortled. "Leave the deep thinking to the men, Gloria."

"Bastian, I've had a great education. I may not have graduated from Harvard, but I know a thing or two about the world."

"Gloria, please be serious. Your education doesn't matter one way or another to our understanding."

He placed a cool hand on her bony wrist. A chill shot through her.

Jerome had touched her there only an hour ago. There had been warmth in his touch, and an honesty—those elegantly long fingers, callused at the tips from pounding the piano keys. Every time he came near her, she could feel the heat sparking between them. Unlike now, when all she felt was cold, cold, cold.

She promptly drew back her wrist. "What 'understanding' are you referring to?"

"I don't know why you insist on playing the fool." He hunched forward, lowering his voice. "Surely you must know by now why we're getting married."

"Please, illuminate me."

"Gloria, you know damn well your parents have arranged this *understanding*. I was planning to save you the humiliation, but I heard about your misconduct last week at your party. I hope you got whatever it was out of your system. We certainly can't afford to jeopardize our engagement with bad publicity. Especially considering your mother's situation."

"Wait, what do you mean by my mother's situation?" she said, a lump rising in her throat. Nobody knew about her parents' pending divorce, not even her best friend. Her mother wouldn't dare tell anyone.

"It's a business transaction." Bastian stared at her unflinchingly. "Now that your father is about to ruin your family's reputation, I am going to ensure that you have an honorable last name to replace your own. Pure and simple."

Gloria swallowed hard. Sure, she was having doubts about Bastian, but in the beginning he had said he loved her. And she'd thought she felt the same way. All those dates, and parties, and dinners together; the romantic summer courtship.

"Nothing is ever so simple," she began, trying to keep down her rising voice. "What do you get out of this?"

"What do you think, Gloria? A fortune. A position of responsibility at your father's firm. And an annoying wife. Really, must we discuss this now?"

"No, you're right." She closed her eyes and moved her head in time to the classical music that the club's pianist was playing. "Who is this?" she asked.

"Vivaldi," Bastian said, distracted. "Gloria, we can live a good life together once you start behaving yourself. I know this is only a phase you are going through, but—"

"The 'Winter' movement," Gloria said with satisfaction.

Bastian shook his head. "It's the *presto* section from 'Summer.'"

Gloria started to tell Bastian he was wrong, but she listened closely and realized that he was, in fact, correct.

She sank back in her chair. How could she have gotten so mixed up? She'd listened to *The Four Seasons* dozens of times.

"You're right, of course," she admitted. Bastian was always right, wasn't he? She had mistaken the piece—and, glancing about the room, she realized that she'd mistaken everything else around her—for something she cared about, something she wanted. Only, the truth was that she'd never cared about or wanted these things at all. Fancy restaurants, expensive dresses, classical music—they could disappear from her life and she wouldn't blink.

All she really wanted was jazz. All she really wanted was Jerome.

His voice interrupted her thoughts. "The service has really gone downhill lately," Bastian was saying to her while the waiter stood beside him. "I must speak to the manager about this. Do you know what you'd like for the main course?"

Bastian might have had a fancy last name that would save Gloria from social ruin, but she was well aware of what she, as a Carmody, brought to the table. "Yes, I know exactly what I want." *I want so much more than this,* she thought.

"Finally, a little decisiveness," he said.

The waiter leaned forward. "For *madame*?"

*"Mademoiselle,"* she corrected him. "I would like a slice of the dark chocolate *gâteau*."

Bastian gave the waiter a patient smile, then said to Gloria, "Dear, we can have that after dinner."

"I don't want it after dinner. And seeing that my father is paying for it, you really don't have much of a say in the matter." She widened her eyes and rested her chin on her hand.

Bastian snapped his menu closed and handed it to the waiter. He didn't utter a single word for the rest of the meal.

The cake, Gloria thought, was delicious.

# CLARA

Clara pulled up to the Carmody mansion in a taxi just as it began to rain. Of course she didn't have an umbrella.

She paid the driver, opened the door, and, covering her head with her minuscule clutch, was about to sprint into the house when she recognized the brand-new Cadillac blocking the end of the driveway.

It belonged to the last person she wanted to see right now: Marcus Eastman. For a guy with so many friends and ex-girlfriends, he seemed to turn up by himself an awful lot.

She bolted for the doorway but was drenched before she was halfway there.

Safe from the rain, she stood dripping under the awning. She needed a moment to collect herself. She felt about as wrecked as the *crêpe de chine* floral print sheath that clung wetly to her body.

She'd just come back from dinner with an old New York acquaintance. Well, not an acquaintance of hers, but of the Cad's. After the last mysterious note, she hadn't been able to rest easy until she found out whether the notes were from him, whether her deepest fears were true. Was it the Cad who was stalking her? Or the Petty Crook? Or the Bootlegger? Or someone she didn't even suspect, someone holding a grudge? There were too many possibilities. Clara had to start crossing them off her list and find this person before he—or she—found her.

So she'd arranged a secret meet-up with one of the Cad's friends. He was an architect named Barton Bishop, who had recently picked up and moved to Chicago to work for Frank Lloyd Wright. She'd concocted a story for Mrs. Carmody—an opportunity to join the Chicago Socialites League!—and slunk out to meet him for dinner at the Cabin Club, a snooty private supper joint downtown.

But her investigation was a total washout. Barton didn't know *anything,* especially not about the Cad, her number-one suspect. Worse, Barton actually had the nerve to hit on her!

In the taxi on the way home she asked the driver to roll down his window. "Don't be startled," she told him, "just keep driving."

"I beg your pardon?" the man said. He was gray-haired and friendly-looking, like her grandfather.

"Just keep driving," she repeated. Then she screamed. She shouted and pounded her fists on the upholstered seat and hollered until she was out of breath and empty of anger. The noise from the car made couples on the sidewalks clutch at each other and stare as the taxi rolled past.

And then she was done. She composed herself. "Thank you."

"Are you sure you're not sick, miss?"

"I'm fine," she said, but on the inside, she was afraid. Deathly afraid.

What did this mystery person want from her? Did he want anything at all, or did he just want to mess with her head? Were the notes really from the Cad, or from someone worse?

Watching the rain wasn't going to get her any closer to an answer. Time to get into her pajamas.

Clara walked into what seemed like an empty house. It was nine o'clock, which meant Mrs. Carmody must be in bed and Gloria must be doing homework in her room. Clara took off her pumps, which had been brutally chafing her heels all evening, and walked through the east wing to the master coat closet.

"Just in the nick of time," came a voice from down the hall. Marcus walked toward her, holding a large open container of ice cream with two spoons planted in the top. "The ice cream is almost melted."

"I'm really tired, Marcus. Not to mention soaked." The ice cream looked good, and so did he. Surprisingly casual in a navy-blue sweater, dungarees, and loafers, he was even cuter than she remembered. "I'm going to dry off and go to bed."

"Why are you so tired?" he asked suspiciously. A clap of thunder echoed in the hallway. "Where were you tonight?"

She hesitated. "I went out to dinner."

"With whom?"

"Just a friend, Detective Eastman. Don't you have anything better to do than loiter around Gloria Carmody's house?"

Marcus scowled. "You were out on a date, weren't you?"

"What makes you think that?"

"Male intuition," he said, wiping away a drop of water that was trickling down the side of her face. "I am particularly in tune with mine."

"Marcus, I'm going upstairs."

"I'm coming with you."

"You can't!" she protested as a streak of lightning lit up the hall. "My aunt would never allow you in my room—"

"I have the run of this house, always have. My parents were never around and Mrs. Carmody practically raised me." He scooped a spoonful of ice cream into his mouth. "Gloria's like my sister."

Clara felt an unexpected pang for him.

"Besides," he went on, "don't flatter yourself: I'm here for one reason and one reason only."

"Which is?"

"Henri's homemade ice cream."

Clara's willpower was weak when it came to ice cream.

"Fine," she said casually, wringing out her hair with her hands. "You can come upstairs, depending on one thing."

"What?"

"The flavor."

◆◆◆

"I'm decent," Clara whispered, opening her door a crack. "You can come in."

Marcus was slumped on the floor of the dark hallway outside her room, right where she had left him a few minutes before. She'd told him she needed privacy to change out of her wet clothes—which was true—but she also was petrified there would be another cryptic note waiting.

She had cased the room but found nothing. Thank the Lord.

Now Clara eyed Marcus's slim frame as he preceded her into the light of her room.

Marcus sized her up in her plush, terry-cloth robe. "You look brand-new."

"I *feel* brand-new." She was still toweling dry her hair as she stood awkwardly before him. "Though I really should remove my stockings." She looked at her legs. She shrugged, realizing she was more nervous around him than she'd thought. "So . . . this is my room."

Marcus gave her a wounded-puppy look. "You don't remember I was here before?"

She thought back to their initial encounter, her first week in Chicago. "That's right," she said, walking over to the old Victrola Aunt Bea had parked here and putting on a Marion Harris 78.

The opening strains of "After You've Gone" filled the room. Clara had been aiming to make the temperature in the room more casual—just two friends hanging out—than romantic, but somehow that had backfired.

Best to shrug it off. "You left me with quite the first impression," Clara said, trying not to reveal *too* much. "I'm still not over it."

"You mean you found me irresistibly attractive?"

"More like irredeemably aggressive."

"I thought I redeemed myself after our date!" Marcus protested, sliding down to the floor and leaning against the bed.

She raised one eyebrow. "Date?"

"When we went to the movies. To see Buster Keaton."

"I thought that wasn't a date," Clara said. "I thought you were merely saving me from Ginnie Bitman's tea party."

Marcus plunked the carton of ice cream between his bent

legs. "It was a date for me. At least, I wanted it to be. It was the best date I've ever been on."

Clara didn't know how to respond. She thought for a moment, then decided her shrewdest move would be to ignore his comment. "I think I'm finally ready for that ice cream."

"If it's not soup by now." He held out a spoon, gesturing for her to sit. Clara kept the distance between them wide. "I like Neapolitan," he said, scrutinizing the chocolate, vanilla, and strawberry stripes, "but I do hate having to choose."

"Agreed." It felt so natural, sitting here with him. "Is Gloria home?" she asked, suddenly registering that Gloria's door had been closed when they had quietly snuck upstairs. It was strange how often Gloria seemed to be mysteriously absent recently. And at odd hours.

"Claudine said she was over at Lorraine's, doing some group project," Marcus said, sounding bored.

"A 'group project' is the oldest excuse in the book," Clara said, skimming off the top of the strawberry ice cream with her spoon.

"And how would you know?"

"I *did* go to high school, Marcus," she said. "And I wasn't born yesterday. In fact, I do believe I'm older than you."

"Older, maybe. Wiser? Not a chance." He gave her a wry grin, shoveling all three flavors onto his spoon and lifting it to her mouth.

"I have my own," she said, waving her spoon in his face. His gesture was sweet—very sweet, in fact—but Clara couldn't let this evening go in that direction. She had to keep reminding herself that Marcus had some sort of "plan" with Gloria and Lorraine. He couldn't be trusted. She dunked her spoon into the chocolate, avoiding his eyes. "So, seriously, what were you doing over here if Gloria isn't even home?"

"So, seriously, you're not going to tell me who you were out with on your date?" Marcus shot back, licking the rejected spoonful. "Whoever it was, he clearly didn't satisfy your sweet tooth."

"I told you, he was just a friend!" Clara insisted. "An old friend—"

"From back east?"

"You could say that."

"Oh no, don't tell me"—he gasped melodramatically—*"Pennsylvania."*

Clara shrugged, neither agreeing nor disagreeing, tapping her hands against her thighs to the beat of the song.

"You definitely didn't have half as much fun on your date tonight as you would have had with me."

Clara playfully knocked her knees into Marcus's. "And what if I did?"

"Impossible," Marcus said. "I want to hear exactly what happened. Step by step, blow by blow."

"I can't. It really was . . . indescribable."

"Fine, I'll describe it for you," he insisted. "He arrived fifteen minutes early, smelling of his mother's rose water."

She wrinkled her nose. "Try again."

"Fine, his grandmother's. Because he has a fetish for the way Gran smells and thought that was a good way to impress you."

She played along. "It was strong. I had to roll down the window."

"And he was wearing a tweed blazer. The first red flag for a bad date."

"The rose water was the first red flag."

"Oh, but you'd snuck a cigarette earlier, and you didn't smell that until you got into the closed cabin of the car. And almost choked to death."

Clara held her hands up. "Guilty as charged."

"He drove like his grandmother, too. In fact, it was his grandmother's car—a wheezy old Model T that she's driven only on Sundays to get to church and back."

"That's the meanest thing you've ever said to me. God forbid I should ever be caught dead in one of those." Clara laughed and remembered how good it felt just to do that. "Besides, I have proof: I came home in a taxi."

"The taxi became necessary when the old tin lizzie broke down along the lakefront."

"Oh no," Clara dismissed. "I don't *do* lakefronts."

"I should hope not: Lakefront parking is so beneath you. But he wanted to get you alone in the struggle buggy—"

"I'm not a backseat kind of girl, Marcus."

He looked offended. "You don't need to tell *me.* Who necks in a car anymore? Not I, certainly."

"Why, Marcus, do I detect a hint of jealousy?"

"Don't insult me." He stood, dropped his spoon, and said, "Come on, let's dance."

"Here?" she asked hesitantly, looking around as if someone might be watching. Someone *might* be. But it wasn't that. No, it was that she knew herself all too well. Being in the strong arms of this boy was begging for trouble. "I'm too worn out."

"Don't be such a Goody Two-shoes. Come on!" He pulled her up to her feet just as "A Good Man Is Hard to Find" came on.

*How ironic,* Clara thought, and was about to protest when his hands met her hips. She tensed up, her arms stiffening. "Marcus, I don't know if this is—"

"Shhhh," he said, taking her hands and placing them around his neck. "Just relax."

Clara had never danced like this before, with anyone. At the jazz clubs and parties of New York, it was never about the dance itself but about how many men you could dance with in one night, flinging yourself from one pair of arms to the next. It was sweaty, out-of-breath, heel-clacking dancing. Comparatively, this was not dancing at all: This was being held.

And for a moment, leaning against Marcus's broad shoulder, Clara felt protected. Nothing from her past could harm her—no notes, no threats—while they were moving, together, to the tender longing of Marion Harris's voice and the synchronized rhythm of their breathing.

His face moved closer to her neck until she could feel his breath in her ear. "What if I *were* jealous?" he whispered, breaking the silence between them.

The song had ended, and the record player emitted a soft pop every few seconds, barely audible in the calming patter of the now lighter rain against the windowpanes.

Clara didn't know what to say. If Marcus *was* jealous, she didn't want to encourage it. Or maybe it was just a line that a playboy would easily pull out of his hat. She slid from his embrace.

"I'm serious, Clara. I can't stop thinking about you," he said, his eyes darkening. "I've never felt this way about anyone before."

"I'm sure that's not true. You've had a hundred girlfriends, from what I've heard—"

"Don't believe everything you hear." Marcus paced the room for a quick second before turning back to her with sudden urgency. "And besides, I'm telling you how I feel about you now. The past isn't important."

"Do you really believe that?" It was nice to think the past didn't matter.

"I believe in clean slates," he said with conviction. "And I believe in being honest about my feelings."

"I appreciate your honesty, but—"

"I don't want your appreciation, Clara. I want you to tell me how you *feel*."

She searched his pleading blue eyes for some flicker of

insincerity, but they were unblinking. She didn't want to hurt him. But she didn't want to get hurt, either. Her wounds had yet to be stitched up; they marked her heart like unraveled dress seams. "I don't know," she said finally, shaking her head.

"That's bushwa, you *do* know," Marcus said. "Why do I feel as if you're lying to me?"

"I'm not," Clara said weakly, but it came out sounding like a lie. *So many lies,* she thought. *When will they stop?* "It's just too complicated. You're Gloria's best friend, and Lorraine likes you—"

"Forget about Lorraine. I like *you,* Clara. I'm smitten by *you.*"

He touched her cheek then, and Clara leaned into his palm. She wanted so much to lose herself in his embrace—

But she couldn't. *He doesn't like* me. *He likes Country Clara.*

"You have to stop thinking about me like that, Marcus. For your own good." Though she knew it was exactly the opposite. She wasn't a man-eater anymore; she was afraid. She went to the door, opened it, and gestured for him to leave. "I'll only cause you trouble."

He walked to her. Clara thought for a second that he was going to kiss her. But he stopped mere inches before her. "You already have."

◆◆◆

A few minutes later, Clara heard Marcus's car start up in the drive. She felt her heart tighten in her chest like a fist.

As she was mindlessly rolling down her stockings, one got caught on her topaz cocktail ring and tore right down the front. Heat pounded through her temples. She took both stockings in her hands and tore them savagely.

But she wasn't finished. Nothing could stop this wild animal rage.

Clara dumped the contents of her dresser out onto the floor: brassieres, scanties, satin tap shorts, stockings, garters, silk teddies—everything went flying, including three pieces of cream-colored paper. She picked them up, shredding the first, then the second, until they fell like scattered snowflakes across the pink carpet. If it hadn't been for *him,* for his false promises and false hopes, she could have kissed Marcus, she could have been open to his affection.

But her heart had been locked up, and *he* had kept the key.

She was about to rip the last of the notes when she stopped: The photograph of her in New York fluttered to the floor.

Out of breath, she picked it up. The last remnant, the only artifact of her previous life. Evidence of the only time when she had ever been truly happy, when life had been without beginnings or endings.

She slipped it safely inside a pair of lacy red panties. She used to wear them beneath her favorite sheer red dress, which she had left behind in New York. She folded the underthings up, placed them back in the bottom of the drawer, and slid the drawer back into the dresser.

She slowly swept the cream-colored scraps of paper into her cupped palm. Gathered in her hand, they were no more than flimsy fragments of fractured words—*found, I, you, inside.* She took them into the bathroom and dropped the scraps into the toilet.

And then she flushed them away.

# LORRAINE

Heart-to-hearts were not Lorraine's thing.

But that was why she figured Gloria had called, asking to come over, on a Saturday morning. Which, in theory, should have thrilled Lorraine: Hadn't she been wanting her best friend back, or at least the opportunity to confront Gloria about all the secrets she'd been keeping?

Of course, that had all been before Lorraine had kissed Bastian.

Just admitting she'd done such a thing was difficult enough. Especially because her memory of the visit was so hazy. This was what she remembered: a sofa, a hand on her knee, a scratchy face against her cheek. Then that holy moment when their lips hovered on the brink of meeting.

But their clothes had remained on, so nothing besides a

kiss had really happened. And now that Gloria was coming over, Lorraine had to decide: to tell, or not to tell? But aside from the fact that Gloria was marrying a man who would potentially cheat on her, how would Lorraine explain her presence in Bastian's penthouse?

Gloria would not forgive her.

This would throw their friendship over the edge of a cliff. But Lorraine had known Gloria since they were eight years old! Surely Gloria would feel more allegiance to her oldest friend than to some guy—even if he was her fiancé.

Lorraine made up her mind: She needed to confess and be absolved.

When the doorbell rang through the bright halls of the empty house, Lorraine ran downstairs to the foyer, calling out, "I'll get it, Marguerite!" If Lorraine wanted to shout, she could: It was only her and the servants in the house this weekend.

Lorraine nervously opened the front door with a bright grin. "Good morning!" she said, about to give Gloria a kiss on the cheek.

Then she took in Gloria's pale, sleep-deprived face. Her sea-glass eyes were dulled, with puffy purple smudges beneath. Even her skin was pasty, her burnt-orange hair almost dirty. "Glo, you look positively—"

"Ruined!" Gloria cried out, her lower lip trembling.

"I was going to say tired." Then the crying began. "Whoa, whoa, whoa! Hey there, waterworks!"

"I don't know what to do!" Gloria wailed, the tears streaming out of her eyes and all over Lorraine's silver silk kimono. "I've made a mess of everything!"

"That's impossible. The Gloria Carmody I know couldn't make a mess if she tried." Lorraine ushered her inside. Lorraine never really noticed how empty the house was until someone like Gloria showed up. Ever since her sister, Evelyn, had gone off to Bryn Mawr last year, the house had felt too big and too cold. "You are going to tell me everything, but first let me get you some coffee. How does that sound?"

"Sure," Gloria said with a sniffle, wiping her nose on her celery-colored sleeve.

"Go sit in the sunroom. I'll be back in a second."

In the vast kitchen, Lorraine instructed Marguerite, the head housemaid, to make a strong pot of coffee and to slice two pieces of that lemon meringue pie with the graham cracker crust. Lorraine was on a faddish Hollywood eighteen-day diet, but nothing calmed a girl like comfort food, so she figured she could depart from the diet for the fourth day in a row to help Gloria in her time of need.

What a lucky break!

Now Lorraine could prove that she was the devoted best friend, provide a shoulder to cry on, and shower Gloria with unconditional love and attention. That way, when the time came for Lorraine to confess her own mess, Gloria would be quick to side with her.

She found Gloria where she had sent her, sitting droopily

on a chintz-cushioned bench in the solarium. It was a pretty room, all glass walls and wrought-iron benches and great big leafy things that Lorraine had tried and failed to learn the names of—a tree was a bush was a plant, as far as her brain was concerned.

Marguerite followed her in with the tray of coffee and pie and placed it on the table in front of the girls.

"Mmm, I feel better already," Gloria said, surveying the pie. She seemed calmer, though the crying had left her cheeks blotchy.

Lorraine handed her a fork. "Now spill."

"Whatever I am about to tell you, promise not to judge me?" Gloria said, scraping up a dollop of meringue.

"Consider this the no-judgment solarium."

"Keep in mind, I didn't keep this from you because I don't trust you—of course I do! You're my best friend. I guess it was just"—Gloria let out a deep sigh—"if no one else knew, it was as if it weren't really happening."

Gloria then launched into a minor epic about the Green Mill and Jerome Johnson. The story had all the makings of a racy romance, but it ended up much tamer than Lorraine had imagined. Or, to be perfectly frank, had hoped.

"Glo, you can tell me," Lorraine said, licking her fork. "What is *really* going on between you and Jerome? It's a little hard for me to believe he just *gave* you this job."

"What do you mean?"

"The man has *piano* hands, Glo," Lorraine insisted.

Gloria slouched down on the cushioned bench, squeezing a pillow against her chest. "Okay, so he's touched me—"

"I knew it!"

"But in a completely professional way."

"Say no more!" Lorraine exclaimed, tucking her knees beneath her on the bench and bouncing a little. "I mean, *do* say more. Say everything."

Gloria poked her. "Raine, I'm being serious. It's not like that. He's tough with me—sometimes a little too tough."

"That's an obvious indication that he likes you. Men who don't know how to deal with their feelings channel them into meanness," Lorraine explained, thinking of how Marcus behaved toward her. "No matter how old or mature they may be."

"But can I tell you something daring?"

"More daring than the fact that Jerome is *black*?" Lorraine said, breaking off a piece of the thick pie crust.

Gloria blushed. "Lorraine!"

"Well, someone had to say it!" Was Gloria really going to ignore the biggest issue of all? "I'm not blind, you know. What would your mother say if she ever found out?"

"Nothing, because she never will," Gloria said, kneading her hands. "I know it makes absolutely no sense, but I'm really *attracted* to him. I can't help it. In a way I've never felt about Bastian."

The inevitable mention of Bastian made Lorraine squirm. "Not even in the beginning?"

"No. There was never the same spark, I guess you could say." Gloria frowned. "Not like the one I feel when I'm around Jerome."

Lorraine had felt a spark from Bastian. Their kiss had been electric. She picked up her coffee and gulped it down. "Ow!" she cried as the liquid scalded her throat. She wagged her burned tongue. "For crying out loud!"

"Are you okay?"

"I always tell Marguerite not to make it *très* . . . hot! Why is it so hard to follow the rules? I mean, instructions." Lorraine daintily set the cup down, trying to regain her composure. "I'm sorry—continue. Bastian. I thought you were so in love with him. All those times you called me, after your dates. And coming into homeroom starry-eyed . . . ?"

Gloria looked down at her empty hands. "I was in love with the idea of him—with the whole checklist. Not actually *him*. But really, it was an arranged marriage from the start—he *never* loved me, even when I thought he did."

Lorraine narrowed her eyes. "I don't understand."

"I'm just a business deal he signed off on, Raine. A deal he made with my parents! They're getting divorced, and my mother thinks it will save our name, or some hokum like that—"

"Back up: Since when are your parents divorcing?"

"Since my father had an affair." Gloria stabbed her fork into the pie. "I swear to God, if Bastian ever touched another girl, I would get a gun and shoot him dead. And the girl, too."

Lorraine winced. "But, Gloria, you aren't exactly the picture of fidelity, fantasizing about a black musician—"

"Fantasizing and doing are two different things, Raine. I thought my father was a decent man. I thought Bastian was a decent man. But now I'm not so sure."

This was Lorraine's big moment—it was now or never. Gloria *had* to know the truth. If she had already turned against Bastian, wouldn't knowledge of the kiss (described, of course, to make Lorraine look like the victim of his forceful advances) only confirm these suspicions?

"If that's the case, then you should know something," Lorraine began slowly, picking at her cuticles. "This is hard for me to tell you, because the last thing I want to do is sound jealous."

"Jealous of which—the arranged marriage or the black musician?"

"Jealous of—of—" The confession was on the tip of Lorraine's tongue.

But she knew that girls were like elephants when it came to men: They never forgot. If Gloria went through with the marriage, every time she kissed Bastian, she would automatically think of Lorraine—and she would never trust her again. So Lorraine might as well say *au revoir* to their friendship—now, when it was getting back to what it once had been and always should be: the two of them curled up on the cushions together, taking turns at baring their souls.

No. She wanted Gloria back. Best friends before boyfriends. Always.

"Jealous of none of the above!" Lorraine announced. "I've just been feeling left out, Glo, as if you've been deliberately excluding me from your life. The Green Mill with Marcus was one thing—"

Gloria's brow furrowed. "Oh, God, that was the beginning of the end."

Lorraine needed to lay on the guilt. "You know I would have never let this happen to you had you not hidden it from me."

"I'm so sorry, Raine—"

"Because you know I've *never* hidden anything from you."

"I know you haven't," Gloria said. "I really am so sorry. I shut you out when I needed you—but now I need you more than ever. I have no one else."

"So now I have to ask the difficult question." Lorraine eyed Gloria's mammoth diamond. "What have you decided to do?"

Gloria fell back against the cushions. "I don't think I *have* a decision to make. I'll be Mrs. Grey before I know it, whether I like it or not."

If Gloria meant to go through with that loveless marriage, Lorraine certainly wasn't about to stop her. She'd have her best friend back for good. "You and I both know that's the wisest choice, at the end of the day."

"Just promise me you'll still be my bridesmaid?" When Lorraine hesitated, thinking of having to face Bastian across the aisle at the wedding, Gloria added, "Chanel is designing the bridesmaids' dresses!"

Lorraine drew Gloria into her arms. "You know I'd never say no to Chanel," she declared over Gloria's shoulder. "I do, Gloria! I do!"

◆◆◆

"I didn't even know your house *had* a library," Gloria said, scanning the floor-to-ceiling mahogany shelves of books. "Or that your father drank."

"Every father drinks," Lorraine said. "Or wishes he did." She was poking around in the glass-fronted bookcase where her father kept his first editions.

"What *are* you looking for?"

"Daddy has a first edition of *The Secret Garden,* which he had Frances Hodgson Burnett sign to me. Though he kept it for himself."

"That seems selfish."

"That's my father. Ah, here it is!" The book was in a musty pile at the bottom of the bookcase. "This is where he hides the key. He thinks he's clever." She opened the front cover and shook, and a heavy iron key fell from the binding.

"Well, *my* father never drank," Gloria said reflectively, flipping through a copy of something called *Arms and the*

*Man*. "Or he never did with us, anyway." She shuddered. "But he probably did with his slutty New York chorus girl."

"Can you imagine barney-mugging someone our father's age? All that saggy, wrinkly—"

"Raine, stop!" Gloria covered her ears. "I may need to go wash my brain out with soap."

Lorraine moved aside the *S* volume of the *Encyclopaedia Britannica*. "*S* for *secret.* You may be seeing a theme here." Behind the volume was a large keyhole, and she inserted the iron key and turned. With a soft thunk, the entire bookshelf swung outward and a light came on.

"Wow," Gloria said. "It's almost pretty."

The shallow cabinet behind the door contained more shelves, these holding drinking glasses and decanters of liquor. The glasses and decanters were dusty, and the labels—where there were any—were hard to read, but the cut-crystal glasses and the old decanters glittered in the light like jewels.

Lorraine could tell that Gloria was impressed. "This morning calls for one thing and one thing only."

"Running away?" Gloria said. "A duel between Bastian and Jerome with me as the prize?"

"No, a Buck's Fizz!" Lorraine's older sister, Evelyn, had told her the Bryn Mawr girls made them in the morning before going to football games. It sounded fun and sophisticated. She handed a few bottles to Gloria, then hitched up her skirt and revealed her lavender garter.

"Oh, damn—I forgot! Your dear mother confiscated my favorite flask. I usually keep it here, snug against my leg."

Gloria winced. "Sorry, Raine—I'm sure she's hidden it somewhere in the house. I'll get it back for you."

"No matter. Daddy has plenty." Lorraine tapped her fingers against an array of flasks on the shelves. "Eeny meeny miny Tiffany!" She plucked out a slim sterling silver one and uncapped it. Setting it atop *The Secret Garden*, she poured some cognac into it. "But first I need to refuel."

Gloria watched her curiously. "Don't you mean refill?"

"Refill, refuel, refresh, same thing."

"Since when do you carry a flask, Raine? Wait, let me rephrase that: Since when do you carry a flask on a Saturday morning?"

"Where else would I carry my booze? Seriously, Glo, I can't very well hide *this* in my garter!" She hefted the cognac bottle.

"But won't your father notice it's missing?"

"The only thing he would realize was missing from this entire house is in the *other* cabinet." Lorraine pulled down another book and slid another key from its binding. "First edition, *War and Peace,* in Russian. He is *so* obvious. I'm sure the key to my mother's chastity belt is in his copy of *Lady Chatterley's Lover*!"

"Raine! Your mother does not have a chastity belt!" Gloria laughed, and Lorraine felt it as a personal victory.

"Not that I know of, but she doesn't need one. Have you seen her without her makeup?"

Gloria laughed again and covered her mouth.

Working a hidden latch, Lorraine eased aside another bookcase. Racked in rows along the wall behind it were a score of guns. "Bang, bang, you're dead."

There were guns of all shapes and sizes—shotguns and long rifles and one with a flared end like a trumpet. "What in God's name is *that*?" Gloria asked, all thoughts of Bastian and Jerome gone at last.

"It's called a blunderbuss," Lorraine said. "I think they're used to kill elephants."

And tucked in between the rifles were handguns. There were enormous revolvers and short snub-nosed pistols and cute little two-shot Derringers. The cabinet reeked of oil and gunpowder. Gloria sniffed loudly. "These smell—have they been *fired* recently?" she asked.

Lorraine took a nip of cognac—really, it went well with the pie and coffee—and said, "Sure. Daddy likes to have target practice out back. Always keeps the guns loaded even though Mommy tells him someone's going to get hurt one day."

She dragged her hand along the lean, oiled muzzles, triggers ready for an index finger.

Gloria fidgeted nervously. "When did your father join the Mob?"

"Are you kidding? My father was a member of a Princeton eating club," Lorraine said, taking down a smaller automatic pistol. "He just collects them." She held the gun at arm's length and sighted down the barrel. "Bang, bang," she repeated.

"May I?" Gloria said, and Lorraine handed over the pistol. "It's heavier than I thought it would be."

"I know," Lorraine said. "First you have to do this." She showed Gloria how to unlock the safety catch.

Then Gloria took the pistol and pointed it at the wall. She fingered the trigger.

"Whoa there!" Lorraine almost shouted. "It's loaded!" She took the gun away. "You've got to be careful with these things!"

Lorraine replaced the gun, closed both bookcases, and slipped the keys back into their respective books. Then she palmed the flask and headed toward the door. "Come on."

Gloria was still staring at the bookcases.

"Glo? Did you hear what I said?" Lorraine flicked the lights on and off. "Fizz time."

"Right, Buck's Fizz," Gloria said, taking a step back from the case. "What are we celebrating, again?"

Lorraine wrapped her arm around Gloria. "Loyalty, of course."

And for the first time in her life, Lorraine wished she meant what she said.

# GLORIA

Gloria had arrived.

"Red's here!" Evan, the trumpet player, blared his horn from the corner of the greenroom, announcing Gloria's arrival. "It's about time!"

He was the only one who seemed to notice. There was a cozy chaos going on backstage; everyone else was busy getting ready by seeming not to get ready at all.

Evan grinned and shrugged. Then he went back to softly playing along with a record that was spinning on the gramophone—Joe "King" Oliver and his band. Over in the corner, Tommy the bass player, already dressed in his cheap tuxedo, was in the middle of a heated discussion with Chuck the drummer, who was lying on the couch in his undershirt and suspendered trousers—"If that's three-quarter time, daddy-o, then you're Frederick Douglass," he said, before accepting a bottle of bourbon from Chuck and taking a sip. Two light-skinned black flappers sat, bored, in the center of the room, smoking pencil-long cigarettes. One was in a sequined, ruffled black getup with a peacock feather jutting out of her hair; the other wore a canary-yellow number with rhinestone trim. Their legs were bare and shamelessly resting on the edge of the coffee table. Sitting between them on the coffee table itself was the band's trombone player, Bix, but he seemed blind to the room, just kept working the slide, drawing out notes and bending them and then scowling at his instrument as if it had betrayed him. The room was a swamp of smoke and popcorn, booze and sweat, but there was a preshow energy buzzing like cicadas on a hot summer morning.

Gloria stood in the doorway, out of breath from the stress of sneaking out of her mother's house and finding her way downtown. This time, she had told her mother she was going with Clara to a showing of a new movie.

Now she was here, with a half hour till the first set, her pianist nowhere to be seen.

"Does anyone know where Jerome is?" she asked. She had to repeat herself at a shout before anyone noticed.

The band members shrugged, but the girl in the yellow dress nodded. "He always disappears before a show," she said in a husky voice.

Evan walked over. "Want me to find him for you?"

"No, I'll find him myself," Gloria said. She was carrying a dress bag and a case of makeup that felt as if it weighed a hundred pounds. She needed to put it down before she collapsed.

Was she expected to change in front of all these people? She knew musicians were loose and uninhibited, but she needed a moment to herself to focus and warm up. "Is there maybe a bathroom or a closet or just a dark corner somewhere I can change? Alone?"

"At the end of the hall—the diva gets her own dressing room." Evan winked, knocking her cheek lightly with his fist. "You ready for your big debut?"

Gloria gulped. "Yeah, if I don't keel over."

"If you do, just make sure you aim for the floor, not the drums. Those things cost a fortune!"

◆◆◆

The "hallway" was just a narrow space that ran behind the back curtain to another little area where a mop sat in a bucket, and where chairs were stacked in an untidy pile. Gloria opened one door and found a foul-smelling bathroom. Behind another door was a tiny square room that held a sink, a clothes rack, a mirror ringed with lights over a small counter, and a wobbly stool. There was wiring exposed in the ceiling. Well, what did she expect, the lounge for the Ziegfeld Follies?

In the doorway, Gloria suddenly tuned in to the muffled roar of the crowd beyond, which only made her heart pound faster, joining in with her already buzzing head and jittery limbs.

She caught her breath in the stuffy dark. *This is it,* she told herself. *This is the night when everything changes.*

"The star's dressing room!" said someone behind her.

Startled, she fumbled and dropped her dress bag, set down her case, and turned.

Three people had come backstage: Carlito Macharelli, a tired-looking young woman, and a child in a pin-striped suit. Gloria squinted into the dark. No, not a child, but a tiny little man, like a gangster made on a smaller scale. The midget openly eyeballed her. It was unnerving, so she turned the full wattage of her smile on his boss.

"Mr. Macharelli!" Gloria said.

"Call me Carlito," he said. He gestured at the midget and the flapper. "The little one's Thor. He's small, but he packs a big punch. And this here's one of my newest girls. I wanted to introduce her to you before you went out. Give her a little backstage preview before the big production. Maude, say hello to Miss Gloria Carson. She's a farm girl with a real bright future."

"Sure, Carlito," the girl said, and stepped forward.

Maude Cortineau. Gloria would have gasped if she could have breathed at all. She recognized the famous flapper from her first night at the Green Mill, when Gloria had accidentally spilled Maude's drink. Gloria could only pray that her haircut and makeup and fashionable dress would be disguise enough. She didn't want Maude to recognize her and spill the beans that "Gloria Carson" was a fake.

But Maude just stared at the sequins on Gloria's red shoes. She was wearing a wrinkled party dress, a shimmery silver sleeveless number that was belted with loops of black beads and had a fringe that rattled when she walked. Maude looked worn out. And scared. "Pleasure to meet you," Maude said, never looking up. This was not the same girl Gloria had first met: Maude, the sheba of underground Chicago. It was as though the life had been drained from her.

If Carlito could steal the sparkle from Maude, what else could he do?

"Give us a ditty," Carlito said. "Sing us something ah-ka— ah-ka-whatever it is. You know, without music."

Was he serious? "Um, I don't have anything ready," Gloria said.

"Come on, songbird," Thor the midget said. His voice was raspy and deep, as if he gargled with broken glass. "Let's hear you tweet." He produced a pack of cigarettes and lit two, then handed one to Carlito. "I like me the pretty songs."

"I'm not kidding around," Carlito said.

Gloria closed her eyes. She thought of Jerome and let the club's hubbub and the cigarette smoke and the dark of the backstage area fall away. She thought of a silly little song from the Great War, and in a grim, throaty whisper, she sang,

> *"Pack up your troubles in your old kit-bag,*
> *And smile, smile, smile,*
> *While you've a lucifer to light your fag,*
> *Smile, boys, that's the style.*
> *What's the use of worrying?*
> *It never was worthwhile, so*
> *Pack up your troubles in your old kit-bag,*
> *And smile.*
> *Smile.*
> *Smile."*

In the silence afterward, she heard the weak applause of three people.

"She was good, wasn't she?" Carlito asked Maude, squeezing her bare shoulder.

"Sure, Carlito, she was oodles of good. She was hotsy-totsy." Maude at last lifted her eyes from the floor and looked right at Gloria. But there was nothing much left of the old Maude Cortineau in her gaze, and she didn't seem to see Gloria at all.

Carlito snapped his fingers and the midget produced a rose from behind his back.

"This," Carlito said, "is for you. Maybe you can wear it in your hair or something." His expression was cold. "A lot of people are counting on you, kiddo. Make sure you knock 'em dead out there tonight." Without another word, he turned and walked through the curtains, followed by Maude and the creepy little midget.

"I'll knock 'em dead, all right," Gloria said to herself.

In the dressing room, she flipped on the lights ringing the foggy mirror.

Deep breath. *Do something normal,* she told herself. Applying makeup would be a good first step, she thought, getting out her cosmetics case. The more she thought about Carlito and Jerome, the spotlight and the song set, the audience—the more her stomach clenched up.

Now was not the time to panic. Except that she *was* panicking.

She went to the sink, splashed cold water on her face, and studied herself in the mirror. Without makeup, she was all pale eyes, round apple cheeks, and a tiny pimple on her chin. She looked young. She *was* young. What was she doing here, singing for gangsters? Weeks ago she wouldn't have dared set foot inside a speakeasy, and now she was headlining at one. She wasn't the same Gloria she used to be.

She picked the rose up from the counter, sniffed it. But it had hardly any scent. It was old, already wilting, just like everything else in this place.

It helped, slightly, to imagine her friends out there in the audience. She had promised Lorraine she wouldn't keep any more secrets from her, and she was sticking to her vow. And inviting Lorraine meant inviting Marcus. He was the one who'd first brought her to the Green Mill, after all. Clara's presence she could live without, but nothing was perfect. She just hoped that none of them would expose her true identity: Gloria Carmody, fiancée, debutante, socialite. Here she was just Gloria Carson, the mysterious ingenue with no strings attached. "Right?" she said to her reflection.

Gloria still needed to warm up, change into her dress, review the set list, and finish her vamp eyes. At least she had the dressing room to herself.

Until the door swung wide.

Gloria almost poked her right eye out with a mascara brush when she saw Vera Johnson's image in the mirror.

"The boys are wondering how long you gonna be," Vera said, standing in the doorway with one hand on her hip.

"Can you tell them I need a few more minutes? I'm running a little behind."

She assumed that was cue enough for Vera to leave. Instead, the girl sauntered into the closet-sized space as if she owned it. "Don't need to tell them nothing. It's a girl's prerogative to make a man wait."

Vera's eyelids were heavily lined Cleopatra-style, with a thick fringe of jet-black false lashes. A copper snake with rubies for eyes was wrapped around her slender upper arm, offsetting her bronze sateen dress and darker skin. She was beautiful. Gloria felt like an ugly, pasty ghost in comparison.

"Don't overdo the makeup," Vera said. "Face like yours is waterproof."

They'd never had a conversation before, but it was obvious to Gloria that Vera hated her.

Yes, Gloria loved it when Jerome looked at her; and yes, she shivered when his fingers grazed the piano keys, making some of the most beautiful music she'd ever heard. But Jerome wasn't her *boyfriend*. She had an engagement ring tucked away in her jewelry box back on Astor Street. Their singing lessons had been platonic, except for the occasional touch of his fingertips on her arm or her ribs, but those touches meant something only to her. To Jerome they meant nothing at all. He was black, she was white. He was poor, she was rich. It could never work. So why did Vera treat Gloria like a vamp out to steal her brother away?

Vera took a tube of lipstick out of her beaded clutch and used her pinkie to smooth the coral pigment onto her plump lips. "I hope you're not going to wear *that* onstage," she said, motioning to Gloria's skimpy champagne silk slip. "Although I suppose that'd be one way to distract your audience from actually listening to your voice."

Obviously Vera had no interest in hiding her claws.

"Ha, ha," Gloria said. "I was about to put on my dress when—"

"When your worst nightmare walked right on in?"

*Right.* This girl did not back down. Gloria ignored her

and opened the dress bag. It was satisfying to see Vera's eyes widen as Gloria extracted her gown. It had taken Gloria two full weeks of scouring the racks of the city's tony dressmakers to find the perfect debut outfit; she'd even skipped a European history exam to get it altered at a tailor's in Chinatown. It was one of a kind: hand-sewn and fresh from Paris, a rich deep green covered in dazzling emerald sequins. Its scooped neck revealed her collarbone and a white swatch of skin above her breasts, which she'd wrapped and flattened. Finishing it off were a green headband with an enormous cloth flower, a single bangle, and a double strand of pearls she'd liberated from her mother's jewelry box.

"That must have cost you a pretty penny," Vera said, fingering the beadwork. "How does a girl from some little country town afford this kind of fancy?"

"It's on loan," Gloria lied, trying to steady her hands as she traced her eyes in black kohl. "From a friend."

"Didn't you just move here?" Vera didn't miss a beat. "I don't know what kind of 'friends' you been making, but I hope you don't consider my brother one of them."

"You know full well that Jerome—I mean, that Mr. Johnson and I have a strictly professional relationship."

"Then why'd you just look so hot and bothered when I mentioned him?"

"Are you trying to tell me something?" Gloria asked, surprising herself. "Or are you just trying to be a bitch?"

Vera broke into a half-impressed smile. "Both."

"Why don't you like me?" Gloria wasn't perfect, but people had always liked her.

"I don't like you for my brother. I see how you look at him. Don't do anything stupid like fall in love with him. Or else."

Gloria felt her cheeks pinking. "Or else . . . what?"

"Baby, you don't even want to go down that road with me."

Just then, the boy in question barged in.

Jerome looked positively debonair. He was holding two cups of champagne, a cigarette dangling from his mouth, a black bow tie loose around his neck. He was wearing an untucked, unbuttoned shirt, revealing his tight white undershirt. Gloria sucked in a sharp breath. And she'd thought musicians were supposed to be scrawny.

"I need a moment with our singer before we go on," Jerome said, frowning at Vera. He didn't seem particularly happy to see her. "Alone."

Gloria realized that she was basically nude. "Get out!" she yelled, shielding her chest with her arms and turning toward the wall. "I'm not dressed!"

"Don't worry, I won't look," Jerome said, covering his eyes. Only Gloria could see that he was smiling.

Vera pushed her brother through the door. "Wait outside until I call you back. And don't you dare come in until I do." She slammed the door and clapped her hands together. "Come on, girl, we don't have time to waste."

"Thanks, but I can finish up by myself," Gloria said.

"You're stupider than I thought," Vera said. She picked up the green dress. "Did you look at the hooks and eyes on this fancy dress you bought? Ain't no way you're going to be able to fasten that on your own."

Gloria remembered the saleswoman's helping her try it on. "Oh."

"That's right, 'Oh.' Now finish up your face so we can get you into this thing and out there onstage. Lots of people are depending on you."

"So everyone keeps telling me." Gloria slid out of her slip and stood up. "And like I said: I didn't buy that dress. I borrowed it."

"Uh-huh. And whoever loaned it to you just happens to be your size. And leaves the price tags on her clothes." Vera pinched the little white tag between her fingers.

"Um . . ." Gloria didn't know what to say.

Vera waved her off. "You think I care about that? All I care about is my brother keeping his job. Now let's get you dressed."

◆◆◆

"My eyes are closed, promise," Jerome said after his sister had vanished back into the club. He blindly took a step farther into the room. "Here. This will help loosen you up." He held out the glass of champagne with one hand, the other still covering his eyes.

She took the glass and said, "You can look."

He took his hand away and slowly looked her up and down, then whistled. "I hope you can sing in a dress that tight." Gloria felt every inch of the silk-and-sequin dress covering her body—and she felt every inch of her body that wasn't covered.

"It's not like I'm wearing a corset," she said, though the dress felt like one.

"You most definitely are *not* wearing a corset," he said, letting out a low laugh.

"Do you really want to make me more nervous than I already am?"

"I'm kidding. And nerves are a good thing."

"They are?"

"Sure. It's high-voltage energy that you can harness and direct into your performance." Jerome moved one hand to her shoulder. "Don't worry. Just sing. You're gonna knock 'em dead tonight."

"Why does everyone say that?"

His hand lingered. "Say what?"

"Never mind." Gloria hoped he wouldn't notice her rapid-fire breathing, growing quicker with the pressure of his touch. Why did she always feel so out of control around him? She hated herself for it. No, she hated herself for loving every second of it. She looked at herself in the mirror. She looked good. No, she looked *great.*

"Listen, once you're up there on that stage, you just have

to trust your voice," he said, moving a strand of hair away from her eyes. "And you have to trust me."

She knew it was wrong, so wrong, but in that moment, she prayed he would kiss her—wasn't that some kind of backstage good-luck ritual, like saying *merde*? His lips would be the only reassurance she needed.

She held her breath and closed her eyes.

"Make a wish," Jerome said.

She felt a finger lightly swipe her cheek. "What?"

"You had an eyelash." She opened her eyes, dazed, to see a strawberry-blond sliver poised on the tip of his finger, like a crescent moon against a dark sky. "So you have to make a wish."

*You,* she thought. *You.*

She had an eerie feeling that once she set foot on that stage, there would be no turning back to the way things were before. "I don't believe in wishes. Or maybe I just have too many."

"You're lying, kid," he said. "You already made it: I could see it in your eyes."

Before she could answer, the door was flung open and someone shouted, "We're on!"

"Go on, then," Jerome said, raising his finger again. "We have to get onstage. Make your wish."

So she did. Gloria exhaled a stream of air, sending the eyelash into space.

# CLARA

The notes.

They bothered Clara so much that she could hardly sleep. Most nights, she would violently awaken at four a.m., her body drenched in a clammy sweat, and be unable to fall back to sleep.

Fear would sneak up on her at unexpected moments during her too-empty days, when she was walking through the Art Institute or along the Chicago River. A ripple of goose-flesh would shiver across her skin, and she would be certain her note-sender was nearby—around the corner or behind her, watching and waiting.

She had her suspicions about who might be sending the notes. While she couldn't be sure, somewhere deep inside her heart, she knew. Why was he doing this to her? What exactly was he trying to prove?

Something needed to change, but the only thing in her control was her appearance. So Clara determined to shelve her goody-goody façade. Just for a short while—specifically, for Gloria's limited engagement at the Green Mill.

Gloria would have performed her first show without Clara in the audience had it not been for a complete coincidence: The telephone had rung.

Clara had been alone in the house, and fearing it was her note-sender finding another way to torment her, she'd answered.

The person on the other end was no one Clara knew, but a man named Evan calling with a message for Gloria.

As soon as Gloria got home from school, Clara cornered her.

"Someone called for you this afternoon," she said, standing outside her cousin's bedroom door. Gloria was still in her school uniform. She kicked off her stiff brown shoes.

"Oh?" asked Gloria, dropping her books onto her bed and herself right after them.

Clara strolled inside and sat beside her.

"What are you doing?" Gloria asked. "I'm busy."

"You don't look it," Clara said, pushing the books aside and lying beside her. "Besides, shouldn't you be getting ready for rehearsal?"

Clara had read the description in books, but had never

seen it until now: The color drained from her cousin's face. "I have no idea what you're talking about," Gloria said.

"I think you do. Someone named Evan called, telling you to swing by the Green Mill for some new sheet music. And to tell you that rehearsal was bumped forward an hour."

Gloria sat up. "Oh, damn! What time is it? I've got to get ready!" She rushed over to her bedroom door and kicked it shut. "What do you want from me?"

"The truth, for starters," Clara said. "After that, we'll see."

Gloria nervously ran her fingers through her hair. "Why would I tell you anything? You're practically best friends with my mother."

"Not fair," Clara said. "And not true. If I were going to rat you out, I could have told Aunt Bea already."

For a moment, Clara thought Gloria was going to sock her. Gloria balled her fists and let loose an angry little scream. "Why must you snoop into my business? What did I ever do to you?"

Clara raised her hands in surrender. "I'm not your enemy, Gloria. I'm just doing time here. You need to trust me."

"Fine, but you have to promise not to tell anyone. Really promise—my life is on the line."

"Cross my heart and all that jazz," Clara said.

Gloria sucked in a big lungful of air and screwed her eyes shut. "Okay, here goes: I'm the new lead singer at the Green Mill."

Clara whistled. Her bland-as-bread cousin was headlining

at the hottest speakeasy in Chicago? Clara had to give Gloria some credit. The girl was wilder than she'd initially thought. "Brava," she said, clapping softly. "That's so much better than anything I could have imagined."

Gloria nodded, her eyes aglow. "It really is, isn't it?"

"So that's where you were sneaking off to? Rehearsal?"

*"Yes!"* Gloria squeaked. She looked happier than Clara had ever seen her.

"Look at you," Clara said. "I'm impressed."

"No one else knows," Gloria gushed. "Except for Raine, of course. Oh, and Marcus."

Marcus.

"You can come if you want," Gloria offered. "To my first show. I mean, safer to have you there, where I can see you, than here with Mother, where you might blab."

Clara was surprised to be invited. Flattered, even. And only the slightest bit suspicious. "Sure," she replied. "There's no place I'd rather be."

But that was a problem. Clara wanted to attend her cousin's debut as herself—her real self. Everyone in Chicago thought she was Country Clara, so she couldn't exactly show up at the Green Mill all vamped up without causing a stir. But she didn't need to go as some dowdy hick, either—where was the fun in that? She needed someone she could blame for Clara's getting all dolled up.

She needed Lorraine Dyer.

So she made a plan.

Flatter Lorraine.

Convince her that it would be *so unfortunate* to show up for Gloria's debut with Country Clara in tow.

Ask if Lorraine could find it in her heart to share her style and expertise to help Clara look a little bit more modern.

Let Lorraine take credit for transforming Clara into a flapper.

◆◆◆

The night of the debut, Clara went to Lorraine's house.

Lorraine's mother opened the door. "Oh, hello, Clara," she said. She was like a tidier, older, more serious version of her daughter. She wore a darkly elegant dress and had her hair pinned up in a sleek French twist.

Lorraine was standing behind her, blank-faced as a little girl.

"I'm off to the opera, Lorraine, dear. Please don't give Marguerite any trouble." Mrs. Dyer blinked at Clara. "A pleasure to meet you, and my apologies that I have to run. I hope we see more of you soon." She swept out the door and into a waiting car, which motored away.

"My parents attend a lot of events," Lorraine explained in passing.

They got ready in Lorraine's room, Eddie Cantor playing on the gramophone, two tumblers of gin poised on the dresser next to an almost embarrassingly huge spread of makeup. Lorraine rested her elbows on her vanity and held down the bottom rim of her eye so that she could blacken the thin pink line with kohl.

Clara watched from the edge of the bed. Lorraine really was a striking girl, but her strong features were the complete opposite of the dainty, fair femininity that was so in fashion these days. Lorraine's glossy black bob was blunt-cut and her bangs nearly reached her wide-set eyes, which were a dull hazel. She was tall and angular, with a coltish way of holding herself—as if she had yet to grow into her long torso and longer limbs.

Clara got up and went to stand behind her. "I wish I had your body. Your hips are practically half my size."

Lorraine's grin was huge and instantaneous. "Really?" she asked, squeezing her waist. "I think my hips look like teacup handles."

"No, I'm so jealous!" Clara exclaimed. "And your chest—you're so lucky you don't have to bother with some horrible compression device."

Lorraine turned sideways in the mirror, admiring her mosquito-bite boobs. "It's just the dress," she said, straightening her red Callot Soeurs frock. It was sleeveless, long—almost to her ankles—but incredibly sexy, with satin trim and beading around the waistline. "The French always know how to dress a woman's body."

Clara made a face at her own dress, which was something of her aunt's. She'd worn it purposefully, hoping Lorraine would be embarrassed by the prospect of being seen with Clara in it. "I feel like I'm going camping in mine." She held out the extra material until it looked like a tent.

"Do you want to borrow something?"

Clara did her best wide-eyed grateful look. "You wouldn't mind?"

"I have a row of dresses just sitting in my closet, most still with the tags on—it's really not a big deal. Besides"—Lorraine sighed impatiently, her eyes traveling to Clara's *passé* frock—"last season is one thing, but last century is something else. Sure, this is Gloria's night, but that doesn't mean *we* can't look *très chic, oui?*"

"Oh, that would really be swell!" Clara exclaimed. This was too easy. "But do you really think I can pull it off?" she asked. "I mean, obviously I'm not half the smarty that *you* are."

Lorraine paused before swiping at her lips with a vampire-red lipstick. "Don't worry." She smiled brightly, absorbing Clara's admiration like a human sponge. "I can't promise miracles, but I can promise mascara."

◆◆◆

"What happened to you?" Marcus asked Clara as the girls sauntered into the Green Mill. He looked stunned.

He wasn't the only one. They both got long, lingering looks. Lorraine wore a red boa draped over her sparkling dress, the expensive fabric shimmering in the light. Her long silk gloves were as black as the kohl around her eyes. Even Clara had to admit the girl looked stunning.

And Clara was stunning, too. Her backless dress was a shade lighter than her honey-blond locks. She looked like a film star.

"I don't think Marcus likes my new look," Clara said demurely. He didn't look half bad himself, in black trousers and a short gray jacket over a navy-blue embroidered vest. A sharp-looking bow tie completed the ensemble.

"No, I mean, it's— You're— You look . . . different?" he said, rubbing his knuckles under his chin in contemplation.

"I take complete blame," Lorraine cooed, linking arms with Clara. "Doesn't she look like the real McCoy?"

"Clearly, I learned from the reigning *queen,*" Clara said, tossing her head back regally. Lorraine did look good—if a bit overdone—but Clara could see that Marcus was still focused on her.

Not that she was complaining. Every girl in the club was vying for his attention. Amid a sea of dark-haired, well-manicured businessmen and mobsters, Marcus was the thrilling opposite—young and blond and full of life.

Of course, Marcus wasn't only a pretty face. (Clara almost wished he were—it would make life a lot simpler.) He had grown on her. Yes, she had wanted to eschew another romantic entanglement, but perhaps some things were simply unavoidable.

Marcus glowed at her. Suddenly, in a flash of memory, she saw *him*—the Cad, not Marcus—before her, smiling that dazzling smile, seducing her as if it were a game. Clara blinked, and the club came back into focus.

Allowing herself to get comfortable with Marcus was not going to be easy.

Gloria was supposed to come on soon, so they all moved to a reserved booth near the corner of the stage. Gloria's doing, otherwise they would have been standing in the back. The booths near them were filled with gangsters in dark suits and flappers in dresses so brilliant they were nearly blinding.

"You think I should go back and check on our girl?" Lorraine said, taking a sip of a toxic-looking drink—a yellowish mixture with something creamy on top. "It's almost eleven-thirty."

"These types of things always start late," Clara said casually. And then caught herself. "I mean, that's what I've always read in the rags. The start time is just a ploy to get people into the room."

"Country Clara dons my flapper dress and suddenly she's the expert!" Lorraine laughed obnoxiously. "If I didn't know any better, Clara, I'd think you'd spent your whole life in a club!"

Clara laughed nervously. "We don't have speakeasies in Pennsylvania," she said, crossing her arms over her chest. "Too many Amish."

"Says you!" Lorraine retorted with a guffaw.

Marcus nudged Clara's knee under the table. "Well, I think she looks like a baby doll." He winked at her. "Beauty must run deep in the Carmody blood."

"Speaking of the other Carmody, I really do think we should go back and check on her," Lorraine said. "Clara, dear. You're family. Why don't you go?"

Clara sighed. Lorraine's ploys were as transparent as a sheet of glass. Clara felt bad for Lorraine—lusting after someone who clearly wasn't interested never ended well. Telltale signs of desperation were etched across Lorraine's face: a little too much makeup, tiny beads of sweat lining her forehead, eyes darting back and forth all around the club, trying to avoid their sole real target: Marcus.

Clara wished she could take Lorraine aside and smack some sense into her. *Marcus isn't interested,* she would say. *You're a smart, fun, pretty girl—you'll find someone else.*

Instead, Clara decided to give Lorraine exactly what she wanted: time alone with Marcus. Besides, things were getting a little too comfortable with his hand on her knee. She needed a breather.

"You know how sensitive Gloria is—let's let her be. But I wouldn't mind refreshing all of your drinks." Clara stood up and gathered Lorraine's and Marcus's empty glasses. "Any special requests?"

"Why don't I go with you?" Marcus offered, sliding out of the booth.

"Absolutely out of the question! It would be completely

improper of you to leave a girl as beautiful as Raine here at the table by herself." And before Marcus could protest, Clara sashayed off.

She slithered through the crowd, drinking in the dark ambiance of the club, and shouldered her way to the bar.

She rested one hand on the stained mahogany. It felt so familiar and easy to be standing there. Not at the Green Mill, of course, but at a speakeasy in general. As if she could step back into her old life as easily as she might order a drink.

"One Pink Lady, one whiskey sour, and . . ." She realized she hadn't ordered a drink for herself since New York. "And one dirty martini. More dry than dirty, though. With two olives."

"Gotta get more vermouth from the basement," the bartender said. "You mind cooling your heels?"

He disappeared just as there was a bustle on the stage. The band members were taking their places. Clara felt a swell of excitement. What could be better than sitting in the dark and listening to good music? Only sitting in the dark and listening to good music with someone you loved.

A handsome black man, whom Clara recognized from last time as the pianist, took the microphone. Jerome Johnson.

"Ladies and gentleman, sheiks and shebas, tonight is a very special night." His voice immediately sent a hush over the rowdy crowd. "Not only because the Jerome Johnson Band has a new member to introduce to all of you, but because"—he paused, ensuring that he had the attention of every last person in the room—"tonight is also this young lady's Chicago debut. So please, give a very warm welcome to Miss Gloria Carson."

Gloria emerged through a curtain at stage left. When she stepped into the light, the entire room seemed to breathe a collective sigh of awe. Perhaps it was the novelty of seeing a young white girl amid an all-black band. Or perhaps it was because she was radiant, like a shimmering mermaid who'd just emerged from the water. Her green dress hugged her curves and made the red waves of her hair look fiery. She held herself with a sophisticated poise and grace that Clara had never before seen her display—she commanded the stage, and she hadn't even opened her mouth yet. When had she learned to do *that*?

The piano began its introduction, and the rest of the band joined in on the fourth measure. And then Gloria opened her lips and took over the room.

*"Since you turned my love away*
*My glad rags ain't the same*
*I dress myself up in the blues*
*And rue that dire day.*

*But now I'm back to tell you*
*I've changed my wicked ways*
*I'll be your true-blue lover, babe—*
*If you'll only let me stay."*

Gloria's voice fit her image perfectly—it was sultry, with glimmers of soulfulness and deep hints of sadness. She began singing in a way that was almost conversational, but then plunged into her lower registers. As the song explained how a man had broken her heart beyond repair, she gradually took her voice even lower, to a throaty whisper, a smoky growl.

"Miss? Your drinks?" The bartender was back and had already prepared the round.

"Put it on Marcus Eastman's tab, please."

The barman carefully slid Clara's martini across the bar so that it wouldn't spill all over everything.

That was when she saw it: Speared between the two olives was a piece of torn paper.

Clara's hands began to shake, and some of the martini sloshed out of the glass. *Not here, not tonight,* she thought. She ripped the note off the spear.

*I see you*

In her mind, she could hear him saying it. Over the crowd, over the band, over Gloria's voice at the microphone, each word resonated like an alarm in Clara's head. She wanted to remain calm and collected, but she felt panic rising within her, about to burst in a hundred directions. Frantic, she scanned the room. There were people everywhere, in every corner, but they were all watching the stage.

All except one.

The pair of eyes was devastatingly familiar. Those same eyes that had once held so much love and now held so much betrayal.

She turned back toward the bar, taking a huge gulp of her martini. She had played and replayed this moment in her mind endlessly. Her journal was filled with unsent letters, saying everything she'd never said. Settling scores and placing blame. Granting forgiveness. She was the one who'd left the city without a goodbye—she had been too hysterical to face him. Hysterical and heartbroken. And scared.

"Excuse me, miss, but did you drop this?"

She could feel him next to her, the sleeve of his suit against her arm. He placed the crumpled note on the bar in front of her. She turned to him, wanting to appear hard as rock, to look unshaken and *over it.* But his presence undid her.

"I told you I never wanted to see you again," she managed to get out.

"Clara. Clarabella." He took a step closer and folded her into his arms.

She wanted to push him away, to beat her hands against his chest—what if Marcus and Lorraine saw her?—but it was futile. The more she resisted, the weaker she felt, until she collapsed against him and heaved a small cry, letting go of everything she had been clutching so tightly all these months.

"I've been waiting for this moment since the day I last saw

you," he said into her hair. "I've been thinking about you every second since you left me."

"*I* left *you*?" Of course, it was so like him to twist everything. Lies. Yes, she had run off, but that was only after he had turned her away.

"If you hadn't, I wouldn't have had to track you halfway across the country."

"You're unbelievable." He looked older than she remembered, though it suited him. Still that same overpowering stature. That same Cheshire-cat grin deepening the cleft in his chin. "If you really wanted to see me, you would have called me. Directly. Not played your sadistic games and sent me cryptic notes."

"Cryptic? I thought they were *nice*. I was trying to give you some space."

"You're delusional," Clara snapped.

"I didn't know if you'd want to see me," he said, his voice deepening.

"I didn't." She swallowed her resolve with another gulp of her martini. "I don't."

She was different now. Stronger. If playing Country Clara had taught her anything, it was to have a little self-respect. To regain the dignity she'd had before he ruined her life.

"The least you can do is have a drink with me."

"I already have a drink."

"Clara," he said, "when has that ever stopped you before?"

He kissed her then, on the corner of her mouth. As his lips

lingered there, soulful and soft, she didn't resist. Her head was screaming *No, no, no, remember what he did to you!* But she was hostage to her body, which had a memory of its own.

For a moment, the room around her dissolved, and those months of raw, red heartbreak were forgotten. It could have been spring in New York City again, when she was seventeen, wild, reckless, and hopelessly in love with Harris Brown.

All before she'd learned the truth about him. And the truth about herself.

# LORRAINE

Lorraine felt like the eel's hips.

She'd made peace with her best friend, she was feeling quite slender, and she was sitting in the most coveted spot in the Green Mill: next to Marcus Eastman.

She even felt a swell of maternal pride, watching Gloria onstage. Yes, she was jealous, but even she had to admit the girl could sing.

She knew Gloria was taking a huge risk. She'd muttered something to Lorraine about the pianist's sister threatening her, and something absurd about how performers here lasted only as long as they were in good with the gangsters who ran the place, but Lorraine had only laughed. She was Gloria Carmody, for Pete's sake! What mobster—or black girl, for that matter—would dare mess with society's darling?

Look at her up there now.

Even though Gloria was nervous, there was a serenity about her. Her face was still, but her body seemed fluid, swaying with the music, her voice spinning into gold as she closed her eyes and sang.

The black pianist was now in the middle of a rousing solo, sending jolts of electric shock through the crowd. Gloria stepped away from the microphone and rocked from side to side while he tickled the keys. Lorraine could practically feel the music in her bones. There was no greater aphrodisiac than hot jazz.

Time for Lorraine Dyer to remind the world who the daring one was here.

She slid a cigarette out of her case and brought it to her lips. "Scorch me?" she asked, trying to rein in Marcus's attention.

He lit her cigarette with a silver lighter from his jacket pocket, but his see-through-blue eyes were focused on something behind her. Not wanting to seem paranoid, Lorraine tried a different tactic. "Doesn't Gloria sound divine?" she asked, taking a deep drag. "I had no idea she had it in her."

"Yeah," he said, distracted. "She's hitting on all sixes."

"Remember the last time we heard her sing, at that unbearable Christmas party— Marcus!" Lorraine interrupted herself. "What the hell are you looking at?" She followed his gaze to Clara at the bar. "Geez Louise, do you need another drink that badly? Are you on a toot?"

"No," he said. "It's that guy. The one she's talking to. Doesn't he look familiar?"

Lorraine rolled her eyes. "She's *allowed* to talk to other men, Marcus. Just because she's a hick doesn't mean she can't flirt." Lorraine gave the man a second look. "You weren't just feeding me a line—that's Harris Brown!"

"Who?" Marcus clasped his hand on Lorraine's wrist.

Now she had him. If Marcus needed gossip, Lorraine was the source. "Harris Brown? Second son of the famous New York millionaire politician? He's a big-deal playboy in the naughty New York high-society world. And looking at him, I can certainly see why. *Rowr.*"

Marcus's eyes grew wide. "What the hell is Clara doing talking to him?"

Lorraine shrugged. "Who cares?" It certainly was odd that such a catch would be making time with Country Clara, but the girl *had* gotten a new look, and a darn sweet one, if Lorraine did say so herself. "Good for her, I say." She glanced back at the bar in time to see Clara pulling away from a kiss. "Looks like our very own Mrs. Grundy is getting *quite* a healthy dose of loosening up."

Marcus was out of the booth and on his feet, his mouth twisted into a hard line of anger. "I'm going to take that joker for a ride."

"You absolutely will not!" Lorraine pulled him back down. "Our plan is finally kicking into gear! Clara is dipping her toes into scandal. Now, would you stop getting yourself into such a lather, and . . ." The words were barely out of her mouth when the truth hit her. The more she looked at Marcus's face, the deeper the realization sank in. "I can't believe this," she said. "This isn't a game for you anymore, is it?"

"I don't know what you're talking about," Marcus mumbled into his glass.

"Do you need me to spell it out?" Lorraine persisted. "You've fallen for her. For *her.* For Clara."

"Stop beating your gums—"

"Oh, I'm the one? This was part of our plan, remember?" Raine's head was swimming. She had to say something, anything, to get Marcus's attention away from Clara, to focus it back on her—where it belonged, whether he knew it or not.

"I'm going to New York next year," she blurted out.

Marcus pulled his eyes away from the bar with a flicker of curiosity. "What are you talking about?"

"I'm going to Barnard next year. Barnard. It's a college."

"I know what it is."

"It's in New York. Barnard College of Columbia University in *New York City.*"

"And I know *where* it is, Raine."

Now that her secret was out, she couldn't make herself shut up. Her mouth just motored along on its own. "I got accepted and it's really a big deal—I mean, I don't need to tell you it's a big deal, you know it is—and I just thought you might want to know. Because, well, since you'll be in

New York, too, you know. At Columbia. Across the street from me—I mean, Barnard. It's across the street from Barnard. And—" But she was thankfully saved by a loud burst of voices from the front of the bar. Equal parts embarrassed and infuriated, Lorraine turned see what was going on.

It was none other than Sebastian Grey.

He was like a man on fire, waving his arms and shouting. "Do you know who I am? I can bring all of city hall down on this den of sin with a snap of my fingers!"

"Oh my God," Lorraine gasped, impulsively clutching Marcus's arm.

Marcus had already caught an eyeful. For the first time that evening, they were on the same page. "Talk about a crasher."

The guy Bastian was yelling at was the same one who had tried to pick up Lorraine the last time she was here. Carlito Maccarelli. Lorraine wanted to warn Bastian, but it was more fun to watch.

Carlito looked irked but calm. "I'm the manager here. I'm asking you to quiet down."

"I will *not* quiet down! Because of *that*!" Sebastian pointed at the stage, where Gloria stood, a hand shading her eyes. She was trying to see past her spotlight and into the darkness of the club. "Do you know what that is?"

Carlito straightened his tie. "Yeah, a shapely pair of stilts with some pretty fair pipes."

A half dozen thugs who'd quietly gathered behind him all snickered. Suddenly, Bastian seemed to take them in and come to his senses: His face paled. He cocked his arm back, but the gangster's men were one step ahead.

A woman screamed, and there was an earsplitting crash.

Bastian had been shoved backward and sent sliding across a table, glasses tumbling off and smashing onto the floor. He fell to his knees, then shakily got up.

"That's it!" he shouted. "I'll have you closed down for violating the Prohibition!"

"Good luck with that, you stuffed shirt," Carlito said. He combed back his hair with the flat of his hand. "In the meantime, what can we do for you? You're upsetting our customers."

"I've come for what's mine," Bastian told him, stalking off toward the stage, Carlito's goons following.

Lorraine's brain was racing—she hadn't said anything to Bastian when she had gone over there drunk, had she? No, she would never do that to Gloria, even in her most incoherent state. "*You* didn't tell him, did you?" she asked Marcus.

"Me? Are you kidding? He and I hate each other."

"I don't get it—who would do such a thing?" She looked up at Gloria, luminously absorbed in the glow of the spotlight. After the initial ruckus, the band had kicked into a rousing rendition of "Ain't We Got Fun," playing as if there were nothing wrong at all. A handful of couples took to the dance floor.

"Marcus," Lorraine pleaded, "we can't just sit here!"

But it was too late.

Gloria spotted Bastian ripping through the crowd and stopped singing midverse. The musicians continued playing, but without a vocalist the music sounded stripped bare and lost, just a car crash of individual noises.

Jerome frantically signaled to Gloria to keep singing, but that powerful version of Gloria, who'd just been onstage commanding the room, had vanished.

Bastian pounded up the stage's steps, and the music came to a jumbled halt. He violently grabbed Gloria's arm. "What the hell do you think you're doing?" His voice carried over the microphone to the entire club.

"I'm singing!" Gloria replied, trying to break away from his grip.

Jerome shot up from the piano.

"Don't you dare touch me, boy!" Bastian barked.

"Jerome!" Gloria shouted, catching Bastian's arm as he cocked his fist.

Jerome seemed to grow taller. He placed a protective hand on Gloria's back and gently positioned himself between her and Bastian as if to shield her. "What do you think you're doing with my singer?" he said to Bastian, remaining calm. The club had gone silent.

"Please, Bastian. Please, let's talk about this later. Not now. Not in front of all these people!" Gloria cried. "I beg you!"

Ignoring her, Bastian glowered at Jerome. "I'm her fiancé, colored boy. And where do *you* get off questioning *me*? You forget your place just because you can play a rag?"

Jerome dropped his hand from Gloria's back, took a step backward, and made fists.

The audience reacted as if they were watching a boxing match: They collectively *ooooh*ed. "My bet's on the piano player," Lorraine overheard a girl say.

Gloria turned to Jerome, who had stepped back, a strange look glazing his eyes. "Jerome, don't! I can explain—"

Still staring at Bastian, Jerome said, "You're welcome to get her on out of here. I think all of us are sorry about the mistaken identity." Even Lorraine could feel the flame in his gaze—hatred? betrayal? disappointment? Maybe all of those things. "Your fiancée should never set foot in this club again."

"Don't worry," Bastian responded, "you won't ever see her back here."

Standing between the two men, Gloria seemed to shrink.

Lorraine couldn't bear it. She pushed through the crowd.

"Gloria!" Lorraine called out as she reached the dance floor. "Glo!"

Bastian was dragging her to the edge of the stage. "Come *on,*" he said furiously.

"You're hurting me!" Gloria cried.

Lorraine climbed up and was at her side in a moment. "Let her go!" she said, pulling at Bastian's fingers, trying to break his grip. "She's coming home with me."

That was when she felt the slap.

There was a burst of light as the palm connected with her cheek, and then a sharp sting, like a lit match against her skin.

At first she thought it was Bastian who'd hit her. But as she recovered from the shock of it, holding her smarting cheek, she met Gloria's boiling eyes.

"How *could* you?" Gloria asked.

"Glo?" Lorraine said, wildly confused. "No. It's not—"

All at once, the world around her—the roaring crowd and the blinding, dizzying stage lights; the music that was now blaring from the gramophone—didn't matter. All Lorraine could see was Gloria, whose face said: *You* betrayed me, *you* ruined my life, *you* destroyed everything.

Lorraine felt her knees begin to shake. "Gloria. I'm your best friend in the world. I would never—"

"I will never speak to you again as long as I live," Gloria said coolly.

And then Gloria surprised both Lorraine and Bastian: she snapped her elbow back into Bastian's gut, and he lost his grip. She ran, leaping from the stage and pushing her way across the dance floor, not stopping for anyone or anything.

Lorraine tried to go after Gloria, but the crowd had already closed behind her. By the time she emerged at the other end of the club, Gloria had disappeared.

It was pointless to chase her now. Lorraine spotted Marcus heading for the door. "Do you think we should follow her home?"

He wouldn't look at her. "I always knew you were screwy, but I had no idea you were a traitor."

The word stung like a cut doused in alcohol. "Marcus, I swear to God, it wasn't me! I didn't tell Bastian. You have to believe me."

"Why should I?" He dropped his cigarette on the floor and stormed toward the door.

*Traitor.* The image of her kiss with Bastian flashed through her mind. *Traitor.* She hadn't told Gloria. *Traitor*.

She felt a hand on her back.

"Are you all right?"

Carlito. The mobster who had been dealing with Bastian. His gray eyes, framed by short black lashes, seemed kinder than she remembered. "I'll be fine," she said. But she was lying to herself: She was never going to be fine again.

"I saw what happened." He fished out a handkerchief, filled it with a few ice cubes from his glass, and held it up to her red cheek. "That was one helluva hit you took up there."

"She's my friend," Lorraine said, the ice soothing her burning cheek. "This feels good. Thanks."

"Don't mention it. What a rotten business this can be. I

had half a mind to have that guy thrown out. Did you see the way he gave me the high hat?"

"I did. Talk about disrespectful," she said, taking over the handkerchief-holding duty.

The gangster blinked at her with interest. "My thoughts exactly. That's what's wrong with this world—not enough respect. Between strangers, between friends, between a man and a woman." He squeezed her arm gently. "If you need anything, I'll be in the back. Anything at all."

Lorraine felt exhausted. "Really, I'm fine." She held out the handkerchief.

"Keep it," he said, folding it into her hand. "The next time I see you, I don't want to see a mark on that beautiful face of yours."

When he walked away, Lorraine unfolded the handkerchief. A monogrammed *M* was sewn into the corner. She lifted it to her nose and breathed in a masculine cologne.

She sniffled.

She had never felt so alone before, so irreversibly alone.

And then she sniffed: *Smoke.*

She looked down. At her feet was Marcus's cigarette, smoldering, its orange spark slowly fading yet still aglow. She covered it with the toe of her shoe, then ground and ground it into the sticky floor until it was no more than an ashy corpse, its light burned out for good.

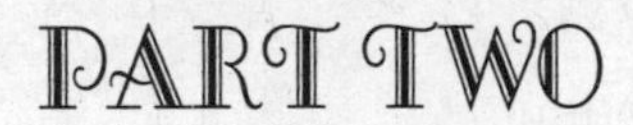

# PART TWO

# SPEAK LOW

I don't want to live.
I want to love first,
and live incidentally.

—Zelda Fitzgerald (1919)

# GLORIA

This was what Gloria remembered: stepping into the spotlight and seeing a crystalline image of her future, where she was meant to be—next to a piano, in front of an audience, a song streaming from her soul. It felt more like home than the house she'd grown up in. Onstage, she could actually *move* people in the moments it took to sing a ballad. That was more than a society wife could do in a lifetime.

But the spotlight had been turned away.

Part of her knew that the truth would have come out eventually. Pictures of her and Bastian were all over the society papers and gossip columns. How long could she have pretended to be a small-town singer? But she'd never thought it would happen so quickly. Life had teased her with a taste of freedom and then cruelly snatched it away, leaving her empty-handed. And alone.

All the girls at Laurelton Prep heard one version or another of the story.

Gloria had gone back to school on Monday—the only place she was allowed to go now, because her mother had grounded her for just shy of forever. Gloria was surprised to discover that she'd achieved a kind of tawdry celebrity. Girls laughed and whispered behind cupped hands when she passed in the hallways, and quieted when she came into a classroom.

During her midday history class, she noticed something being passed back and forth between girls. Gloria, from her seat in the third row of desks, leaned over and snatched it from the grubby hands of Malinda Banks, a junior with the sad hint of a mustache.

"Hey!" Malinda said, but Gloria didn't pay her any attention. It was a page from the Chicago *Daily Journal.* The gossip column "The Chatterbox." Right at the top of the page, Gloria spotted her own name in boldface type:

Chicago sweetheart **Gloria Carmody** was caught without her pretenses—and without her engagement ring—performing the other night at an undisclosed location. Under the name Gloria Carson, the 17-year-old was discovered by her fiancé, Harvard graduate **Sebastian Grey,** fronting an all-colored band. "He ripped her right off the stage," reports an anonymous source who witnessed the performance. "It was so embarrassing. For both of them."

"Gloria has always been a loose cannon," says a friend of the Carmody family. "You wouldn't guess it by looking at her, but she has a hidden life. I've heard that this isn't the only colored band she's performed with." What other secrets is the young chanteuse withholding? Better find out, Sebastian, before it's too late.

In other news, **Elizabeth Downing** was spotted in Hyde Park last—

"Honestly," Gloria said, looking up from the page. It was only after every head had turned to stare that she realized she'd spoken out loud.

"Yes?" Miss Trimbal, the history teacher, asked. "Did you say something, Gloria?"

"All I did was *sing*. Is that such a crime?" Gloria glared at Malinda, then at every girl in the room.

"It's not that you sing," called a voice from the back—Anna Desmond, that greasy-haired cow—"but whom you sing *with*. And that you lie about it. Because everyone knows there'd be only one reason to lie about singing love songs with a colored man—"

"That's quite enough, class," Miss Trimbal said, ringing the tiny bell she kept on her desk. "I will remind you not to air your dirty laundry in public. Doing so only makes the sinner feel self-important and—"

That was when Gloria had gathered her books and stood up.

"Gloria Carmody, where do you think you're going?" Miss Trimbal asked, but Gloria knew that any answer was beside the point.

She stormed out of the room and into the bathroom down the hall, where she locked herself in one of the stalls and began to cry. The worst part? She couldn't even go to Lorraine for comfort. They hadn't spoken since that night at the Green Mill.

Everyone at school acted so high and mighty, but it soon became clear to Gloria that they all wanted a piece of her story: They wanted to know whether she was involved with the Mob and whether she'd witnessed any killings; whether she could pull strings and get them into the Green Mill; and one girl asked her straight out whether she was "knocked up with that colored boy's bastard," and Gloria had slapped a person for the second time in her life.

Gloria had never realized how much she depended on Lorraine to survive an average day. Between in-class note passing, lunch, after-school shopping, and nightly chats, the girls had been in constant communication.

Luckily, Lorraine didn't show up for school on Monday or Tuesday, so Gloria hadn't had to deal with her. But when she set foot in homeroom on Wednesday, a textbook clutched to her chest, Lorraine was there in her wrinkled uniform and heavy makeup, looking haggard and hungover, as if she'd been on a bender for days. A cross between a chorus girl and a corpse.

Gloria had the urge to smack Lorraine's face with the book she was holding.

Instead, she avoided her.

Gloria's entire life was a mess. Her irate mother's most optimistic prediction was that Bastian would forgive her for the sake of the "greater plan." Gloria could have her old life back and never speak again of singing, or carousing, or standing at the front of a band of black musicians as if she were no better than your average harlot.

"What does that even mean?" Gloria had snapped. "What's an 'average' harlot, Mother?" They were in the dining room, eating an overspiced meat loaf. Clara watched from across the table, speechless.

"Do not sass me," her mother had said. "You know full well what I mean."

"Right," Gloria answered. "That I should aim to be an above-average harlot. A superior harlot!"

"Gloria! To your room this instant!"

She'd gone upstairs without dinner that night. Again. She'd flopped across her bed, as she had each of the nights since her Green Mill debut (if you could even call it that), and listened to Bessie Smith sing "Downhearted Blues" over and over.

She felt an actual pang in her chest at the thought of never seeing Jerome again. Or leaving him with the indelible image of her as a fraud, as the rich little white faker he'd pegged her as from the start. A daddy's girl. Except that her father wasn't even in the picture, just wreaking havoc on their lives from a distance.

She had to do something—anything—soon, or she knew that pang would eventually consume her. She just didn't know *what* she could possibly to do to redeem herself.

So in the meantime, she went over to the record player and moved the needle back to the beginning of "Downhearted Blues."

Gloria was on her bed, staring at the beige ceiling, when Clara popped her head around the cracked-open door. "Glo, you-know-who just telephoned for you."

Lorraine had been incessantly calling the house, but Gloria refused to speak to her. Raine had even sent over a series of telegrams that had said "I'm sorry," "Please forgive me," and "Did you get my first telegram saying that I'm sorry?" but Gloria had thrown them in the garbage. She was in no mood to read a bunch of self-justifying excuses and tiresome apologies. After all the years they had been best friends, after everything they had been through together, how could Raine have ratted her out? She had always been a little crazy, that much was true, but never in a cruel way.

And now Gloria was grounded, getting ripped apart by the papers, while Lorraine was free as a bird. How was that fair?

"I hope you told her the usual," Gloria said, hugging one of her frilly pink pillows to her chest. "As in, 'Don't call this house again, you bitch.'"

"I left out the bitch part, but otherwise, yes," Clara said, gliding into the room. She was wearing a floral silk robe that Gloria had never seen before—it looked European, with bold red poppies covering the black silk.

"Where'd you get that robe?" Gloria asked.

Clara froze for a split second. Then she wrapped the robe even tighter around herself. "It was a gift." She went to the record player and stopped the song midchorus. "Someone needs to put you out of your misery."

Gloria threw the pillow to the floor. "Good luck trying. I'd rather just wallow."

"Trust me, I wasn't volunteering for the job. Although I'll bet I know the one person who could get it done."

Gloria looked at her cousin suspiciously.

The girls weren't enemies, but they hadn't crossed over into "friends" territory yet. True, Gloria hadn't been the most welcoming of relatives, but . . . No, the truth was that Gloria had been terrible. She had plotted to get rid of Clara before she'd even arrived. Then, once Clara had shown up, Gloria had either been rude or had ignored her cousin completely.

Looking at Clara now, Gloria regretted her actions. Was it too late to make amends? Even Marcus liked Clara, and he was the world's harshest critic when it came to girls. So what if her cousin lived on a farm? It didn't make her a bad person. It might even be nice to have a relative her own age who was also a friend, especially now that Lorraine had shown her true colors.

"If you say Sebastian, you are officially banned from my room," Gloria said, attempting a joke.

"I have no problem with that," Clara said, eyeing the volcanic disaster that was Gloria's bedroom. Every surface was covered with piles of dirty clothes, books, old coffee cups, bowls of melted ice cream with cigarette butts floating in the dregs. "You might want to let Claudine in here one of these days, if she doesn't faint first."

"You're right," Gloria said. She hadn't let the maid in for nearly a week, but living in squalor really wasn't helping ease the situation. "So, who *are* you talking about?"

"J.J.," Clara said. "Would you like me to spell out what each *J* stands for?"

"No, that won't be necessary," Gloria said, her stomach somersaulting. "What about him?"

"That's what I was hoping you'd tell me."

"There's nothing to tell," Gloria said.

"Oh, honey, I'm not as stupid as you think." Clara picked up a hairbrush from the floor, sat on the bed beside Gloria, and began to brush her unwashed, matted hair. "You have a rock from a man who looks like Bastian Grey—a man every girl and her mother are lusting after—yet you're locked up in your room looking like hell, playing a Bessie Smith song over and over? Can you get any more classically lovesick than that?"

"What would you know about it?" Gloria asked defensively. "Did some farmer steal one of your sheep or something?"

As soon as she said it, Gloria started laughing. Then Clara laughed, too. "I know this is shocking, but even where I come from, there is such a thing as falling for the wrong person."

"In *Pennsylvania*?"

Clara put down the brush. "Listen, it's about time I told you: I didn't move to Chicago just to help plan your wedding. I needed to get away from someone, from my own past—so that I could start fresh. Someone I was in love with but never should have been." She closed her eyes. "I'm no more of an expert on the subject than any other girl. But this much I know: Love is worth everything. If you really love someone, you'll have no regrets. Even if it turns out badly."

"But how do you *know*?" Gloria asked. "How do you *know* if it's love? How do you know if it's anything at all?"

"All you have to know is whether you're willing to find out." Clara took Gloria's hand. "Or whether you're ready to give up on it."

"No." Gloria thought of Jerome, of his hands around her waist during that first voice lesson. Of him teaching her how to sing, how to feel. "I'm not ready to give up. Not yet."

"The only time I've seen you look truly alive was when you were up there with him, performing together. It was pretty magical."

The tears came like a hot spring then, from a place inside Gloria that Jerome had shown her. "I *need* to find out whether Jerome and I are meant to be. Otherwise, I'll never forgive myself."

"Then what are you waiting for?" Clara asked, gently wiping Gloria's wet cheeks, her eyebrows arched with a hint of mischief. "Your mother won't be home for another few hours."

◆◆◆

Gloria did something she had never done before: She took the bus. By herself. At night. To Bronzeville.

She'd never even set foot in Bronzeville. But she figured if she was going to take the biggest risk of her life, she couldn't do it in a cowardly fashion. She couldn't ask someone to drive her. She had to go by herself and show up at Jerome's door and be willing to bare her soul. Otherwise, there was no point in going at all.

She'd "dressed down" for the bus—an old cloche hat, a plain long-sleeved white blouse, a skirt that was dark and modest—but hadn't dressed down enough: None of the women were wearing heels, and most wore demure skirts that reached to midcalf. Like the men on the bus, they wore sensible shoes, shoes for walking and working. They were coming home from work, Gloria realized.

An older woman stood up and offered her a seat. Gloria tried to say no, but the woman insisted with a smile, saying,

"A lady shouldn't be standing." It was as kind as anyone had been to Gloria in days.

The other thing about the riders was this: Nearly all of them were black.

At first, she felt as if she stuck out and that men and women alike would stare at her with contempt. Old stories from school came to mind, and she clutched her purse in front of her and tried not to meet anyone's gaze. But the ride was long and her patience was short. Soon enough, she was looking up at people.

A few glanced at her now and then, always turning back to a book, or a newspaper, or some knitting. No one much noticed the white girl in the fancy clothes. It was as if she didn't matter to them at all.

And Gloria realized that was true: She *didn't* matter. These people had lives—real lives, in which they struggled for things they cared about. A lovesick girl in a bad hat? There were more important things to worry over.

When she reached her stop, Gloria joined the passengers stepping down from the back of the bus.

She was shocked to find the streets full of activity. Astor Street, where she lived, was always eerily quiet. But here, noise was everywhere. Children playing stickball, running to the sidewalks when a car passed. Older women with baskets of laundry on their hips loudly gossiping on the corners. And there were black teenagers, leisurely sitting on stoops and smoking cigarettes, and couples walking hand in hand.

As she passed, she felt some people stare at her. This was different from the train. She kept her eyes cast modestly downward and prayed she wouldn't get lost.

Any trace of warmth had disappeared from the air, and a windy November chill had settled in. Still, she was drenched in sweat by the time she arrived at the address Evan had given her.

Jerome lived in a run-down three-story building on a block of brownstones. There were empty flower boxes in some windows, shirts drying on the fire escapes, music coming from slightly opened windows. It was a nice place. As nice as it could be.

Jerome had told Gloria once, during rehearsal, that he had moved out of his parents' house a year before, at eighteen, having earned enough money from playing piano to start life on his own. His father didn't approve of his career and wanted him to take over the family business, a grocery store on Garfield Street. Vera, who was Gloria's age, still lived in their childhood home. Their mother had died when they were young, and Jerome's sister was his only link to his father, whom he no longer talked to.

She pressed the buzzer for 2B, next to the initials *J.J.*

Her heart raced.

There was no answer.

Her finger was poised on the button, about to buzz again,

when she froze. She took a step down the front stairs and caught her breath. *It wasn't meant to be,* a voice said crisply in her head. *It was never meant to be.*

There was nothing to do now but go back home.

A cruel shiver of defeat ran through her. She knew life was a series of near misses, but this one was tragic. The reality of never seeing Jerome Johnson again sank into her, and she staggered and gripped the railing and thought, *No!* She knew in that moment, clutching the rusty banister, in this all-black neighborhood with everyone staring at her, that she wanted him. Needed him. Only felt alive when she was beside him. Loved him with all of herself, with whatever she had in her to love him with.

That was when the front door opened and the dark silhouette of Jerome Johnson stood before her.

She wanted to run back up the stairs and into his arms. But the look on his face quickly killed that fantasy.

"I'm glad you're here," she said, her voice seemingly detached from her body.

"What do you want?" He was wearing only a white T-shirt and a pair of old slacks.

"I'm—" she started, seeing that his eyes held no sympathy. "I'm freezing."

He was about to protest when he saw that she had no coat.

"You can come in," he said, "but only for a second."

Without a word, Gloria followed him inside. The interior hallway was dark, the wallpaper peeling, the carpeting worn.

His apartment was small but charming, with a bohemian air that Gloria hadn't expected. Hundreds of books and records were stacked on the floor, and a few bold unframed paintings hung on the walls. At one end was a tiny kitchen—just a sink and a burner and two cupboards—and at the other was an alcove that curved around a corner, leading to what she assumed was his bedroom. An old baby grand piano took up nearly half the room. She went to it, running her hand over the piles of sheet music strewn across the top.

Jerome watched her.

She wanted to appear comfortable, even though she was so *un*comfortable. She turned to him. "See, I've warmed up already."

"What do you want?" Jerome demanded again, staying on the other side of the room. "I hope you didn't come all the way out here to see me. Is your driver waiting, Miss Carmody? Or should I say, Mrs. Grey?"

"I deserve that. No, my driver isn't waiting. I took the subway. And I am still *Miss* Carmody," she added.

Jerome didn't respond. He folded his strong arms across his chest.

"May I have some water?" she asked, not knowing what else to say.

"Sure," he said. "Get it yourself. We don't have maids here."

Gloria shuffled over to the kitchen, took a glass out of one of his cupboards, and turned on the tap. She was used to

Jerome's rough manner, but this was entirely new. He was angry at her. Which meant he was hurt. Which maybe, just maybe, meant he actually loved her.

"Thanks," she said, taking a long sip.

Jerome rocked back and forth on his heels. "When you're ready to tell me what you want, you let me know," he said. He walked to the window, sat in a chair, and lit a cigarette.

Gloria had grown so used to men making everything easy for her. She never had to know what she wanted, only what she didn't want. Now the opposite was true. "I want to explain."

"Why should I believe a word you say?" He exhaled a thin stream of smoke, unimpressed. "You've already lied to me once. What makes you think I would trust you?"

"Because before, I had everything to lose," she said. "But now that I've lost everything, there's nothing left to hide."

Jerome just kept staring out the window.

She walked across the room and sat in the chair next to his. "Please," she said, placing a hand on his knee.

"You don't owe me anything." He didn't brush her hand off, but he didn't grasp it, either.

"You're right, I don't. We don't owe anything to anyone but ourselves and the ones we love," she said defiantly. His eyes widened at the word *love*. "But just hear me out."

She told him everything.

About her background, her family, her schooling. She told him all about Bastian, how the engagement was nothing more than a business deal with her parents. About her father, and how he had basically deserted her and her mother, leaving them to fend for themselves, make their own reputations and fortunes. How everything now rested on her shoulders. And how her world was slowly coming apart at the seams, but how singing had temporarily sewn it back together.

His face showed nothing as she talked—no emotion, no reaction, no flicker of understanding. She began to feel that she had misjudged those moments together, during rehearsal, in the dressing room. That almost-kiss—maybe it truly had been only about the eyelash. Had this all been in her head?

"So," she said, "do you believe anything I've just said?"

"Not yet," Jerome countered.

Her heart plummeted.

She had to remind herself that whatever happened, at least she had given it a good try. "I don't know what else to say. I just told you everything there is to know."

"Not everything." He stubbed his cigarette out in an ashtray, then placed it on the floor. There was nothing separating them. "You haven't told me what I should call you."

He knew her name now. He knew her *real* name. What was he getting at? "Oh!" She let out a short laugh. "Gloria Rose Carmody."

"Gloria Rose, Gloria Rose," he repeated, as if tasting the

words in his mouth. "Now, *that* is a killer stage name. Next time you sing, that's how you should be billed."

"I doubt there'll be a next time."

"You have a beautiful voice, kid." He stared straight into her eyes. "I would hate to see you give it up."

"Then you need to keep teaching me."

Jerome got up and moved closer to the window. "I don't think that's such a good idea."

"Why not?"

"You *know* why not," he said. "You should find another teacher."

"I don't *want* another teacher!" She went to him. If she didn't say it now, she never would. "I want *you.* That is what I want. That is what I came over here to tell you."

Jerome's eyes blazed as Gloria touched his shoulder. He stroked her hair gently, tilted her face up to his. "You can't know that yet. You can't know what that means."

"Then show me," she said, pulling closer. "Show me."

He wrapped his arms around her. When their lips finally met, it was as if they had been waiting for this one kiss their entire lives.

# CLARA

"Did you know that the Green Mill is named after the Moulin Rouge—the Red Mill—in Paris?" Clara said to Marcus, gazing at Henri de Toulouse-Lautrec's *At the Moulin Rouge.* In the painting, a bunch of top-hatted men and well-dressed women sat around a table, while in the foreground, a goblin-faced woman seemed to be giving the viewer the evil eye. It was unnerving.

"Well, look at you, scholar," Marcus said, nudging Clara.

"Consider me your personal tour guide."

"I must say," Marcus murmured, "I'd rather be at the Green Mill than the place in this painting. None of these people look like they're having any fun at all."

They were at a special exhibition at the Art Institute of Chicago. And it was quite a big event—bigger than Clara had expected. The main exhibition hall was packed with so many people decked out in their finest that Clara would have wagered that all of Chicago's elite were here, drinking seltzer and squinting at paintings.

Clara, too, was dressed to the nines, wearing one of the only valuable pieces she had managed to salvage from her New York stash. It was a boxy silk Chanel, and it had cost one of Clara's beaux a small fortune. The skirt was almost too short to wear out in polite society, but Clara looked beautiful in its intricate black and bronze patterning, and beauty excused lots of things.

"Have I mentioned how incredibly gorgeous you look in that dress?" Marcus said again.

"I think that makes twelve times," Clara said. "But who's counting?"

A week after Gloria's Green Mill fiasco, a week after Clara had met the ghost of her past face to face, Marcus had called, inviting her to this opening.

She'd eagerly accepted. Now that Clara had finally seen Harris Brown, the tiny sentimental part of her that was still clinging to his memory had been exterminated. She could move on with her life, full speed ahead. She could be around Marcus and not feel those endless questions nagging at her. She was free.

"Can I tell you a secret?" Clara asked Marcus now.

"You seem to be full of them," he said as he pulled her toward a waiter holding a tray of shrimp.

"What's that supposed to mean?"

He dipped a shrimp into the bowl of red cocktail sauce and popped it into his mouth. "Nothing. So what's your secret?"

"It's my dream to go to Paris and hobnob with all the literary expatriates." She searched Marcus's face for a reaction but couldn't read his expression. He hadn't been in touch with her all week—no phone calls, no house calls—and then this invitation had come, albeit at the last minute. Had Marcus spotted her talking to Harris at the Green Mill? Was that why he'd been absent? "So have you been?" she asked, sipping her ginger ale. "To Paris, I mean?"

"I'm thinking of taking a trip there next summer—all around Europe, actually."

"How original of you." But then, realizing that sounded snotty, she added, "To get it all out of your system before you get tangled up in the Ivy?"

"I have nothing I need to get out of my system. Do you?"

"Um, simmer down, Columbia." She linked her arm in his. "Besides, I'm jealous. I've only been as far as—" She stopped herself before she said the obvious.

"As where?"

"As here, I was about to say. Chicago."

"Are you sure about that?" He removed her arm from his and dramatically turned toward her. "No detours in between?"

"I don't know what kind of detours you mean, but—"

"Clara Knowles, I didn't expect to see you here!" That high-pitched squeal could belong to only one person.

"Why, Ginnie, what a surprise!"

"My father is on the museum's board of trustees," Ginnie said, blinking her close-set brown eyes.

Clara had leaned in for a cheek-brushing kiss when Ginnie spotted Marcus and practically pushed her off to one side. "Marcus! I didn't even— I thought you weren't—" Ginnie stammered breathlessly, twisting her hair around her finger.

"Lovely to see you again, Virginia." He took Ginnie's hand in his while she fanned herself with her other hand. "Actually, we were just talking about you."

"You were not!" Ginnie snatched her gloved hand back and clapped both hands together with glee.

"We were," Clara confirmed, happily playing along. "We were just discussing how lovely your high-tea party was the other week, and how sorry we both were we had to leave so abruptly—"

"On account of Clara's delicate stomach," Marcus reminded Ginnie.

"Food poisoning," Clara said, grimacing. "It really was the worst."

Ginnie wrinkled her nose. "Really, you don't need to say any more! I'm just so happy that you're feeling better!"

Marcus placed a hand on Ginnie's arm and whispered loudly, "We suspect it was Mrs. Carmody's undercooked salmon."

Ginnie giggled. "It was so sad you had to leave before the clown arrived."

"Buster Keaton?" Marcus asked.

"No, Daddy couldn't book him," Ginnie said, staring dumbly at Marcus. "But wasn't that so sweet of you, Marcus, to escort Clara home?"

"*So* sweet." Clara took a fresh drink from a tray passing by and gulped it down—sparkling cider. *Ugh.* She wished it were champagne.

Suddenly, Ginnie looked from Marcus to Clara and back again, pursing her lips in thought. "Are you two here . . . *together*?"

Marcus said, "Yes."

"No," Clara said simultaneously.

Marcus and Clara locked eyes for a brief, tense moment.

"I invited her, yes," Marcus said. "As my date."

"So you *are* here together!" Ginnie gaped, growing more excited than jealous.

Clara felt herself blushing. "I guess so."

"But Gloria's not here, is she?" Ginnie asked, her face suddenly serious.

"No, unfortunately she couldn't make it," Marcus said, looking past Ginnie now, as though scanning the crowd for someone.

"Because she's still grounded?" Ginnie made a big show of looking in both directions. "For singing at that seedy *black* place?"

"You could say that," Marcus said coldly. He patted Ginnie on the back and gave her a little push. "Again, it's been *so* lovely to see you, Ginnie!"

They made their way toward Van Gogh's lonely *The Bedroom.* But before they could reach it, Marcus had to say hello to half a dozen couples. The girls seemed to know him and gave Clara a cold eye, and the boys were all like Freddy Barnes—young, rich, and not yet out of high school. In fact, Freddy was at the center of a bunch of them.

"I say, Eastman," he said as they walked past. "This is the second time I've seen you with that bird. You two been nesting?"

"You are as witty as ever, Freddy," Marcus said. "Which is to say, not at all."

Freddy bowed toward Clara and said, "I'm just teasing. We're all happy to see Marcus here settle down. After he quit student government and disappeared, we feared vile Ginnie Bitman—"

"Tedious Ginnie Bitman!" one of the other fellows chimed.

"Nightmarish Ginnie Bitman!" another added.

"Clearly, words fail us," Freddy said. "But we feared for his manhood with that chunk of lead."

"As you can see, my manhood is intact. Now, if you'll excuse us." Marcus's hand at her back steered Clara away. "Those guys," Marcus said. "What a laugh factory."

"I didn't know you were in student government!" Clara said.

"I was impeached. It's too tragic to dredge up now."

"Well, if you ever need a girl to stand by your side as you're dragged through the mud, I think you could do a lot worse than Ginnie Bitman."

"Really? I don't know. She may well be the worst of the worst."

"In other words, exceptional. And perfect for you."

He placed his hand over his heart. "My boyhood dream: fulfilled. Ginnie Eastman." Then he cleared his throat. "And what about you, Clara? Who's your pick?"

"Oh no," Clara laughed. "I don't have a litter around me like you do, with little Ginnie and her friends all wagging their tails."

"But you do have some bigwig New York politicians. What would you call them?"

Clara froze. So he *had* seen her and Harris that night. The thought made her sick to her stomach.

She peered up into Marcus's honest face—there was no anger there. No, he looked wounded. He *liked* her. This beautiful boy liked her. She was not going to allow Harris Brown to ruin her life again—once was enough.

Clara took a deep breath. "What you may have seen the other night: It wasn't how it looked."

"A man like that kisses you and it's not how it looks? I'm not stupid, Clara."

"Of course not. But there's more to it, and I—"

"Why, *there's* my little troublemaker," a woman cooed, appearing out of nowhere and putting her hands all over Marcus, fussing with his jacket and his tie.

For a middle-aged woman, she was attractive. Her platinum-blond hair was piled up in a pretty bouffant, and she looked elegant in a floor-length black lace gown. She seemed weirdly familiar. With a shock, Clara realized this was Marcus's mother. She had his forceful self-confidence and spoke in a distinctive breathless rush, emphasizing words with a jab of her cigarette holder.

"I've been looking *all* over for you! I wanted to introduce you to Mr. Kent, remember? On the board of trustees? He practically owns half the real estate in New York, so he could be a *very* useful connection for you next year." She finally noticed Clara. "And who is *this* darling little thing? Don't tell me you are Beatrice's *niece*? The one Marcus has been going on and *on* about?"

"Guilty as charged," Clara said. The longer she was in Chicago, the more people wanted to meet her. It was nice to feel wanted. "And excuse me for saying so, but it's obvious whom Marcus gets his good looks from."

"*And* she's a doll?" Mrs. Eastman said to Marcus. "Well, excuse *me* for saying so, but ever since *this* one over here was a little boy, I always thought he was in *love* with your cousin Gloria—they were *so* attached at the hip. But then when she got *engaged*—"

"Mother!" Marcus protested. "Really, please stop—"

"And you just *dropped* into my boy's life like an *angel* falling from the sky," she continued. "I just had this *feeling* about you two. This cosmic feeling."

"Oh, Mother," Marcus muttered.

"Maternal instincts are the best instincts," Clara said, smiling. This woman was wild, and charming. Clara liked her enormously.

"They may not be the *best,* but they are always right," Mrs. Eastman said, straightening Marcus's bow tie while he fidgeted. "Now, don't mind *me,* I'll leave you two *alone* to enjoy my exhibition. Well, not *my* exhibition, I'm only on the *board*. Oh, look, there's Betsy von Tipper—I hear she's having an *affair* with her *dentist.* Betsy!"

Marcus and Clara watched her dash off to cheek-kiss a woman in a purple gown that looked like a Persian rug.

"Wow," Clara said, "your mother is—"

"A face stretcher?" Marcus offered.

"Marcus, that is not a nice thing to say about your own mother! I was going to say the cat's pajamas." Lillian Eastman might have been a little overwrought, but she was certainly more interesting than most other women her age. "So what did you tell her about me?" Clara asked. "I hope only good things."

"Of course." Marcus regarded her sternly. "Unless everything I told her was a damn lie."

His tone shocked her.

"I mean, I know it's none of my business, seeing that we're . . ." He trailed off.

"We're what?" *We're an* item? *We're crazy about each other? We're meant to be?* That was what she wanted to say, but instead she said, "Tell me."

"We're *nothing,* Clara. Maybe that's the problem." He tugged at his bow tie as if it were strangling him. "If you want to kiss some other man, I have no right to say you can't. But a man like Harris Brown—" He yanked hard and his tie came completely undone. "How do you even know a man like that?"

Hearing his name come out of Marcus's mouth made her cringe. She wanted to tell him that she was over Harris, that she was proud of her new self for not going off with him to "catch up." She wanted to tell Marcus that she had changed. That she wasn't the same girl she had once been in New York. That she liked the new woman she was becoming.

But Marcus didn't know any of that, and as she looked into his wounded blue eyes, she wanted it to stay that way. "Why don't we go visit the Cassatts—"

"I have a better idea." He led her through the maze of diamond-encrusted women and tuxedo-clad waiters, right past the room with the Cassatts and into a closed-off part of the museum. Finally, they hopped over a barricade blocking off a dark corridor of Renaissance art. The party was a mere buzz in the distance now, and they stood in the eerie darkness, out of breath, alone.

"Is this your subtle way of telling me you prefer images of the Virgin Mary to mothers bathing their children?" she asked, trying to make a joke. But he didn't laugh, just paced back and forth in front of an enormous dark portrait of the Madonna. "You're acting a little bit like a crazy person."

"Because you've been *making* me crazy!" he said, exasperated. "Ever since I saw you kiss that character at the Green Mill!"

Clara's dress suddenly started to feel too tight. She couldn't breathe.

"Maybe I shouldn't tell you this—maybe I should be suave and pretend I don't give a damn—but I *do,*" he said.

"No, I want you to be honest with me," Clara began, only to realize how dishonest *she* was being.

"Why won't you open up to me? Can't you see I'm trying, here?" He ran his fingers through his hair. "But you're just a closed book, aren't you? You won't let anybody in."

Clara wanted so much to tell Marcus the truth—he deserved the truth, not a twisted sliver of it—but what would he think of her? How would he ever respect her? She looked at him, at the softness and concern that lived within his eyes. He was the first guy in her life who'd ever really cared for *her*—not some girl who was part of a social equation, who fit a need and a style of the moment, but *her,* Clara, with all her stupid jokes and her fears and her mistakes.

If she told him about her sordid past, she would risk losing him. And she couldn't risk losing anything again. "I want to tell you," she said, on the verge of tears, "but you'll hate me if I do."

"I could never hate you, Clara," he said. His hands traveled to the back of her neck, and he drew her to him, to his soft lips. "I want you to let me in, Clara."

And for the first time in her life, Clara had a true kiss—one that wasn't about someone taking advantage of her, wasn't about her lying with her lips. It was about wanting to kiss no one else in the world. It was a kiss that shook her to her foundation and woke her up again, shook her alive.

◆◆◆

Sitting on the steps outside the museum, sharing a pilfered bottle of sparkling cider, Clara told Marcus how she'd run away from Pennsylvania to New York, and the wild flapper life she'd lived there—the jazz, the booze, the boys. How she was trying to reinvent herself and stay out of reform school in the process. And she told him all about Harris Brown—well, mostly all. There were some things—one horrific thing—that Clara couldn't bring herself to mention.

"So you didn't know he was engaged to the other woman?" Marcus asked, passing her the bottle.

"No, I knew," she said quietly, ashamed. "The two of them were all over the papers; their engagement was a big deal. It was impossible *not* to know unless you were living under a rock."

"I don't understand," he said. He rubbed his jaw. "Why would you want to put yourself in that position?"

"I feel strange talking to you about another man," she admitted, though she was relieved to have it all off her chest. She looked down at her black patent-leather pumps, so tiny next to his large brown suede loafers. She *was* holding back, but the rest of the story she would never tell him—never in her life.

"But what's he doing here? Men like him don't come chasing a girl halfway across the country if they're through."

Clara hugged herself. "His fiancée broke off their engagement when she found out about me. He's here because he couldn't find anyone else who would have him."

Marcus looked up into the dark night. A full moon hung in the sky, hoarding all the light. As he gazed at it, Marcus's face looked angelic, almost too pure for the story she was telling.

"Listen, if you want nothing to do with me after this, I understand. But please, please, be discreet. The Carmodys have enough trouble. The last thing they need is another scandal." Clara felt drained and exhausted, but at least she had come clean. That was more than she had done in a long time.

Marcus stood up to leave. Of course he was leaving. Despite his faults, Marcus was a good, respectable guy. He wanted a sweet, innocent girl. Not a reformed flapper whose past hounded her at every step.

Clara took one last look at Marcus. Oh, how she wanted

to kiss him! But instead, she would have to let him go. "You can go if you must. That's all I wanted to say."

She closed her eyes, hoping that when she opened them, Marcus would already be gone. She couldn't bear seeing the rejection in his face. She waited a few seconds and then blinked. He was still there.

"I'm not going anywhere," he said softly. "I just wanted to give you my coat."

Marcus knelt down and wrapped her in his coat, and then in his arms. It felt so incredible to be held by him.

Clara rested her head against his broad shoulder. She wasn't used to kindness. Nearly all of her secrets had been revealed, and Marcus was still there, holding her, with no intention of leaving.

"I just have one more question, and I want you to be honest with me." He paused. She could feel the warmth of his breath on her neck. "Do you still love him? Now that the engagement is broken off, you could be together."

"No," she said. "I don't love him. I don't think I ever really did. I didn't know what love was, back then. I think I wanted to feel things just for the sake of feeling them. But now I have a much better idea."

"Oh?" he said, trailing his fingertips up her arm. "What kind of idea?"

"Something like this," she said, and kissed him again until the moon had sunk past the horizon and the night sky over Chicago was spangled with stars.

# LORRAINE

"What are you drinking?" Bastian asked her. "Or rather, how sloppy do you want to get?"

"I didn't come over here to socialize with you," Lorraine said, holding down the hem of her dress as she crossed her legs. "Or get 'sloppy,' whatever that means."

"No need to play coy with me, Raine." He lined two tumblers up on the bar. "You lost that privilege the last time you were here."

"I'd prefer to forget. In fact, consider it erased from the record." She was at Bastian's apartment with a mission, and under no circumstances would she deviate from it. Or risk a repeat of last time.

"I much prefer to remember it." He tapped his head. "Chiseled in stone."

Lorraine studied Bastian's face—the dark eyebrows, the square jaw, the oh-so-kissable lips. Sure, he was gorgeous. But he was a liar and a creep. He was also her only route to vindication. For better or for worse, she needed him.

She had come here to uncover exactly how Bastian had known that Gloria was performing at the Green Mill. She hadn't told him, and yet she was the one getting all the blame. Her friendship with Gloria was in the garbage; Marcus wouldn't look at her, let alone talk to her.

In the past, it had felt good to be bad—especially since Raine was always in the shadow of prissy, perfect Gloria. But who had she become? Did she even *like* that Lorraine anymore?

Maybe Marcus was right and Lorraine Dyer was worthy only of scorn. She had crossed a line somewhere, and now something had to change. Whoever that despicable girl was who had sat on this couch two weeks ago, kissing her best friend's fiancé, it was no longer Lorraine. She was going to change. Starting now.

Bastian walked over to the couch with the two glasses of brandy and stood over her. He looked handsome and smug. She hated him more than she'd realized. "What brings you to my neck of the woods? Didn't get enough of me last time?" He handed her a glass, which she immediately placed on the coffee table.

He sat down next to her, stretching out his arms and legs so that he crowded her against the armrest. "You don't mind, do you?" he asked, lighting a cigar. "Oh, I forgot—you're not attracted to men who treat you well."

Lorraine slid to the corner. He seemed to be plastered already. "Why is Gloria under the impression that you don't drink?"

"Oh, it's more than just that. Gloria also thinks"—he counted on the fingers of his raised hand—"that I do not smoke, or go to speakeasies, or stay out late, or . . . indulge in other extracurricular activities," he said, sliding closer to Lorraine. "Activities I know *you're* always game for."

Lorraine was speechless. Bastian was even more of an oilcan than she'd thought. Contempt from Gloria and Marcus she could accept, but from Bastian—it was too much. "You— I— You're despicable."

He just laughed. "Me? I'm sorry, but am I misreading things? Here you are again, late at night, full of gin, on my sofa. What is a man to think?"

Too infuriated to speak, Lorraine began to stand up. But Bastian's hand shot out and caught her arm and yanked her back down.

"Get your hands off me!" she cried.

"You didn't seem to mind before."

Lorraine pulled her arm from his grasp and straightened her dress. She had to stay focused. "I'm not here to play games with you, Bastian," she said. "I came here only to find out who told you about Gloria, and then I'll leave you alone."

Bastian threw back his drink. "Oh, is *that* all you want?"

"Please," she said, trying to appeal to whatever goodness was buried deep inside him. "Gloria thinks I ratted her out—"

"Correction: Everyone thinks you ratted her out."

"I don't care about everyone! I care about my best friend. Gloria's friendship is important to me."

"So important that you'd consider sleeping with her fiancé?" he said, exhaling a trail of smoke rings.

"How could you even—" She could feel her cheeks flushing. Maybe this was a better tactic. You caught more flies with honey. "Bastian, please try to understand the situation I'm in. I'll do anything—"

He leaned forward. "Anything?"

She made herself smile. "Well, *almost* anything."

Bastian leered and stubbed out his cigar. "I'm a businessman, Lorraine," he said, placing his hand on her knee. "I speak in the language of transactions. Goods and prices and fees for services rendered. Now, understand, I am more than willing to negotiate with you."

Lorraine caught his hand before it reached her thigh and dug her nails into his flesh. "Tell me who it was," she said, trying to push him off.

"I only believe in fair trade." He twisted her hand back, pinning her against the sofa. She thrashed wildly. "You're a real bearcat," Bastian said.

"You have no idea," Lorraine said, kneeing him in the groin. Bastian yelped like a little dog and released her.

Lorraine peeled herself off the sofa. Nothing was worth the price of her dignity.

She downed the brandy. "Thanks for the drink," she said, slamming the glass back on the table.

"Do you know why your little boy crush Marcus will never want you?" Bastian gasped, still curled in a ball. "Because you're easy, Lorraine. You've got easy written all over your face."

Coming to Bastian's had been a complete and utter mistake.

"You don't deserve a girl like Gloria," Lorraine said. "And I'll make sure she finds that out. I'll tell her everything you're up to, and let's see if she still wants to marry you then."

"What makes you believe she'll listen to you now?" Bastian asked. "She won't even speak to you."

Lorraine didn't bother to answer. She turned and walked out the door.

◆◆◆

Lorraine ran. She slipped off her heels and ran in her stockinged feet all the way up North Lake Shore Drive and didn't stop until she rounded the corner onto Astor Street and spotted the Carmodys' looming estate.

But the house was dark. Of course. Tonight was the seniors' Honor Society induction ceremony, which Gloria was sure to be attending, along with her mother. Lorraine had already gotten into Barnard; she didn't need her Honor Society key. It didn't unlock anything, anyway.

Maybe this was a blessing in disguise.

Lorraine wasn't an avid reader of crime novels, but she had pieced together this much about the betrayer:

1. she had to be in Gloria's inner circle;
2. she had to know Bastian Grey; and
3. she had to have a motivation to harm Gloria.

*She, she, she* . . . What made her think the traitor was female? A man could easily have wanted to break up Bastian and Gloria's engagement, if there was a romantic interest at stake. But this had all the markings of girl-jealousy. Lorraine had a gut instinct about it. Some might call it intuition, but Lorraine knew it was just one bad girl recognizing the work of another.

Since Lorraine was here anyway, she might as well take advantage of Gloria's absence. She put her heels back on and straightened her dress. She needed to find something—a single clue, a smoking gun, a note about Bastian—anything to prove that Lorraine wasn't the one who'd spilled about the Green Mill.

The Carmodys' tired old French maid answered when Lorraine knocked on the door.

Claudine was a wispy slip of a thing who had a rodent-like distrust of everyone around her. Lorraine prayed that the scandal between her and Gloria hadn't filtered down to the hired help just yet, even though they usually seemed to know everything before anyone else. *"Oui, Mademoiselle Lorraine?"*

*"Claudine, est-ce que je visite la chambre à Mademoiselle Gloria? Je,* um, forgot *mon* book there *le* other *nuit* and we have *un examen* tomorrow."

Claudine regarded her suspiciously but let her in all the same.

The house was unnaturally quiet except for the sharp *tock* of Lorraine's heels on the parquet floor. The grand hall was dark with shadow, the lights dimmed, and Lorraine was grateful when she reached the carpeted stairs. She glided up silently.

Just before hurrying into Gloria's room, she paused. A door on the right, cracked open an inch, had caught her attention. The bedroom of Clara Knowles. Sweet, innocent, goody-two-shoes Clara Knowles. A girl who seemed to be so clueless, so harmless, yet had somehow managed to win over Marcus—and everyone else—as if she had cast a voodoo spell.

The spell had even worked on Lorraine, hadn't it? When they had been getting ready for the club together, Clara had pretended she had never seen kohl before. And then with the help of a few tips from Raine, Clara had suddenly metamorphosed from dowdy caterpillar into va-va-voom butterfly? Fat chance.

That night, Clara had carried herself like a real flapper, as if it were second nature. Her confidence couldn't have come from just a slash of red lipstick. Where was the quaint country girl then?

Something was wrong with this picture, and Lorraine was determined to find out.

Clara's room looked surprisingly normal—and boring. A few snoozy clothes carelessly strewn on the bed, a few jars of makeup out of place on the vanity. On her nightstand was a copy of Fitzgerald's *Flappers and Philosophers,* Wharton's *The Age of Innocence*, and Edith Hull's *The Sheik*—saucy! And, over her bed, a poster for Douglas Fairbanks's *Robin Hood.* Fairbanks—now, there was a man.

Lorraine pulled her eyes away from the poster. What was she even looking for? If Clara truly had been so savvy as to pull the wool over everyone's eyes, she certainly would know how to hide her tracks and burn the evidence.

The grandfather clock downstairs chimed ten o'clock. The Honor Society ceremony was sure to have ended, and the Carmodys would be arriving home any second. She had to work fast.

Nightstand first: vanilla body lotion, coconut cuticle oil, blemish cream, a playbill from the theater—boring, boring, *boring.*

On to the next: underwear. Lorraine felt no shame digging through Clara's garters and her brassieres. Sometimes you had to stoop in order to rise. Probably too obvious a place to hide anything important—what did Lorraine have in her own underwear drawers? A pair of BVDs from the beautiful actor she had almost lost her virginity to; a napkin on which Marcus had once sketched a drawing.

There! In the back right corner, amid a sea of bland cream and beige, was a pair of lacy fire-engine-red panties. Jackpot. Lorraine extracted them carefully. And what came fluttering out? A photograph worth a trillion words.

A flapper with some handsome swell in a speakeasy somewhere.

No, wait—the flapper was *Clara,* with . . . Harris Brown. Lorraine gave a low whistle. Clara had been a full-on flapper. She was in a beaded headdress displaying a pixie bob, her vampish face tipped back in drunken revelry. He was kissing her neck, holding a cigarette. She was leaning across him, her bare legs splayed out across the booth. The table was littered with bottles of booze. On the back of the photo, written in tiny black lettering:

*Times Square*
*September 1922*

Oh! Clara *wasn't* a rube from some little town in the middle of nowhere. She'd been to New York. She was a party girl—a flapper supreme. And judging from the looks of things, she'd had some sort of romantic tryst with Harris

Brown. Country Clara was just an act—a good one, Lorraine admitted to herself, but an act nonetheless.

What would everyone think when they found out that Chicago's newest, sweetest socialite was a boozer and a woman of the world? What would Mrs. Carmody think when she found out her niece was taking her for a sucker?

Lorraine knew that where you uncovered one lie, others were sure to be lurking: If anybody was down and dirty enough to tell Bastian about Gloria and the Green Mill, it was the vixen in this photograph. Lorraine did a little jig for joy. Clara thought she could outsmart Lorraine Dyer, leave Lorraine taking the blame for everything. Well, Clara's show was finished.

What would Marcus think when he learned that the pure, virginal maiden he'd fallen for—a girl he'd originally meant to compromise—had seen more scandal than he would in his entire lifetime?

*"Mademoiselle?"* Claudine's mouselike voice squeaked from the doorway.

Lorraine clasped her hands together in prayer, the photograph between them. "*Je pense que* Gloria gave *le book* to Clara, *parce que* I did not find it in *sa chambre.*" She pointed nervously to the stack of books on Clara's nightstand. *"Quel dommage!"*

*"Oui, dommage,"* Claudine repeated, not budging from the

door. "You know, my English, it is better than your French? You may speak in the English to me. I understand."

Claudine escorted Lorraine all the way down the grand staircase to the front door. "Oh, and Claudine!" Lorraine exclaimed on the front step. "Don't worry about telling Gloria I was here. I'd rather tell her myself, *non?* I mean, *s'il vous plaît.*"

Claudine blinked. "As you wish, *mademoiselle.* Gloria, she doesn't listen to me when I speak to her anyway."

As soon as the door shut behind her, Lorraine peeled the photograph off her sticky palm and slipped it into her purse.

The temperature had dropped significantly, and a November wind sliced through the night air. The moon was full and fat and orange, and as she walked the few blocks home, Lorraine felt the first hint of winter rattling in her bones. Yet there was a strange heat boiling within her: the picture of Clara in her black-fringed purse.

Her encounter with Bastian tonight had left *him*—not Lorraine this time—the hurt one. Her visit to the Carmodys' had left *Lorraine*—not Clara this time—with the upper hand.

And so with each step toward home, Lorraine made her plans and swore on the harvest moon: She would never be anyone's fool again.

# GLORIA

It was lunchtime at Laurelton Prep, and Gloria was sitting by herself, picking at a chicken croquette. She wished she'd joined geriatric Miss Tucker in the home ec room, learning how to sew a button, instead of forcing herself to endure the dining hall: the tables around her, packed with gossiping, chewing girls, now seemed unbearable.

Over the past two weeks, she had made a habit of hiding out in the library during her lunch period, a much-needed forty-three-minute respite from the unending cattiness of her fellow students. Today the library was closed for some reason, and because of the rule that kept students on school grounds during lunch, Gloria'd had no other option.

She was trying to read but for the past ten minutes had

been stuck on the same line from Edna St. Vincent Millay's *A Few Figs from Thistles.*

Every line sent her mind spinning off with thoughts of Jerome. She spent her days thinking about him. *Obsessing* over him. How she hadn't seen him since that night at his apartment, a week before. How the longer she was apart from him, the more she doubted what had transpired there: Had those words—that she *wanted* him—really come out of her own mouth? Had they really, finally kissed? A kiss that was so perfect and so pure that even now the memory of it made her weak.

If only tonight, at seven-thirty sharp, wasn't the engagement party that her mother had been planning since the day Gloria met Bastian.

Gloria felt something hit the back of her head, followed by obnoxious snickering. She froze. *Don't stoop to their level and turn around,* she told herself. *Keep your eyes on your book.* But then she felt it again.

Spitballs.

Gloria turned, her cheeks warming, to face her nemeses: Anna Thomas, Stella Marks, and Amelia Stone. Those braided, brunette prom-trotters were out to make Gloria's life a living hell. She was in no mood for this today.

Gloria extracted the two gooey white wads of paper from her bob. "I think you lost something," she said, flinging the spitballs back at them.

"Oh no, those are yours to keep," said Stella, her thin lip curling up and revealing the gap between her front teeth. "But speaking of losing, I think I saw your dignity sitting in the lost and found? You might want to consider picking it up."

The girls broke into another round of laughter.

"I guess you aren't going to audition for the school musical anymore?" Amelia asked.

"Of course I am," Gloria retorted, though she knew she probably wouldn't. All through high school, it had been her dream to star in the musical, open to seniors only. This year Laurelton was putting on Rogers and Hart's *Poor Little Ritz Girl*. But if she couldn't have Jerome at the piano, she didn't want to sing at all. Still, she wasn't about to tell the girls that. "Why wouldn't I audition?"

"Well, there aren't any roles for *colored* boys," Anna said, with a slurp of her milk. "Since we know how much you love them."

This was just too much. Gloria closed her book. "You're right," she said, her face growing hotter by the second, "I do *love* them."

She stormed out of the dining hall and down the corridor, away from all those wretched girls. She couldn't stay in this school another second.

But there'd be no getting out of the engagement party tonight. She had already successfully apologized to her mother, convincing her it had all just been a common case of cold feet. And she had apologized to Bastian, reassuring him that she would never sing in that "den of sin" again. One sickeningly phony "I'm *so* sorry" after another.

But she would never, for the life of her, apologize to—

"Gloria!" Lorraine was standing in the hallway, right in front of her locker.

Gloria tensed up. "May I please get to my locker?"

Lorraine looked like a haggard scarecrow, her cheeks gaunt, dark purple shadows beneath her eyes. "Please, will you just listen to me, so I can explain that I never—"

"There's nothing to explain!" Gloria snapped.

"But if you'll just let me talk to you, before your party tonight—"

"My *party*?" Gloria glared in disbelief. "I hope to God you know better than to show up to my party tonight. For your own sake," she said, reaching behind Lorraine's back. "Now, please get out of my way." She shoved Lorraine hard to the right.

Gloria grabbed her coat, slammed her locker shut, and charged down the hallway and out of the building, not caring whether the headmistress or anyone else saw her break the school rule. She didn't stop until she had hopped into a taxi and was speeding uptown toward the only person she wanted, needed, to see right now.

◆◆◆

She was chilled to the bone when she stepped out onto North Broadway. The night before, there had been a brief rain, and then the temperature had plummeted, coating the streets in slick sheets of treacherous ice.

Gloria didn't realize how nervous she was until the taxi rolled up in front of the club. She knew he would be there—Friday-afternoon rehearsals were mandatory—but she hadn't been back to the Green Mill since that fateful night when Bastian had exposed her as a liar, a sham, a spoiled brat playing dress-up.

And now she had returned. She took a deep breath and knocked on the unmarked entrance.

The familiar slit slid open, revealing a brown eye. "It's Gloria, the—the ex-torch?"

"What do you want?"

"I . . . I've come to see"—she was about to say Jerome, then realized that might not be such a good idea—"to see about something I left in the club. The last night I sang here?"

The Eye squinted at her for a second; then its owner said gruffly, "Don't go anywhere."

The slit closed. Which gave her just enough time to remove her engagement ring. Taking it off had once been the first step of her costume change—when she was in the throes of rehearsals. Now, sliding it off and tucking it into her school satchel, she felt like the fake that she always had been.

The door opened, and Gloria stepped into the familiar darkness.

The music was a magnetic force, pulling her toward it. She stood quietly in a back corner, enraptured, soaking in the sound that had been filtering through her dreams at night. Jerome's body swayed with the slinky syncopated rhythms, his eyes closed, as if the notes transported him to a place unknown to anyone but him. She could watch him play forever.

His eyes flickered open and he caught sight of her.

At first she couldn't tell whether he was smiling at her or it was a trick of the light. But no, he *was* smiling at her. The band wasn't yet dressed for tonight's performance; they looked as if they'd just stepped in off the street. Jerome and the bass player were wearing tweed caps, and everyone wore khaki pants or dungarees and wrinkled linen shirts that looked as if they'd been slept in.

The song ended. Jerome stood up from the piano bench and was about to step off the stage when the bass player stopped him and whispered something in his ear. Jerome looked back at Gloria, but this time, the smile was gone.

Gloria hung back. Suddenly she felt awkward, standing there still in the gray and white of her school uniform. She didn't belong here. And then it dawned on her: *She had no place.* She didn't belong anywhere. Not here, not in school, not back on Astor Street. Nowhere.

Jerome came over, his hands casually tucked into his trouser pockets. "Hey," he greeted her coolly. No kiss, no touch. "I'm surprised to see you."

"I know I should have told you, but—"

*"Surprised,"* he continued, cutting her off, "because I thought your big party was tonight. I saw it in the paper."

Gloria felt her body go cold. "It is," she said flatly. "But I wanted to see you. If that's all right. I can leave if you—"

"No." He took a step closer, and she could see something in his dark eyes, like a secret unsaid between the two of them. Then he whispered, "I've missed you."

Gloria barely had time to let this sink in—even though his words were exactly what she needed to hear—because Evan, the trumpet player, stomped over.

"We gotta wrap this up before they start getting ready for tonight," Evan said to Jerome, without so much as a glance toward Gloria.

"Hey, Evan," she said. "You sounded really good up there just now."

Evan rocked back on his heels. "Why is she here?" he said to Jerome.

"Beats me," Jerome said, crossing his arms. "But I'm thinking the same question."

"I lost one of my grandmother's earrings that night," Gloria explained, touching her bare earlobe. It was the truth: She hadn't realized it until she got home, after she'd managed to stop crying and look in the mirror at her distorted face. "It was my good-luck charm," she added, which was also true. Until now.

"Yeah, well, good luck finding it." Evan smirked, then lightly punched Jerome's arm. "Remember, first set's early tonight—Carlito's trouble boys are coming for dinner. Be here at seven."

"Got it." Jerome tipped his tweed newsboy cap as Evan walked out of the club. Jerome eyed the stage, where the bass player and drummer were still dawdling. "This way," he said to Gloria.

She followed Jerome to the stage. "Hey, Chuck. Hey, Tommy," she said sweetly.

"Hey," they both mumbled back.

"Gloria lost her earring," Jerome explained. "So we're just gonna take a quick peek backstage, see if she dropped it back there. All right?"

Chuck raised his eyebrows.

"Come on," Jerome said to her, walking to the backstage door.

Gloria hung her head as she passed the stage, embarrassed. She knew she owed them all an apology—and an explanation—but this was not the time or place.

Jerome held the door open, and Gloria, eyes still fixed on the floor, stepped into the pitch-black, narrow hallway. The door slammed behind them. For a split second, she was reminded of her first voice lesson with Jerome. The first time they had ever been alone. The first time Jerome had ever touched her—

Something touched her waist, and she jumped, gasping loudly.

"Shhhhh," came Jerome's voice, at a rock-bottom register, as she realized it was his hand. Then both hands, pushing her gently against the wall. She wrapped her arms around him, clutching the broad muscles of his back. His body radiated a soothing warmth, and Gloria felt something expand deep within her.

She felt his lips, gentle against her cheek. She couldn't stop herself from meeting his lips with her own.

She broke off at last and whispered, "What are we doing?" She opened her eyes and tried to make out his face in the dark.

"Looking for your earring," he said, tugging at her earlobe with his teeth.

Gloria squirmed, letting him linger there for a second longer before taking hold of his biceps and pushing him back. "I'm serious," she said. "What are we doing, Jerome?"

It was all too much for her, these extremes. To go from her prep school dining hall to *this*—when she didn't even know what *this* was—and then off to the engagement party tonight. And Jerome, from cold to hot in the snap of a finger.

Jerome sighed in frustration. She felt his body next to her, leaning against the brick wall. "What would you say if I took you on a date? A hot date."

"Now?" She couldn't tell whether he was serious or kidding.

"Don't worry, I'll get you home before you turn back into a pumpkin."

◆◆◆

"Are you sure this is all right with you?" he asked, holding her numb fingers.

Gloria gazed out at the frozen pond filled with skaters. "I—I—" she stuttered, unable to get the words out of her mouth. "What happened to the 'hot' part of the date?"

"Pond froze up early this year. We ain't even had a proper snow yet."

When Jerome had whisked her away from the Green Mill, Gloria hadn't been imagining anything in particular for their date. But an ice-skating rink had been the furthest thing from her mind. Not that she minded, of course—the important thing was that they were spending time together. After three weeks apart, she was finally in his presence, in his arms. It didn't matter what they did.

She checked her watch, making sure she could return home in time to play the role of dutiful daughter and soon-to-be-wife. It was early yet—not quite four.

"No, is it all right with *you* that . . . you know what I mean." Jerome lifted her cupped hands to his lips and filled them with his warm breath.

She paused, her eyes still glued to the frozen pond. "I haven't skated in years."

Gloria hadn't ice-skated since she was twelve and her father had taken her to a private gala in the Chicago Arena. But she knew this was not what Jerome was hinting at.

"You know what, why don't we go somewhere else that's less—"

"No!" She stopped him, tugging at his arm. "If you can teach me how to sing, then I'm sure skating will be a cinch."

"Yeah, I'm sure you'll fit right in," he said, pulling her in the direction of the skate shack. Not one white person was skating on that ice. In fact, not one white person was anywhere in sight.

Jerome had taken her to the South Side. But after all, where were they supposed to go and be together—high tea at the Blackstone? It was absolutely out of the question to be with him anyplace where white people predominated. Being around Jerome at the Green Mill was one thing. He'd been a musician, she'd been a singer—sort of. But being with him in public was another story entirely: holding hands, touching, kissing . . . It simply couldn't happen. A black boy and a white girl would draw a whole lot of attention—and not the good kind.

Boys and girls whizzed past them, running and laughing with each other but pausing to notice her. She felt their gaze, but in a much different way than when she'd performed.

She looked at Jerome. Was this what life was like for him every day in places that were mostly white? How did one deal with it—with standing out when all one wanted to do was blend in?

They sat on a bench, and Jerome tied her skates for her. He must have sensed her unease, because he leaned in and whispered, "I've seen you face much tougher crowds than this before. And they loved you, remember?"

"It seems as if all that never happened now, doesn't it?" she said, grasping his arm as they wobbled toward the pond. Twice she almost fell flat on her face, and they weren't even on the ice yet. "As if it was part of some dream."

"How about now? This doesn't feel real to you?"

"I don't know what is real anymore."

Jerome took her hand. "Then let's see if we can change that."

Holding hands, they stood at the edge of the pond. As the skaters circled past, she could feel their eyes—couples, parents, kids—all, all of them, homing in on her and Jerome. She could hear the whispers, too, not so different from the first day she'd gone back to school after the Green Mill Incident.

What was she doing here? If she could barely survive being stared at during a fun activity like ice-skating, how could she possibly consider life with Jerome beyond the rink? She didn't know any mixed-race couples—did they even exist?

Without another word, he led her onto the ice.

Jerome pulled on her arm and slingshotted her past him. She couldn't help herself: She shrieked.

Behind her, he hooted and scrambled to catch up while she struggled to keep her balance. And then she had it—she was upright, and it wasn't all *that* hard, was it?—and he was beside her, still laughing. "What's so funny?" she asked, but he only laughed harder.

And she was laughing, too.

Maybe it was her easy glide across the ice, or the biting chill of the air against her face, or the soothing warmth of his hand in hers—but suddenly, her mind emptied until it was as smooth and placid as the ice beneath her feet. She felt the way she had in those first few uninterrupted moments on the Green Mill stage: blissful and full of something that felt like promise.

Then it began to snow.

Tentatively at first, a few soft flakes from the whitewashed sky. The skaters all stopped, wherever they were and whoever they were with, and just looked up. Palms extended, eyes filled with wonder, childish squeals of delight. In that holy moment, Gloria experienced the same joy as everyone around her.

By the time they'd circled the pond a few more times, the snowflakes had become the first hint of a snowstorm. The first of winter, earlier than usual this year. It wasn't even Thanksgiving yet.

Gloria and Jerome tumbled off the ice, out of breath and laughing as though nothing in life had ever been more fun. They crashed onto the nearest bench and leaned against each other in exhaustion.

Snowflakes caught like crystals in Jerome's long black lashes. Gloria impulsively kissed his eyelids, the wintry flakes melting in her mouth.

"You shouldn't do that in public," he said, looking around

to see if anyone had noticed. "What did you go and do that for?"

Gloria shrugged. "For my hot date."

He crouched in front of her and began unlacing her skates. "You know what they say about the first snow?"

"Hmmmm . . . a cue to migrate south for the winter?"

"If only."

"Why, you don't like it here?"

"That's one off," he said, moving to her other skate. "This town is a part of me, whether I like it or not. My family is here, jazz is here. But I've got a traveler's blood pumping in my veins—I'm ready to shake things up somewhere else, like—"

"New York?"

"Yes!" he said, seeming surprised by Gloria's suggestion. "That's exactly where I had in mind. What made you say that?"

"I didn't think you meant Cuba. Though now"—she shivered—"even that doesn't sound like such a bad idea." She paused for a moment. "But couldn't you just see us in New York?"

*"Us?"*

She didn't know what she had meant by it, only that she liked the way it sounded. *Us.* "Can't you see it?" she asked. "Taking our act to a brand-new city? To Greenwich Village, or Harlem, even—we would be the talk of the town. J.J.'s Jazz Band, featuring Gloria Rose."

"I like the way it sounds."

"And with nobody to hold us back—no parents, no Green Mill mobsters, no catty former best friends, no—"

"Fiancés?"

It hung in the air like a dirty word. "Don't talk about him—I don't want to ruin this perfect date."

"Perfect?" he said. "You're telling me, Miss Gloria Rose, that *this* is your perfect date?"

"Yes," Gloria said. "That's precisely what I'm telling you."

"I know a way to make it even more perfect." He raised himself up. "How 'bout some hot cocoa?"

"Now you're speaking my language," she said.

He led her to a small shack next to the ice-skate rental that sold coffee and hot cocoa for two cents a cup. As they stepped up into the line, the girl working the stand looked startled.

"Well, look who decides to show up." She appeared to be about Gloria's age, with bewitching almond-shaped eyes that glistened beneath a black knit cap. She was wrapped in a battered black peacoat.

"Max." Jerome shifted his weight and dropped Gloria's hand. "How are you?"

"That question's coming a little too late, don't you think?" she said. "Would have been nice if you'd asked it a month ago."

"I've been real busy—"

"Yeah, I can see that." Her gaze shifted sharply to Gloria. "Too busy playing with little rich white girls?"

"Careful, Max. Don't talk about things you know nothing about."

"You're right, I know nothing but what I heard—about some redhead shacking up at your apartment last week. At night." She cut her eyes at Gloria. "Must have been total make-believe."

"We came here for a hot drink, not for your icy tongue." His voice had dropped at least an octave.

"I'm sorry, but read the sign: We only serve hot cocoa and coffee. *Dark* drinks. *Black* drinks."

Dumbfounded, Gloria stared at the girl. She had asked for "real" and she'd gotten it, hadn't she? She wasn't welcome here; she and Jerome weren't welcome anywhere. And this was nothing but some stupid girl selling hot chocolate.

"It's fine," Gloria said. "I'm not even thirsty—"

"No, it is *not* fine!" Jerome threw a nickel onto the counter, rage glistening in his eyes. "You will serve us two hot cocoas, just like you've been serving everyone else." Max was about to respond when Jerome placed an arm defiantly around Gloria's shoulder. "Now."

Max clucked her tongue but placed two cups of cocoa on the counter. She made a small gesture of presentation with her gloved hands. "I hope it's to your liking," she said smugly to Gloria. "Enjoy it while it lasts, honey."

Jerome took their cups and they headed back toward the street in silence. It was dark now, and the snow was still lightly falling. Except for the distant squeals of the remaining skaters and the occasional passing car, an eerie quiet had settled over the frozen city. Jerome handed her one paper cup.

"I don't even want this anymore," she said.

"That girl, she's a friend of my sister's," he began apologetically. "I don't want you to think she was anything—"

"You don't have to explain. I don't even want to know." And really, she didn't. She'd never actually considered the other women in Jerome's life. Surely there had been many; he was surrounded by throngs of them at the Green Mill every night. But who was she to talk? She had a diamond burning a hole in her purse—

The engagement party! She had completely forgotten! She could not be late, under any circumstances. It was 5:15. If she hopped into a taxi now, she could be home by 5:35, in the shower by 5:45, hair dried by 6:15, dressed by—

"Come here." Jerome tugged her by her coat sleeve into an alley off the street, then looked carefully around to make sure they were alone.

He kissed her softly. "You know, I never told you what they say about the first snow," he said. "Whoever you're with during that first snow of winter will be the person who will change your life in the year to come."

She laughed. "You made that up."

"Hey, Red, where's your faith?"

They left the alley and went to the corner, and he hailed a taxi for her. He took the paper cup she was still holding from her hand. "Now, go enjoy your party," he said softly.

As the taxi drove off, she watched him through the window. He poured their drinks onto the ground, turning the snow the color of cocoa, before walking away.

◆◆◆

"I *can't* do this."

Gloria slumped on the edge of the bathtub, wrapped in a peach-colored towel, her hair dripping water down her back. A half hour before the party and she had made no move to get dressed. "I don't have a fake smile left in me."

"Take a deep breath," Clara said, inhaling dramatically to demonstrate. She had been reading aloud the list of all the reporters expected to be in attendance. Now she folded it up and tossed it on the marble vanity. "I won't attempt to fix your feelings, but the least I can do is fix your appearance. Don't move an inch!"

"Where would I go?" Gloria mumbled as Clara whizzed out of the room.

Gloria had been doing just fine until she'd begun to shave her legs in the shower. She'd spotted a ripe bruise blooming on her knee—right where she had fallen on the ice with Jerome—and her mind had gone back to the afternoon. Bastian would *never* have taken her ice-skating.

Sopping wet, Gloria dragged herself out of the bathroom and belly-flopped onto her bed.

"Up! Up! Up!" Clara clapped her hands briskly as she

reentered the room and quickly shut the door. "Didn't I say not to move?" She climbed onto the bed and jumped up and down.

"I get the point!" Gloria forced herself to sit up.

"I brought the goods; all you need to do is sit still and do what I say." Clara waved a flask under Gloria's nose. "You need a dose of medicine."

Gloria seized the flask, turning it over in admiration. It was brushed gold, with a butterfly engraved across the front; *C & H* was etched on the stopper. "Where did you get this?" she asked, unscrewing the top and sniffing the contents.

Clara made a *tut-tut* sound. "No time for asking questions, only time for following orders. Now, drink up."

Gloria did as she was told. It felt as if her esophagus had been swiped with the lighted end of a cigarette. "Are you trying to poison me?" she demanded, coughing. "What the hell is this?"

"The Green Fairy." Clara sniffed at the flask herself. "Though why they call it green when it tastes like black licorice, I have no idea."

"Are you speaking English?"

"Absinthe, my dear." Clara repositioned Gloria at the edge of the bed.

Gloria could feel the alcohol spreading through her, making her feel loose-limbed and calm. She could almost feel it in her fingertips. "I can't be owled in front of those reporters!"

"Would you rather they see you in the charming state you're in now?"

"Point taken." Gloria swigged another mouthful.

Clara set a small black leather valise on the bed and unlocked the brass clasps. Inside was a veritable cosmetics shop: powder tins, lipstick tubes, rouge pots, foundation jars, rows of pencils and brushes.

Gloria blinked. "Are you starting a stage career?"

Clara laughed. "This family is only big enough for one showgirl. Now close your eyes." She unscrewed a jar of milkweed cream and rubbed it onto Gloria's cheeks.

"This stuff smells vile."

"The things we do for beauty," Clara said, dabbing and blending concealer under Gloria's eyes and around her nose.

"Can I ask you something?" Gloria said.

"As your makeup artist, or as your life advisor?"

"As my cousin."

"Now, that's a hat I haven't worn in a while." Clara dipped a puff into translucent powder and blew on it, filling the air between them with a chalky cloud.

"What about for Marcus?" Gloria asked curiously. "What hat do you wear for him?"

"I thought we were talking about *you* right now."

"We are, in a roundabout way," Gloria said, spotting the eyelash brush that was nearing her face. "And please don't poke my eye out with that thing."

"I'll tell you why I like Marcus." Clara stroked black

mascara over Gloria's pale lashes. "With Marcus, I feel I can be the girl I *want* to be. Not *was* in the past, or *should* be, or whatever . . ."

"Are we talking about Marcus Eastman here?" Gloria felt the exact same way when she was with Jerome, but that didn't change the impossible circumstances.

Clara dragged Gloria to her feet. "Come on, let's get you dressed," she said, leading Gloria behind the Oriental dressing screen and lowering Gloria's dress over the edge like a descending curtain.

It was the most extraordinary dress Gloria had ever seen. A sheer champagne netting flowed over intricately woven gold silk, with a metallic chiffon sash at the dropped waist that tied in a bow at the hip. The skirt was a billowing waterfall of chiffon, ending at her ankles. The dress was elegant but still true to the flapper's look-at-me appeal—although Gloria had to admit she hadn't felt like a flapper since her last night at the Green Mill.

"So I've been thinking about your difficult situation," Clara began. "Listen, love is a roll of the dice, just like anything else. And sometimes, love alone is not enough to sustain a life together—in the same way that money or status alone is not enough. Look at Bastian. Look at your parents! Money and status have done nothing for them but tear them apart."

Gloria poked her head around the screen, the dress halfway on. "So you're saying I lose either way?" Clara's eyes now looked as stormy as Gloria felt. "Are you all right?"

"I told you: No time for questions!" Clara shooed her back behind the screen. "Except for one, and I get to ask it: Who will ultimately make you happiest?"

Gloria emerged once again, fully dressed this time, and Clara gasped. "Oh, Gloria!"

"You like it?"

Gloria was about to dash over to the pier glass in the corner of her room, but Clara stopped her. "Don't look yet! We need to fix your hair first." Gloria followed her into the bathroom.

She thought about Bastian, and she thought about Jerome. This whole question of love versus duty suddenly seemed ridiculous. It wasn't that simple. Was love "right"? Was duty "right"? She looked at her nails and knew her answer. In the end, duty didn't stand a chance. The love she felt for Jerome—and *yes,* it was love, why pretend it was anything else?—defied everything she had been taught to think or feel or do. A future with Bastian would be unbearable.

Clara massaged some pomade into her bob. Then she spun Gloria around and stepped aside. "Now would you take a look at yourself?"

Gloria looked into the mirror and sucked in her breath. "Clara!" she exclaimed, leaning closer to the mirror in disbelief. "How did you *do* this?"

Clara dusted a speck of powder off Gloria's cheek. "It's all you, babycakes. You have an inner glow."

Gloria did. Her cheeks radiated a peachy luminescence,

seeming to brighten her eyes to a spearmint green and her hair to a gold-flecked copper. It was as if she were seeing herself in color for the first time. "Are you sure this isn't the absinthe?"

"Hold that thought!" Clara dashed out and came back a second later with the butterfly flask. She placed it in Gloria's palm. "I want you to keep this."

Gloria traced the mysterious *C & H*. "Clara, I can't—"

"Consider it my engagement gift to you. Tuck it somewhere safe, like your garter, and use in times of need," Clara said.

Gloria impulsively hugged Clara. "Thank you," she said into the shoulder of Clara's dress. She was finally grateful to have Clara here. "Thank you for everything."

"Hey now, don't smudge your face! Or my dress!" Clara teased, holding Gloria at arm's length. "Last word of advice for the night," she said. "Make up your mind and never look back."

Gloria nodded. Clara was right about life and love. Gloria was going to have to make a choice, and she was going to have to make it quickly—with no regrets. Before an irreversible choice was made for her.

# CLARA

Clara leaned over the banister and peered down the stairs.

The house was alive with people and noise—hundreds of guests eating, chattering, and laughing; bright darts of music from Isham Jones and his all-white jazz orchestra, specially hired for the occasion. Usually, the place was so empty: only her, Gloria, and Aunt Bea—and the help. Tonight, however, the house was thick with fancy faces—gray-haired old members of the Chicago elite, gray-faced friends and family of Sebastian's, pie-eyed acquaintances of the Carmodys. Even a few local celebrities had been invited, but no one expected them to show up.

Gloria's engagement party had begun.

From her perch at the top of the grand staircase, Clara

could see it all. In the foyer, Mrs. Carmody's man, Archibald, had roped off space to either side of the door, where he herded the reporters and photographers. With every new guest he announced, there was a stutter of light as a dozen explosions of flash powder went off, and then the shouts of the reporters trying to get a choice quote for their stories. In the house proper, waiters in white tuxedos glided masterfully among the guests, carrying silver trays of drinks and appetizers raised high on their gloved hands.

And the guests themselves were resplendent. There were girls on the verge of flapperdom in sparkly dresses, bronze and gold and silver, with long white gloves on their arms and pearls looped around their necks, and older women swathed in floor-length gowns of georgette, crepe, and satin, their hair done up, diamonds and other jewels dripping from their ears and fingers. The boys and men looked all the same in white tie and tails.

Claudine had transformed the front sitting room into a hat-check room. Even from here, Clara could hear the poor girl crying out *"Oui, monsieur!"* again and again. And on every surface, piles upon piles of hothouse flowers: plush white peonies, statuesque white calla lilies, soft petals of purest white everywhere.

"Oh God," Gloria said, coming up behind Clara and standing next to her. "Save me."

Clara gave her cousin a nudge. "Just remember to stay calm. This is *your* party, after all."

Gloria said nothing, just gazed at the mob below and looked sick.

"Come on," Clara coaxed her. "We can't hide up here forever."

Together, the girls descended the staircase.

Their descent caused a ripple in the crowd below, a low *"Ohhhh"* that seemed to fill the foyer and drive everyone to silence. "There they are!" someone shouted. And then there was clapping—such loud and sustained applause that it seemed to rock Gloria midstride. For a moment she looked nakedly terrified.

"Just smile for the cameras," Clara said.

The clapping continued until they'd reached the bottom of the staircase. It was a long way down. Clara was about to say, "See? That wasn't so bad," when someone shouted out: "Smile, Gloria!"

*"Smile, Gloria,"* Clara repeated in a silly voice. Gloria turned and looked at her, and they both started laughing. What a ridiculous scene this was. An engagement party for a girl who didn't want to get married—because she was in love with a black musician, who, if he'd shown up tonight, would have been turned away the moment he stepped onto the property.

Bastian had been waiting at the bottom of the steps, looking especially tall and broad-shouldered. His face was smooth shaven, his dark hair brushed back in a wave. He took Gloria's hand, and the couple posed for yet more photographs. Then they were engulfed by the crowd.

Suddenly, all the cameras were on Clara.

Clara blinked away the afterimages of the photographers' flashes and searched the crowd for Marcus, but all she saw were stuffy Chicagoans in fancy dress. The orchestra was playing something soft and mellow in the living room. Clara could hear it and wished she were there, with Marcus, having fun and away from these high-society wolves.

"Miss Knowles! Miss Knowles!" cried a woman reporter in a fur-trimmed suit. "What a beautiful gown! Who made it?"

"Oh, beats me, really," Clara said, looking down at her dress, a sheer midnight-blue sheath that fell to her knees and was hemmed with a silk and beadwork band. It was slightly out of fashion but still beautiful. She could have told the reporter that it was Chanel who'd designed this gown, but Country Clara would have had no idea.

"Clara, dear, there you are!" Aunt Beatrice swept through the crowd and kissed Clara on each cheek. For once in her life, Clara's aunt was in something chic—a modest black dress, her neck wrapped in diamonds. She looked happier and younger than she had in ages. *Aunt Bea looks elegant,* Clara thought. She told her as much.

Aunt Bea gave her a quick hug. She seemed genuinely happy to see Clara, so unlike when Clara had first set foot in this mansion. The threat of reform school was only a ghostly memory.

"I was just about to tell this reporter about my gown." Clara did a little twirl. "Of course, I can't take credit for my ensemble tonight. If my aunt hadn't been so generous, I would have come looking like a ragamuffin! We country girls don't know a ton about fashion, but I've been learning so much."

Aunt Beatrice waved her hand in the air. "Oh, nonsense! You became the toast of this town all on your own." She patted Clara's arm and whispered, "That there *will be* a wedding is thanks, in no small part, to you. I'm glad you came to Chicago, dear. Your parents would be very proud."

Clara felt tears come to her eyes. She hadn't thought of her parents in ages; in her mind, they would always be disappointed in her. But maybe her aunt was right, and now they could finally stop being ashamed of her.

"Miss Knowles, will you stand for a photo?"

"Of course," Clara said. She smiled without showing her teeth, one hand propped on her dropped waist.

A few more reporters threw out questions, but she called to them, "I'm sorry, but I need to get a bite to eat before I perish from hunger!"

She was lying. She had eyes for only one thing, and it wasn't caviar. It was Marcus.

He was waiting for her, leaning against one of the

cream-colored walls and looking more dashing than he had when she'd first laid eyes on him—if that was even possible.

"Hello there, handsome," Clara said, tugging at his silk tie.

He kissed her cheek. "Don't think I didn't see your little pose over there, Miss Clara. Did they teach you in Pennsylvania how to make those sultry eyes for the camera?"

"Marcus! Don't you dare say that dirty word here," she said, taking a sip of his seltzer.

"I wasn't aware that *sultry* was a dirty word."

"I meant *Pennsylvania*."

Marcus crinkled his adorable brow. "And yet I may need to say it one more time when I ask you what your parents will think of me, back on the farm in *Pennsylvania*." He gulped down his drink, then took two crab-cake hors d'oeuvres from a passing waiter's tray and popped them into his mouth.

"You're an animal," Clara said, laughing. He wanted to meet her parents? He wasn't even her boyfriend yet. Or was he? *Baby steps,* she reminded herself. "I thought we were taking this slowly."

"We are," Marcus answered. "Slowly, slowly, slowly. That is the name of the game." He ran his fingers through a loose tendril of her hair. Every time he touched her, she felt weak. "Did I tell you how beautiful you look tonight?"

Marcus took a second glass of seltzer from a waiter, then casually poured the water into a potted plant. He produced a flask, from which he poured a golden liquid into the glasses. He handed one to Clara. "An event like this calls for champagne. Unfortunately, all I have is whiskey."

"That will have to do." Clara raised her glass. "Should we toast to something?"

"We must!" he said, raising his own. "To . . ." He squinted at her. "Now, this may make me sound like a flat tire, but how about to leaving the past in the past, and living for the future?"

"I'll drink to that." Clara wrapped her arm around his, and thus entwined, she and Marcus clinked their glasses together. "How is it you always know the right thing to say?"

"Me? I'm a bumbling idiot around you!" Marcus said. "Speaking of, would you follow this bumbling idiot somewhere more private?"

"Pos-i-lute-ly," Clara said.

No one would notice if they disappeared for a moment. The photographers and reporters were still locked on Gloria at the other end of the hall, who was sitting on a plush chair that looked like a poor man's throne, gingerly holding Bastian's arm in a chaste manner that probably looked proper but that Clara knew was because of her distaste for the man. Questions were coming fast from the reporters. Bastian answered all of them while Gloria stared into space.

At the edge of the crowd Clara spied Ginnie Bitman. She looked positively horrifying in a baby-blue dress, but she was talking to a boy—a real, live boy!—who seemed . . . not completely uninterested. Sure, he was funny in the face, but Clara felt a swell of pride for the girl.

Marcus took Clara's hand in his. He led her down the hallway past the kitchen, where the caterers had noisily set up camp; past one of the guest bathrooms and its overpowering stink of lilac-scented soap; and toward her uncle's library. That room had been virtually closed since he'd abandoned the family for his Manhattan fling.

And then it dawned on her: a secluded, dark room—

No, she didn't want to be that girl to him! She didn't want him to think that just because she had been promiscuous in the past, she would fool around with him now. It was important to start this relationship off right.

*Relationship?* She stopped dead in the hall and pulled her hand from his.

"What is it?" Marcus asked, his face flushed.

"Nothing," she said. "Sorry. I just got . . . confused."

So that was how she was feeling. *Relationship.* She used to run away at the mention of that word, but now . . . She looked at Marcus and grinned until her cheeks smarted.

She thought of the "plan" she'd overheard Lorraine and Gloria discussing the first time she'd met Marcus. Was this the final step? A dark room, humiliation before a crowd of hundreds?

"Maybe we should go back," she suggested.

"Into that stuffed-shirt hell? God, why?"

"I just thought that, well—" There was no easy way to voice her suspicions.

But all Marcus did was say, "I guess this hallway will be private enough, then. Clara Knowles, you *are* the most exquisite girl in this gaudy old house. And don't you dare protest that compliment, it's not allowed."

"Compliments. Flattery." Clara tilted her head. "Why are you so sweet to me?"

"Me? Sweet? Don't ruin my reputation." He dug inside the pockets of his tailcoat and fished out a red box with a signature gold-scripted *Cartier* stamped across the top. "But if you already find me too sweet, maybe I should reconsider giving you this."

"Marcus!" she said, a little breathless, and then, not knowing what else to say, said his name again.

"Perhaps you should open it first." He laughed, holding the box before her, but underneath his confidence, Clara could see he was unsure of himself. He wanted her to like him just as much as she wanted him to like her. The way this felt—the two of them equal, neither with the upper hand—was something new and altogether scary, but also wonderful.

Tentatively, Clara opened the box.

Inside, a glittering diamond and platinum bangle bracelet, with rubies scattered between the pavé diamonds like a red constellation, stared back at her. It was the most gorgeous, most delicate thing she had ever seen. She was stunned into silence.

"I can't tell if that's a good or a bad reaction," Marcus said, shifting from foot to foot.

"Good," she managed to croak. "Definitely good."

He removed the bracelet from the box and gently took her wrist in his hands. The simple touch of his fingers made her weak. "If you'll allow me the honor."

While Marcus clasped the bracelet around her wrist, Clara studied his face. What had she done to deserve this? To deserve him? The universe was giving her a second chance, and this time nothing would make her mess it up. She flung her arms around him. "Marcus, it's too thoughtful, and beautiful, and really way too much."

"Clara, my Clara. It reminded me of you when I saw it," he said, kissing her forehead. "A little delicate beneath all that beauty."

She kissed him then, raking her hands through his silky hair. He lifted her off the floor and swung her around. She laughed and planted kisses on his cheeks and ears and neck until, as the room spun dizzily around them, she noticed a dark figure in the entrance to the hallway.

Clara cried out, and Marcus came to an abrupt halt.

"What's wrong?" he asked.

She clumsily slid down to the floor, her heels hitting the parquet with an echoing clack. Her face must have said everything. Marcus followed her horrified gaze toward the one and only Harris Brown, standing there in a smart-looking tailcoat. Watching.

Harris strolled down the center of the hallway toward them, seeming to fill the space, seeming somehow larger than himself.

A sudden rage expanded in Clara like a balloon, inflating until she felt she would burst. "What the hell do you think you're doing here? You weren't invited!"

"I'm in politics, remember?" Harris said, sporting the cocky grin she used to love and now was repulsed by. "I'm always invited."

Marcus stepped forward. "I suggest that you find your way to the nearest exit right this second, or else—"

"Or else *what*?" Harris laughed.

"I'm warning you, Harris," Clara said, trying to steady her voice, "leave now before things get messy." She would not let him back into her life. This was her city now, her home, her party, her boyfriend—

"But you *love* messy, don't you? Some things never change, baby doll." Harris stepped closer, sizing Marcus up. "Oh, Clara, you poor thing. Don't tell me your life here has driven you into the arms of this little pretty boy. He barely looks old enough to tie his—"

Marcus lunged at Harris and slammed him up against the wall.

But if Harris knew anything, it was how to fight dirty.

He jabbed his knee into Marcus's gut, flipped him around, and punched him square in the eye.

"Stop it! Stop!" Clara screamed, trying to tear them apart. But it was no use.

Harris, clutching Marcus by the neck, held him stiffly against the wall. "I broke my engagement because of you, Clara. You know I love you—I always have. I came here to take you back to New York, to start a life together—"

She wouldn't hear any more.

She sprinted blindly back down the hall, needing to get away from it all, from both of them. How many nights had she lain awake wishing Harris would say that to her, those exact words?

She stared down at the bracelet on her wrist. She didn't deserve it.

There was a loud crash.

Clara stopped, and the world around her came sharply into focus: the main foyer, a large silver tray rattling at her feet, pâté-covered croquettes scattered everywhere, and a hundred pairs of gawking eyes. "I'm sorry," she muttered to the waiter she'd plowed into, dropping to her knees to pick up the platter. "I'm so sorry—"

"Just who I'm looking for!"

The guests parted, and Lorraine staggered into sight.

Clara barely recognized her: Raine's cheeks were smudged with black mascara, her mouth a smear of red, her cream-colored dress wrinkled and dirty. Clara was thankful that someone worse off had wandered in at the right moment to take the attention away from her—until she realized Lorraine was addressing her. "If it isn't Clara Knowles, the Queen of Hearts herself, gracing us with her menday—mendaysh—mendacious presence!"

"Lorraine, are you all right?" Clara asked, but she could smell the booze from where she was standing.

The guests and reporters circled around them as if they were about to watch a boxing match. Clara had to defuse the bomb that was Lorraine. "Raine, why don't we find a nice quiet place to—"

"No! I want everyone to hear what I am about to say." Raine's words were slurred and sloppy, and she wavered on her feet. "I want everyone to know what a fraud you are."

Before Clara could respond, Gloria ran up to her former best friend, a panicked look on her face. "You were not invited to this party!" she spat, glaring at Lorraine. "You need to leave this instant."

"It's her!" Lorraine pointed her finger at Clara as if they were in the middle of the Salem witch trials. "*She* shouldn't have been invited to this party. *She* was the one who told Bastian everything. *She* was the one who ratted you out—who told him about the Green Mill. It wasn't me, Gloria! I swear. Just ask him—"

"She's lying!" Clara insisted. She turned to Gloria. "I

swear to you, Gloria, I never said anything to Bastian. You are a liar, Lorraine."

"Oh yeah?" Lorraine said, her face twisting. "Then what is Mr. High-and-Mighty Harris Brown doing here? Explain that to everyone! Then we'll see who's the filthy liar!"

Lorraine pointed somewhere behind Clara. But Clara didn't need to look to know who was there. A wave of whispers rippled through the crowd, and the reporters scribbled furious notes.

Lorraine ambled around the circle, angrily pushing people out of her way. "When I saw you with Harris Brown at the Green Mill, Clara, I thought, *How does a stupid rube of a country girl from Pennsylvania, a girl who stinks of manure and doesn't know a garter from a garter snake, know a big politico in New York like that?*"

"You're drunk, Lorraine," Gloria said. "Please, will some of the able-bodied men here carry out this piece of trash?" She looked around for Bastian, but he was nowhere in sight.

"Ah-ah-ah!" Lorraine said, dodging the one man who went to comply. "I called a few of my contacts at Barnard—did I tell you I'm going to Barnard? It's in New York City. Near Harlem, which my father is not happy about."

"We know where Barnard is," said Marcus.

"My friend Shelly, who can spot a cad from a mile away, knew what a notorious playboy Harris Brown is."

Clara's mouth felt as if it were stuffed with cotton. "Stop," she said weakly. She wished somebody, anybody would stop this girl. She looked from Gloria's face to Marcus's, to Mrs. Carmody's, to the faces of random guests she didn't even know. No one was saying anything. Everyone was staring at Clara, eyes wide, waiting for her to respond. "Please, stop her—"

"And guess what I found out? Surprise! Clara Knowles is not who she says she is!" Lorraine lost her balance and fell backward to the floor with a loud thud.

Everyone gasped, and then there were fresh bursts of bright light as the photographers started snapping away.

Lorraine was splayed out with her skirt bunched up around her thighs, her pink floral underwear showing. Almost as quickly as she fell, she rolled to her knees, straightened up, and pointed at Clara with one unsteady finger. "You are a little tart, Clara Knowles. A smutty little vixen. What do you have to say about *that*?" Lorraine placed her hand demurely on her chest and burped. "Excuse me."

Clara froze. Lorraine was clearly a mess, but she wasn't wrong, either. She had found out about Harris. She'd exposed her "Country Clara" lie. What else did she know? Clara's knees were trembling now, and she found herself making her way to Marcus. "Make her stop," she said, tugging at his sleeve, trying not to break down completely. "Please."

Marcus strode into the circle. "You aren't welcome here, Lorraine. Leave at once—"

Raine did a jazzy dance step in the middle of the foyer.

No one even laughed—people were appalled by her behavior, and the crazier she acted, the more nervous Clara got.

"Oh, Marcus," Lorraine said, "my silly little Marcus. We're just getting to the best part of the story—the part that you will *especially* want to hear." There was an authority in her voice that made Marcus step back.

Clara's head was filling up with air now, as if it were about to float away from her body. "Lorraine, I'm begging you—"

"Everyone thinks *I'm* a bad girl, showing up in places with too much makeup and too-short hair and a little too potted in booze." She stared directly at Clara. "But ladies and gentlemen, sweet, innocent Clara Knowles was having an affair with Harris Brown. Bam! Zip! Pow! Even though he was *engaged to be married* to that French heiress. And you want to know how their sordid affair came to an end?" Lorraine raised her arm and pointed at the ceiling. "She had his *baby*! Clara Knowles had Harris Brown's *bastard child*!"

The words struck Clara like an open hand.

And then she was blinded by light, burned and baptized by a hundred dazzling explosions as a dozen cameras clicked, capturing her pain, her shame, her grief, for all the world to see.

# LORRAINE

This was not how it was supposed to happen. *This was not happening.*

And yet it was.

Everything was a confusing jumble in her head: the faces, their jaws dropped open; her dress smeared with fingerprints and dirt; Marcus and Gloria and that lying, two-faced Clara. And there were noises in there somewhere, too—her voice rising with a frenzied shrillness, saying what? She wasn't sure. Then there was the taste of the alcohol turning sour in her throat.

And now Clara was crying. Fat tears of repentance, rolling down her perfect dewy cheeks, turning her into a pixieish martyr. The Mary Pickford–like darling of the press who could do no wrong. Lorraine remembered what she had said. Yes, she had revealed everything—everything!—and announced to the world that Clara Knowles was a fake, a liar, a sham.

So why wasn't Clara running away in shame?

"It's true," Clara said. "Everything she says is true."

That wasn't what Lorraine was expecting.

"I might as well come clean, here and now. I don't want to lie anymore."

What else could possibly be left for Clara to confess?

Lorraine had dug up everything. She'd gotten the lowdown from her friend Shelly Monaheim at Barnard. Shelly's brother had gone to Harvard with Harris, knew him the way Lorraine knew her own hand—and Shelly had delivered *all* the dirt, every sordid detail. Clara's affair with Harris. The baby.

Clara was ruined, and Gloria would finally understand that it was Clara who had spilled the details about the Green Mill, that it was Clara who had lied to everyone she'd ever met, that it was Clara who had betrayed her. Lorraine was the one who was truly devoted to Gloria, and now her best friend would simply have to take her back.

Wouldn't she?

But Clara wouldn't shut up. Why wouldn't she shut up?

"I was seventeen and I—I was stupid. I was new in the city, and I was swept away by the excitement and the lights—and by a man, yes. Harris Brown. He swept me off my feet, and—" A sob choked her, and Lorraine thought, *About time.*

"No one wants to hear all the sordid details!" Lorraine said, but her mouth didn't seem to be working right. Anyway, everyone—Gloria, Marcus, even Mrs. Carmody—shushed her.

"And I got pregnant." Clara paused and looked down, sucked in a deep breath.

A whisper spread through the crowd. Was there a sympathetic edge to that whisper? What was going on here?

"She's a whore," Lorraine slurred—she recognized what was happening now, realized she might have had a little too much liquid courage before coming here.

But the crowd ignored her. Clara had everyone's attention.

Clara's voice grew steadier. "But I lost the baby." She looked up and wiped away tears. "I lost it. I lost *her*. I miscarried in the thirteenth week." She blew her nose and turned to Lorraine. "But thanks, Lorraine, for reminding me of who I used to be. I thought I would be able to escape my painful past by coming here, but I can see now I was wrong."

Lorraine struggled again to figure out what was going on. The crowd around them was murmuring things—wicked comments about Lorraine—that she couldn't bear. No, no, no—why was Lorraine being cast as the villain?

Clara turned to Gloria. "And for the record, cousin: I swear on my life, I didn't say a word about the Green Mill. I owe everything to you, Gloria. And I would never do anything to jeopardize your *true* love." Gloria clasped her hands, teary-eyed.

"Oh, come *on,*" Lorraine said, finally fed up. "Do you all believe this act? She's a liar!"

Clara turned back to Lorraine, tears sparkling in her eyes. She looked sad, not angry. "I only lied about my past. I'm not as coldhearted as you are, Raine."

*Coldhearted?*

She must have meant someone else. Lorraine felt only love for Gloria, and everyone knew that. Didn't they? Lorraine had tried—was trying—to make sure of Gloria's happiness! That was why she had come here tonight.

Wait. Why *had* she come here? The memory was hazy now: Lorraine had been going over her notes from Shelly, figuring out just how best to break the news to Gloria.

And then, because she'd been feeling a bit nervous, she'd gone for a drink at a speakeasy called Sub Rosa—a glass of wine that had turned into three or maybe four glasses. The wine was to bolster Lorraine's courage—telling Gloria the scummy truth about Clara was going to be difficult, very difficult—and a way to distract herself from the engagement party that was going on without her.

There'd been a man with a mustache there, and he'd been very friendly. Maybe too friendly, now that she thought about it. He had kissed her, his rough hands dropping fast to her garter.

She had slapped him and run out to the street, her skirt twisted halfway around and riding up her legs. But she didn't want him to catch her—the nerve of that man!—so she had run for all she was worth, but hadn't noticed all the ice on the street from the cold snap.

And she had slipped and fallen on the frozen pavement and torn her stockings and the skin of her knee, and it had *hurt,* but there was no one there to help her, so she swallowed her tears and another slug from her flask and then found her car and got in. And that was when she saw it:

REDEMPTION

The word blinked in red. Followed by:

TRUTH

In green.

If that wasn't a message from somebody up above, she didn't know what one would look like. Sure, the sign was on the front of some sort of crazy downtown church—what kind of person went to church under a neon cross?—but she wasn't going to be picky right then about where she found her divine inspiration. So she had fired up the car and driven off toward Astor Street with a mission in mind.

But somehow it all had gone terribly wrong.

Clara was gone now, had rushed off in a storm of tears, Marcus running after her. The party was breaking up, the reporters slipping their notepads back into their bags. Guests were gathering their coats. Members of the orchestra were packing their instruments.

"I think it is high time that you leave this house, Lorraine Dyer. I want you to listen very carefully: Don't you ever set foot under my roof again." Mrs. Carmody's hands were at the small of Lorraine's back, pushing her toward the front door. Lorraine tried to resist, but the old biddy was like a force of nature, and anyway, Lorraine had lost a shoe somewhere.

Then they were on the porch, and Mrs. Carmody was handing the shoe to her, and Lorraine felt cold and confused and terribly, terribly alone.

"I've put up with a lot from you, Lorraine Dyer. I know your parents are mostly absent from your life, and I always wanted you to feel welcome here. But now look what you've done. This is the final straw. Never again go near my Gloria. For as long as you live."

◆◆◆

Sitting on a bench, shivering, Lorraine gazed up at the sky through bare branches.

Her nanny used to bring her and Gloria here to Astor Square Park when they were young girls—it was within walking distance of both of their homes—and they would play for hours. Now she was smoking a cigarette, alone, sober, her head still hammering. Her dress was filthy and ruined. She was the one who felt like crying now, but the raw wind was stinging her eyes dry.

She could barely make sense of what had transpired. If Lorraine had been in Clara's shoes, surely she would have fallen prey to a man like Harris Brown—so handsome, so powerful. But a miscarriage? No girl deserved that kind of trauma.

She took out her silver Tiffany cigarette case, only to find it empty, gleaming at her almost malevolently, as if playing a cruel joke. She chucked it as far as she could into the darkness of the park.

She put her hands to her temples. There was a throbbing rhythm like feet tapping on her head. No, wait, those were actual footsteps. Heavy, like a man's. And she was alone, at night, in a deserted park. Dressed like a floozy, and without the energy to run.

"Lose something?"

She recognized the voice immediately. But she was more surprised by her initial reaction—of relief?—than by the fact that it was Bastian Grey. He waved her cigarette case like a fan as he stepped out of the shadows. His bow tie was loose around his neck, and his shirt was hanging out over his formal trousers. "Or was that just your unconventional method of quitting? I hear it's good for the lungs."

"Since when are you concerned with my health?"

"Oh, don't worry, I'm much more concerned with your *un*healthy habits." He sat down next to her on the bench.

"Although, as far as I know, you have yet to display any healthy ones."

Bastian's motives were always suspect, but it was nice to have a warm body against hers—his mere presence distracted her from the unbearable tension of being alone. Plus, he had cigarettes. "Care to corrupt my lungs a little more?"

"The pleasure is all mine," he said. He retrieved his own cigarette case and lit two in his mouth before handing her one. "Nice show you pulled tonight, by the way. You should really consider taking that act on the road."

She wasn't in the mood for his sarcastic banter. "Why did you follow me here?"

"I'm a gentleman at heart, Raine. And if Marcus was so gentlemanly as to follow the victim, I figured it was only fair to follow the villainess."

*Marcus.* No matter what she did, Marcus would never want her. The realization was terribly sobering and made her body ache all the more.

She found herself leaning into Bastian's wool coat, but quickly pulled away. "Fair? Since when do you believe in fairness?"

"Don't they say all's fair in love and war?"

"All is *un*fair in love and war."

"You know what I think your problem is?" He turned to her, brushing a strand of hair out of her eyes. "You don't know who your enemy is."

She shivered at his touch. No, the problem was that everyone was her enemy.

"See, you chose to make war with the wrong person," he continued. "In this town, bad press is the best press of all."

Lorraine cringed. "Yeah, well, I didn't know Clara was going to steal the story."

"She actually came off pretty sympathetic," Bastian said. "Everyone has a skeleton or two in his closet. Most people sympathize." He cocked his head. "What they don't necessarily like are the people who open the closet doors. Scares them."

"If you're trying to say I did the wrong thing, can it. Gloria deserved to know. Everyone deserved to know. Clara is a con artist."

Bastian smirked. "Maybe she is, but she's not the one who told me about the Green Mill."

Lorraine was shocked. Somewhere along the way, she had miscalculated.

"At any rate," Bastian continued, "she certainly has her claws securely into pretty boy Marcus Eastman. I wonder what they're doing as we speak."

Lorraine rubbed her arms. "I don't care. I'm moving on to bigger and better things—I'm waiting for New York."

New York. The city that never slept. New York would be where she would start over. Barnard would be her new home, where no one knew about her life in Chicago.

Columbia was right across the street, filled with dozens—no, hundreds!—of gorgeous, smart, rich boys. Surely she would find one of them to date, to love, one who wouldn't ignore her the way Marcus did or treat her like some little floozy, the way Bastian did. New York was where her life would change—and unlike Clara, she wouldn't mess things up. Lorraine would do it right.

"And what will you do in the meantime?" Bastian casually draped his arm around her. "You're too beautiful a girl to be by yourself."

His arm brought her back to reality; instantly, she removed it. "Don't even start with me, Bastian."

"Come here," he said, in almost a whisper. "Do you not trust me at all? I said, come here." He gently pulled her against him, rubbing her arms to warm her up. "You were shivering."

"Oh, thanks." What was she thanking him for? This was just a ploy, some sick sexual ploy to draw her close to him—had she learned nothing from the past two times in his apartment? But her body was numb, and her fingers were numb, and her heart felt numb, too. She would let him warm her up, but that was all.

He rubbed her hands together, as if he were trying to spark a fire from two sticks. "Better?" he asked.

"A little," she said, pulling her hands back and placing them in her lap.

They sat for a moment in silence, listening to the wind in the bare branches of the trees. Then he said, "I may have gotten a bit . . . out of line the last time I saw you—"

"'Out of line' is an understatement," Lorraine said coldly.

"You're right, and I'm sorry. You deserve to be treated with respect."

"Respect?" She wiggled away. The outside of Bastian might have been gorgeous—that dark hair, those smoldering eyes—but his insides were surely rotten. "Cut the bushwa!"

"I'm serious, Raine. The Greys and the Dyers go way back. And if we can't treat each other with respect, how do we expect the dirty lower classes to?" His expression nearly made Lorraine sick.

She looked at him squarely. "You are such a—"

"A what?" His eyes shimmered with amusement. "What title do you think *you* deserve after tonight? Good Samaritan? Savior? Oh, Saint Lorraine, please have a drink with me," he pleaded. "Let me bask in your holy presence, and accept my paltry mortal offering."

"And what is your offering, exactly?"

"A drink. At my place."

Something inside her knew better than to accept Bastian's offer. His intentions weren't pure, and she was pretty sure he wanted to sleep with her. And while she didn't want that to happen, Bastian was making her feel as if she hadn't messed up her entire life half an hour earlier. Surely in the morning she would be grounded forever by her parents. She might even make the society papers alongside Clara.

Tonight might very well be her last night of freedom. Why not enjoy it?

"*One* drink," she said. "That's all."

Bastian grinned and raised two fingers in a mock pledge of honor. "You make the rules, Miss Dyer. I simply follow your lead."

All thoughts of Clara disappeared. All thoughts of Marcus vanished. Gloria, Mrs. Carmody, even Lorraine's parents—gone. She could feel herself changing, something dark inside her rising, forcing its way to the surface. "Well, in that case," she said, her voice newly energized, "let's get sloppy."

# GLORIA

Now Gloria understood everything.

That was why Clara was here. To escape. All her talk about romantically following her heart was a sham—Clara had followed her heart, and look where it had led her: to shame, to loss. To disaster.

Gloria wouldn't repeat her cousin's mistakes. She'd go to the club and say goodbye to Jerome. Quick and simple. No room for failure. No room for regret.

Surely, her feelings for Jerome were nothing more than a childish infatuation—like Clara's for Harris Brown. Gloria might have thought she shared something special with Jerome, but they had no future together. Where would they live? Where would their children go to school? Even though her life with Bastian might be dull, it would be respectable.

Gloria had said as much to Bastian in the aftermath of the engagement party. He had forgiven her, saying, "I'm happy to see that you've come to your senses." Then he had kissed her goodnight and gone home.

Gloria wouldn't be causing scandals or getting her name in the gossip columns as Mrs. Sebastian Grey III. Her mother would be secure. There was so much that made *sense* about the wedding.

Nothing about her and Jerome made sense at all.

So why was she standing here the next day, paralyzed, at the entrance to the Green Mill? She had rehearsed this. She'd written out a script during study hall, treating it like a cut-and-dry English class assignment:

*Our worlds are too different, Jerome. There's too much at stake, too many people who could get hurt. We need to be mature adults and admit what this really is: nothing more than the thrill of the forbidden. But we both know it's wrong. A setup for disaster. A mistake.*

Leif opened the door at her knock. The club was nearly deserted.

"Red! What are you doing here?" he asked.

"Forgot something backstage," she said. "Is Jerome here?"

He shrugged and went back to the bar. "He's around here somewhere."

She strolled past the bar as if she belonged, and climbed

onto the stage. In the dressing room, she found the dress she'd changed out of for her debut. It lay crumpled in a corner on the floor like a snakeskin coiled up on the side of the road.

She picked the dress up and clutched it to her chest, breathing in. It smelled like dust and varnish. Like this dingy little room in the Green Mill. *Don't cry,* she warned herself. *Do not cry.*

"Well, if it isn't the doll I've been waiting to see."

She turned to the door. It was Carlito Macharelli, in an impeccably tailored dark suit as usual. Even in the dull light of the dressing room, his dark hair shone. When he pushed back his coat to rest his hand on his hip, Gloria caught a glint of light on metal: a pistol in a holster.

She'd had only a handful of encounters with him after her audition. A few times, he had sat in on the band's rehearsals, observing silently from the dark back of the room, visible thanks only to the red coal of his cigar. And then he'd come backstage that first and last night to wish her good luck, with Maude and that midget.

Now he was blocking the doorway, wearing a smile she didn't trust. "That was some act you pulled the last time you were here."

"I know," Gloria said, edging toward the door.

"Let me tell you, you stirred up more bedlam than this club has seen in years. It takes one hell of a girl to do that."

"I've been meaning to apologize," she said uneasily. It had

been more than three weeks already, but the horror of it was still as vivid as yesterday.

"*Meaning to* and *doing* are two very different things."

"I know. That's part of why I'm here. I never meant to cause any trouble—"

"There's *another* reason?"

She couldn't mention Jerome. "To pick up my dress," she said, holding it up as if it were an exhibit in a trial. She could smell Carlito's Brilliantine. It smelled like menace. She had never spent this much time alone with the gangster, and the club was empty. She studied Carlito's face. Was he dangerous? Where was Maude—had something happened to her? "I left it here."

He chuckled and stepped closer, shutting the door behind him. "You know, I'm a very forgiving man, Gloria. In fact, I pride myself on my ability to forgive. But what you did that night caused a lotta trouble. And cost a lotta dough."

"I know, it was all my fault—"

He put a finger to her lips, silencing her. His closeness made her intensely uncomfortable; she could smell the tobacco on his breath and practically taste the Scotch oozing from his pores. "That fiancé of yours is a pretty powerful man in this town, isn't he? If it wasn't for him, you wouldn't be in such a fortunate position."

Gloria didn't want Carlito to sense her fear. "I am truly

sorry, Carlito," she began. "I had no intention of causing trouble. All I wanted to do was sing."

"But you ain't a singer, baby, you're a socialite." He traced her lips with his finger. "Girls like you should know better than to play with fire."

Gloria was now backed up against the wall. The dress, clutched against her chest, was the only barrier between them. "I said I was sorry—"

"An apology ain't enough," he said, his eyes fierce and terrifying. "Even out of the mouth of a beaut like you."

With one hand he caught her by the waist, his thumb digging hard into her left hip. With the other, he wadded up her dress around her hands. "There is a way to make it up to me."

"Stop it! Please!" she cried out, attempting to push him away, but she was no match for his strength. He kissed her hard on the mouth.

"Stop!" she screamed in the second she managed to break from his kiss. He was tearing at her now, crushing her. "Stop, please!"

His tongue felt like sandpaper. She closed her eyes, hoping he would stop. *Please let him stop.*

And then, suddenly, he did.

Gloria opened her eyes and watched as Carlito stumbled back against the far wall, violently yanked away from her. And then watched as his head snapped to the side from the force of being struck again.

He fell like a tree at the feet of Jerome Johnson.

Relief and excitement flooded through her. "Jerome!" she gasped.

"Hush," he said. "We've got no time for anything but getting out of here. So just be quiet and come on."

They walked quickly and quietly out of the dressing room and back into the heart of the club. The bar was still empty.

Standing directly before the front door, though, was Thor, the midget Gloria had met backstage on the night of her performance.

Thor rocked back and forth on his heels and stared at them with a smug expression. He was dressed in a tiny dark suit and a black hat. His arms were crossed in front of him. Despite his stature, there was something scary about him.

"Where's Carlito?" Thor asked.

Gloria glanced at Jerome. "We don't know. If you'll excuse us, we have to get going."

The midget removed a pistol from his jacket, grasping it with both hands. "Nobody goes anywhere till Carlito says they can. Now put your hands up in the air, where I can see 'em."

Gloria and Jerome reluctantly raised their hands. Carlito was bound to come to at any moment, and then what? He would hurt Jerome. From the corner of her eye, Gloria saw Leif coming at Thor from the side. The bartender snapped his leg out and kicked the gun clear across the room.

"What the—"

Leif swept Thor up and tucked him under his right arm. "I never liked you, little man," he said.

*"You're dead, bartender!"* Thor screamed, squirming and kicking.

"Oh, right," Leif said. "Forgot something." He fished a dirty handkerchief from his pocket and stuffed it into Thor's mouth. "There, that'll shut you up. I got just the place for you. Empty cupboard behind the bar."

"Leif!" Gloria cried out. "What are you doing? You're going to get in trouble!"

"Saving your caboose is what I'm doing. I figured you two might need some help," Leif said. Thor stopped kicking.

Jerome said, "Thanks, Leif. We owe you."

Leif broke out in a toothy grin. "Don't worry about me. I was done with this place a while ago. Good luck, Red." He turned to Jerome. "Take good care of her."

"I will," Jerome said. He was already pushing open the door, the cold air rushing at Gloria and filling her lungs.

"Come on," Jerome said. "We're not clear yet. Now we've got to run."

They pounded along the pavement, holding hands as they barreled down the avenue past curious onlookers. What did the bystanders think, seeing a young black man running hand in hand with a young white woman? Gloria realized she didn't care. She clutched Jerome's fingers as tightly as she could, never wanting to let go.

If it hadn't been for the wrinkled dress clutched in her other hand, she would have completely forgotten that she had come to the Green Mill to say goodbye.

◆◆◆

They had reached the entrance to the Navy Pier. They hadn't spoken a word since they'd run out of the Green Mill.

The Navy Pier was practically deserted, the frigid weather driving away the usual hordes of tourists. There were only a few straggling couples, the women tucked beneath the men's arms, strolling in silence.

Gloria peered out at the lake, the water shining like a sheet of metal. "You shouldn't have done that," she blurted out. "Carlito will have you killed."

Jerome inched closer, wrapping a hand around her waist. "Would you rather I'd left you there, for him to take advantage of?"

"No, but—"

"Then what was I supposed to do?" he asked. "I love you. I had no choice." Jerome pressed his nose against Gloria's. She felt so safe in his arms. "I'll see to it that that creep doesn't lay a finger on me, or you, ever again."

Even though she was scared of Carlito, Gloria was taken aback. "Wait—did you say *love*?"

"Didn't you know that I've fallen for you, Gloria Carmody?"

he said somberly, planting a soft kiss on her forehead. "I love you."

"I don't understand—"

"What's to understand? I love you. Simple as that. *I love you.*"

Gloria stared at him, her eyes wide and unblinking. His words seemed to sink into her body. She wanted to say them back to him—because she did love him back, didn't she?—but the sentence stuck in her throat. She remembered the first time she'd said "I love you" to Bastian: They had taken a carriage ride through Lincoln Park, during that innocent spring when she'd thought she knew what love was.

What a fool she had been.

Jerome took the dress from her and draped it over his shoulder. They walked toward the water. "Listen, I need to say something," he said. "And I don't want you to interrupt or protest or argue.

"You deserve a life of happiness, Gloria. There is plenty of suffering in the world—the last thing we need to do is pile more trouble on top of the heartbreak life dishes out to you.

"And after tonight, I think I gotta be the one to say it: I'm no good for you."

"Jerome, wait—"

"No, listen. I may love you, but I can't promise you a life of happiness. I can't promise you any kind of life at all. And that's why you got to do what you originally planned, and marry Sebastian."

"You don't mean that—"

"Yes, I do! You'll have your family, and you'll have your friends. You'll have beautiful children who will go to good schools—"

"Stop it! Stop!" She couldn't listen to another word. She stared into Jerome's eyes and felt her entire body tremble. "How can you say that to me! How can you tell me you love me and then send me away!" She buried her face in her hands.

"Gloria," he said, wrapping her in his arms. "Gloria, look at me."

"Jerome, what's the point of living if it's going to be easy? I've already wasted seventeen years of my life on that. I don't want to spend the next seventeen doing exactly the same."

"Then what *do* you want?"

She was silent.

"Say it," he demanded. "Tell me what you want."

It was as though a veil had finally been lifted and everything was perfectly clear. "I want to leave Chicago," Gloria said.

"Then that's what you should do."

"No, Jerome. I want to leave Chicago with *you.*"

For the first time since she'd met him, Jerome looked scared. "We have to be realistic, Glo—"

"You and I can't stay here! We'll both die—you'll end up gutted in the basement of the Green Mill, and I'll end up trapped in a dead marriage. You said you loved me. Did you mean it?"

His eyes widened. "Of course I meant it. I love you, Gloria. I've never loved anyone more in my entire life."

"Then that's all I need to know. Let's go to New York. We can figure out the rest once we get there."

"You know what New York will mean for us, don't you?" he said. "We'll be slumming it. No more mansions. No maids or drivers. No more country clubs or Paris dresses—"

"I've had all that, and look where it got me."

Jerome thought for a moment. "If you mean what you say, if this isn't just some crazy whim, I'll be waiting for you in front of my apartment tonight at ten sharp. We can catch the midnight express train to New York City."

She threw her arms around his neck. "I'll be there."

Jerome let out a laugh. "You are wild, Gloria Rose Carmody. You know that you're sounding crazy, right?"

"Then why do I feel the most sane I've ever felt in my life?" She kissed him and drew back. "And, Jerome?"

"What?"

"I love you, too."

◆◆◆

There was just one more thing she needed.

"He's at his weekly bridge match, Miss Carmody," the doorman at Bastian's said.

"That's all right, Martin." Gloria beamed winningly. "I just need to leave a surprise for him, if you don't mind."

The elevator opened onto Bastian's small foyer. Gloria unlocked the front door with her key and stepped into the hallway. It was empty, quiet. She caught sight of her face in the gilded mirror hanging over the hallway table. Her cheeks looked cherry-stained from being outside; there was a brightness in her eyes she didn't recognize. She looked good. Happy.

Then she heard Sebastian's voice, booming from his office. Not out playing bridge after all.

"All the more reason to clean house, Carlito. Don't want to give him time to rally his black gang or get out of town. Just hit him as soon as possible. Yeah, it's the address I gave you in Bronzeville. Two B. You take care of him, and I'll take care of her. She's a little bit of nothing."

Gloria put her hand over her mouth, stopping her breath. Carefully, with her other hand, she opened the drawer in the table under the mirror, feeling for the red velvet pouch she knew was tucked away in the back. Bastian had informed her that he kept it there "for security," in case of a burglary.

Once she was safely back in the foyer, noiselessly shutting the front door behind her, she took her hand away from her mouth and breathed in.

Bastian knew Carlito? They were working together? Carlito was a gangster. Why would he be taking orders from her fiancé? And how did Bastian know where Jerome lived? She had to get to Jerome. She had to warn him. Save him.

The elevator arrived.

Bastian's voice echoed through the door. "Hello? Is someone there?"

The pouch was heavy in her hands—much heavier than she'd expected. She dropped it into her bag just as the elevator doors hissed open.

In the lobby, Martin the doorman asked, "Did you leave Mr. Grey's surprise?"

"I sure did," Gloria said, trying to mask her nerves as she pictured the small black pistol resting inside her purse.

# CLARA

Clara stared into the gaping mouth of the suitcase on her bed. Her clothes were packed in tightly pressed and folded stacks, courtesy of Claudine. That was all her life in Chicago had amounted to: a few dresses that fit into a too-small valise.

"It's not that we don't want you here," Mrs. Carmody had told her the day after the engagement party debacle. "But you understand, don't you, Clara? Our family is about to have a scandal of its own, what with my husband's affair. We're ill equipped to deal with yours." She went on to explain that she wasn't going to send Clara off to the Illinois Girls' School of Reform. "My dear, that was only ever a threat. I've spoken to your parents, and they've agreed to let you come home." Aunt Bea pressed her palm against Clara's cheek. "I think you've suffered more than enough."

It was strange, being asked to leave. The Carmody mansion had come to feel more like a home than her real home in Pennsylvania. In many ways, Clara had even come to like Chicago more than New York. She'd finally found a place where she belonged. Sure, that sense of belonging was based on a character she had created—good old Country Clara—but toward the end, she'd been enjoying herself so much, she'd nearly forgotten she was acting. In a lot of ways, she had become what she'd pretended to be. And she'd liked that role.

Her mementos were scattered across the floor: a program from the Art Institute opening (first kiss with Marcus); a ticket stub from the Buster Keaton movie (first date with Marcus); a strand of fake pearls borrowed from the Unmentionable (Lorraine).

And then there was the red Cartier box.

Clara opened it and fastened the delicate ruby-and-diamond bangle around her wrist. After the engagement party from hell, she had shut Marcus out. He'd come around the Carmody house more than a few times, but she couldn't bear to talk to him. What was the point?

The bracelet winked at her with an icy glint. She had to give it back to Marcus. It felt strange on her wrist.

Pattering mouselike footsteps came from the hallway, followed by the faint click of a door. Gloria. Whatever Gloria's feelings were about Clara, she'd be gone by the morning, on a train back to Pennsylvania. This was the perfect—and only—opportunity to say goodbye, and to pass off the bracelet for Gloria to return.

Summoning whatever strength she had left, Clara knocked quietly on Gloria's door and pushed it open.

It was the mirror image of her own room: vanity at the foot of the bed, dresser on the far wall, walk-in closet in the corner opposite the door—and a half-filled suitcase open on the bed. What was going on?

Gloria was hovering over the suitcase, hastily stuffing in a wadded-up nightgown. She looked ravishing in a gold lamé dress that shimmered like a burst of sun, a gleam in her eyes that said she planned to get exactly what she wanted. Gloria was no longer playing the part of a singer at a speakeasy, no longer a rebellious child who had bobbed her hair to spite her parents.

Clara's cousin had truly become a flapper.

"A word of advice if you're planning to come with me to Pennsylvania," Clara said, stepping into the room and shutting the door behind her. "Ditch the dress. A bit showy for a train ride."

"It's not just a dress, it's a Paul Poiret," Gloria said. She dug through her drawers, throwing clothes like salt over her shoulder. "And I wouldn't make my New York entrance wearing anything else."

Gloria was going to New York? Clara was about to

question her, but then remembered how she'd felt when she'd decided to run away from home two years before. "When are you leaving?"

"Tonight."

"Have you thought this through?"

Gloria didn't answer. She just kept combing through drawers and casting things into the open maw of the suitcase. "I've thought plenty. Staying here isn't an option. I hope leaving is not a mistake, but even if it is, it is mine to make. Mine and Jerome's."

Clara couldn't stop herself. "Oh my God, are you pregnant? You can tell me if—"

"What? No!" Gloria paused, horrified. "I haven't even—you know—yet. With anyone."

Clara perched on the edge of Gloria's bed. Clara thought of her old feelings for Harris, then her new ones for Marcus. It was like comparing a watercolor by a five-year-old to Monet's water lilies.

"A word of advice," Clara said. "Once you give it up, you can't get it back. And everything gets even more complicated than it already is."

"Listen," Gloria said. "I really appreciate your trying to act the older sister and everything"—she scooped a pile of brassieres off the floor—"and I'm sorry if everything didn't work out the way you planned. But that doesn't mean it won't for me. I'm sorry if that sounds harsh, Clara. I certainly don't mean for it to."

Gloria pressed down the top of her suitcase, trying to close it, only there were too many clothes. "I love Jerome. If our love won't be allowed to exist here, then we have to find a place where it will. Where we can start fresh."

"If that's how it is," Clara said, studying her cousin's face and walking over to the bed, "you're going to need a little help."

Clara took some of the items off the top of the stack in the suitcase—a red cashmere sweater, a knee-length white cotton skirt—and tossed them onto the floor. "You need to pack lightly. All these clothes are just going to weigh you down. Just buy whatever else you need once you get to New York," she added, scrutinizing the newly thinned-out contents. "Please tell me you packed money."

Gloria nodded.

"Are you sure you have enough?"

"I hope so."

Clara remembered how hard it had been when she'd first arrived in New York, with only a hundred bucks to her name. But then, she had survived, hadn't she? Pounding the pavement along with everyone else and scrambling to pay her rent, sure—but the scramble was part of New York's hardscrabble charm.

"Listen, you're going to take over Manhattan." Even though Gloria was leaving, Clara had never felt closer to her cousin. "And who knows, maybe I'll see you there one day soon."

Gloria squeezed Clara affectionately. "There's something I want to give you." Gloria began to stomp around the room, kicking at the piles of clothing on the floor, until she found what she was looking for.

The gold butterfly flask.

"Didn't I tell you that's yours to keep?" Clara asked.

"I know, but I figured you might want it. To remember . . ." Gloria trailed off, a sadness darkening her face.

"Everything I want to remember, I already have," Clara said. "Besides, it's a long train ride." Clara stuffed the flask into Gloria's clutch.

Gloria buried her head in Clara's shoulder. "What would I have done without you?"

Clara tugged at a strand of Clara's hair. "Something tells me you would've gotten along just fine. Now, you'd better get a move on! Don't waste your tears on me." She dragged Gloria's suitcase, significantly lighter, off the bed and handed it to her. "And don't worry about your mother—I've got you covered. For a few hours, at least. Remember to use the servants' entrance."

Gloria planted a huge kiss on Clara's cheek. "I'll send you a telegram once I'm there, all right?"

Clara walked Gloria to the servants' door, where they briefly hugged one last time.

Then Gloria was off, suitcase in hand, rushing toward whatever journey awaited her. "Good luck," Clara whispered into the darkness.

◆◆◆

Clara went back to her room. She had stuffed Gloria's bed with pillows so it looked as if she were sleeping there, in case her aunt woke up or Claudine decided to check on Gloria in the middle of the night. Aunt Bea would realize Gloria was gone in the morning, of course, but by then Gloria would be most of the way to New York.

Clara felt happy for Gloria, who was at last becoming someone worth knowing, and sad for herself, who'd become someone nobody wants to admit to knowing.

She thought about that morning's papers, about the photos and the headlines (she couldn't bear to read more than that): Lorraine pointing at Clara; Gloria, shocked, in the background. BELLE OF THE BALL HAS SECRET PAST! and SHOCKING SECRETS UPSTAGE THE ENGAGED! and "SHE HAD HIS BABY!" CRIES DRUNK. There had been other pictures inside, Claudine had told her, but those were mostly of Lorraine struggling to get up off the floor.

Clara stripped off her clothes and cranked open the hot tap on the bath. Then she upended the French lavender bath salts her aunt liked to buy but asked the girls to "save for a special occasion." This was a special occasion if she'd ever seen one. The spigot gurgled and ever so slowly began to fill the tub.

Wrapped in a towel, Clara collapsed onto her bed,

throwing a hand over her eyes. That was when she felt the cool metal scrape of the bracelet on her eyelids.

She had completely forgotten! She waved her wrist in the air above her head, following the diamonds back and forth. She would never get the bracelet back to Marcus in time now. She supposed she could ship it to him from home.

Home. Home wasn't Pennsylvania. It no longer was Chicago. Really, if Clara was honest with herself, it was New York City.

Where Gloria was bound.

There was a soft knock on her door.

Gloria must have forgotten something. "Hold on!" Clara called out, relieved to have a second chance to remove this damn bracelet. She turned off the tap, retied the towel around herself, and went to the door. "Thank God you came back," she said, "because I forgot to ask you to—"

"Forgot to ask me what?"

"Marcus!" Clara stumbled back in shock, clutching the top of her towel to prevent it from falling. "What are you doing here?"

He stepped into the room. His blond hair was swept back, and he was wearing a light blue cardigan and light brown trousers. He looked as if he hadn't slept since the engagement party last night. There were purple circles under his eyes, and his cheeks were sprinkled with light stubble.

"First, tell me what you wanted to ask me." His voice gave her goose bumps.

She wanted to ask him a million things: *Do you hate me? Can you ever trust me again? Have I ruined my chances by lying to you? Can you ever look at me without thinking of Harris? Without thinking of his baby? Do you love me? Do you love me?*

But instead, she extended her arm like a frustrated child. "My bracelet! I can't undo it."

He gently took her wrist in his hands. "Did you ever consider that it may not want to be undone?" He opened the clasp and then snapped it shut again, still on her arm.

"Hey!"

"Just be quiet for once."

Marcus led her to the bed and sat her down, then sat beside her. Clara held her breath as he spread her palms open on his lap. "I knew it," he said, tracing her life line with his fingertips.

"You knew what?"

"Oh, nothing," he said. "I just learned for sure what your answer will be to my question, that's all." He tapped her hand. "It's so obvious, really, that I don't even need to bother to ask."

"Ask what?" Clara was confused. Happy and confused and scared. She stared down at her hands. They just looked like hands. A little wet, maybe, from messing about with the bathwater. "Marcus, just take your bracelet and leave me be. Please."

"Is that really what you want?"

"Does it even matter what I want? You already know everything there is to know. There's nothing left. I have nothing left," she said, her eyes fixed on the bracelet.

"Look at me, Clara," he said.

"I can't." She shook her head. "I can't."

He gently caught her chin with his finger, raising it so that she was staring straight into his eyes. "I want you to look at me." There was a dreamy cast to his eyes, like the sky seen through wispy clouds. "Now, was that so hard?"

"I didn't think you'd want to see me again, not after the other night—"

"I'm here, aren't I?"

"But why? To see me in my shame?" She swallowed a sob. "You finally got what you wanted: To see Country Clara made the victim of a scandal. To send her running out of Chicago. That was the plan, wasn't it? When I first arrived?"

Marcus looked ashamed. "It was. Originally. But that was before I knew you. I don't want that anymore."

"So what do you want now, Marcus?"

He smiled in a maddening way and took her wrist again in his hand. "I want you. Clara, will you"—he paused, his finger poised on the clasp of the bracelet. "Will you move to New York with me next summer? After I graduate."

"What?" Clara sprang up from the bed. She wished more than anything that she weren't dressed in a towel. "Is this some kind of joke?"

"Clara," Marcus said, exasperated, "if I don't act now I may never see you again."

"Did you not hear what Lorraine said last night? Don't you know what this means for my reputation in Chicago? New York? And, frankly, everywhere?"

"I don't care what you did or didn't do before me. I just care about you, now. I love you. I'm in love with you, Clara," Marcus said, pulling her back down to the bed so that she was practically sitting on his lap. "I had some time to think about everything. And the thing is, when I imagined what my life would be like without you, well . . . I didn't see anything at all."

There was so much to say that Clara felt nearly paralyzed. She ran into the bathroom and wrapped herself in a flannel robe.

"Do you remember meeting me, for the first time, in this room?" Marcus asked when she came back.

"How could I forget?"

"I remember thinking there was something different about you—something just beneath the surface, a veil of mystery waiting to be lifted. It made me want to kiss you, right then and there."

"But you didn't."

"No, I didn't," he said, stroking her hand. "I am a gentleman, after all."

She wanted him to kiss her. She wanted to kiss him. "What if you don't like me . . . the real me?" she asked nervously. "What if, when I'm myself, you no longer want me?"

"I'll always want you, Clara."

"But how do you know?" she asked. "How do you know for sure?"

"How about this?" Marcus asked, sitting upright. He straightened his cardigan and stuck out his hand. "We'll start from scratch. Hello. I'm Marcus Eastman. Who are you?"

Clara laughed. "Oh, Marcus. Come on. Don't be silly."

"I'm serious!" he said. "Introduce yourself. Your real self."

Clara was about to laugh again, but then she realized that this was exactly what she wanted: a fresh start.

"My name is Clara Knowles," she said, placing her hand in Marcus's.

He shook it vigorously. "Lovely to meet you, Miss Knowles."

"Likewise, Mr. Eastman."

They both started laughing and fell backward on Clara's bed.

"There's only one problem," Clara said in all seriousness, still holding on to Marcus's hand.

"What's that?"

Clara ran her fingers through his thick blond hair and across his cheek. This was it—the moment when she would take the biggest risk in her entire life. Which was saying a lot. She grinned. "How am I possibly going to wait till next summer?"

He just laughed. "It won't be too long." He kissed her.

"The next time you kiss me," Clara said, "the next time we kiss—it will be in Grand Central Station. I'll have come in on the overnight train."

"Your hair will be pushed up into a wide-brimmed hat. I won't recognize you at first."

"But then I'll pull off the hat, and I'll shake out my hair—"

"Like a starlet in some terrible movie." He made a face.

"In a fabulous movie, thank you very much. That's when you'll see me on the platform. At first, you'll be struck speechless. I'll break into a run and throw myself into your arms, and you'll swing me around, and I'll kick up my legs and everyone else will turn and stare, jealous of us and of our love."

"My God," Marcus whispered. "Clara Knowles, I do believe you're a romantic."

And suddenly she knew it was true. She *was* a romantic. When had that happened?

"Do you still want me to undo your bracelet?" Marcus asked.

"If it's all right with you, Mr. Eastman," Clara said, "I think I'll keep it on for good."

# LORRAINE

Sitting at home and moping was not an option. Going out to the newest speakeasy, called Cloak & Dagger, *was*.

Even if Lorraine had to go by herself.

She figured it was preparation for Barnard—surely all the girls there were so confident that they could go stag all over the city and no one would even bat an eye.

She had her driver drop her off at a run-down Italian restaurant off State Street. Her friend Violet had written out the instructions on the back of a missal she had in her purse, and Lorraine followed them exactly: Walk to the back of the restaurant, bypassing all the couples; push through the double doors as if you belong, then charge through the tomato-splattered kitchen, ignoring the cooks; turn left at the far wall, stride past the reeking garbage bins, and go straight up to the large, scary-looking man in front of the metal door.

"I'm here to see a man about a dog." Lorraine tried to growl, only the noise came out more like a whimper. The man—who was dressed all in black—gave her a quick once-over, then let her in without a word.

Cloak & Dagger was cozier than she had expected: a small, dark room, lit by what looked like a thousand little votive candles in tiny glass spheres. A winding iron staircase led up to a second-floor wraparound balcony. Tucked into the far corner of the room was the bar, but it was more like a very tall desk. An even taller man—the bartender—slouched against the desk, smoking a cigarette. A scratchy jazz record played in the background, and a few couples on the minuscule dance floor were moving as slowly as the winding curlicues of smoke rising from their cigarettes.

Lorraine liked this mellow, sultry atmosphere. No one seemed to care much about anyone else. With one or two martinis in her, she could forget why she was here alone in the first place: because her life, as she knew it, was ruined.

Her parents had come home after two weeks away and had spoken to her just long enough to tell her they'd read about her behavior in the gossip columns, were grounding her until she graduated, and furthermore, weren't speaking to her. Nor were any of her friends.

She casually strolled toward the bar. Unlike the Green Mill, this place was thinly populated. But she didn't miss the drama of a crowd. No more trying to please others. No more Gloria. No more Bastian. No more . . . anyone.

She needed to drown her sorrows in something pretty and brightly colored and alcoholic. Maybe even something pink. She took off her mink capelet and draped it over a tattered stool.

"You're breaking my rules," she heard the bartender say over the music. Lil Hardin's voice was singing something sultry.

The bartender was lean and muscular, in a tight sweater vest and stovepipe-narrow trousers. He looked dangerous and appealing. Lorraine was sick of pretty boys like Marcus and privileged, snot-nosed brats like Bastian. She needed someone new and different who would think *she* was new and different. Someone lean and muscular and wearing stovepipe-narrow trousers.

"I thought places like this didn't have rules," Lorraine said. The bartender's eyes were depthless and dark. "Isn't that why I'm here?"

"I'm sorry," he said. "I thought you were here to flirt with me."

"Am I that transparent?"

"Not at all," he said, leaning slightly over the bar, "unless we're talking about your dress."

"I don't remember giving you permission to look at my dress," Lorraine said with a coy smile. She was wearing a brand-new Jeanne Lanvin—shipped from her mother's personal shopper at Bergdorf Goodman. It was mostly sheer, nude netting, with burned-out velvet flowers rising up the center. "You never told me what rule I'm breaking."

He lined up four shot glasses on the bar. "Don't worry," he said eventually, pouring a clear liquid into the glasses. "I'm only teasing."

He pushed two across the bar toward her. "There are four. Two for each of us."

Lorraine squinted at him, uncertain.

He laughed. "I'm sorry—would you rather I pour you a big glass of milk?"

His mockery was childish—she knew it was childish—and yet it got under her skin. She didn't want him to think she was a little girl. Yes, she was a teenager, but— "Cheers to . . . ?" she asked, raising a shot glass.

"To finding each other!" he said, clinking his glass against hers. He downed both shots in a second.

Lorraine followed suit. "A chaser would have been nice," she said, wincing from the burn.

"I have the perfect thing in mind." He winked, then called to a man smoking alone in the corner. "Frank, take over for a sec? We're out of lemons." He stepped out from behind the bar and took Lorraine's hand. "Come on," he said.

Lorraine felt the alcohol slither through her body like a hot snake. She clung to the bartender's hand as if they were a couple. What was his name? She forgot. Or maybe she had never asked. She thought he was leading her to a far table, but he passed it and pulled her into the dark, to a door she hadn't noticed.

"In here," the bartender said, hitting the door with his shoulder. It opened onto a cramped storage space stacked high with boxes of corn, beans, tomatoes, and peppers.

"I don't see any lemons—"

"I found the lemons I'm looking for right here," he said, squeezing her shoulders as he pushed her against the wall. "Just relax."

He kissed her before she could make a move, and his hands felt their way down her back, all the way down, until he reached the top of her thigh and pulled her leg around his.

Lorraine pushed him off and slid away. She'd had enough. Kissing a man only reminded her of when she'd kissed Bastian, and of all the kisses she would never share with Marcus.

The bartender stepped back. "Hey, where do you think you're going?"

"I forgot my wrap," she said.

She had to get out of this place, but she'd left her capelet on the stool. She probably had about two minutes before the bartender followed her out. She spotted her capelet where she had left it, draped over a stool at the bar, and immediately went toward it.

But a man in a fedora, sitting at a table against the wall, snatched it up first.

"Hey!" she cried. And then she saw the man's face under

his hat. He immediately seemed familiar—and strikingly good-looking, in a dark way—though she couldn't quite place him. But she knew those gray eyes from somewhere.

Still, she was in no mood for games, especially when it came to her fur.

"I'm not about to beg for it, but I'm not about to freeze to death outside, either," she said, her hand outstretched.

"Where you running off to?" he said, exhaling a steady trail of smoke.

She crossed her arms. "Somewhere hotter than this joint."

"You don't like it?"

Lorraine didn't know where this conversation was going, but it was better to play Sophisticated Flapper than Silly Little Girl. "I mean, I've seen better."

"That's too bad," he said, putting out his cigarette in his half-empty drink. "Because I own this joint. So now you're obliged to have a drink with me."

Lorraine was about to protest, but then she realized she was dealing with a gangster.

"Fine," she said, sliding clumsily onto the bench next to him. "One drink." That phrase sounded familiar: She remembered saying it to Bastian before they'd gone up to his apartment.

The bartender walked back into the room. He glared at her but didn't come over, probably because she was sitting with his boss.

"Two martinis," the gangster called out. And a few moments later, a tray was set on the table in front of them.

"I know you," he said to her.

"I doubt that."

"No, sure I do. Your name is—"

She took one of the glasses and swigged a mouthful.

"—Lorraine."

Just hearing her name roll off his tongue gave her chills. This was the guy who had come up to her the night of Gloria's debut, after Marcus had rejected her and Gloria had accused her of spilling the gravy to Bastian. Who'd been kind, giving her his beautiful handkerchief.

Carlito Macharelli.

"You were friends with that redheaded singer. Your girl is in one fine mess with that colored boy. And so is her little tabloid-darling cousin." He leaned forward into the light, and Lorraine could see him clearly for the first time. He didn't look so good. Someone had hit him.

"She's not my friend anymore. I don't know anything about what she's doing." The words were sad, Lorraine thought, because they were true.

"That's okay." He took a revolver out of his coat, popped the cylinder, and calmly loaded it with bullets while he went on. "I know everything there is to know. I know that you came here alone. I know that your little friends think you were the one that squealed. And soon I'll know where your ex-friend and her boy are holed up."

The threatening tone of Carlito's voice made her nervous.

"Can I have my fur back, please?" she said, trying to stand up.

His arm shot out, blocking her. "But let me tell you something you don't know," he said. He relaxed his arm, and Lorraine sank back onto the bench. "See, you're actually sitting pretty."

She was unsure what he was getting at. This was the Mob she was dealing with. What did they want with Gloria? Best to remain neutral, or at least inscrutable. "I'm sitting right here."

"Exactly. You are exactly where you should be. Here with me."

She looked him directly in the eye. "So, what's your point?"

"My point is," he said slowly, taking his time to light up another cigarette, the light throwing shadows across his face, "I believe our interests are very much aligned. We're more alike than you think, Lorraine."

Lorraine might have been at a low point, but she could hardly imagine how she and Carlito Macharelli had anything in common. She knew all the stories about Al Capone and his gang—this guy was dangerous.

"I hardly think so," she said, tilting her head back ever so slightly.

Carlito looked amused. "No?"

Lorraine licked her lips—it was best to match confidence with confidence. "I'm much prettier than you are," she said.

Carlito chuckled, then seemed so surprised that he'd actually laughed that he chuckled again. "I like you, girlie," he said. "You got . . . sass."

Lorraine was about to say thank you when two heavyset men lumbered up to the table. "Carlito, let's go. We found 'em. We should get rolling."

*Found who?* Lorraine wondered.

Carlito snapped the cylinder back into place and dropped the gun into his coat pocket. "That's the best thing that's happened to me all night." He put his hand on Lorraine's. "No offense, peach, but I gotta run."

"None taken," Lorraine said. And then, on impulse, "When will I see you again?"

"I expect you'll see me next week at the Green Mill."

"Who says I'll be at the Green Mill?" Lorraine asked. "I'm a busy girl, you know."

Carlito smirked. The entire right side of his jaw was purple. "Not too busy to accept my help when I'm offering it. Which is rare. You got nothing right now, baby. But I'm gonna change that." He leaned down, touching his lips gently to the side of her face.

"You've got yourself a deal," Lorraine said with her eyes closed. Only a moment passed, but when she opened them, Carlito was already gone.

# GLORIA

It was 7:53 p.m.

She didn't feel like wearing a garter tonight. Her gold-beaded dress, cascading in waves of crystalline fringe, covered the intersection between her sheer stocking and bare thigh.

She slipped her right foot into one of her two-tone Mary Janes, her left foot into the other. The thin black straps went across her ankles, the silver buckles tightened with a pinch.

From the munitions strewn across her vanity, she carefully selected her weapons and placed them in a gold mesh evening bag: vamp-red kiss-proof lipstick, silver powder compact, tortoiseshell comb, ivory cigarette case.

She stared into the mirror. Everything was perfection: green eyes smoldering, cheekbones rouged and accented, lips outlined and plumped. Tonight, even her skin shimmered with something almost magical.

As she dabbed a final drop of perfume into the crease where her shiny bob skimmed her neck, Gloria decided the garter would be necessary after all. Of course it would.

And then, before snapping her bag closed, she added the small black handgun.

Now she was ready.

◆◆◆

A little more than an hour later, at 9:04 p.m., Gloria was parked outside Jerome's apartment, her bag in the trunk. She was early.

She sat in the car in the dark, her heart beating like a wild bird in a too-small cage. She could just as easily turn the key in the ignition and drive back where she'd come from; her decision was not yet irreversible. She knew, though, that the second she opened the car door, her new life would begin.

Sneaking out of her house without saying goodbye to her mother? Leaving her engagement ring on her dresser? Stealing her mother's car? Doing those things had been *easy.* So why was she finding it so difficult to get out of the car?

Jerome finally made the decision for her, by opening his front door and peering at her car. "Gloria?" he called.

She hurried up the steps to him.

"I worried you wouldn't come," he said.

She understood, staring at his face, his anxious eyes, that he wasn't truly sure that *she* loved *him.* That she would risk everything for him. Leave Chicago. Leave her old life.

Well, he was wrong.

Jerome stepped back and stared at her for a moment, his hand to his chin.

Gloria felt suddenly naked. "What's the matter?"

"Nothing," he said. "Absolutely nothing. You just look . . ."

"Sexy? Silly? Stupid?" Gloria blurted out, crossing her arms and trying to hide her shimmery dress.

Slowly, Jerome came forward until he was standing directly in front of her. He placed his hands on top of hers—they were big, his hands, and strong, and were filled with magic, Gloria thought—with music. She wanted those hands to play the piano just for her, to hold her for the rest of her life.

"I was going to say that you look like the genuine article. Not like that girl playing at dress-up," Jerome said, the cool tone of his voice nearly making her swoon. "Gorgeous. Confident. Dangerous, even." She thought about her purse, and what it held inside.

He set his hands on his hips. "Gloria Carmody, you are a true flapper."

◆◆◆

Gloria helped Jerome stuff dress shirts into his suitcase, piled jazz records into a steamer trunk, waited for him to put on his shoes and do the buckles.

She found herself touching her bare ring finger. Everything had happened so quickly. She didn't even really know whether they'd be living together in New York—let alone whether they would be sleeping in the same bed. She didn't know any couples who had lived together before they were married—it was virtually unheard of. Especially since they had never . . .

"What's wrong?" Jerome gave Gloria's shoulders a squeeze.

"Nothing!" she said, too quickly. She closed her eyes, trying to relax into his hands. "I'm just worried—about Carlito, about making the train, about New York City. All of it."

"I wasn't going to tell you this till we got to New York, but it looks like you could use a boost to your confidence. I've been talking to a buddy of mine who owns a jazz club up in Harlem. He's opening up a new piano bar down in Greenwich Village, and he happens to be looking for an act to headline. And since he says I've been getting some buzz on the jazz scene, he'll try me out."

"Jerome! That's unbelievable!" She couldn't help throwing her arms around him. "A job! Already!"

"But the best part is still to come. I told him about you."

"Me? Why?"

Jerome squeezed her hands. "I told him I knew this red-headed torch who had the voice of a songbird. And you know what he said? That a black pianist with a hot white chanteuse would be the talk of the town. He said that's exactly what New York needs, something to spice up the nightlife and cause a stir."

Gloria tackled him, pushing him onto the sofa and kissing him wildly. "We're going to be just fine," she said, pausing and resting her head on his chest. She could hear his heart beat, slow and steady and strong. "We're going to be just fine."

"Of course we are." He rubbed small circles on her back. "I really wasn't sure you'd come tonight. I got Vera coming by to drive me to the station in case you didn't show."

Gloria picked her head up. "Hey, if we're going to do this together, you have to trust that I'm going to be there."

"I know," he said. "But part of me still feels guilty, like I'm taking you away from the life you should be living, from the easy life you deserve—"

"We are going to New York so we don't have to feel ashamed about being together."

"It's not going to be all that different there," he said. "People are still going to raise their eyebrows at a white girl with a colored boy. Still going to hate us for it."

He was right, but she didn't care. She kissed him. "I love you," she whispered.

He kissed each of her eyelids. "I love you, too."

She began to unbutton his shirt, slowly. "Gloria," he said softly. "We gotta go. What are you—"

"No more words," she said, unbuttoning the last button. "Just kiss me."

So that was what he did.

And in the long moments that followed, it seemed as though the world beyond the cracked walls of the apartment dissolved and the midnight train would wait for them forever.

◆◆◆

By 10:16, they were outside, packing the luggage into the car. It was dark. There were light flurries of snow in the air, and the crescent moon glowed dimly through a pale yellow veil of clouds. Jerome closed the trunk, and the hollow thump resounded down the silent street.

"Ready to go?" Gloria asked.

"Ready as I'll ever—" Jerome stopped, his mouth widening into an oval. "Shoot, I forgot something."

"Can't you leave it?" she said, looking at the watch on his wrist. "You already locked up the apartment, and we need to make sure—"

"This won't take long, I promise," he said, giving her a quick peck on the cheek. "Just wait right here."

"Jerome!" she called after him, but he was already sprinting back up the stairs. He disappeared into the building.

Gloria leaned against the car, tapping her foot impatiently against the powdery pavement, trying to warm up. The snow felt cool against her face. Her pulse was still racing, pounding in her temples and all the way down to her feet.

She hugged herself against the cold. Jerome was taking forever.

She just wanted their lives to start already—in the car, on the road, on the train, en route to their final destination. Her heels clicked on the pavement like chattering teeth against a fork. She tugged her dress down as far as it would go, trying to warm her legs, her purse dangling around her shoulder.

Footsteps, coming fast from behind her.

Two figures emerged from the snowy dark.

Gloria felt her throat close up. "Jerome," she tried to call out.

But then the men were there, pushing her against the trunk of the sedan.

"Don't make a sound, girlie."

The accent was unmistakable. She twisted her head around, meeting his ruthless gray eyes as he pressed her body into the car. The rest of his face was wild, teeth exposed as if they were fangs. His companion was a guy she recognized from the club, whose name she couldn't recall, whose body was as thick as a side of meat.

"Please, Carlito," she whimpered, and felt a gun jab into her side.

"Didn't I say not to make a sound?" Carlito wrenched her

arms back, cutting off her circulation, the gun poised at her ribs.

Gloria felt no pain. All she could think was *Jerome, Jerome, Jerome.*

"So you like the black boys, huh?" Carlito whispered into her ear, his breath stinking of tobacco and booze. "How do your mama and daddy feel about that? Their little girl running off with—"

Gloria kicked backward, hard.

Carlito grunted and stumbled back just as Jerome came bolting out of the front door.

"Gloria!" Jerome shouted. But before he could reach her, the other mobster pounced, hurling him to the ground.

Then Carlito was on her again, slamming her back against the car.

Jerome swept his leg around and knocked the gangster off his feet. The minute he was down, Jerome leaped up and kicked at the guy, but that was all Gloria heard before Carlito smacked her head back down sharply against the trunk.

Gloria yelped. She couldn't help herself: It hurt.

Then Carlito was yanked off Gloria and flung away.

Gloria put a hand to her head—it was bloodied—and turned and saw Carlito lying in the snow, Jerome standing over him.

Jerome came to her and gingerly touched her head. "Are you hurt?"

"Watch out!" she shrieked as Carlito rose up behind him.

Carlito backhanded Jerome in the face so hard it spun Jerome around. He tripped backward into the curb and stumbled to his knees.

Carlito lunged. "Stop!" Gloria shouted.

But Carlito didn't stop. He punched Jerome in the eye, then snapped his knee against the side of Jerome's head. Jerome keeled over and lay on the sidewalk, coughing. "You should have known better than to mess with me," Carlito said. He let loose a vicious kick, and Jerome curled into a ball. Carlito laughed. "Tony," he said, "take out the trash, will ya?"

Gloria hadn't seen the other mobster—Tony—quietly get up and come to Gloria's side with his pistol outstretched. He shuffled over to where Jerome lay on the pavement.

Calmly, Tony drew back the slide on his pistol, unlocked the safety, and swung the weapon toward Jerome's head.

Gloria screamed out in horror. "No!"

A shot rang out.

The world became hushed, peaceful almost, save for the crunch of something hitting the snowy pavement. Then there was just the silence. Gloria looked down at her shoes: They were like two black petals against the pure white snow.

She was suddenly conscious of the gun in her hand, of its dark weight. She let it go and dropped to her knees. The snow seeped through her stockings, but all she could feel was the sound of the shot, vibrating through her body. She was shaking now; somebody was shaking her.

"Gloria!"

A face she knew. Arms raising her up, holding her close. *You're alive,* she thought, clawing at Jerome's chest. *How are you alive?*

Red ribbons stretched toward her like fingers in the snow. A body lay facedown, unmoving. At her feet, the gun was cool and dark and dead, like a second body.

She had killed a man.

She gasped and the world snapped into focus. Her hand was numb from the pistol's recoil, and there was a stink of burned gunpowder in the air, and she was cold, so cold. "Oh God," she whispered.

"It's going to be all right," Jerome said softly. "I promise."

But how could it be? "No," she mumbled.

"Gloria," Jerome said, taking her shoulders in his hands. "You saved my life."

Gloria's head wouldn't clear. "Where's Carlito?" she asked.

"I don't know," Jerome said. "He took off running right after you—after the gunshot."

Before she could fully take that in, another set of footsteps was pounding toward them.

"Vera?" Jerome said. "It's just Vera, Glo. It's only my sister."

Gloria couldn't look away from the body. It was snowing harder now, the flakes coming down furiously out of the darkness. The gangster's corpse was fast becoming shrouded in white, but the red didn't go away. It just got darker.

Vera reached them, out of breath. She stopped when she spotted Tony's body and covered her mouth with her hand. "I thought I heard a shot, but I didn't—" She looked from Gloria's slack face to Jerome's bloody one.

"Carlito came out of nowhere," Jerome said. "With one of his goons. They knew we were leaving, I think. Someone must've tipped them off."

Vera looked around nervously. "Wait, what are you doing with that?" she asked, spotting the gun at Gloria's feet.

"They were going to kill me. Gloria got the drop on them."

"It's Bastian's gun." The words came out of Gloria's mouth before she knew what she was saying.

Vera's face shut down completely. "Leave," she said quickly. "Leave now. I'll take care of everything."

"Vera, I can't let you—"

"I said, *leave!* I'll get Fred and Doug to get rid of the body. Ain't no cop going to dig too deep to figure out what happened to some two-bit gangster. You two need to go, and fast."

Jerome gave his sister a quick kiss on the cheek. "I'll write you from New York."

Jerome slid into the driver's open door and turned the ignition. The car shuddered and rumbled to life.

Gloria stood frozen, her eyes locked not on the body but on the red snow.

"Gloria." She felt Vera gently shaking her arm. "You have to go, before the police come." Vera guided her around to the passenger-side door. Before she opened it, she put her forehead against Gloria's. "You take care of my brother for me, okay? I'm trusting you."

It was the nicest thing Vera had ever said to her.

"Okay," Gloria heard herself say. "I will." And then the door of her mother's car was shut, and with Jerome at the wheel, they drove slowly down the street, the snow filling their tracks as quickly as they made them.

◆◆◆

They had made it.

On the platform at 11:52, awaiting the midnight train, Gloria stood half a car's length away from Jerome. They didn't want to appear to be together in case anyone saw them. He had cleaned up the best he could in one of the bathrooms at the station, but his lips and cheeks were cut, and a bruise was taking over his right eye. He had pulled a fedora low over his face, and the hat's brim hid the worst of it.

As the clock ticked closer to midnight, she walked past the other people on the platform and up to Jerome. "I don't care who sees us together," she said.

"Good," he said.

“What are we going to do?” she asked. This was not how she’d imagined starting her new life with Jerome. This was not how it was supposed to be.

“I want you to listen to me,” Jerome said. “As far as you’re concerned—as far as *anyone* is concerned—I killed Tony.”

“But, Jerome—”

“*Listen* to me,” he said. He moved his face close to hers. “I killed him, and that’s that. The Mob and the police will both be after me—I’m nothing but one more worthless black man to them, better dead than alive.

“So I have to run. But even when I get to New York, Carlito and Capone’s guys will try to track me down. I’ll be living as a fugitive.

“But you, Gloria,” he said softly, “you don’t have to suffer. You can stay here, safe.” He stared hard at his hands, then back up into her eyes. “I love you, Gloria. And because I love you, I can’t let you come with me.”

Gloria felt her chest crack open. He was right—she knew he was right. As long as Carlito lived, any life they had together would have to be forged in the shadows. And it was all her fault. If she hadn’t gone back to the Green Mill, she would have never run into Carlito, and he would never have attacked her, and Jerome would never have had to defend her, and—

A piercing whistle.

The train pulled into the station with a hiss of steam.

Gloria looked up into Jerome’s eyes. “I love you,” she said, and the words swept everything else away. Her fear of Carlito's revenge, her worries about their uncertain future, everything.

The conductors went down the line, opening the cabin doors.

"All aboard!" one conductor called out. "Midnight train to New York City! Final stop: Grand Central Terminal!"

Jerome took a risk and kissed her cheek, a farewell kiss, and pried himself away. "Be a good girl, now," he said, shouldering his trunk and picking up his suitcase.

Jerome moved down the platform, as if in slow motion, leaving Gloria behind.

"Jerome!" she shouted out, but he had already climbed the steps to the train, stopped, turned around to gaze at her.

"I almost forgot," he said, digging into his pocket. He produced an earring—her grandmother's—the one she had lost that night in the Green Mill. He held out his hand. "That's what I went back into the apartment to get."

Gloria ran to him and mounted the steps. "I'd rather be with you—wherever you are, no matter how bad things are—than anywhere in the world without you."

"Are you sure?"

The whistle blew its warning cry. Around them, people flooded into the train cars, taking seats, putting away their luggage. "It won't be easy," Jerome said. "Easy is over with. I won't hate you if you say no. I'll understand."

Gloria gazed at this man who had changed her life, who

had opened himself up to her, who had taught her how to sing—not just on the stage, but in life. This man she had killed for. She thought about their being together in New York, with Carlito hunting them. She thought about being alone in Chicago if she stayed.

*Make a decision,* Gloria thought. *It's now or never*.

"All aboard!" the conductor cried.

# EPILOGUE

## VERA

"I told you never to come here," Bastian said as the elevator doors shut. "That was our deal."

"That was before you *broke* our deal," Vera said, storming into his apartment. "Before my brother almost ended up dead."

Bastian closed the door. "Now I'm going to have to make up a story about needing a new cleaning lady."

"Fat chance of anyone believing *those* horsefeathers at two in the morning."

Vera knew it was risky. Not only coming to an all-white neighborhood, but to an engaged, rich white man's apartment. At night. But she had no other choice. She was responsible for what had just happened.

The two of them had never been alone before. It made her very uneasy.

In the past, they had met on a pair of benches along the east side of Washington Park, or in one of the Chinatown eateries in Hyde Park, where no one would take notice of a white man eating dinner with a black woman.

"May I take your coat, Miss Vera?" he said with mock hospitality.

"Can the act," she said, not wanting to expose the skimpy dress she was wearing beneath her coat. She'd gone straight from work at the Green Mill to say farewell to her brother. She hadn't expected the blood, the body, or Jerome's battered face.

"Then may I at least get you a drink? It might warm you up," he said, walking over to a bottle he had sitting out.

"I don't want your booze, Mr. Grey," she said, staying close to the door. "You know why I'm here."

"Be so kind as to enlighten me."

"One of Carlito's men is dead. I don't think he was showing up at my brother's to wish him a good trip to New York."

"I already know," Bastian said, taking a sip of his drink. "News travels fast when your brother murders the pal of one of the most powerful gangsters in the city of Chicago."

"Jerome killed this guy?" Vera bit her tongue. So Carlito was blaming Jerome. Probably because no one would bat an eyelash if he killed a black man in vengeance. But a rich white society girl?

She had a hunch Bastian didn't know it was his own

gun that had killed Carlito's man. "I can't believe I ever trusted you."

Bastian laughed scornfully. "Is that so?"

He strolled across the room and stared down at her. He didn't hide his contempt. "Let's be honest with ourselves, Vera. Was I the one who investigated the new singer at the Green Mill? Was I the one who ratted out my brother about his planning to run away with her to New York? Was I the one who gave me his address to make certain that the two lovebirds split up for good?"

He gulped down the dregs of his drink. "Shall I continue?"

"No one was supposed to die." Vera felt her insides wither. Bastian was right: She had only herself to blame. She'd been convinced Gloria was going to ruin her brother's life.

She'd been wrong.

Jerome had almost lost his life because of what she'd told Bastian. And now her brother and Gloria were on the lam, and a man was dead, and it was all because of Vera.

She had to fix this.

"*You* sent Carlito to kill Jerome tonight, didn't you? You didn't care who got hurt. You just wanted to punish Gloria."

"Of course." Bastian tilted his head. "Silly, stupid Vera. It's a little too late for remorse, sweetheart."

"Don't you dare call me sweetheart!"

"What would you rather I call you? Judas? A traitor to your own flesh and blood?"

"That's enough!" Vera wanted to strike him, to tear into

him with every ounce of strength she had in her body. "I was trying to *save* my brother—"

"Then you should have known better than to involve me."

"Gloria could have been killed," Vera said, backing toward the door.

"I don't give a damn about Gloria," Bastian said. "It's her money I want to marry."

Vera couldn't stay in this apartment for another second, for fear of doing something she might regret. "You won't get her *or* her money. I'll make sure of it."

Bastian smiled wickedly. "And how are you going to do that?"

Vera opened the door, looked back at Bastian, and smiled, because she knew what he did not: that she had his smoking gun tucked away in her purse, linking him to the murder outside her brother's apartment.

"Just you wait and see," Vera said.

And then she firmly closed the door on him.

Find out what happens next in

INGENUE,

the second novel in the sexy, dangerous,

and ridiculously romantic Flappers series . . .

. . . where revenge is a dish best served cold.

Turn the page for a sneak peek.

# VERA

Fashion kills.

Crouching for long periods of time was never fun, but doing it in patent-leather T-strap heels was murder. Vera usually tried to wear more comfortable shoes when she was following someone, but there'd been no time to change. She'd been working at the Green Mill when she'd overheard Carlito Macharelli mention a meeting on the docks with Sebastian Grey.

She'd immediately called a cab.

"Follow that car!" she'd ordered the driver.

A normal cabbie would never put himself at her disposal for this sort of activity—a black girl? Telling a cabdriver to follow a wealthy white man?—but Wally was not a normal cabbie. He was that rarity: a black man with his own taxi and license. He was a family friend and happy to help her clear her brother's name. "Jerome is like the son I wish I'd never had," Wally liked to say. Most nights, he waited outside the Green Mill until she was done with her shift to take her home.

Tonight they followed the taillights of Carlito's Rolls-Royce all the way through downtown and to the docks—a place Vera usually avoided. This area was dangerous. Vera already worked in a Mob-run speakeasy; she didn't need the added threat of being around when the gangsters unloaded the hooch.

She asked Wally to let her out a block behind where Carlito parked the Rolls in the vacant lot. The hulking shadows of ships loomed to the east, but here the docks were still and silent.

Vera edged close to the Rolls, dodging from shadow to shadow until at last she found a hiding place behind a stack of tied-up crates. Already, there was Bastian Grey—she could see his smug features as he lit a butt from his silver cigarette case. He ambled out on the pier and stood smoking, staring out at the water.

She was sweltering on this warm summer night, thanks to her black, knee-length trench coat, but Bastian looked at ease in the heat, irritatingly handsome in a brown suit, his cheeks freshly shaven, his dark hair slicked back and parted. He was a looker, that much Vera couldn't deny.

"What do you want?" Carlito called out as he walked up, the lights from the pier warehouse catching his gray pinstriped suit and black fedora.

Carlito was her boss and had once employed her brother, Jerome, as the piano player at the Green Mill. But then Carlito and Tony Pachelli, one of his goons, had tried to kill Jerome. And Gloria, Bastian's high-society fiancée, had shot Tony dead. And then Gloria and Vera's brother had had to flee Chicago to save their lives.

And it was all Vera's fault.

Vera had been the one feeding Bastian information about Jerome and Gloria. Vera had been the one determined to break up their secret affair. Just because Vera hadn't known that Bastian was telling everything to Carlito didn't mean she was any less guilty.

That was why Vera was here, crouched behind a stack of crates, hoping to learn something incriminating about Carlito and Bastian—something she could use to barter for her brother's life.

"What do *I* want?" Bastian flipped his cigarette in a bright arc across the lot. "*You're* the one who told me to meet you here."

Carlito stepped backward. "No, I didn't."

"Secret notes and midnight meetings." Bastian walked a few steps away. "I'm tired of your little games, Macharelli." Only a young man as despicable as Bastian Grey could work with mobsters *and* show a proud distaste for them at the same time.

"This isn't a game," Carlito said, casting a quick glance over his shoulder. "And I didn't send you a note. That means someone else did."

"Don't be absurd," Bastian said, lighting another cigarette. "Why would anyone go to the trouble of dragging us out here?"

Vera was leaning forward to hear better when she felt a hand crawl over her mouth. "What are you playing at?" a woman's voice whispered.

She wanted to struggle against the stranger's hold, but she couldn't give herself away. She felt herself being turned around to face her attacker.

Vera stared into the eyes of Maude Cortineau, Carlito's moll. When Maude had been a flapper, she'd barely paid attention to anyone outside her glamorous inner circle. Since she'd gotten with Carlito, she stuck to his side and spoke only when she was spoken to.

"I'm *trying* to eavesdrop," Vera whispered back. If Maude had been planning to bust her, she would've done it already.

"Shut up, Vera," Maude hissed. "I was waiting in the car, and I saw you running around behind these crates like you didn't have a care in the world. If Carlito sees you, you're in deep trouble. Don't be an idiot. You don't want to end up like me."

After dropping out of her bluenose prep school, Maude had become the queen of the Chicago flapper scene. Sequins, feathers, gold lamé—she wore it all. Her makeup was always flawless and her headband always settled perfectly over her blond bob.

But now her beaded red dress hung over her bony body

like a burlap sack. Deep shadows lurked underneath her kohl-rimmed eyes. Carlito had sucked the life out of her: The flame that Maude had once been famous for had been snuffed out.

"Maude! Where the hell are you?" Carlito called from the other side of the crates.

"Just be smart and hide," Maude said, clacking away in her heels, back to Carlito's Rolls. Carlito was pacing by the car as Maude ambled up, smoking a cigarette. She was the perfect portrait of boredom.

Carlito banged his fist on the hood. "I told you to stay in the car!"

Maude dropped the practically new cigarette. "I wanted a ciggy," she replied in a soft, defeated voice. "I know how you don't like anyone to smoke in your car, Daddy."

"Get in," he said. "We gotta go, and fast. This is a setup."

"You're being silly, Macharelli!" Bastian shouted. "No one is after us!"

But Carlito ignored him. He slid behind the wheel, cranked the engine, and sped off with a squeal of tires.

Vera let herself relax against the crates, leaning out to check on Bastian. How could she have been so stupid as to ever trust him? *Those eyes,* she thought. When she'd first met Bastian, his green eyes had seemed sincere—swoony, even. Arrogant, of course, but that was to be expected from a rich white boy like him. She hadn't realized the heartless steel his irises really concealed until she'd accused him of sending a man to kill Jerome and he'd just smiled and called her "silly, stupid Vera."

And in all honesty, that was exactly what she was.

Vera opened her purse and felt the comforting, cool metal of Bastian's pistol inside. She'd carried it often since she'd found it at Gloria's feet that night. Bastian certainly didn't know it was his own gun that had killed the gangster, that his own fiancée had pulled the trigger.

Vera had never used a gun before, but if a dame like Gloria could use one, then so could she. Vera loved Jerome every bit as much as Gloria did, and would go just as far, if not further, to protect him.

She snapped the purse shut and looked back toward the docks.

Footsteps, approaching from the other side of the dockyard. The figure wore a long black overcoat and a hat with a wide brim. Vera watched the person walk down the pier.

"Sebastian Grey?" Vera was shocked to hear the voice of a woman.

Bastian turned from the water. "I don't believe I've had the pleasure—"

"Skip the formalities. I'm looking for Macharelli. And the piano player, Jerome Johnson."

"Do I look like their keeper?" Bastian breathed out a cloud of cigarette smoke, and then his face brightened. "You're too pretty a woman to be chasing after trash like Carlito. But if you must know, he took off a minute ago."

The woman made a swift movement, and Bastian raised his hands in surrender. "Where to?" she demanded. "And where's the piano player?"

"No need for guns," Bastian said, slowly backing up. "Carlito went home. And Johnson? No one knows where he disappeared to. He sent his kid sister a postcard from a post office box in New York, but that's been a dead end so far."

"Thank you," the woman said. "You've been most helpful."

Then Vera heard the unmistakable sound of a gunshot. Two.

Instinctively, she cowered, knocking her heavy purse against the crates.

The killer turned at the noise, her features hidden by shadow. All Vera could see was the silver pistol, pointed directly at her.

The third gunshot in as many minutes rang out over Lake Michigan.

The bullet slammed into a wooden crate so close to her head that Vera felt splinters hit her face. She didn't wait for another bullet. She just turned and ran.

It wasn't far to the edge of the dockyard, and the wall of crates was between Vera and the shooter. But Vera was wearing heels, and she'd never been able to run in heels.

Until now.

She waited for the crack of the gunshot and the bullet in

her back as she crossed the lot, as she turned and ran the block to Wally's cab, as she banged on the window to wake him from his nap.

"What's the rumpus?" he said as she clambered into the backseat.

"Drive!" she said. "As fast as you can."

Wally didn't need to be told twice. He turned the key, gunned the engine, and took off.

When he dropped her at the club, it was already locked up for the night, but that didn't slow her down: She fumbled through her purse, found Jerome's old keys, and slipped the brass master into the lock.

Whoever the killer was, she wouldn't miss the next time.

◆◆◆

All that had been hours ago.

Vera had made a pot of coffee. She'd sat down in a booth to try to figure out what to do next. And once she'd been sure she was alone, she'd cried. She'd cried for vile Bastian Grey, and for her brother, and for herself. She was only seventeen. She was supposed to be in school, not fleeing killers. Her mother had been dead for years, and if her father found out about the mess she'd gotten herself into, it would probably kill him, too.

The only reason this place was a safe haven right now was that it was morning, much too early for anyone—the band, the girls, the owners—to be there. That would change in a few hours. Vera needed to gather her things, figure out a plan, then scram.

But she couldn't stop shaking. Maybe she could wait just a little longer. Just until her nerves settled.

Then she stiffened in her seat: a jangle of keys outside the door. She needed to hide.

But by the time she'd slid out of the booth, the door was already open.

"What are you doing here?" a man's voice exclaimed.

Vera's heart slowed. The voice wasn't the cool steel of a thug's, but warm, buttery, and familiar: Evan. The trumpet player in the band and an old friend of Jerome's.

Despite the early hour, Evan was already dressed for the day in a soft white dress shirt and brown slacks. He looked the slightest bit amused, thanks to the way his lips naturally turned up at the corners. His face was smoothly shaved, his cheeks and jaw incredibly angular. He removed his brown derby hat as he flicked on the light and walked into the room.

"What are *you* doing here?" Vera asked, shutting her purse. "What time is it, five in the morning?"

"Five-thirty," Evan replied. His eyes widened as he took in Vera's appearance. She was still wearing her sleeveless gold dress, though it was a wrinkled mess. Evan picked a splinter of wood out of her hair. "What happened to you, Vera?" He pointed at the booth. "Take a load off, girl." He went behind the bar and ran the tap.

When he came back, he handed Vera a tall glass of water. She held it out in front of her: Her hand wasn't shaking.

"It's water," Evan said. "It's for drinking."

Vera smiled for the first time that night and gulped down the entire thing.

"Thank you." She leaned back in the booth, feeling a bit more herself. "Now, I think you were just about to tell me why you're here about ten hours earlier than usual."

"You're welcome," Evan said. He sat down opposite her and ran a hand through his sleek dark hair—Vera could smell the Brilliantine. "Truth is, Vera, I'm taking off."

"You were just going to ditch the band?"

"Aw, it ain't much of a band anymore. Tommy's been talking about joining up with a piano player at another club, and Bix never wants to practice. Without Jerome or a decent singer, this ain't a good gig anymore. I just came by to get my trumpet."

Vera couldn't help feeling hurt. He'd been planning to leave without saying goodbye?

Evan reached out to pat her hand. "I was going to tell you. I just wanted to sneak my horn out of here early, before anyone was around. Or at least it was *supposed* to be before anyone was around." He gave a wry grin. "Now, what are *you* doing here?"

Before Vera knew what was happening, words started spilling out of her. She told him how she had betrayed Jerome and nearly cost him his life. How Bastian and Carlito had been lured to the docks, and how the killer had shot Bastian dead. And she told him how she'd nearly caught a bullet herself. "And the woman asked about Jerome," she said. "Bastian knew about Jerome's post office box in New York City. He knew Jerome had sent me a postcard."

"He sent you a postcard?"

"Months ago. I—I carried it around like a dog with a bone. Someone must have gone through my purse when I was working. Someone must have told—" She swallowed heavily. "And now the killer knows he's in New York."

Evan reached over and tilted her chin upward, forcing her to look at him. "That is not your fault. But don't you worry—I'll help you sort this out."

She turned away from his hand. "I'm dealing with it all right on my own."

Evan raised his eyebrows at her torn dress and dirty face. "Yep, you're doing just fine."

Despite herself, Vera laughed, and then she stood. "I'm gonna go clean myself up a bit."

She washed the grime off her face in the ladies' room. Now she'd gone and involved Evan. He was the one person besides her father she really cared about in Chicago, and she'd repaid his friendship by putting his life in danger, too. In the dressing room at the end of the hall, she stuffed her makeup kit, red hairbrush, and silver clutch into a large black shoulder bag she found on the floor.

Then she looked at the clothes rack and winced.

She couldn't very well run away with only a bag full of sparkly flapper dresses. Still, she chose three of her favorites and packed them. And then, murmuring an apology, she swiped a few of a fellow cigarette girl's simple day dresses, including a pale yellow number that she slipped over her head. It was a little tight, but not in a bad way. Finally, she slipped her feet into a pair of black ballet slippers. With her T-strap heels packed in the bag, she slung it over her shoulder and said goodbye to this place.

She found Evan behind the bar. His beat-up trumpet case and a tan briefcase sat on the floor near the booth.

Two glasses of water sat on the table. Evan carried over a pair of plates from the bar and set them down. "Isn't that Betty's?" he asked, glancing at her dress.

"Not anymore," Vera replied as she sat down.

"Fair enough," Evan said, taking a seat. "I figured you might be hungry. Sorry it's not the greatest breakfast—I worked with what was available."

Vera looked down. A ham and cheese sandwich. There was even a pickle next to it. Evan was kind as well as handsome. And unlike her, he remembered the importance of things like drinking water and eating regular meals.

She grabbed the sandwich and devoured it.

Evan cleared his throat. "So, what's the plan now? Send a note to Jerome?"

Vera pushed the plate away. "There's no time for a note. Somebody's got to stop this woman." She opened her bag and pulled out Bastian's gun. "I'm going to New York."

Evan dropped his sandwich. "What the hell are you doing with a gun, Vera?"

She sighed. "Long story, and I'm not particularly in the mood to tell it."

"Then save it for the train ride to New York," Evan said. "No way am I letting my best friend's sister head into danger by herself. I'm coming with you."


Published by Delacorte Press, an imprint of
Random House Children's Books,
a division of Random House, Inc., New York.